IT STARTED WITH A PROPOSAL

SUSAN MEIER

HIGHLAND FLING WITH HER BOSS

KARIN BAINE

MILLS & BOON

First published in Great Britain 2024
by Mills & Boon, an imprint of HarperCollins*Publishers* Ltd,
1 London Bridge Street, London, SE1 9GF

www.harpercollins.co.uk

HarperCollins*Publishers*, Macken House, 39/40 Mayor Street Upper, Dublin 1, D01 C9W8, Ireland

It Started with a Proposal © 2024 Linda Susan Meier

Highland Fling with Her Boss © 2024 Karin Baine

ISBN: 978-0-263-32126-5

03/24

IT STARTED WITH
A PROPOSAL

SUSAN MEIER

MILLS & BOON

CHAPTER ONE

ANTONIO SALVAGGIO SAT in his favorite Manhattan restaurant with his favorite date, June Bronson, a petite blonde with a bubbly personality. Nights with June were always upbeat, positive, sexy. Every time he was in New York to see the family conglomerate's lawyer, he called her.

So why was he staring at the tall brunette hovering in the corner of the Tuscan style restaurant? Her hair had been pulled back in a bun at her nape. Her conservative beige skirt and matching sleeveless sweater made her blend into the mural of a vineyard on the wall behind her.

Though it was Sunday, she was also working. She had to be. Her focus and concentration were on a table in the middle of the room. Others might not have noticed that all the seating had been moved at least six inches away from that center table, but Antonio came to Sabato every time he was in the city. He saw the discreet distance.

A young woman with a violin appeared out of nowhere, stopped by the center table and began playing something soft and romantic. The guy seated with a woman who was clearly his girlfriend pulled a ring box out of his jacket pocket, rose from his chair and got down on one knee.

Ah. That was why all the tables had been moved a few inches away from that center table. The guy dressed in a black suit was proposing.

The restaurant fell silent. Waiters stopped pepper mills mid-turn. Forks stopped midbite. The hostess bringing in a pair of new diners came to a quick halt, putting out her arm to stop the couple following her. The air in the room shimmered with something intangible, something special.

The guy said, "Will you marry me?"

His partner's eyes widened before she blinked back tears. "Yes!" She jumped out of her seat. "Yes!"

He caught her in his arms to kiss her when he probably should have been sliding the ring on her finger. The brunette in the beige skirt hustled over. She took the ring box from his hand, extracted the ring and gave it to him, along with a significant look.

He jerked back from the kiss and put the ring on his new fiancée's finger.

Then, to everybody's surprise, a choir dressed in judge's robes danced in from the kitchen singing the alleluia chorus. After a second of silence, a burst of laughter filled the room.

"She's a judge," the future groom explained to the crowd, grinning as if he'd just won the lottery.

Another round of laughter erupted followed by a round of applause.

"She seems awfully young to be a judge."

Antonio murmured, "Hmmm," in response to June's comment, but his eyes were on the woman in beige. She'd obviously planned the proposal, gathered the chorus, hired the violinist. She'd noticed the groom's little faux pas of not immediately putting the ring on his girlfriend's finger. That was probably the choir's cue to enter. So, she'd hurried over and kept the proposal on track. Then she'd gone back to her spot in the corner, blending into the Tuscan-themed mural on the wall, as she studied the happy couple who accepted congratulations from diners near their table.

Antonio watched them too. He should have shuddered in revulsion—marriage was an outdated institution as far as he was concerned. A messy divorce had cemented that idea for him. Yet he couldn't stop thinking about that proposal. Low-key enough to be romantic and sincere—but with a spark of interest with the alleluia-singing judges—it was exactly what his grandmother wanted from him.

"Antonio?"

He faced June again. "Sorry."

She batted her eyelashes. "That was very romantic."

He snorted—but sadness tightened his chest. His grandmother had breast cancer and she was dragging her feet about scheduling her treatments. She'd been depressed since Antonio's grandfather died six months ago. It was difficult to get her to do anything. But scheduling those treatments wasn't just "anything." If she didn't pull herself together and start treatment, her depression would end up making her cancer, and therefore the treatments, worse.

An itchy sensation raced along his skin. Every argument he or his father had made seemed to have fallen on deaf ears. But it seemed wrong to stand by and do nothing. GiGi was a good woman, a wonderful woman, who'd raised Antonio after his mother left his dad—left *him*. They had had visits with his mother, but they were few and far between. Because she was an alcoholic, his dad preferred that she come to Italy to spend time with him, but she liked the privacy of her own home. Probably to hide her drinking.

She rarely came to see him, and his grandmother had become a mother to him. Gretta Salvaggio hadn't asked for anything in return. She just wanted her grandson to be happy. Unfortunately, in her way of thinking, happy meant married—with children. She believed children made life worth living.

He thought of his defunct marriage and rolled his eyes. After the first six months, there had been nothing happy about it.

"Have you ever thought of doing something like that?"

Antonio's blood ran cold. Clearly June hadn't seen the eye roll. "You mean propose?" Dear Lord, he hoped she wasn't hinting. They'd gone out four or five times in the past six months. They weren't really a couple. They were...

They were...

They were...

Friends with benefits?

She also knew he had other "friends." She had to. They didn't keep in touch when he returned to Italy after his appointments with the law firm where she worked. He only called her when he came to the city.

They were casual.

And if this was "the" conversation about where this relationship was going, then he'd have it. "You know I don't believe in marriage."

She sniffed.

He frowned. "Do *you*?"

She shrugged. "Sure. Someday. But I love romantic gestures like that proposal."

So that's what she was hinting at. She wanted a little romance.

He was about to make a mental note to do something romantic, something that didn't spell commitment, when he saw the newly engaged couple leaving the restaurant, stealing kisses as they walked to the door. It struck him that he'd never see them again. He would have no way of knowing if they ever actually got married.

Neither did any of the other people in that restaurant. All they saw was a proposal.

His brain woke up and quickly drew some conclusions. He didn't ever want to remarry, but his grandmother was old-fashioned. She wanted him married. Settled. Preferably with children.

But looking at that couple, he realized he didn't have to get married to make GiGi happy, to give her a burst of energy that would get her moving to schedule her treatments. All he needed was a really romantic proposal that she could see— or watch on YouTube.

YouTube.

He laughed out loud.

"What's funny?"

"My grandmother is sick."

June looked at him as if he were crazy. "What?"

"I'm sorry. I don't mean to sound flip. My grandmother is having some health problems and I just figured out something that will raise her energy enough that she can go through treatment."

June's face scrunched in continued confusion. "Okay."

He knew his explanation had been vague, but that was because he didn't talk about personal things with casual dates. Still, his plan was a good one. He adored his grandmother. She'd been depressed since Antonio's grandfather's death. But the cancer diagnosis seemed to have sucked the very life out of her.

And now he had the plan to revive her.

He rose. "There's something I have to do." He glanced around for the nondescript brunette in the beige skirt. "You can take the limo back to your apartment."

She stood up and leaned against him seductively. "Will you be joining me?"

"Sorry. This thing I'm thinking about might take a while." He kissed her. "By the time I could get to your apartment you'd be asleep. I'll see you next time I'm in town."

She smiled prettily. "Okay. Thanks for dinner."

She headed for the door. Not angry. Not upset.

Their relationship really was the epitome of casual. Still, he decided to send her flowers in the morning. He glanced around looking for the brunette again. He found her in the foyer near the maître d'.

"Good evening."

Gathering her purse and briefcase from the bench by the door, she looked over at him. "Good evening."

"Are you a party planner?"

She studied his face. Maybe gauging his sincerity? But all he saw were her eyes. Green. Not brown-green, but real green. In a face that could only be described as classically beautiful. Pert little nose. High cheekbones. Full lips.

"Yes and no. I plan marriage proposals mostly."

"There's market enough that you can be that specific?"

She sighed. "It's a big city."

"I know." He couldn't believe he was asking stupid questions but just looking at her made him feel funny—like a guy who could trip over his own feet. Which was ridiculous. Italian billionaires raised on vineyard estates were suave. *He* was suave.

"I'm sorry. I just saw that guy ask his girlfriend to marry him and it was pretty clear you'd set it up. I'd like for you to plan a proposal like that for me."

Her face brightened. "Oh! I'm sorry. I thought you were about to ask me to rent a bouncy castle for a bunch of five-year-olds."

He laughed. "No. I have no children." But at thirty-three he could be a father. Which was why his GiGi was always hounding him. She said time was passing him by.

He shook his head to clear it. What the hell was happening with him tonight?

She smiled apologetically. "Don't get me wrong. Kids are great. Kids' parties are fun. But it's been a long day for me."

It gave him a little comfort that they had both gotten off on the wrong foot.

A group of diners arrived, bringing warm June air in with

them. Realizing they were standing in everybody's way, Antonio said, "Can I walk you to your car?"

"I've got a ride share coming."

He pointed at the door. "Can I wait with you outside?"

"Why don't you just come to my office first thing tomorrow? I'm in at seven and I don't have anyone scheduled until nine o'clock." She handed him her sedate, classy business card.

Riley Morgan
Making Wishes Come True
Remember your proposal forever

He handed her one of his business cards too, but he winced. "Sorry, that card's got my company information on it, and we're headquartered in Italy. But I'm staying at the Intercontinental. If something comes up tomorrow morning and you can't see me, you can reach me there. I'll want to reschedule. This proposal is very important to me."

She smiled as she tucked his card in her pocket. "Trust me. I can help you figure out the absolute best way to propose to your girlfriend."

"Oh, it's not for my girlfriend. It's for my grandmother."

She frowned. "You're asking your grandmother to marry you?"

"No, my grandmother is ill, and I want the kind of proposal that will make her so happy she'll find the energy to fight."

Her eyes widened, then filled with sincerity. "I'm so sorry."

The softness in her voice warmed his chest. She was pretty, polite, sweet and so sincere it was affecting him in the oddest ways.

He tapped her business card against his hand. It was time to get the hell away from her and gather his wits. The proposal idea was perfect. He wouldn't ruin it because he was acting all wrong, probably because he was tired.

"Since we're meeting so early, maybe we should have breakfast?"

"I'd rather meet in my office. I can show you pictures. We can talk about venues."

"Okay."

She smiled again, so pretty his heart pounded in his chest. The sense that he'd never met anyone like her tried to take over his brain, but he reminded himself he met beautiful women all the time. But this one wasn't as beautiful as she was classic. Like a woodland fairy. Happy and wanting to make others happy.

He shook his head, clearing it of some of the weird thoughts and feelings as he walked out into the warm Manhattan night.

He'd been up for a day and a half. With the time differences he'd gotten to New York almost the same time that he'd left Italy. Technically, he'd gained eight hours in this day. Because of an emergency, he'd worked every one of them even though it was Sunday. He needed sleep. Then he could deal with the pretty green-eyed woman who would help him revive his grandmother.

Riley Morgan left the restaurant glancing at the business card Antonio Salvaggio had given her. She had never met anyone who'd made her feel what he had in a thirty-second conversation. He was gorgeous, dressed like a man accustomed to the finer things and loved his grandmother. That's all she remembered because she kept losing her breath.

She knew why she'd been off balance. When he looked at her, something inside her woke up and demanded attention. That sounded dreamy and romantic and more than a little bit tempting. But when a woman had employees to pay and marriage proposals to plan, she couldn't afford to trip over her own tongue.

She went to bed still chastising herself for losing her cool just because a guy had the accent of a god and the most beautiful dark eyes she'd ever seen—mostly because he'd been with a woman. She'd assumed that was why he wanted a proposal planned.

Actually, she wasn't a hundred percent sure what he wanted.

She finally fell asleep around midnight and woke super early Monday morning with ideas floating around in her head. She dressed in slim pants and a lightweight summer sweater and by the time she arrived at her office, she was absolutely ready to get out the photos and videos of her best events. She made both tea and coffee in the breakroom and had the local bakery deliver a dozen Gourmand pastries.

Her assistant arrived ten minutes later, and she poked her head into Riley's office. "Good morning."

With her flowing red hair and long limbs, Marietta Fontain looked more like a dancer than an office assistant, but Marietta was one of the best.

"Good morning. I have someone coming in in a few minutes. I gave him my card at last night's proposal and told him to stop by at seven."

Marietta smiled. "Okay, boss. I'll be ready."

"You always are. I'll probably be busy with him for an hour. Is there anything I need to know before he gets here?"

"No. I'm putting Vince and Montgomery on the Islee proposal this morning. I haven't yet done the workup of what this proposal entails, but maybe I could do that with them?"

"Good idea. I actually want them to oversee the event itself."

Marietta gasped. "You're taking a day off?"

"No. I'm going to watch from the back of the venue to make sure they can manage the whole thing on their own."

"Ooh. Clever."

"Don't get your hopes up that training more people means

I'll take a day off. I like being at events to make sure everything goes as planned. But you never know what life's going to throw at you. Just in case I ever get sick or need a day off, I want to know all employees can handle an event on their own."

"I love that you think ahead."

"I'm successful because I think ahead."

"Well, thinking ahead is one thing. Doing everything yourself is another. Once those two get up to speed, we'll all be trained. You could trust us for two weeks while you go to the Bahamas or something."

The main door opened. Marietta pivoted to race back to the reception area. "That's my cue."

Riley took a breath. She might have been overwhelmed by Antonio Salvaggio's presence the night before, but this morning she would be all business.

CHAPTER TWO

WAITING FOR MARIETTA to bring Antonio Salvaggio back to her office, Riley took a seat at her desk and pulled up the spreadsheet of that week's schedule. Her company had six proposals. All preplanning had been done. Flowers were ordered. Music had been scheduled. Two violinists. One mariachi band. One string quartet. And two without music.

"Riley?"

She glanced up to see Marietta in her doorway. "Mr. Salvaggio is here to see you."

Antonio Salvaggio stood behind Marietta, smiling. Her stomach fell to the floor.

He was even better looking than she remembered. Today he wore another expensive suit and a smart tie. He was the epitome of a successful businessman, but he somehow made being a businessman look yummy.

"Good morning."

Oh, God, that voice.

She resurrected her smile and rose from her desk. "Good morning."

Marietta scampered away, but turned halfway down the hall and mouthed, *Oh, my God!*

Riley had to swallow a chuckle. "Have a seat."

"Thank you."

As they both sat, she said, "Can I get you some coffee? Tea? A pastry?"

"No. Thank you. I had breakfast at the hotel."

"Then let's get right to your proposal."

"I want something memorable."

"Everybody does." She thought about the woman he'd been with the night before and tried to figure out a way to ask for specifics without reminding him of their clumsy conversation at the restaurant door. "You said the proposal was for your grandmother?"

He shook his head but before he could say anything, Marietta walked in with two cups of coffee. Obviously, her assistant wanted another look at their new client.

"Just in case you change your mind about something to drink."

"Thank you," Riley said as Marietta set the two china cups and saucers on her desk before walking to the door, where she turned and mouthed *Oh, my God!* again.

He took a breath. "Yesterday was a marathon day for me. I'd flown to Manhattan from Italy and spent the whole day with lawyers going over bullet points for a business deal that was falling apart. Which is why I babbled when I tried to explain my idea."

Liking that reasoning, she said, "I had a long day too. I babbled a little myself."

He laughed, his rich voice making the sound deliciously sexy. "My grandmother is depressed. My grandfather died six months ago and she's still grieving. I understand that. But she was diagnosed with breast cancer a few weeks ago and she seems to be ignoring it. When my dad stepped in and instructed her personal assistant to work with the doctor to schedule her chemotherapy, she exploded and refused to go to the appointments. I know this all goes back to her grief, so last night when I saw that proposal you had arranged, I thought of how her fondest wish is to see me married. I don't want to get married, but it hit me that if I did a fake proposal and put it on YouTube, it could excite her enough that she'd come back to life again."

"I see."

His enthusiasm died. "You don't do fake proposals?"

"We haven't to this point, but I don't see why we couldn't do one."

He picked up one of the cups of coffee. "Believe me. I know this probably sounds idiotic, but my grandmother raised me after my parents divorced and my mother returned to Norway. I would do anything to bring GiGi back to her old self at least long enough to get the care she needs."

Her eyes softened along with her voice. "I think that's extremely kind. But how are you going to explain things when you don't actually get married? Won't your grandmother be upset?"

"She's never to find out the engagement was fake. Once she's on the road to recovery, I will simply tell her that things didn't work out with my fiancée. As long as I get engaged in the States to an American girl—someone she doesn't know and won't run into—I don't see how she will discover otherwise."

She sat back. "The idea does make me feel like I'd be doing a good deed."

He nodded and her chest tightened. Good grief. She'd seriously give up her company to see what it would be like to kiss him.

"Don't worry. It might be a good deed, but I'm happy to pay you."

She pulled herself together. "That's not what I meant. You're a good grandson. I totally understand what you're doing and why. I just feel that I need to point out that this might backfire."

"I won't let it. If it does, I'll be the one to deal with it."

The sincerity in his serious dark eyes told her he was as good as his word.

"Okay, then."

"Okay." He shifted on his chair. His smile warmed again. "Do you have any idea of what we'll do?"

"We can do anything you want. I think if you keep it simple like last night's proposal in the restaurant, your grandmother's more apt to believe it."

"Simple is good. But I was thinking maybe something in Central Park. It's green and lush in June. It would be a pretty space. Also maybe have mandolins playing in the background before I get down on one knee."

"I can do that." She sat forward. "I can also have potted flowers brought in for added color." She thought for a second. "Do you have a budget?"

He laughed. "Spare no expense."

She remembered his suit from the night before, the pretty blonde in the exclusive restaurant, and smiled. "Okay. Let's look at some pictures."

She hit a few buttons on her laptop and pulled up folders of other proposals she had done. She rose and sat on the seat beside him, setting the laptop on her desk between them so he could see what she had.

Opening one of her Central Park proposals, she said, "I like the idea of doing it in a pavilion." She glanced at him to see his reaction and when their gazes met something like lightning shot through her. They were close enough that she could touch him, and she swore she could feel the heat of his body—

She looked away and clicked on a picture of a proposal in Dene Summerhouse, reminding herself that he might be planning a fake proposal, but he had been having a cozy little dinner with a pretty blonde the night before. This attraction was totally one-sided or wishful thinking.

"As you can see, the gazebo itself is a little stark. So, I'd bring in pots of flowers for color." She pointed at the second picture. "We can have the mandolin players over here. And depending on whether or not you have a long speech planned—"

"I don't. As you said, the simpler the more believable."

"Then the whole thing can take two minutes. Unless you'd like to add a dance at the end."

"At the end?"

"After you propose, it would be romantic to share a slow dance. Particularly since you're already bringing in musicians."

"I like it. My grandmother would definitely think that was romantic and we'd still keep the whole thing under five minutes."

He smiled at her, and her nerve endings crackled. She could smell his cologne. If she moved her arm just a fraction their elbows would brush—

She cleared her throat and looked away to break the connection. "Okay. So, all we need is the when."

"I'm leaving town Wednesday morning. If we do it tomorrow night, could we have it up on the internet by the time I get home?"

She carried her computer back to the correct side of her desk and glanced at her calendar. "I don't see why not. Our proposal tomorrow is in the afternoon. The evening is open." She smiled her professional smile. "Once it's recorded it's only a few clicks on a keyboard to get it up online. I can probably text you the link right then and there. Unless you want the video edited. Then you won't have it until morning."

"No editing. I think the more honest the video, the more my GiGi will believe it. She'd love it if there was some kind of blunder. It would tickle her and probably make it even more believable. In fact, maybe we could slide one in."

She shook her head. "We'll keep it simple, but no deliberate blunders. Even if it is a fake proposal, I have a reputation to maintain." But the reminder that he really wasn't getting engaged rippled through her—

She squelched it. The man lived in Italy. She lived in Manhattan. Plus, he was one of those strong, decisive types. She liked sensitive lovers.

She almost slapped herself upside her head.

Why the hell was she thinking these things?

He rose. "Okay. We'll see you tomorrow night then."

"Yes." She hesitated but only for a second. All this had gone too easily. She ran down a mental list of what she needed and basically their short conversation had covered all the bases. Still, given that he really wasn't getting engaged, she couldn't assume he was a lovesick puppy who would do the normal prospective groom things.

"Don't forget to bring a ring."

He laughed.

"I'm serious. It's the most important part of the proposal. Putting the ring on your fake fiancée's finger will be ninety percent of the believability. I also want you to remember that there needs to be some longing glances and a good kiss right after you put the ring on her finger."

He snorted and raised his eyes to the heavens. "Got it."

She didn't want to insult him by telling him to practice the longing glances or the good kiss. She'd seen him kiss the woman at the restaurant. Even if she would only be his fake fiancée, Riley knew Antonio Salvaggio knew how to kiss.

She felt a few seconds of honest-to-God jealousy for the pretty blonde who would be standing in as his fiancée, if only because of that kiss, but stomped it out. She handled her love life the same way she handled her business. Carefully. Intelligently. A fling with a hot Italian guy might get her motor running but without the proper preplanning or thought, it could really blow up in her face. The same way this proposal could blow up for Antonio if they didn't do everything correctly.

She would get her head in the game and make this proposal beautiful and romantic…

And believable.

After Antonio left, her mom stepped into her office. Short and sweet but with a bit of a bossy side, Juliette Morgan sat on the chair Antonio had just vacated. "And who was that?"

This is what happened when you shared workspace with your mom's home nursing agency because rent in Manhattan was so high.

"A customer."

Her mom groaned. "Too bad. That guy is gorgeous."

"And he's from Italy. Too far away to date."

"So, you thought about it?"

She laughed. "Mom, I'm planning the man's proposal."

"Fake proposal," Marietta said as she entered Riley's office.

Riley gasped. "Marietta! That's not supposed to get around."

"Your mother's a nurse. She knows all about confidentiality."

Her mom studied her before she said, "I do know all about confidentiality, but I've also never seen that look on your face before."

"And I told you. He's from Italy. Here on business. I am never going to see him again."

"Except on Tuesday night for the proposal," Marietta interjected.

Her mom examined her for a few more seconds. "I came in here to ask you to have dinner with me on Tuesday night. I guess that's out of the question now."

Riley glanced at her calendar. "Not if we make it a late dinner. What's up?"

"Just some doctors I'm wining and dining for referrals."

She groaned. "They're not single are they, Mom?"

"No. Old and settled. But it's simply better to have you at dinner to keep the conversation from getting too boring."

She sighed. "I hate to sound like I'm old and cantankerous, because I'm only fifty, but sometimes these dinners are so dull I could weep."

Riley laughed. "Got it." She pointed at her mom but spoke to Marietta. "If you want to bug someone about taking a vacation. She's the one you should be bugging."

Juliette sighed. "I do not need a vacation. I just need someone to help me keep dinner light and amusing on Tuesday. Can you come?"

"Proposal is at seven, while it's still light out. It's going to be simple, and the client wants one take. He thinks bloopers will make it more believable." She shrugged. "I can be at the restaurant at eight. Eight-thirty at the latest."

Her mom rose. "Good." She walked toward the door but stopped and faced Riley again. "Wear something pretty. Not those beige pants and sweaters you always wear. We're going to The Milling Room. You'll need to fit in not blend into the woodwork."

Riley laughed even though it meant she'd have to bring something fancy to work and change before the Salvaggio proposal, so she wouldn't waste time going home after it. But that was fine. She and her mom had struggled after her dad died. His parents evicted them from his condo, and they were always two steps away from being homeless. All that time, her mom had gone without so Riley could have things. Then she'd started her home nursing agency and taught Riley that having control of your destiny was the only way to go. Now, Riley was a business owner too.

She owed everything to her mom. If Juliette wanted Riley to wear a pretty dress, then she would wear a pretty dress.

Because of the tight deadline, Riley had taken charge of the entire Salvaggio proposal herself. Twenty minutes before she had to leave, she slipped into a pink lace dress for her mom's dinner. She pulled her hair out of the bun and styled it around her shoulders before applying extra makeup and sliding into white sandals.

Clipboard in her big purse, she raced to the lobby to catch the cab that would take her to Central Park. Just off Fifth Avenue, Dene Summerhouse was easy to enter and just as easy to leave, so Riley wouldn't have any trouble getting to the dinner with her mother.

As she was overseeing both the flower arrangements and the mandolin players, Antonio Salvaggio walked up the path to the gazebo. He looked mouth-wateringly handsome in a light-colored suit with a pale blue tie. Both of which accented his dark good looks.

She greeted him warmly. "The blue tie is perfect. It works with your coloring and will show up on the video."

He glanced around the big gazebo. "For as quickly as we planned this, everything looks great."

"As we discussed, this is a simple proposal. You could have gone crazy with music and singing judge choirs or had the cast of a Broadway play sing a love song."

He laughed.

"But we decided on simple."

"Yes." He caught her hand and held her gaze. "Thank you."

Electricity skittered up her arm. With all that sincerity focused on her, his touch could have made her stutter. She forced herself to pull herself together and be professional. "My bill's already in your e-mail inbox."

He snickered and let go of her hand. "I still appreciate it."

She surveyed her crew and the pavilion. "Everything's ready. Do you have the ring?"

He patted his jacket pocket. "Right here."

She didn't need to see it to check off that item on her list. He was clearly organized and thorough, going at this like a businessman. "Do you know what you're going to say?"

"Just 'I love you. Will you marry me?'"

She nodded. "Short and sweet. Exactly what we want. So, where's the bride?"

He frowned. "Bride?"

"Sorry. Where's your fiancée?"

He continued to look at her as if he didn't understand.

"The woman you're going to ask to marry you."

His mouth fell open a little bit. "I thought you were bringing her."

"I don't even know who she is."

"That's the point. There is no one. So just like the flowers and the mandolin players I thought you'd provide someone to fake propose to."

This time her mouth fell open. "I assumed you'd bring the woman from the restaurant."

He squeezed his eyes shut. "No."

"Okay," she said, thinking on her feet. There were three cute young women arranging the flowers, but they were dressed in dark trousers and golf shirts with a florist logo on the breast pocket.

"I..." She looked around.

He tapped her shoulder to bring her attention back to him. "You're here." He looked down at her dress. "And you're dressed for it."

Damned if she wasn't. She squinted as she thought about her mom telling her to wear a dress—

She couldn't—

She wouldn't—

Could her mom have set up a dinner just to get her to wear a dress to this fake proposal?

She couldn't have. She wouldn't have known Antonio didn't have a fiancée. Still, it wouldn't be the first time Juliette had tried to matchmake.

Antonio's voice brought her back to reality. "Please. We've gone to all this trouble already."

She took a breath. "You're right. It's no big deal and technically I am dressed for it."

"And you look beautiful."

Her heart fluttered before she could remind herself that he'd only told her that because he wanted a favor.

She forced a smile, then turned to Jake, the videographer. "I'm going to be playing the part of the fiancée," she said, holding her smile in place as if it was no big deal that she was standing in for the role. Because it wasn't. This was a job. Period. Nothing more.

"Once I get to the center of the gazebo, you start filming." She faced the mandolin players. "Same instruction to you. Once I get to the center of the gazebo, start playing. I want the video to begin with me standing there, waiting for my Prince Charming with music in the background."

The three guys nodded. Jake scrambled to get into position for the best angle for the simple video.

She handed her big purse and clipboard to one of the flowerpot positioners. The woman looked confused, but she took them.

Riley started up the stairs but stopped suddenly. She faced Antonio. "I'll walk to the center and turn around. Jake will start filming. The guys will start playing. Count to five, then walk up the stairs and meet me in the middle."

He nodded.

She took a long breath and put her forced smile on her face again. She walked to the center and turned.

Jake said, "Action."

The mandolins sent romantic music wafting through the gazebo.

Antonio started up the steps. He walked to her, got down on one knee and took her hand.

When his warm fingers wrapped around hers, she had to

work to stop her heart from pounding. The man was simply too darned good looking and sexy.

"I love you, Riley Morgan. Will you marry me?"

The words rippled through her as if they were real. Their gazes held. It was like living a fantasy—

But that's all this was. Fantasy. A fake proposal to make his grandmother happy. His motives were good. She was getting paid.

Having seen the reactions of hundreds of prospective brides, she smiled broadly and said, "Yes! Yes! I will marry you! I love you too!"

He took the ring from his pocket and slipped it on her finger.

Had she not been fully immersed in the role she was playing she might have taken a second to gape at it. The diamond was huge. The gold band glittered like the sun.

He rose and caught her around the waist and a realization froze her breathing. She'd told him he had to kiss his new fiancée. But that was before *she* was the fiancée.

Their gazes caught. Time went to slow motion as his face got closer and closer. The breath in her lungs shivered. A tremor ran through her. But her stalled brain finally woke up.

Hadn't she thought she'd give up her entire company for one kiss from him? Well, this was her moment.

Her eyes closed. His mouth brushed hers. She swore she heard the choir of judges from Sunday night's proposal singing the alleluia chorus. His lips were surprisingly soft and amazingly experienced. He brought her closer, making her realize she was all but frozen with shock. She slid her hands up to his shoulders, then slipped them around his neck.

As his clever mouth worked its magic, he brought her closer again. Her breasts bumped his chest. All the air disappeared from her lungs.

The mandolin players shifted songs, as they had been instructed, and the music for their slow dance began. He broke the kiss but instead of moving away from her, he stared into her eyes. She saw his confusion and knew it mirrored hers. Every part of her body was warm and tingling. She could have caught his shoulders and brought him back to kiss him again.

But he slid one hand around her waist and took her other hand to lead her in the dance. They drifted together slowly. Even as every cell in her body wanted every second she could get pressed against him, her brain reminded her this wasn't real.

This wasn't real!

Good grief! They were being videotaped for his grandmother. And she was not acting the part of a happy new fiancée. She was shell-shocked.

She stepped closer to him, laid her head on his shoulder familiarly and almost swooned when the feeling of being pressed against him stole her breath again. Temptation skittered through her. For the remaining two minutes, he was hers to cuddle or kiss or—

Stop.

Seriously.

Laying her head on his shoulder was intimate enough. Especially when his hand drifted from her waist to the middle of her back. The romance of it flitted through her. She told herself one more time that this wasn't real, but the sigh that stuttered out of her was very real.

He was probably the sexiest guy she'd ever met, and they were snuggling. She was allowed to sigh.

It would be good for the video.

CHAPTER THREE

THE MUSIC STOPPED and they broke apart slowly. For the next ten seconds they held each other's gaze. He didn't know what she was thinking but he'd never felt the sensations that had rippled through him when he kissed her. The logical part of him knew his honest reaction would be good for the video, but the male in him was nothing but confused.

He knew all about attraction and seduction. What had happened between them had been...different.

Jake yelled, "Cut!" bringing Antonio's attention to the young man in jeans and a sloppy shirt. He shook his head as he watched the playback on the recorder in his hand. "I think it's perfect."

"I'd like to see it," Riley said, her voice crisp and professional.

Still a bit shell-shocked, Antonio whispered, "I'm pretty sure it's exactly what we want."

His whisper accurately depicted what he felt. A soft, insistent confusion. When he reminded himself this wasn't real, his soul rebelled, confusing him even more. What he'd felt holding her could be as dangerous as it was romantic and wonderful. He'd lost control of that kiss. Following those feelings could mean losing control in bigger, more important ways. Antonio Salvaggio did not lose control. He'd done that in his first marriage, and it nearly destroyed his faith in humanity. Which was what made his reaction so confusing. He knew better.

Jake sauntered over. Addressing Riley, he said, "I texted the video to your phone."

She took her purse from the wide-eyed florist helper who had been holding it and rummaged for her phone. As she pulled it out, it pinged with a text. Two screens later she and Antonio were huddled around it watching the video.

He could see every emotion on her face. Fake surprise when he asked her to marry him became real surprise when he pulled her close to seal the deal with the kiss, which started slowly and built to the unexpected passion that had left him flummoxed. When they'd pulled away, he saw real longing in her eyes. His grandmother would probably see it as romantic. For a second, he did too.

But romance was a mirage. The truth was they'd surprised each other with that kiss. They really were attracted, but they would never see each other again, and these feelings were fleeting. Plus, he couldn't really be upset about never again seeing a woman he only just met. He didn't miss his lovers when they were apart. How could he feel a ping of disappointment over a woman he'd kissed for a video?

When the video ended, he quietly said, "It's perfect."

She smiled at him, back to being totally professional. "It is. I'd say we're done here."

He glanced at Jake. "You'll put it up online?"

"Whatever platform you want."

"Make it private on YouTube—" He didn't want the entire world having access to a fake proposal and he suspected Riley wouldn't either. "I'll send my grandmother the link." Needing to get things back to normal, he shook Riley's hand and smiled at her. "Thank you."

Her face remained professionally pleasant. Though he thought that should jerk him back to reality, it was difficult to pull his gaze away from her.

When he realized he was standing there, holding her hand

like a man bewitched, he dropped it. "Good-bye, Riley Morgan."

"Good-bye, Antonio Salvaggio."

He headed out of the park to the limo that awaited him. "Airport, Simon."

His driver said, "Yes, sir. But I thought you weren't going home until morning?"

He laughed. "Have you ever had one of those moments when you knew deep down it was time to go home?"

"Only with a woman I shouldn't have been dating, Mr. Salvaggio."

Antonio laughed. "That pretty much sums it up. Let's get me out of here."

After watching Antonio disappear down a path that would take him away forever, Riley got to work directing the florist's crew to gather the flowers. The musicians packed to leave. Jake headed back to the office to go over the video again to make sure there were no odd things in the background before he put it up on the internet.

The mandolin players left next. Then the florist's helpers carried out the potted flowers and suddenly she was alone.

She glanced around. Technically, she was done and Antonio Salvaggio, good kisser that he was, was out of her life. She blew out a relieved breath and headed out of the park, but the sun caught her left hand and the enormous diamond winked at her.

She froze.

He'd forgotten to take back the ring!

Or she'd forgotten to give back the ring.

Damn it!

She was not walking around Manhattan wearing what she was certain was a million-dollar ring on her finger! She had to return it to him.

She quickly called her mom. The call went to voice mail, which was good. Because when she didn't arrive for dinner, her mom would check her phone and find the voice mail and Riley wouldn't have to make a long explanation.

"Sorry, Mom. I can't make dinner. The proposal took an unexpected turn and I have to fix it."

There. That gave her mom enough information that she wouldn't make her doctors wait for dinner.

She took a cab to her office and pulled up Antonio's file on her laptop. Thank God she had his hotel information as a way to contact him. She quickly called the front desk, and they connected her to his room.

No answer.

She attempted to reach him for an hour and eventually gave up. He could have gone to dinner or a club—or on a date with the blonde.

She winced, telling herself that was none of her business. Getting this ring back to him was.

With the hotel number in her phone, she tried three more times on the cab ride to her apartment. When she used her left hand to open the door, the damned diamond winked at her again. Sighing, she dropped her purse on a living room chair. If nothing else, she could take the darned thing off.

She wrapped her fingers around the slim band to pull off the ring, but it didn't budge.

Groaning, she tried again. Nothing.

She took a seat to give herself better leverage and pulled one more time. Nope. Not even moving, let alone sliding off.

She tried three times, but it wouldn't come off.

It was stuck.

Using an old trick she'd learned from her mom, she put a little cooking oil around it and tried again. It didn't budge.

Tired and more than a little annoyed, she left it on while she showered, put on pajamas and slid into bed. She tried Antonio's hotel room one more time, then remembered she had his business card. Surely, his cell number would be on that.

She whipped it out of her purse only to discover his cell wasn't on it, only the number for his office in Italy. Seeing that, she remembered that was why he'd given her his hotel information. The business card was no help.

She sighed again and eventually fell asleep, though the ring weighed down her finger like a bolder.

Waking early, she dressed quickly and headed to his hotel. At the desk, she said, "I need to see Antonio Salvaggio. Can you call his room for me?"

The clerk hit a few keys on her computer and frowned. "He checked out."

"He checked out? Already? It's not even seven o'clock!"

The clerk looked at her computer screen. "He called last night and said he wouldn't be returning. Housekeeping is packing his things to ship to him."

She stared at the clerk. "He left last night?"

With a sigh of annoyance, the young woman said, "Yes."

"So, if I had something to give him like a signed contract—" She shifted the truth a bit because she couldn't go around with a million-dollar ring on her finger, and she also couldn't drop it in the mail. She knew the hotel had his information. If not his cell number, an e-mail. If he was still in New York, a signed contract could cause the clerk to contact him. "You wouldn't be able to give it to him?"

"Not really. Unless you want me to fly to Italy."

"You don't have a cell phone number?"

"We have his office number…the reservations were made by his company."

Disappointment overrode the clerk's complete lack of concern. "Okay. Thank you." The clerk might not have to fly to Italy, but it looked like she would.

Forty minutes later, her mom sat across from her in her

office, sipping coffee in between guffaws of laughter. "I'm sorry, sweetie, but that whole thing about a fake proposal was bizarre."

"It made perfect sense, Mom. His grandmother is still depressed over losing her husband and now she's facing chemo. He knows the video will cheer her up."

"He does realize he's going to have to do a lot of lying over the next few months."

"Not my problem." She waved her hand in dismissal and the ring shimmered in the morning light as if laughing at her. "My problem is getting this stupid ring back to him."

"That's hardly a stupid ring. It's gorgeous. And you're not going to be able to drop it in the mail."

"I know."

"There are services though. You know, delivery companies who handle special packages."

"There are only two problems with that. I can't get it off my finger and I don't want to have it removed by a jeweler for fear we'll damage it. If we have to have a jeweler remove it, I want Antonio with me while they cut the band."

"Looks like you're going to Italy."

She groaned. "I can't! It's a busy time for me."

"I hate to break to you, but the quicker you get to Italy, find the guy and get to a jeweler together, the better."

Riley covered her face with her hands.

"Oh, come on. You're the only person I know who could grouse about going to Italy. Especially when you've been talking about expanding. You say you want to offer proposals in Tuscany, but you don't have any contacts. So go to Italy. Make the contacts with the florists and vineyards and violinists."

She opened her fingers to peek at her mom. "I do want to expand."

Her mom rose from her seat, taking her mug of coffee with her. "Yeah, you do. Why not make your airline ticket open ended? Once you get there you can contact Antonio about the ring, then check out vendors and venues. In between phone calls and meetings, you can take in the sites. Maybe meet a good-looking guy and have some fun."

She snorted. "I might take a few days, but only for work."

"Take some extra time to relax."

"No."

"Why not? You have a very capable staff. Put Marietta in charge. She's been training for this since the day you hired her."

It was true. All the staff had been trained and Marietta could stand in for Riley for a day or two...a week or two really.

Not that Riley intended to take extra days, but this was a really good opportunity to do the legwork she needed to do to expand her business.

She shook her head, then turned to her computer so she could look up Antonio Salvaggio. She had the number for his office in Italy, but what was the point in calling? She had to fly to Italy anyway. It would be much easier to just show him the ring and explain that they needed to go to a jeweler.

Luckily, his family was so rich he wasn't merely listed in the general information websites for his family's companies. He was also in several magazine articles that mentioned he lived in the mansion on the family's enormous vineyard with his father and grandmother.

It finally dawned on her that she couldn't go to his house. *She* was the fake fiancée in the video. If she went to his house, she might run into his grandmother. Oh, boy. That would be peachy.

She would have to go to his office.

She called the airline.

The time difference for Antonio's trip home always screwed up his internal clock. He'd slept on the plane but when he arrived home it was time to have dinner with his father and grandmother, who had a million questions. He'd sent them the link to the video proposal at the airport so he wouldn't have to field their reaction calls while he was in the air. Now, it was time to handle the fallout.

He knew enough about Riley that he could give real answers to GiGi. Except he didn't tell her Riley was a *marriage proposal* planner. He'd told her she was an *event* planner. Which, technically, was the same thing.

His father had given him an exuberant slap on the back and both he and GiGi had asked when they would get to meet this woman who'd finally gotten him to see that love was real.

He'd laughed and told them he wasn't sure when she'd be in Italy, though he threw them a bone by conceding Riley was special. But walking into his office on Thursday morning, he'd frowned, flummoxed again about the sensations and feelings that had raced through him when he'd kissed her. That kiss— one fake kiss—was not an indication that the all-encompassing state called love was real. Love was hormones. Love was the fantasy of men who lost control, lost their footing, and let themselves believe a fairy tale because it felt good. And eventually when the happiness died, and they needed an excuse for making a mistake, love was a much better reason than saying they let their hormones get the better of them.

Which was what had happened in his marriage. Sylvia had been a model so beautiful people stopped on the street to stare at her. She'd been soft and sweet. The paparazzi had loved them as a couple.

Then six months into the marriage, the silent treatment had begun, followed by longer and longer separations for her photo shoots and runway shows.

The sad thing was he'd soon become glad when she left and tired when she returned.

When he'd decided they needed to fix whatever was wrong,

he'd surprised her by showing up at her latest gig and found her in bed with her favorite photographer.

He'd had six months of happiness and endured six months of her anger and sarcasm only to discover she'd left the marriage long before he'd even known it was over—

His phone buzzed as he sat on the tall-back chair behind his desk. He answered on speaker.

"There's a Riley Morgan here to see you."

He froze. "Riley Morgan?"

"From New York."

Their kiss popped into his head, along with the sensation of running his hand from her waist up her back and down again. He knew what she tasted like. Knew what she felt like. And wished he'd had the foresight to run his fingers through her hair. He liked it down, not in that bun at her nape. She looked ethereal—

Stop.

He pulled himself together, shoved all that nonsense out of his head. "Please send her in."

Twenty seconds later his door opened and his assistant escorted Riley Morgan into his office. Today she wore jeans and a simple top. She should have looked relaxed and comfortable. Instead, she caught his gaze with wary eyes.

No one ever looked more beautiful.

He thought of his ex. One of the most stunning women in the world. And he reminded himself beauty was only skin deep.

"Thank you, Geoffrey."

His assistant left. He and Riley stared at each other.

Finally, she said, "We have a problem."

This he could handle. "No. We don't. Whatever happened on your end, my grandmother is glowing, and my dad's the happiest I've ever seen him. Fix whatever is wrong because we're good here."

She held up her left hand and the diamond he'd slipped on her finger sparkled at him.

He'd been so confused he'd forgotten the ring.

The oddest rattle of happiness raced through him. She'd brought the ring to him herself? Almost like an excuse to see him.

Try as he might to sound businesslike, his smile ruined it. "You could have found a courier."

"I can't get it off."

His gaze fell to the ring. "Oh!"

"I tried the easy stuff. But I think a jeweler is going to have to cut it off. Since it's clearly expensive I didn't want to go to that extreme without your approval."

Motioning for her to take a seat, he tried to think of something clever to say and couldn't. Too many things buzzed around in his head. Complete lack of concern for the expensive ring. Disappointment that she hadn't been looking for a reason to see him again. And the oddest spike of interest that she'd be in Italy at least for the day. They could go to a jeweler, get the ring removed, have lunch somewhere romantic—

"Do you have a jeweler?"

He snapped himself back to the present. "Of course. A man doesn't have a grandmother whose birthstone is a diamond without having a jeweler who has a file on everything she already owns."

Riley laughed. "You know there's a part of me that would like to get to know this woman. Not only is she taking charge of her own life, but she got you to fake a proposal and now I find out she gets her own way on jewelry too."

He settled back into his chair. "Yeah, she does."

"Sounds like a firecracker."

He caught the gaze of her stunning green eyes, felt the connection of being in cahoots with each other, as well as having kissed and danced. Complicated, unwanted pleasure filled him again. For as much as he was curious about why he kept experiencing things with her that he never had before with another person, he also did not like things he couldn't explain.

So, no romantic lunch.

Trip to the jewelers, yes.

Lunch? No.

If he was smart, he'd drive her to the airport immediately after they got the ring off and send her home.

"She is definitely a firecracker." He reached for his phone. "Let me call Rafe," he said referring to his jeweler. Before he had a chance to hit the contact number, his office door burst open and his short, wiry GiGi burst in. Dark hair peppered with gray, and a bright red pantsuit made her look like the firecracker Riley guessed she was.

She gaped at Riley. "It's true! You *are* here!"

Riley's gaze jumped to his. He jumped out of his chair. "GiGi! What a nice surprise!"

"I was early for my hair appointment," GiGi said, examining Riley as she walked over to her. "And I thought I'd stop in to kill some time. When I got here, Geoffrey told me you had someone in your office. After I prodded, he admitted it was Riley. So lovely to meet you, dear."

Riley cautiously rose from her seat. "If I'd known I was going to meet you, I'd have worn better clothes."

GiGi's head tilted. "You look comfortable."

"Well, the flight from New York is long. I wasn't about to wear heels."

GiGi laughed. "You missed my Antonio." She patted Riley's cheek. "How sweet…and romantic."

Grateful, Riley had kept up the ruse, Antonio said, "And I missed her." He walked over to Riley to slide his arm around her waist. She automatically stiffened, but quickly relaxed.

He frowned. While his entire body filled with happiness at touching her, she'd stiffened?

Not that he cared. He *didn't* care. They were strangers who'd faked a proposal for his grandmother. Right now, this was all about his grandmother.

Excitement brightened GiGi's pretty face as she said, "Can I see the ring?"

"Of course!" Riley held out her hand. "It's beautiful, isn't it?"

GiGi's eyes filled with tears and every moment of discomfort and confusion he'd experienced because of this ruse became worth it.

"It's beautiful." She caught Riley's hand. "And you are beautiful. I feel like I'm looking at a mirage."

"No mirage, GiGi," Antonio said, though he had to fight back a wince at the lie.

She unexpectedly hugged Riley before patting Antonio's cheek twice. "You surprise me," she told him. "But it's the happiest surprise of my life."

She stood on tiptoe and kissed the cheek she'd just patted. "You two can tell me all about it at dinner tonight. I want to hear everything. How you met. When you kept company. How you kept all this a secret."

Once again, Riley picked up the ball. "Well, we haven't actually known each other long. But when something works, you know it."

His grandmother beamed. *"Si!"* She glanced at her watch and headed for the door. "I need to go, or I'll miss my appointment. But I have to say your engagement filled me with joy…and now I've gotten to meet the woman responsible. This is my lucky day!"

She left Antonio's office and silence reigned for a solid minute.

"Actually, what was *lucky* was that you couldn't get the ring off."

Riley snorted. "If the ring had been off, we could have said that I'd come to Italy because I'd had a change of heart and wanted to break the engagement. And the ruse would be over."

"I don't want it to be over, remember? Not until she starts her treatments. Besides, it's perfect. You live in the US so we can go about our lives normally until Gigi is done with her chemo. She hasn't made arrangements for the treatments yet, but from the joyful look on her face when she met you, I saw shades of happy GiGi coming back. She'll make them soon, then I can keep up the ruse here in Italy until she's well again. When I make trips to the US, I'll say the trips are to see you, not merely for business. All you have to do is come to dinner at the vineyard tonight to make the story look legit."

She frowned. "I don't know… It's getting complicated now."

He caught her hands. Electricity shot through him. He worked to ignore it by remembering the important reason he'd planned all this. "Please?"

She took a breath and expelled it quickly. "Since we're going beyond our original arrangement, how about a new deal?"

Not wanting to be indebted to anyone, he liked that there was something she needed from him. "Anything."

"I didn't just come to Italy to return the ring. I'm planning to expand my business by offering proposals here in Tuscany. Since I'm here anyway, I was going to scout locations, look for vendors, that kind of thing. Can you get me an in with some of the vendors? You know, put in a good word for me so prices don't go through the roof because I'm from the US. Even if you can't do flowers and musicians…what I really need is a beautiful vineyard to host the proposals."

"I could fix it so that you could use *our* vineyard for proposals if you do this favor for me." He smiled again. "At dinner tonight, you could actually see the place. I'll even give you a tour."

Approval lit her pretty green eyes. "All right."

His chest blossomed with happiness that tried to steal his breath. He warned himself that getting too close to her was playing with fire, but he couldn't shake the sense that having real feelings for each other would help them that night.

"You'll pick me up for dinner?"

"Yes."

The warmth that filled him at the idea of spending more time with her should have been a warning to tread lightly. But he was a grown man, not interested in the relationship they were pretending to have. She would be wonderful with his family at dinner. He had no reason to believe otherwise since she'd played her part very well—even when his grandmother surprised them. He would keep his deal about the vineyard, and tomorrow he would instruct Geoffrey to help her find florists and musicians suitable for her business. When she was done with her research, he would send his limo to take her to the airport so she could go home.

There was nothing to worry about.

CHAPTER FOUR

As GOOD AS his word, Antonio arrived at her hotel around six to pick her up. He got out of the white limo to allow her entry and smiled when he saw her, sending her heart rate through the roof.

"You look wonderful."

She glanced down at her simple pink sundress. "This was the only thing I brought that I thought would suit. But I can easily explain to your grandmother that I packed light. I didn't have anything fancy to wear."

"Makes sense." He motioned for her to enter the limo and got in behind her. "Thank you again for doing this."

"You're welcome. But it's not purely a favor. Don't forget your offer about your family's vineyard."

"I haven't. Mostly because it will be good PR for us too."

She peeked at him. "Oh, yeah?"

"The more people who come to the vineyard, the more positive word of mouth we get."

"Your word of mouth is always positive?"

"Our vineyard is exceptional. We have a luxury wine tasting room, but we also have a gazebo for those who enjoy being outdoors."

"Both sound perfect for proposals."

"And if neither of those work for you...there's a cobblestone path along the perimeter of the vineyard. It's beautiful through the summer."

It surprised her that he'd thought this through, but having just planned his own "proposal," he probably remembered what she'd told him as they were flipping through the pages of her venue book.

Satisfied with their deal, she took a breath and watched the scenery go by. Rolling hills, lush with green grass and rows of grapevines told her why people loved Italy.

"This is amazing."

"Are you speaking generally or for your business?"

"Both. It's gorgeous! If I lived here, I'd never leave."

"I feel the same way about Manhattan. I was born and raised in what most people consider paradise. But Manhattan is a paradise too. Wonderful restaurants. Broadway. Central Park. If I lived *there*, I would never leave."

She laughed. "You're saying the grass is always greener on the other side?"

He faced her. "Something like that." He smiled. "We always want what we can't have."

Unexpectedly intimate, the smile sent a shiver through her which she barely suppressed. If she really thought about this, he was forbidden fruit. That was probably why he seemed so interesting. Adding that to the connection they had because they were doing favors for each other, her emotions went haywire.

Of course, doing favors for each other technically made them friends. Which was a much better explanation for why she was so happy around him.

That conclusion stopped the weird sense that something personal could be growing between them. Yes. Their kiss had been amazing and dancing with him had been like a fairy tale, but now they had an arrangement. A deal. Anything "personal" between them was nothing more than the friendship developing as a result of their deal.

When they arrived at the vineyard, she had to stifle a gasp.

Not just at the beauty of the grounds, but also the villa. The spectacular two-story yellow stucco mansion rambled as if sections had been added to the main house, giving it depth and interest.

"It's lovely."

"It's a monster," Antonio said, helping her out of the limo. "It's been in my family for hundreds of years. It seemed every generation built an addition as a way to add their stamp to it. I persuaded my grandmother that we had enough space, and rather than add on, she tore out the original pool and created a patio that's perfect for parties."

She laughed. "I hope you realize, she's a gem."

"I do." He closed the limo door. "Dinner won't be for at least an hour. Not until my father gets home. I should have told you to bring a swimsuit."

"It's probably better you didn't." She hooked her hand around his elbow, making them look like the couple they were supposed to be. "You'd have never gotten me out of the water. I don't take vacations. A pool sounds like heaven right now."

He chuckled, but quickly sobered. "Are you ready for this?"

"Absolutely. We can amuse your grandmother until dinner, eat, and then you can give me the tour of the wine tasting room, gazebo and path. I'll take a few pictures on my phone and shoot them to Jake who'll start a book for proposals in Tuscany. And I'll go back to the hotel."

"Sounds like a plan." He took a breath. "And really, I'm glad I could help. You truly are going above and beyond for me."

They entered the front foyer and she sighed with appreciation. A curved mahogany stairway led to the second floor. A crystal chandelier caught the sunlight.

"GiGi! We're here!" Antonio called, disturbing the sedate elegance.

GiGi appeared at the top of the stairs and descended like the mistress of the manor that she was, her sheer maxi dress billowing around her. When she reached the bottom, she kissed both of their cheeks. "Let's enjoy the patio."

"I was just telling Riley about your remodel."

"Remodel?" She cut Antonio a stony look. "Rebuild is more accurate. At the very least it's a total redesign."

Antonio removed his jacket and a man in a white coat suddenly appeared to take it before scampering away.

GiGi led the way down a corridor that revealed sitting rooms and a huge formal dining room before they reached French doors. She opened them on an infinity pool overlooking the vineyard. Then she sat on a chaise shaded by an umbrella.

Riley stared. She rarely got out of Manhattan, so she'd never been on such a huge patio. A long row of French doors lined the entire back wall of the house, granting entry to the patio from most of the downstairs rooms. Yellow stones that matched the stucco surrounded the pool.

There were enough umbrella tables and seating areas for a hundred people beside a huge, covered bar. Beyond that was the vineyard. Lush and green. She had no idea where the winemaking facilities were, or the gazebo or the path Antonio had spoken of, but they appeared to be far enough away that her proposal clients wouldn't disturb the Salvaggio family. They probably wouldn't even know they were there. Which was undoubtedly why Antonio felt comfortable offering those spaces for her use.

Antonio glanced around. "It might be a little warm for me out here in a long sleeve shirt."

GiGi waved him off. "Go. Change out of that suit. Dinner will not be formal. In fact, if you want, we can eat out here."

Riley suddenly felt like a peasant in her simple sundress and sandals and worried GiGi had changed their plans for her.

As Antonio left, Riley glanced down at her clothes, wincing. "I packed light."

GiGi laughed. "You look lovely. And we don't have formal dinners unless we have a guest." She sat up. "*You* are family."

Relief filled her and she sat on the chaise beside GiGi's. "This is a beautiful home."

"It's a monstrosity. But it's our monstrosity. It's been in the Salvaggio family forever." She took a slow breath, suddenly moody. "Even though I came here as a young bride and have been here decades, it still feels wrong to live here without my Carlos."

Riley saw the sorrow and grief etched in GiGi's face and remembered the grief her mother had endured after Riley's dad died. "Carlos was your husband?"

She nodded. "You would have loved him."

The French doors opened.

GiGi said, "That was quick."

When Riley turned, she saw Antonio walking out in shorts and a T-shirt. He looked happy and approachable, but so different that she laughed. "Well, that's a side of you—"

He gave her a warning look.

"That I don't see often enough," she finished, pulling back from saying she'd never seen him dressed casually. No matter how new their engagement, a real fiancée would have seen him in much less than a suit and tie.

He walked over, leaned down and kissed her forehead before lowering himself to the chaise on the other side of GiGi.

She knew he'd kissed her because it was something a fiancé would do and told herself not to swoon over gestures of affection. They had a whole night ahead of them.

Antonio grimaced. "I should have gotten some wine before I sat."

"I would love a glass of white," GiGi said.

Not wanting to be trouble, Riley said, "That's good for me too."

Antonio rose and walked to the covered bar. He stowed a bottle of wine in a bucket of ice and set it on a fancy cart. He added four wine glasses, then wheeled the cart to their seating area.

He filled the first glass and handed it to GiGi, then poured a glass for Riley.

Their gazes caught. "Thank you."

"You're welcome."

An unholy sense of rightness rattled through her, but she reminded herself it was simply the connection of doing favors for each other. Not just the ruse but his offer of helping her. They were friends. Business associates.

She took a sip of her wine, as an older gentleman came out of the French doors. Every bit as tall and handsome as Antonio, he headed toward their grouping of chaise lounges.

"Enzo!" GiGi said. She motioned to Riley. "This is Antonio's fiancée."

Antonio rose from his chaise. "Dad, this is Riley Morgan. She's from Manhattan. Riley, this is my dad, Lorenzo Salvaggio."

She rose as he reached her chair, extending her hand to shake his. But the dark-haired gentleman caught her in a bear hug, almost causing her to spill her wine.

"What a pleasure!" he said excitedly, as he released her far enough that he could hold her at arm's distance and study her. He turned to Antonio. "You do the family proud. She is lovely." He faced Riley again. "This also explains how he could keep your relationship a secret! You live across an ocean."

Antonio chuckled. "Surely, you didn't think I flew to Manhattan twice a month just to see lawyers."

His father laughed. Antonio poured him a glass of wine.

"So, you are from Manhattan?"

"Yes. I run an event planning business."

"That's interesting."

Realizing Antonio's father was smart enough to put two and two together if they didn't handle this right, she smiled. "It's a fun challenge. Every event is different. I also have five employees. But if the business keeps growing the way I mapped out in my five-year plan, I'll be adding two more every year."

Enzo beamed at her. "Impressive."

"Thank you."

As if Enzo's arrival was a signal, the kitchen staff quietly began preparing one of the umbrella tables for dinner.

When they were done, Enzo rose from his seat. "It looks like they are ready for us, and I am starving."

"Me too," Riley said, so comfortable with Antonio's family that she should have at least wondered about it, but she didn't. She got along with Antonio, who was basically a stranger. Why wouldn't she get along with his father and grandmother?

They took their wine glasses to the table. As they sat, Antonio went behind the bar for another bottle. A young woman served antipasto.

When everyone was settled, Riley tasted her first bite and groaned. "This is fabulous."

GiGi pointed at her. "I'm thinking you don't eat enough."

She shook her head. "Trust me. I do. I have one of those metabolisms that runs like a race car. I can and do eat a lot."

"Or maybe it's that you work too much," Antonio suggested.

"I don't think I do," Riley disagreed but it was a great way to continue their conversation about her business, including the fact that she shared office space with her mom, so they didn't touch on anything too personal that might trip them up. She didn't want to make a mistake or lie to his grandmother any more than they already were.

Dinner, Florentina steak and pasta, was served and the conversation about her business continued through the meal. Riley noticed GiGi losing her energy, winding down from the day, and wasn't surprised when she refused dessert.

"I'm just feeling tired." She smiled at Riley. "We talked so much about your company, we haven't heard about anyone in your family except your mom."

"That's because it's just my mom and me," Riley said, setting down her gelato spoon.

GiGi's eyes softened. "I'm so sorry. Your father...?"

"Unfortunately, my father passed when I was seven." Empathizing with GiGi and realizing she might need to know she wasn't alone in her grief, Riley added, "I was a kid, but I still remember the loss like it was yesterday. My mother seemed to grieve forever."

"*Si.*" GiGi nodded. "I understand."

"But she's good now. Her business made her wealthy. She's busy and happy. She flits all over Manhattan like she owns the place."

Everyone laughed.

GiGi said, "What does her husband think about that?"

Confused, she tilted her head. "Her husband? You mean my dad?"

"No, her new husband. She was young when your father died. Did she not remarry?"

"She never married at all." Riley shook her head. "She and my dad lived together after she got pregnant. They believed they had all the time in the world to get married. Turns out they had only eight years together before he died."

GiGi clutched her chest. "That is sad."

"It was, but it was long ago."

"So long that she could have found someone." Serious and solemn, GiGi held her gaze. "Did she never want anyone but your dad?"

Riley had indulged this conversation hoping to help GiGi see that her future wouldn't always be filled with grief. Instead, it seemed she was making GiGi sadder. "What she went through after my dad was rough. She sort of lost her faith in people."

And that was worse.

Now she was going to have to explain why her mother had lost her faith in people. There was no way Antonio's grandmother would relate to the rest of her story.

"Because my parents never married, my father's family refused to acknowledge us. After I was born, my mom went to nursing school. My father paid all household expenses. When my mom got out of nursing school, they kept that up…with my mom using her paychecks to buy things I needed. Meaning, my dad's family believed my mom had no stake or share in the condo he'd bought before they met. Lawyers served us eviction papers two days after he died, and my mom packed and left. She probably could have hired a lawyer to get a piece of his estate. But she didn't want it. She wanted nothing from his family. She had loved him. Not his money. And she saw walking away as proof of that."

GiGi took a breath. "That is romantic and strong."

"Yes, to both."

GiGi rose to leave. "And I understand perfectly."

She did. Riley knew GiGi was a lot stronger than she let on. Though she grieved, there was a strength beneath the sadness. Riley longed to let GiGi pour her heart out about her late husband, but she wasn't really part of this family.

For the first time, the ruse seemed wrong. But she wouldn't let that thought stick. Antonio's fake proposal would ultimately help GiGi.

GiGi studied her for a second before she said, "I'm glad your mamma is happy."

"Yes." The sincerity in GiGi's eyes made her realize again why Antonio didn't want to lose her. She was a wonderful, empathetic person. "Thank you."

Antonio rose from his chair. "I promised Riley a tour of the wine tasting room, gazebo and vineyards." He held out his hand to her. She rose and took it. "We'll be back to say good night."

Enzo rose. GiGi smiled. "I will see you then."

Antonio kept her hand as they walked around a hedge to a

hidden cobblestone walkway. The lights for the path shifted from the patio lights to quaint streetlamps.

The "other" side of the vineyard came into view. A huge building with the same yellow stucco as the house sat in front of even more fields of grapevines. A big tree shaded the gazebo. Lit by streetlights, a path wound from the wine tasting room to the gazebo and along the vineyard.

Just as Antonio had told her.

As they grew closer, she could hear the music that billowed out of the building. A parking lot filled with cars and buses didn't exactly ruin the ambience of the beautiful place, but it did show her she'd probably want to use the gazebo or path for proposals.

"I'm sorry that it's noisy, but this is a typical Thursday."

"Oh, don't be sorry," she said, enjoying the moonlight and the fresh air of the vineyard. Realizing they were far enough away that they didn't need to be holding hands, she pulled her hand out of his but wished she hadn't. She'd probably be in Italy another day or two. Was it so wrong to enjoy him while she had him?

She shook her head to clear that thought. She was not really engaged to Antonio. They weren't even dating. They were now business associates, and she would act accordingly.

Pulling her phone out of her dress pocket, she snapped a few pictures that she sent to Jake. "I need to get the real idea of what the area looks like so I can decide how to handle things. The inside might be noisy, but the outside is beautiful. Romantic."

He laughed.

As they approached the gazebo, she took more pictures, then twirled in the moonlight. "This is the place for evening proposals...and the path by the grapevines would be my choice for daytime."

They continued along the cobblestone, long enough for

Riley to see the area was dreamy in the moonlight and maybe rethink the path for nighttime proposals, then they headed back to the house.

Antonio led her to a family room where GiGi was reading, and Enzo watched a sporting event on a big screen TV.

"I'm going to take Riley back to her hotel."

GiGi balked. "Why is your fiancée staying at a hotel, not the villa?"

Riley almost choked. But Antonio didn't miss a beat. "It's a luxury hotel and I'm not coming back." He wrapped his arms around Riley from behind. "We're still celebrating our engagement."

Clearly pleased, GiGi smiled, but heat went through Riley. She pictured it. She could see them kissing in her room. He would romantically sweep her off her feet and she would melt like butter—

She stopped the vision, but the yearnings remained. The evening had been warm and happy, their walk romantic.

Going back to her room seemed like a logical next step— *No. It did not!*

Thoughts like that shouldn't even enter her mind. Antonio was a stranger—

Well, technically, that was no longer true. She now knew his family. She'd seen his office and part of his home. And while she'd talked to his GiGi, he'd sat back and listened to the story of her life.

They weren't strangers anymore. They knew a lot about each other.

The excuse that gave her a good reason to stay an arm's distance away was no longer true.

She was really going to have to keep her guard up now.

CHAPTER FIVE

WHEN THEY ARRIVED at her hotel, Antonio helped Riley out of the limo. Given that he couldn't go home, he would also have to get a room for the night. This hotel was as good of a place as any.

Stepping inside the plush interior of the pale stucco building, he reminded himself that spending the night in one of the exquisite rooms wouldn't be a hardship, though he wished he'd thought ahead to bring clothes for the next day. Luckily, he had an extra suit in his office closet and could change out of his shorts and T-shirt when he got to work.

"Let's make a quick stop at the reservation desk," he said, directing Riley that way. "I'll need to get a room."

Two steps before they would have reached it, the gentleman ahead of them turned. Antonio's chest pinched, then his father's friend Marco said, "Antonio?"

"Si. Buonasera." He shook Marco's hand.

Glancing at Riley, Marco said, *"Buonasera."*

"Marco, this is Riley Morgan. Riley, this is Marco Ricci. He's a good friend of my father's."

"Your father's *best* friend and your godfather," Marco corrected, reverting to English, as Antonio had done, for Riley's benefit.

Riley said, "It's a pleasure to meet you."

Marco grinned as if he'd caught Antonio in the act of escorting a woman to a room for the night. Then he glanced at her hand.

His gaze jumped to Antonio's. "You are engaged?"

Antonio took a quick breath. He had no choice but to keep up the charade. Marco might live in Paris, but he still did business in Italy with Antonio's father. He slid his arm around Riley's lower back. *"Si."*

"You are *engaged*?" Marco repeated, his voice dripping with confusion.

Antonio laughed. "Why are you so surprised?"

"Your first marriage was a disaster."

And the whole world seemed to know.

It was the embarrassment of a mistake that would follow him forever. "Yes. I was there, remember?"

Marco unexpectedly grinned. "I want to tease you mercilessly about breaking your vow to remain single forever, but your Riley, she is beautiful. And, honestly, I am happily surprised."

"So were we," Antonio said, knowing from the look on Riley's face that she was drawing conclusions about him and his life. The way he'd realized things about her and her life while she'd talked to his grandmother. "But really, we need to be going."

Marco laughed. "Too bad. I'm on my way to the bar." He pointed behind them to the lounge with glass walls providing a view of every inch of the lobby. "I would buy you a drink to celebrate."

"We're tired," Riley put in, obviously realizing they didn't want to prolong their conversation with his father's best friend. "But it was a pleasure to meet you."

"Si," Marco said. "It was my great pleasure to meet you too."

With that, he turned and went into the bar, taking a seat right beside the wall of glass that faced the lobby.

Antonio held back a groan. Now for sure he couldn't leave Riley's room until Marco left the bar. There was no way the old man wouldn't see him sitting right by the window!

He guided Riley into the first elevator. As the door closed behind them, she said, "What are you doing?"

"Coming up to your room with you. I had intended to get a room at the desk, but with Marco watching from the lounge I'll just call from your room."

She gave him a skeptical look.

"You have to know Marco can't see me leave or the ruse is ruined."

"And you have to know that if he sees you at the desk, he could just think there's something wrong with our accommodations."

Antonio sighed. "It's easier for me to call the desk from your room."

She studied his face for a second. "I suppose."

The elevator stopped on her floor. They walked down the hall. She opened her door with her key card.

As they stepped inside, he understood her apprehension. The tingle of attraction that always seemed to whisper through him when she was around tripled as she closed the door—leaving them alone in a bedroom.

Worse, the room was small, barely big enough for the queen-size bed.

Seeing a house phone on a tiny table between two chairs in a corner, he walked over to it. He picked up the phone's receiver and hit the button for the front desk.

Apprehension filled him again. No matter where he stood, he was by the bed. "You certainly got a small room."

She crossed her arms on her chest. "I'm the only one staying in it. All I need is a bed and a place to shower. I'm going to be working, remember?"

The clerk answered his call with a chipper "Front desk."

He sighed with relief. "Good evening. This is Antonio Salvaggio. I need a room for the night."

Riley put her suitcase on the bed and unzipped it. She pulled out something pink and shear—not quite see-through but filmy. Soft and sexy looking.

Were those her pajamas?

If so...wow.

"I'm sorry, sir. We're all booked."

The clerk's comment brought him back to the present and he frowned. "Really?"

The good-natured clerk laughed. "*Si.* If you'd like a room tomorrow night, I could book that now."

"No. I need a room tonight. Isn't there something you're holding in reserve, something I'd happily pay extra for?"

"I'm sorry. Those rooms are gone too. It was a busy day today."

He wanted to argue, then wondered why. He'd seen the crowded lounge. Besides, there were other hotels in the city.

"Thank you." He disconnected the call.

"They're all booked up, aren't they?"

"We should have guessed that from the crowd of people in the lounge." He took a breath and faced her. "I can't go home."

"I know. Luckily, there are other hotels."

"Yes, but I can't go past the bar until we know Marco's not in there anymore."

"Are you sure he'll see you?"

"He's right by the wall of glass." He sighed. "Besides, Marco sees everything. It's why my father likes doing business with him."

"Okay." She glanced around awkwardly. "I guess you're stuck here for a while." She looked around again. "I was going to shower."

"You still can. You going to another room for a while might make this easier."

"I'll be coming out in pajamas."

Yeah. That little pink filmy thing.

Still, as a gentleman, he said, "I won't look."

Pink pajamas under her arm, she grabbed a couple more things from her suitcase and walked into the bathroom.

He sat on one of the chairs by the tiny table. The sound of the shower leeched into the room. He told himself not to think about the fact that she was naked under a warm spray of water...but the picture formed anyway. He could imagine all her soft skin dampened by the warm water. See himself walk up behind her and kiss her neck—

All right. That was enough of that.

He pulled his phone out of his pocket and began looking for another hotel. He didn't call any of them, only got their phone numbers.

The bathroom door opened. He blinked. Either she was the fastest showerer in recorded history, or he'd been scrolling longer than he'd thought.

"That was quick."

"I don't waste time or water."

He narrowed his eyes, squinting to see her better. "Are those yoga pants?"

"Yes."

"And a bra?"

"Yes."

He gaped at her. "Why? I told you I wouldn't look."

"You just looked, or you wouldn't know I was in yoga pants."

He laughed. "You must be really attracted to me to be afraid to put on your pajamas."

She pulled back the bed's comforter. "Yes and no."

He snorted. That was a sort of honest, sort of confusing answer. "Yes and no? You're either attracted to me or you're not."

"You're a very handsome guy. Of course I'm attracted to you."

"But…"

"But I don't want to be."

He shook his head. "That doesn't count. I don't want to be attracted to you either but I still am."

The room grew silent. She sat on the bed, propping her back up with pillows.

All the feelings he kept having around her intensified. He knew she was attracted to him. The proposal kiss demonstrated that. He'd also seen the way she looked at him sometimes. But hearing her say it made it more real. More earthy—more *possible* that something could happen between them.

"I'm not sure I'm glad we got that out in the open."

E-reader in her hand, she peered over at him. "Out in the open means we're both aware this little thing between us exists so we know to ignore it."

He stretched his legs out in front of him, suddenly confused about why they were fighting this. It wasn't like either one of them was committed to anyone else—and they *were* attracted.

"Why, exactly, do we want to ignore it? Right now, my grandmother is very happy, thinking we're spending the night together. And Marco's probably thinking I'm a lucky guy."

"Oh, you're so funny." She dropped her e-reader and snapped off the lamp. The room became dark as midnight. If that wasn't a sign that she wanted him to go he didn't know what was.

"You do realize that I might have to stay in your room tonight."

"And you realize we already decided that's not a good idea."

He dropped his voice an octave. "You're the one who thinks that. My whole thought process has had a radical transformation. We're adults who are attracted. What's the big deal?"

"The big deal is this relationship is going nowhere."

"Does it have to go somewhere? Isn't a night of blistering passion worth it?"

"Seriously? Are you that vain? It might have been a while since I dated anyone, but I still have a head on my shoulders. I can resist you."

He sunk down in the chair. "Good, then there's no reason I can't stay in your room."

Riley stifled a groan, realizing she had sort of walked into that. She pulled the silky sheet up to her chin and huffed out a sigh. If he wanted to sleep on a chair, he was welcome to it. But she was firmly committed to keeping her guard up around him.

Antonio's voice drifted to her in the darkness. "You are perfectly safe. I don't have to accost women. I have a vibrant social life."

A string of jealousy wound through her. Not just jealousy for the lucky women, but for the fact that he was as busy as she was, yet he still found time—and partners. Of course, he was a rich Italian guy with an accent that probably made women swoon. "I believe that."

"What I'm saying is, if you don't want to explore our attraction, I'm fine with it. You have nothing to worry about from me. As my godfather said, I had an ugly divorce. My wife cheated on me and fought to get more of my family's property than she had a right to. And my parents' divorce was even uglier, mostly because my mom is an alcoholic, and my dad got a court order that her visits with me had to be supervised. I've never seen a divorce that didn't result in fights and hatred. So, I stay away from commitments. Now that I know you're the kind of woman who wants to get married, I'll stay away."

The room remained silent for a few seconds as she settled

her head on her pillow, not happy with him. She understood that a bad marriage and divorce could sour someone on commitment, but that didn't make him smart enough to figure her out after a few encounters. She might ultimately want to be in a permanent relationship, but she didn't think she wore that like a sign. It annoyed her that he so quickly pegged her as someone who wanted to get married, when she didn't advertise it.

"How do you know I want to get married?"

"You're nice. You were great with my grandmother. So open and easy. Talking about your mother as if my GiGi already knew her." He shrugged again. "You have 'nice-and-kind-and-likes-being-part-of-a-family' written all over you."

She sat up. "That's funny, since the last three guys I dated didn't see that at all. They thought I'd be happy just dating forever. The one guy still lived with his mother before he moved in with me. I think he liked my apartment more than he liked me."

Laughing over her joke about her last boyfriend, he rose from the chair. "I'm getting the spare blanket. There's usually one in the closet."

She rolled her eyes. "It *was* funny that my boyfriend liked my apartment more than me, but it made me realize I attract all the wrong men."

"You're trying too hard. You're beautiful, smart and kind. One day the right guy will see all that."

She couldn't stop her chest from tightening when he said she was beautiful. It wasn't the first time he'd said it. But that only validated the fact that he *really* thought she was beautiful. It took her breath away and made her question making him sleep on a chair just because she knew nothing would come of them sleeping together—

That was when the truth hit her.

He was just like her exes. Except he was smart enough to

see that she wanted more out of a relationship than sleeping together and sharing rent.

And maybe that was the warning she needed to get rid of the romantic feelings she always had around him.

Several minutes went by, but try as she might, she couldn't sleep. She flopped to the right, then back to the left.

Antonio's voice again came from across the small room. "So, tell me about your parents—your father's death. It's interesting that your mother never found anyone else. Were they so happy together that it makes you want to find something permanent?"

"Yes and no."

"You really have a tough time making up your mind about things."

"I forgive myself for riding the fence on this issue. My mother put everything into her relationship with my dad. And while I can look back and envy that they had a once-in-a-lifetime love, I saw what happened when she lost that love. She was shattered. The horrible way his family treated her didn't help."

He whispered, "I'm sorry."

"Don't be. As I said, my mom pulled herself together, started her home nursing agency and she is now rich and successful. Happy as a clam."

"So, your reasons for wanting to marry have nothing to do with things you might have missed out on after your father died?"

She sat up and flicked on the lamp by the bed. "That's the confusing part. Even seeing my mom lose my dad, I still want someone in my life. Someone to share my life. You know. Kids. A minivan. A house in the suburbs. Is that so wrong?"

"It isn't exactly wrong, but it might be wishful thinking. The world's a different place than it was when your parents were a couple. Especially since there are much better ways two extremely attracted people could be spending *this* night. And you're letting a fantasy you have prevent us from indulging in an attraction we both feel."

"It's not a fantasy… Lots of people find real love."

"Name two."

"My mother found it with my dad."

He winced. "You can't use your parents because their romance was cut short. Fate didn't give them a chance to go the distance."

"Okay, how about my best friend? She lives in Scarsdale with a man who dotes on her."

He winced again. "It's my experience that men who do too much are overcompensating for the fact that they're having affairs."

She gaped in horror at his train of thought. "What is wrong with you?"

"Nothing."

"Not everybody's as cynical as you are."

"I'm not cynical. I just don't kid myself into believing in things that don't exist." He took a long breath. "Go to sleep."

She might not go to sleep, but she was done talking to him. She flicked off the light again, fluffed her pillow and flounced to her side. But before she drifted off, she thought about the three serious relationships she'd had in the past six years. Her college love, the first guy she'd lived with and the guy who wanted to move out of his mother's house.

If anybody had a right to believe true love didn't exist, it was her.

Damn his hide for reminding her.

The next morning, Antonio woke to her shaking him.

He'd given up on sleeping on the chair and had stretched out on the floor. Their conversation the night before had gotten a little intense. He might have even crossed the line in trying to get her to understand that she might be hoping for a fairy tale that wouldn't ever come to pass.

Actually, that could be what all the shaking was about.

He rolled over. "Enough. I'm awake."

He lifted himself off the floor, remembering something Riley had said about how her other boyfriends hadn't seen that she was looking for real love. He'd heard the disappointment in her voice, and he'd hated recognizing her sadness—which is why he'd wanted her to steer clear of believing in something that would always hurt her. Her desire to find something that didn't exist threw up all kinds of red flags for him. She had a successful business, and she was happy. Her idea that she could find real love could actually ruin a lot of life for her.

That wasn't his business. Was it?

No. They were only pretending to be engaged. If they hadn't been forced together for so long the night before, they never would have had the conversation that made her angry. Because they had, he decided they needed to put some space between them. Meaning, he would let his assistant help her with venues and today they would take care of getting the ring off her finger. That would end their time together.

As she walked into the bathroom, he pulled out his phone and called Rafe.

An employee of the jewelry store answered.

"This is Antonio Salvaggio. I need to speak with Rafe..."

"I'm sorry, Mr. Salvaggio. But Mr. Carabot is on vacation for another week."

He sucked in a breath. Okay so they couldn't take care of the ring today. Having Geoffrey help her with her search for vendors would give them sufficient time apart to forget last night's conversation before they had to see each other to handle the ring.

"Thank you. I will call again when he returns."

He disconnected the call and glanced around, looking for

his sandals, intending to head to his office. But the guilt he felt about their conversation the night before filled him again. It truly hadn't been his job to change her mind about love and he knew he'd kept talking when he should have stopped. What she wanted—what she believed—wasn't his concern.

He slipped into his shoes.

Walked to the door.

And stopped.

He couldn't just leave. She was doing him a huge favor. She'd been good to his family. He owed her an apology.

He sat on the edge of the bed, waiting for her to come out of the bathroom. When the door opened, he bounced up.

"Look, before I go, I just want to say I'm sorry. I pushed you last night, trying to get you to see my side of life and that was wrong."

She shook her head. "I get it. I probably seem like a dreamer to somebody who had such a bad divorce."

"Yes! I did have a bad divorce! I *am* jaded. Sometimes that makes me get on a soapbox. I'm sorry."

She studied his face for a few seconds, then smiled. "I forgive you."

His face scrunched in surprise. He'd expected at least a little scolding. Instead, she said she forgave him. "Just like that?"

She chuckled. "Just like that. It's what people do."

Not the people he knew. His ex could have turned this misunderstanding into a month-long pout.

The funniest sensation skittered along his spine. Relief and confusion spiraled together as she held his gaze with her earnest green eyes.

Something fierce rose in him. He wanted to kiss her so bad, his heart thrummed. But he couldn't. Faking things for his grandmother, he could kiss her all he wanted. Having real feelings, he couldn't.

And maybe that was really why he was off balance, pushing when a smart person would back off. Half the time they were pretending. The other half, they were real with each other. He didn't feel like himself either time, and he wanted to be normal with her. Himself. Not a fake fiancé.

He slid his hands to her shoulders, his eyes on hers, watching for signs of displeasure. But he didn't see any as he pulled her to him for a kiss.

She softened like summer rain. Her arms went around his neck. His arms drifted to her waist, pulling her closer. Relief fluttered through him, along with the notion that this was the smartest thing he'd done all week. He couldn't stand the thought that she had been upset by him—or hurt. It gutted him to think he had hurt her. But she'd forgiven him.

He pulled her closer, luxuriated in the feel of her in his arms, but when happiness began to morph into arousal, he pulled away.

"Thank you for being so good to me. I appreciate you helping me with my grandmother. Today I will tell my assistant to make time to help you with vendors. Come by my office whenever you are ready."

With that, he left her room and walked down the hall, feeling like himself for the first time since he'd met her.

Except he'd kissed her.

He might be happy to be back to behaving like himself, but theoretically kissing wasn't allowed. Particularly since they now knew they weren't compatible. They wanted two different things out of life and the kind of affair he would want with her could hurt her.

Which was why Geoffrey would be helping her with vendors, not him. No matter how attracted he was to her, she wanted the fairy tale. His first marriage showed him it didn't exist, and he wouldn't pretend it did. Which proved they were not a good match.

Not even for an affair.

CHAPTER SIX

AFTER HE LEFT, Riley stood staring at the door. It hadn't surprised her that he'd apologized. His comments about what she wanted out of life had been a step or two over the line. But he'd recognized that and said so. Which put their relationship back on track. Still, that apology was nothing compared to how he could kiss. That kiss had been sexy and breath-stealing—

No. That wasn't what had stolen her breath.

He'd kissed her for real.

His grandmother wasn't around. That kiss hadn't been for the charade. He'd kissed her because he wanted to.

Tingles of possibility tightened her chest. She and Antonio had shared a kiss filled with emotion. A real kiss had sealed his apology and her forgiveness.

She had been correct the night before. They were no longer strangers. Or even friends who'd made a deal to help each other. There was something happening between them.

But he didn't believe in love, and she did.

If she didn't keep her wits about her, they could make a major mistake. One of them or both of them could end up hurt.

She turned away from the door, disappointed that they couldn't explore this. But they couldn't. She wanted real love. Kids. That house in Scarsdale—

Besides, it was best not to screw things up again. After his apology, their friendship was back on track, his assistant would help her find florists, musicians and singers and she would stay away from him before one of them said something else that put his ruse in jeopardy.

She showered, dressed for the day and left the hotel. She'd intended to have breakfast in the restaurant/lounge with the glass wall but at the last minute she remembered Antonio's godfather. She didn't want him to see her eating breakfast alone and she wanted even less for him to join her. Then she'd have to keep up the charade with him. Frankly, she was a little tired of her life being confusing. Now that things had been straightened out, she would avoid walking into trouble.

Except he'd kissed her. For real.

Yeah, but it had been a kiss to seal his apology. Not an attraction kiss.

She ate at a sidewalk café, then made her way to Antonio's office, fortifying herself to see him. For a kiss between friends, it had been awfully sweet and sexy and *emotional*. The sense that there was something brewing between them hummed through her like the music of a favorite song, but she stopped her thoughts, reminding herself that they were in a good place. She would act like a businesswoman when she saw him.

At least she hoped. Her emotions around him were so powerful that it was difficult to control them or even think rationally sometimes. That's why being with him was so confusing. She was an intelligent, logical person yet she still had to fight an attraction that was all wrong.

In the building housing Antonio's office, she took the elevator to the third floor. Antonio's assistant, Geoffrey, jumped out of his seat when she entered. Tall, with dark hair and dark eyes, he didn't look much older than twenty-two.

"Mr. Salvaggio instructed me to find some vendors for you. I took the liberty of letting them know you'd be stopping by and telling them what you were looking for."

He handed her a neatly printed list and she smiled at him.

She'd worried for nothing about how she would react to Antonio. He didn't even come out of his office to say hello.

"Thank you. I'm impressed."

"I can come with you to scope out the vendors if you want."

"No. Thank you." She took a breath, telling herself she wasn't disappointed, but she was.

Which was probably why it was better she didn't see him. All the emotion that kiss dredged up would only get them into trouble. Especially since he didn't believe in love.

Yeah. It was better not to see him.

She forced a smile for Antonio's assistant. "I'll call you if I have questions."

"Come back and let me know how everything went. If there are problems or other vendors you'd like to talk to, I can arrange that."

She would not be coming back. "I'm good for now."

She put the list in her purse and headed out the door, telling herself Antonio's apology and her forgiveness were a good way to end their dealings. It was a clean, effective, happy break. He didn't need her to continue the ruse for his grandmother. He could handle that on his own. His assistant had given her the help she needed with vendors. Technically, their business was done. They could both get on with the rest of their lives.

She barely got to the sidewalk before Antonio came running out of the building. "Riley!"

She stopped. He'd changed out of the shorts and T-shirt he'd worn to dinner—and slept in—the night before. He probably had spare clothes in his office—and was back to looking deliciously handsome.

"Antonio?"

"I didn't want Geoffrey to let you go alone."

"He asked if he could accompany me, but I told him I was good on my own."

He shook his head. "No. You are doing me an enormous favor with my grandmother, and you don't know your way around the city. I promised to give you help with vendors." He glanced around, as if thinking through the situation. "It's so beautiful out, I could take the rest of the day off." He peered over at her. "We could have lunch, then look at Geoffrey's list together."

Her heart stuttered. Had he just asked her out?

After kissing her for real?

She groaned internally at the juvenile reaction and forced her common sense to the front of her brain. He owed her for playing the role of his fiancée. He was not asking her out. He was paying her back.

After that kiss?

"You don't want me to go with you?"

"I do! Really! I just—"

Just what?

Wanted him to define what they were doing? Wanted him to explain why they were going to lunch together when they didn't have to? They had opposite beliefs. She knew they wanted different things. She shouldn't even be considering what his offer meant. She should take it at face value.

Except she liked him. *That* was the problem. She liked him enough to wish that even one little piece of what was happening between them was real.

That was really why she'd gotten so upset with him the night before. She was looking for something real, and he wanted something insubstantial. He'd offered a night of blistering passion. Which, if she thought about it, was all two people could share when they were only getting to know each other.

But she wasn't a night-of-blistering-passion girl.

And that had been the end of that.

Still, he did owe her the help with vendors, and it probably was a good idea to have him come along so she could find her way without constantly consulting GPS. She'd take his offer for what it was. Payback.

"I'd love lunch."

"Great!" He stuffed his hands in his pockets, and they started up the sidewalk. "If I know Geoffrey, he's got Spinelli's Flowers on that list. They're actually just up the street. Maybe we'll pop in there before we eat."

"Okay."

She said it happily, like someone grateful for his assistance, but walking together like business friends felt odd. Awkward. Not normal.

Actually, *this* was their real normal. Everything else that had happened between them was either for the fake engagement or in a bedroom where they were feeling two different things. Right now, he was thanking her for helping him and she would appreciate it.

The muffled sound of a phone ringing floated to her from her purse, interrupting her thoughts.

"That's me." She quickly pulled it out. "It's my assistant." Remembering there was a proposal that night, she clicked to answer. "Hey, Marietta! What's up?"

"I'm so sorry, sweetie, but you need to come home. Your mother's been in an accident. She was hit by a car."

Her heart stopped. "Oh, my God!"

"She was awake enough to consent to surgery on her arm—which is broken—"

"She's in surgery!"

"Her arm was broken really bad. The doctors are telling us that she'll need a pin. Maybe two. She also has a concussion. They don't want you to worry, but they do want you here."

"Of course, I want to be there!" Fear trembled through her. Unlike Antonio who seemed to have people coming out of the woodwork, Riley only had her mom. If anything happened to her—

"I'll be on the next flight."

As soon as she clicked off the call, he said, "What's up?"

"My mom's been in an accident. She's in the hospital—having surgery. I have to go home."

He pulled out his phone. "My limo will take you back to your hotel, then to the airport."

Her imagination began forming all kinds of terrible scenarios. Her mother had gotten a call just like this one the night her father died. Not a kind nurse telling her that her significant other was dead, but a call to come to the hospital. In the twenty minutes it had taken to get there, her dad had died. If her mother's injuries were worse than they were telling her and she succumbed, Riley would be totally alone.

She took a quick breath, stopping her runaway imagination, and managed to hide her fears from Antonio. This wasn't his problem. It wasn't even really any of his business. Technically, they weren't even friends.

"Thanks. I have an open-ended ticket. Let's hope I can get a flight out today."

"I'm sure airlines have contingencies for emergencies."

Her airline did, but the next flight to New York wasn't for three hours. She booked it as she threw her things into her suitcases.

Antonio had waited for her in the limo. He wanted to ride with her to the airport, but she refused his offer. She was too nervous about her mom. She needed a clear head. Not the crazy brain of a woman pretending to be engaged to a guy she was so attracted to that a simple apology kiss had thrown her for a loop.

She had to get home to her mom.

During the two-hour wait for a flight, she prepared herself to see her mother hurt, broken. Italy was seven hours ahead. The flight took seven hours. They had taken off at three o'clock, so she landed in New York almost the same time that she'd left Italy.

Another hour was spent getting from the airport to the hospital. In the elevator to her mom's room, she glanced down to see Antonio's engagement ring. She hadn't been in Florence long enough to get it taken off—

It didn't matter.

Now that Antonio knew it had to be cut off, she could have the ring removed herself and find a courier service that could deliver it to him in Italy.

Technically, their relationship was over.

They'd never see each other again.

The feeling that she missed out on something good with him shuffled through her. She tried to soothe her disappointment with the knowledge that anything she'd had with him wouldn't be permanent. But that gave her small comfort. Meeting him, getting involved with him, had been a once-in-a-lifetime opportunity. A gorgeous Italian billionaire wanted her to pretend to be his fiancée. She'd all but swooned every time he touched her.

She laughed as the elevator doors opened.

It was a miracle she'd kept her wits about her.

She checked in at the nurses' station and they directed her to her mother's room.

She walked in to find two of her mom's employees. Jane Fineman, her mom's assistant and Pete Williams, her second in command.

Pete walked over and hugged her. "She's fine."

"And she can speak for herself," her mother mumbled from the bed.

"Surgery took a few hours," Pete continued. "But apparently, it's pretty routine stuff. She handled it like a champ."

Riley walked to the bed and hugged her mother as well as

she could, given the IV and dressing on her arm. "You scared me to death."

"Hey, I didn't ask to get hit by a car at three o'clock in the morning."

"What were you doing out at three o'clock in the morning!"

"The doctor I was wining and dining likes clubs."

"You went clubbing!"

Riley's mom turned to Pete. "If she's going to be a buzz kill, she needs to leave."

Pete laughed. "Pain meds are making her silly."

Riley sighed. "You guys can go home."

"You all can go home. I would like to get some sleep."

With that, Juliette drifted off and Jane faced Riley. "We really should go. There are schedules to be made, employee problems to handle. Without your mom, everything falls to me and Pete."

Plus, if they'd been the people called by the hospital, they'd likely been here since four or five o'clock in the morning.

"Yes! Go!" Riley said.

Jane gathered her purse and Pete hugged Riley one more time before they left. Riley's mom slept soundly.

Riley glanced around. With everyone gone, the room was silent. She wished she'd bought a magazine or book from the newsstand at the airport, then remembered she had her phone. She found a word game and started playing. If she didn't keep her mind busy, she'd worry about her mom or think about Antonio and wonder if she'd made a mistake by not giving in to their chemistry. She didn't want to think about either of those. Too much had happened in a few short days. Including her mother's accident. Her brain needed a rest.

But thoughts of her time in Italy floated to her mind as she played the mindless game. Being with Antonio and his father and grandmother and being in a quiet hospital room with her mom right now, really brought home how alone she was. If that accident had killed her mom, she would have had no one.

No one.

It wasn't like she hadn't thought of that before. But her mom was only fifty. And she was strong. A little bulldozer. Riley hadn't even considered that she could have an accident. Still, she knew, deep down, that having only her mom as family was what lured her to want a committed relationship. Not the idea of being in love—but the idea of having a family. The kind of family her friends had had when she was in grade school.

Parents, three kids and a dog—or cat. Crazy-busy breakfasts. Outings on weekends. Soccer games. A minivan. Lots to do besides reading in her condo when she didn't have work.

Even as she thought that, GiGi's feelings about Antonio getting married suddenly crystalized. Antonio's grandmother didn't want great-grandkids. Not that she wouldn't love great-grandkids, but her real motivation was that she did not want her only grandson to be alone. His grandfather was gone. GiGi herself was sick. And Antonio's dad was at least as old as Riley's mom. He had a mom, but he didn't speak much of her. He'd said she was an alcoholic, which brought its own problems, including illnesses.

In the blink of an eye, Antonio could be as alone as she was.

The idea amazed her. She'd thought he had people coming out of the woodwork, but just like her people, they were friends, coworkers, not family.

Neither one of them had much family to speak of.

And the people they did have were getting older.

She wondered if he ever thought about that, but decided it was none of her business. Undoubtedly, he thought having friends and coworkers and lovers was enough people in his life. And she supposed it was. Some friends were better than family.

Except Antonio had experienced having a family. She

hadn't. She remembered times with her dad, but the memories were fleeting. Antonio knew what it was like to be surrounded by love, to be part of something, to always have Christmas dinner and summer vacations.

That's what made them different. It was why she wanted something he didn't even consider. His loving upbringing had satisfied a need Riley still had.

Close to eight o'clock that night, just when her phone battery was about to die, Marietta arrived.

She hugged Riley. "How is she?"

"She was well enough to give me a hard time when I got here. Then she immediately fell asleep. She's been asleep ever since."

Marietta nodded. "Has the doctor been in?"

"The nurse told me he had another emergency surgery, but he'd be in before he left the hospital for the day." She paused, then realized why Marietta hadn't arrived until almost eight.

"Did tonight's proposal go well?"

Marietta smiled broadly. "I wondered when you'd ask."

Riley glanced at her mom. "I guess we now know what it takes for me to forget about work."

Marietta patted her hand. "She's going to be fine."

"Eventually. She didn't just break her arm. She also has a concussion. I have to be patient."

"Hospital is the best place for her right now."

Riley sighed. "I guess."

"I know!" Marietta said, then she grinned. "And the proposal was as smooth as pudding."

Riley finally noticed how bright her assistant's eyes were. "You had fun doing it!"

"I did! Now I see why you're so obsessed with work. It was so much fun! They were so happy. It was pure magic."

Riley laughed. "It always is." Antonio's proposal to her popped into her head and sadness filled her. Maybe it was all the emotion of the day, but it seemed a shame that something that looked so good was fake.

Plus, she missed him. She missed a guy she'd met a few days ago. How could she miss him? Why was she even thinking about him? He was out of her life. Poof. Never to be seen again.

Marietta left to get coffee and a sandwich from a nearby vendor. She hadn't been gone two minutes before the tall, balding doctor wearing scrubs came in and told Riley that her mom would be going home the next day, or the day after if there was a complication.

"But I don't believe there will be. The surgery was textbook. We'll keep her here tonight and if she's well enough, then tomorrow she can go home. It will all depend on her concussion status."

"Thank you, Doctor."

"You should go home and get some sleep too. I heard you were in Italy."

"I was."

"This must have been a long day for you."

"Yes." Thirty-six hours already. And she still wasn't home.

"Well, go. We'll talk in the morning."

By the time Marietta returned, Riley was ready to leave. Now that her adrenaline was wearing off, she could have dropped where she stood.

They took a cab. Marietta had the driver let Riley off at her condo building first. The doorman gave her a goofy grin as he opened the door to the lobby for her.

"Evening, Miss Morgan."

"Evening, Oscar."

As she entered the lobby, a man rose from one of the convenience sofas. She stopped. Her mouth dropped open. "Antonio?"

"My grandmother went nuts when she heard that your mother had been in an accident, and she shooed me across the ocean to be with my fiancée."

So tired that she was giddy, that struck Riley as hysterically funny, and she laughed. "The more you try to be a make-believe fiancé, the more your GiGi shoves you into the role for real."

"I do not think it's funny."

"Oh, you should be up for thirty-six hours. *Everything's* funny."

He caught her arm and directed her to the elevator. "Let's get you to your condo."

She clung to his arm. "Good idea."

CHAPTER SEVEN

THE ELEVATOR DOOR opened as soon as he hit the button. They rode in silence to her floor, then walked to the last door on the right, which she unlocked.

Following her, he stepped inside the condo, looking around with approval at the white stacked stone fireplace, dark hardwood floors, and white area rug that matched the white sofa and chair with multicolored print throw pillows.

"Wow. Somebody must be making good money."

She tossed her purse to the kitchen island of the open-concept space. "This condo was my reward the first year my company reached a two-million-dollar profit."

"Two million dollars for planning proposals?"

"Have you seen *your* invoice?"

He laughed. But he watched her closely. She was so tired that her arms moved like noodles.

"Plus, I believed I deserved a nice home for all my hard work."

He wondered if a home was the first thing she'd bought because her father's family kicked her and her mom out of the condo they were living in when he died. But he didn't mention that. She hadn't argued about him coming to her condo with her, and though he could get a hotel room, his GiGi was right. She needed him and he had the relentless sense that he should be taking care of her.

"Come on. Let's get you to bed."

She leaned in and whispered, "I thought you'd never ask."

He snorted. "In the morning, you're going to wish you hadn't said that."

"Why? Are you going to take advantage of me?"

"I told you. I don't have to take advantage of women. I'm assuming this condo has two bedrooms?"

She pouted. "It does."

He shook his head as he helped her down the hall. She pointed at a door. "That's the spare room."

He nodded. "Okay. That'll be my room."

They walked to the second door. "And this will be my room."

"Are you good to shower by yourself?"

Her big green eyes grew serious. "Honestly, I'm so tired that I'm just going to face-plant on the bed."

He laughed. "How about if I come in with you and turn down the covers while you take off your shoes."

"Okay."

Her agreement was so subdued that he missed silly Riley, but he knew her getting back to normal was for the best. As she kicked off her shoes, he pulled down the comforter, then the sheet and plumped the pillow.

"There."

She walked over to him, stood on her tiptoes and kissed him. "Thank you."

The spontaneity of it took him by surprise and he blinked. He'd kissed her and she'd kissed him back, but she'd never kissed him first. So innocently. So honestly. The pleasure of it rode his blood in the oddest way. Not as arousal, as he would have expected. But as happiness.

She liked him.

That was what all her silliness had been about. She'd been too tired to pretend indifference.

A smile formed before he could stop it.

She climbed into bed, pulled the covers to her chin and closed her eyes.

He walked to the door, said, "Good night," then left her room, shutting the door behind him.

In her kitchen, he found nothing to eat. All the cupboards were bare, as if they'd just been installed by the contractor. He opened the refrigerator. Though there was no food, there was a nice assortment of beer.

He frowned. Unless she'd just had a party and this was left-over beer, there might be a man in her life. His chest tightened at the possibility. Then he remembered their conversation in her hotel room the night before. Good God! Had it only been one night ago? It felt like forever. Like he'd known her forever and that conversation was in their distant past.

If there had been a man in her life, she would have told him when he was ragging on her about looking for real love.

He still felt bad about that, even though he'd apologized. But he'd apologized with a spontaneous kiss, that—just like the easy kiss she'd given him that night—told him he liked her.

Still a little flummoxed over the way she'd kissed him, he should get a hotel, lie to his GiGi and make up stories about her mother being fine, but that didn't sit right. He did not want to go through another bout of feeling guilty over her. He would stay at least one day to make sure Riley and her mother really were okay. And if he was staying, the cupboards would not be bare.

Not wanting to dig too deeply into that, he opened drawers looking for takeout menus and found several. He ordered Chinese, then went to the lobby to wait for it and also to have a chat with Oscar.

As soon as he saw him, Oscar straightened. "Mr. Salvaggio? Leaving?"

"No. I ordered Chinese. I thought I'd come down and wait for it."

"I could have brought it up!"

"I actually wanted to ask you where a person gets groceries around here."

Oscar said, "Lots of people order things online. You know, from the usual places. But there's a grocery around the corner."

"If I order online, will it come to you?"

He nodded.

"Riley's mom had an accident and we'll be at the hospital tomorrow." He pulled a few bills out of his wallet. "If you could take a delivery that would be great."

Oscar raised his hands. "You don't have to pay me. That's a service of the building."

"Consider it a thank you."

Taking the money, Oscar nodded. "I'll handle it personally."

Antonio's Chinese food came, and he returned to the condo. After putting his dinner on a plate, he took a seat at the big kitchen island and started scrolling on his phone. He found two sites with one-day delivery, ordered food for breakfast and dinner as he ate. Even if it didn't come until tomorrow afternoon, Riley would have food for breakfast and dinner the following day.

After tidying the kitchen, he went into the living room where he turned on the big screen TV. He should have felt uncomfortable in her house, but the easy way she'd kissed him matched the feeling of ease he had in her home.

It was a bit disconcerting.

But it also felt right. She'd kissed him. He'd helped her into bed and ordered food for the next day. He couldn't remember the last time simple things had given him such pleasure.

Because he liked her too. He wasn't merely attracted to her. He liked her. Comfortable in her living room, he couldn't deny that that meant something. He might not want what she wanted but that didn't have to mean they couldn't have *something*. And more than a friendship. Something real. Something fun.

Maybe his grandmother sending him to Manhattan was a

second chance of a sort? They might not be meant to be together forever, but he couldn't shake the feeling they should
have a romance. A happy and passionate affair. He knew she
didn't want that. But the sense that they were made for *something* wouldn't leave him.

He went to bed not sure of anything, except that she had
considered sleeping with him. She might have been so tired
she was punch drunk, but sometimes when people were vulnerable the truth came out.

She'd definitely thought about sleeping with him.

He couldn't stop another smile because for the first time
since he'd met her, he wasn't off balance.

Riley woke the next morning in the clothes she'd had on the
day before. She gasped and jumped out of bed. Now, her sheets
were covered in airplane germs!

Wasting no time, she walked to the hall linen closet and
when she turned away from getting new linens, she saw her
guest room door was closed.

Her eyes widened. She'd forgotten Antonio!

She raced into her room, changed her sheets, tossed the
airport germ sheets into the laundry, then she showered and
dressed for the day. She was *not* dressing special for him. It
was Saturday. She had to go to the hospital to take care of
everything with her mom. Jeans. A summer-weight sweater.
Comfortable tennis shoes. That was it.

She glanced at her face in the mirror and winced.

All right. So, she would put on makeup. No respectable
single woman in Manhattan went out without makeup. Traveling so much had given her black eyes and saggy cheeks.
Both needed a boost. A little lip gloss wouldn't hurt either.

Satisfied, she took a long breath before she opened her bedroom door and swore she smelled coffee. The scent increased
as she walked into the common area of the house. Antonio
stood in front of the big island.

"Good morning!"

She drank in the sight of him. She'd missed him and he'd appeared in her condo building as if by magic. Nothing would come of this relationship, but she was not going to be stuffy about him being here. Sure, his GiGi had sent him, but he'd come. If she remembered the night before correctly, he had helped her as his GiGi had said he should.

For once, she would take his presence at face value and not overthink things.

"Good morning." She ambled to the cupboard, got a mug and made herself a cup of coffee in the one-cup coffeemaker. "Did you sleep well?"

"Yes. Like you, I'd been up over twenty-four hours."

She winced and took a seat at the center island. "I might have handled it more poorly than you did."

"Your mother had been hurt. You were upset. You had a right to be off your game. How is she by the way?"

"She might be released this morning."

"Oh."

"I'll probably have her stay here with me for a few days."

"If that's a polite way of telling me that my room will be spoken for tonight. I get the hint. Plus, that's a good excuse for me to give my GiGi...that with your mom here I'd be in the way."

Disappointment tumbled through her. She hadn't meant to kick him out. It seemed she was always doing that. Just when things could be normal between them, she did or said something that made her sound less than hospitable.

She tried to fix it. "Or maybe you could handle some business here? You know, get a hotel and do some work?"

"GiGi would like it if I spent a few days here. And my last trip was unexpectedly cut short."

He glanced at her hand.

She looked down at the ring too. "Maybe we could find a jeweler?"

He cleared his throat. "Maybe."

She'd been so preoccupied with joy that he was here, she hadn't noticed he wore a white T-shirt and pajama pants. The intimacy of it almost stopped her breathing.

She now knew what he slept in.

And he knew she'd slept in her clothes.

He sat beside her.

She wanted nothing more than to take advantage of having him here with her, to talk and laugh the way they had when she'd planned his proposal, or at his family's vineyard, but she couldn't think of anything clever to say.

She sipped her coffee. This was ridiculous. Nothing felt right, the way it had in Italy, and she had a mother to attend to. She shouldn't be thinking about Antonio and trying to make something happen between them.

She slid off her stool, taking her coffee with her. "I have to get to the hospital. Doctors get there early, you know. I don't want to miss him and have to wait until night rounds to talk to him."

"Unless your mom is released today."

"I still need to talk to him. My mom's a nurse. She's going to try to buffalo me into believing she's better than she is."

He laughed.

"I need to ask all my questions at the source." Spotting her purse on the counter where she'd left it the night before, she grabbed it and headed for the door.

"Good-bye."

She turned. Realizing she looked like she was giving him the bum's rush again, she softened her tone and said, "Good-bye. Thanks for your help last night."

His eyes shifted, sparked with something so male she nearly lost her breath. "You're welcome."

She raced out of her condo, needing to get away from all that sincerity and those beautiful dark eyes. Things might not be as easy between them as they had been in Italy, but he was still gorgeous.

And…

Had she asked him if he was taking her to bed the night before?

She groaned. She had. The memory came back vividly.

But they were in a fake relationship. The day before, she'd gotten herself to accept that. This morning, if she'd been a little less in control, she could have fallen back in that trap again of thinking something was happening between them.

It wasn't.

She wouldn't let herself think it was.

Antonio stared at the door. He'd seen the longing glances she'd given him, but she'd raced out, as if she couldn't get away from him fast enough. Of course, she was worried about her mother, and he didn't blame her.

He showered and was about to put on a clean shirt and trousers when it hit him that this was Saturday.

Only the most diligent would be working. Without the crises that had brought him to New York the weekend before, he would not work on a weekend.

He sighed, shifted from trousers and a dress shirt to jeans and a T-shirt, then he glanced around with another sigh. He didn't have anywhere he needed to be. But he also didn't feel like hanging out in Riley's condo or taking a walk in the park.

She hadn't told him much about her mother's accident or condition, except that she might be released that day, and the guest room would be needed for her. She'd been so uncomfortable that morning that he'd known better than to ask. But GiGi would ask. He needed more info.

He used his phone to search the internet and found her company's website, along with the phone numbers for her and her assistant. Not wanting to interrupt Riley when she was with her mom, he dialed her assistant.

An hour later, his limo let him off in front of the main entrance to the hospital. He took the elevator to her floor and strode to her room.

Riley bounced out of her chair. "Antonio?"

He walked in, hugged her and gave her a proper kiss, for the benefit of the pretty blonde woman lying in the bed, in case she wasn't in on the fact that their engagement was fake. Having caught her off guard, the kiss was equal parts passion and sweetness, and the idea that this might be a second chance for them again popped into his brain.

She pulled back, dazed. "What are you doing here?"

He displayed the flowers he'd brought. "First, these are for your mother."

The blonde in the bed smiled weakly. "So, you're Antonio."

Riley seemed to come back to life. "Antonio, this is my mother, Juliette Morgan. Mom, this is Antonio Salvaggio... I told you about him."

Her mom closed her eyes. "Yes, you did. It's nice to meet you, Antonio. Thank you for the flowers." Then she took a breath and it seemed she fell asleep.

"She's been in and out like that all morning. The doctor said it's nothing to worry about. All part of recovering from the trauma of being hit by a car." She caught his gaze. "You didn't have to come here."

"Actually, I need some solid facts for my grandmother. I know she's worried, so I thought a real visit was in order."

"Okay—" She glanced at her mother. "As you can see, she's sleeping a lot and the doctor recommended she stay another day."

"She's staying another day?" He shifted his gaze to Riley's. "Meaning, the extra room in your condo will be open again tonight."

CHAPTER EIGHT

RILEY STARED INTO Antonio's eyes and knew exactly what he was telling her. With her mom not coming home with her that night, he could sleep there.

Marietta came racing into the room. "Oh, I see you're here!" she said to Antonio.

He chuckled. For a billionaire, he had an uncanny way of looking perfectly comfortable even in the oddest situations.

"Yes. You must be Marietta."

"We sort of met the day you planned your proposal to Riley."

"Yes. We did. You make great coffee."

She blushed. "I wish I could take credit for it, but Riley had everything set up for you. I just poured it." She faced Riley. "Could I have a minute with you in the hall?"

Riley's heart stopped. "Why? What happened with yesterday's proposal?"

"We should talk about it in the hall."

Riley raced out behind Marietta and said, "Give it to me straight. Whatever went wrong, we can fix it."

"Nothing went wrong. I told you last night that it was perfect, but you were so tired you probably forgot. I was hoping to beat your Italian god to the hospital so I could warn you he was coming. He called and asked for the hospital your mom was in, and I couldn't think of a good reason not to tell him... since he is your fiancé."

Riley groaned. "Fake fiancé."

"I know but it just felt wrong not telling him." She peeked into Juliette's hospital room. "He's such a nice guy."

He was a nice guy. Considerate and gorgeous. Which is exactly what made him so tempting. Until she remembered he was like her other boyfriends. He wasn't somebody who would settle down. Ever. Her mom's accident reminded her that she was alone—that she needed things a man like Antonio couldn't give her. No matter how happy she'd been to see him, she needed to keep her distance.

"He's a great guy, but we're really not engaged. Not a couple. Nothing at all between us."

Marietta looked at Riley again. "Really? Nothing?"

She winced. "Well, not *nothing* nothing. I'm not dead. The guy is gorgeous. And so suave." She almost sighed. "Seriously, mouth-watering sexy."

Marietta laughed. "So, what's the problem? Why aren't you enjoying this?"

Not wanting to admit her weird feelings, Riley gave the obvious excuse. "He's a client."

"No. He's not. His proposal is over."

"Were it not for this stupid ring," she said, waving it at Marietta. "This whole mess would be over. Instead, he's here when he shouldn't be."

"Really?"

"Yes. He's only here because his grandmother told him he should be with his fiancée when her mother is in the hospital."

Marietta gave her the strangest look. "Do you think he's only here because his grandmother sent him?"

She combed her fingers through her hair. His grandmother might have told him to come, but he hadn't needed to actually visit the hospital. "I don't know."

"He likes you. I could hear it in his voice."

"He also doesn't believe in love."

"So, you've talked about it?"

"Yes, when we were deciding we were not letting anything happen between us."

"You talked about *that* too?"

She sighed. "Look, don't go making a bigger deal out of this than it needs to be."

"I'm not making it a big deal. You are. The guy is sexy, good looking. He's also considerate. Under that suave billionaire persona there seems to be a great guy. He came to check on your mother. Give him a chance."

"No. We want two different things."

"Okay. How about this? You've been so stressed lately, why not—you know."

Her face scrunched. "No. I do not know."

"Why not have a little fling?"

She gaped at Marietta. "Because nothing can come of it!"

"Can't you just, for once, have some fun?"

"I need more in my life than fun—"

"You know what? You do need more in your life and someday you'll probably get it. You'll find a guy who wants forever with you. But that doesn't mean you have to mourn until you find him or he finds you. In fact, maybe a little fun would make you happy enough that you'd see other opportunities. Maybe even see the right guy."

She'd never looked at it like that before. Had she been so busy, so intense, that she'd actually missed opportunities?

"Lots of guys have looked at you like they might be interested, but you have this way of being all business with everyone."

"Probably because most of the men I deal with come to me wanting me to plan their marriage proposal."

"Yeah, but a lot of those guys have had friends or cousins. You don't even see them, do you?"

"You're talking about people who come to watch the proposals?"

"Yes."

She blinked. Many people came to proposals. Parents. Grandparents. Friends of both the bride and groom. That's what made the more elaborate events fun. But she never scouted the crowd looking for Prince Charming. She never glanced at the crowd at all. She was too busy working.

Always working.

"I do have a job to do—"

"Yeah." Marietta winced. "But sometimes you're so intense that I think people are afraid to approach you."

She gasped. "I scare people off?"

"Maybe scaring people off is a bit dramatic. It's more like guys take one look at you and know you're so busy, so intense, that there's no point in approaching you."

She blinked. "Oh."

"Oh, honey. I don't mean to insult you. But you never have any fun. And I want you to have fun. You're the nicest, most wonderful person I know. You're so good to your employees we become your friends. But you're not very kind to yourself."

Shell-shocked, Riley said, "Okay. I can see that might be true."

Marietta glanced at her watch. "I've gotta run. Lots of stuff to do today. But think about what I said."

Riley returned to her mother's room, her head down, still gobsmacked. Antonio sat on the visitor's chair, reading his phone.

"Anything interesting on that phone?"

"Just a message that the groceries I ordered for you last night have been delivered."

"You ordered groceries for me?"

"You had no food. With your mother in the hospital, I

thought it wiser not to have to go to a restaurant for breakfast...or to grab a donut."

Weird feelings bubbled up. According to her assistant, she never noticed guys who might be interested in her. Antonio had spent the night with her in her apartment, and he'd bought her food. Because his grandmother had shipped him to New York to be with her or because he was a genuinely good guy?

"You're right. I probably wouldn't have stopped for more than a cup of coffee."

"Under stress like this, you need real food and it's now in your building."

The kindness of the gesture almost overwhelmed her, but she couldn't stop thinking of what Marietta had said. Was she intense? So driven she never noticed other people?

No. Caring for other people was her job. What Marietta had said was she never was kind to herself. And that she never had any fun.

Which was true. A good book was as close as she got to a good time.

"Oscar texted that he'll run the order up to your apartment."

Confusion tightened her chest. "Oscar texted you?"

He tucked his phone into his jacket pocket. "Yes."

"He normally doesn't get that friendly."

He shrugged. "What can I say? People like me."

She winced. "Meaning, I'm the first person you don't get along with."

"You and I were getting along just fine until we got engaged."

She snickered. "That was all your idea."

He motioned to the ring on her finger, suddenly serious. "If we can leave your mom, we can probably find a jeweler and have that removed."

She glanced down at it, "It would be a good idea, but I don't feel right leaving today. The doctor's not supposed to check in until this afternoon." She glanced at her sleeping mom.

He rose from his chair, walked over and hugged her. "Okay. I understand."

It felt so wonderful to be hugged by him that she could have wept. But she had no idea why. Her mother was going to be fine. Still, he had thought she needed a hug, and he gave her one.

Antonio said, "I'll see you at home."

She sniffed a laugh at the way he'd said *at home*. Her home, but he was clearly comfortable there.

"I'll make dinner."

A hug was one thing. Making her dinner was special. No one ever did things like that for her. She was always the one doing things for other people.

She pulled out of his hug. "Really?"

"Sure."

She studied his face, so confused about him she didn't know what to think. "I just don't picture billionaires cooking."

"We're people too. We have likes and dislikes and twenty-four hours to fill every day."

"I thought you had yachts for that."

He snorted. "Seriously? I might not have to work six days a week, but I like to use my brain and my talents."

"Cooking is one of those talents?"

"It's a form of creativity."

"It is."

They smiled at each other. The sense of connection filled her again, except this time it wasn't an ethereal whisper of fate. It was tangible. The intuition that something was happening between them wasn't her imagination. They liked each other and it was blissfully wonderful.

And spectacularly wrong. With all the realizations she had made because of her mom being in the hospital, her feelings were raw, and she was needy. She could fall in love with him so easily.

Or would she?

She knew going in that this relationship would end. And she was a pretty smart cookie. If she looked at this as two people who liked each other, enjoying the limited time they had together, she could hold her feelings in check.

Plus...

What if Marietta was right? What if she was so intent on doing her job that she missed the cues that someone was interested in her? Worse, what if she really was scaring people off—

What if she *did* need a fling with an Italian billionaire to get back her sense of fun?

The talk with the doctor went exactly as she'd thought. Her mom's condition had not improved in the twelve hours since she'd seen him. She would be spending at least another night.

When visiting hours were over, she texted Antonio and told him she was about to get a cab. He told her he'd already sent his limo for her.

The happy sensation filled her again—the knowledge that Antonio was someone special. Not just a billionaire with a great family and vineyard so gorgeous it felt like heaven. But a considerate person.

Oscar grinned at her as she entered her building lobby. "Evening, Riley."

"Evening, Oscar."

"Antonio's upstairs."

"Yes. He texted me."

"Great guy."

"I know."

She entered the elevator. She did know. The man loved his grandmother enough to fake a proposal. He was helping her find venues for her work in Italy. Now, while her mother was in the hospital, he was here with her for support.

She stepped into her condo and smelled the crisp scent of marinara sauce.

He glanced up from the pot he was stirring. "How did things go?"

She rolled her shoulders, not really tired, more like stiff from stress. "You mean with the doctor?"

"Yes."

"He hadn't changed his mind about Mom staying another day."

He nodded, then held out a spoon of red sauce for her to taste. "Try this."

She gingerly took a sip. "Oh." She groaned with pleasure. "That's delicious."

"I'm guessing you didn't eat lunch."

"You guess right."

"Go. Take a quick shower and put on something comfortable. The spaghetti needs eight minutes. I'll wait two before I put it in water, giving you ten minutes."

She laughed and raced back to her room, so eager for a shower she could have kissed him. Removing her clothes, she realized again how easily she thought about kissing him. She paused, thinking that through. Though anything they had would be a fling, it wouldn't be casual or spur of the moment. It would be wonderful, memorable.

Which was exactly what was missing from her life. Something wonderful. Something memorable. Something that marked the end of old, intense, all-business Riley and the beginning of the Riley who would be approachable.

And he stood in her kitchen right now, making her dinner.

Her shower took two minutes, choosing clothes and applying just enough makeup that she didn't look like a ghost took the rest of the time.

She ambled to the stove wearing yoga pants and a cute top, not wanting to appear to have dressed up for him, but also looking enticing enough that she could flirt. Maybe even make a pass at him.

The stove timer went off.

"You just made it. Not a second to spare."

She smiled. "It's the best way to run a business. You can't ever be late…but you also can't appear too eager."

He laughed. "That's true about a lot of things." Wearing her seldom used oven mitts because she didn't have potholders, he removed the pan of pasta from the stove and dumped it into a colander that she didn't even know she had. Then he put the spaghetti on two plates. "I'll let you pour your own sauce. The pasta can cool a bit while we eat our salads."

He carried them to the table. She followed him and saw that the meatballs and sauce were already there. Two plates of salad sat in front of two chairs, and he'd decorated her little table with candles, along with her good silver and the linen napkins that her mom had bought her when she purchased the condo. There was also a bottle of wine. He must have explored the neighborhood before he started cooking.

"This is lovely."

"In Italy, we call this casual."

She laughed as she sat.

He sat too. "So, you said your mom needs time?"

"At least one more day. I reminded the doctor that she runs a home nursing agency, and she employs about a hundred nurses who could care for her, and he said he'll take that into consideration when deciding when she can come home."

"Do you think bringing her home is wise?"

"I think when she finally wakes up for more than an hour at a time, she's going to demand she be allowed to go home."

"Staying up for more than an hour at a time will probably mean she's *ready* to go home."

"That's a good way to look at it."

She dug into her salad.

"And you are fine?"

"Actually, I'm pretty good. Sitting in her room for two days forced me to slow down." She glanced over at him. "Think about things."

He studied her for a second. "You've never done that?"

"I haven't had a vacation in six years. Lots of proposals happen on weekends. When I get home, I take a shower, read a book and think about what's on the schedule for the week to come."

He pointed his fork at her. "If you were in Italy, I'd make you slow down. Enjoy the scenery."

"I enjoyed your GiGi...and the tour of your beautiful vineyard."

"There is so much more to see."

She almost told him that when she returned to Italy to visit the vendors Geoffrey had found for her, she would take him up on that offer. But what they had wasn't about the future. It was an in-the-moment thing. Which was the best way to enjoy it. No promises. No plans. Just let whatever happened happen. That way, no one got hurt.

"Tell me a little bit about you."

His head tilted as if the question confused him. "You've met my family. Seen my office."

"Yeah. But I'd like to hear something no one else knows."

He laughed. "Really?"

"Sure."

"Something silly?"

"No. Something that tells me about who you are."

He took a breath. "Something that tells you about who I am?" He picked up her salad plate, then his and carried them to the kitchen. When he returned, he handed her a plate of pasta, then offered her the bowl of sauce.

"We're so different," she said, explaining her reasoning when it seemed like he might not share. "I'm just trying to get to know you."

"Okay." He thought for a second. "When I was fifteen, I tried to run away to Norway."

Knowing that was where his mother lived, she perked up. "Really?"

"Yes. My father had disciplined me for something, and I decided my mom would be a lot easier on me and I was going to live with her. I thought life with her would be wonderful. She was alone. She always said she missed me. I saw myself moving in with her and nothing but happiness."

She leaned in, eager for the chance to know more about him. "What happened?"

He took a breath. "It's almost a two-day train ride to Norway because there's no direct route. And don't even get me started on the ferry."

"You were bored?"

He snorted. "No. By the time I got there my father was already there. He had taken a plane."

"That's funny!" She peered at him. "Why aren't you laughing?"

He set down his fork, sighed. "That was the day, I met my real mom."

She frowned. "Oh."

"Thinking my mom and I needed some private time, my father left us alone to talk things out." He shook his head. "The two hours I spent with her were…the worst of my life."

"Showing you that living with your mom wasn't a better option than your dad?"

"It was more than that." He took a breath, as if thinking through his answer and finally said, "My mother was a train wreck. Drinking mostly."

Her mouth opened slightly but no sound came out. He'd

said she was an alcoholic, but obviously that one word didn't convey the truth of the situation.

"When my father met her, she was a fun-loving party girl. He adored her. They always had a great time together. They married. She got pregnant and he settled in, but she didn't. Very shortly after that he realized she was drinking a lot. Not just when they went out, or at dinner, but all day. Every day. He soon recognized she was an alcoholic. When they had the fight that ended their marriage, she knew she was in trouble, but she didn't want to get help. She liked herself. Her life... just the way it was. She said she could manage her drinking and my dad was just looking for a way to get rid of her."

He shrugged. "She's my mother and I love her. But the day I visited her, the minute my dad left, she made a drink, then another, then another. She's not managing anything."

"How long did your dad leave you with her?"

"Not even an hour and I suspect he spent the time right outside her apartment complex. That visit—as short as it was—explained a lot to me about my parents' divorce. Explained a lot about my mother. I thought—believed—she loved me and in her own way she did. But the daydream that she was lonely without me was nothing but wishful thinking."

Riley sat back. That visit with his mom might have shown him a lot of things, but it also explained his stance on marriage and love. His dad loved his mom, but that love died. Then his own marriage fell apart. And his relationship with his mother was nothing but wishful thinking.

It was no wonder he didn't believe love existed.

Still, his grandmother had shown him real love. So had his father. "Your dad seems like a nice guy."

"My father is a very smart man, whose only mistake was marrying my mother. He should have seen the obvious when they were dating and engaged. He didn't. He'll tell you that himself. He takes full responsibility."

She winced. "You and your dad have bad marriages in common."

Obviously trying to lighten the mood, he said, "And a love of casinos, good wine and a solid business deal."

"That's enough to make me think you're just like your father."

"I would say yes, but no man in his right mind admits that."

"Ah."

He took the sauce bowl from her. "Now, you tell me something about you… I think I'd like to hear about you and your mom. It seems like you two are also alike."

She winced. "We are. Although one of the things I realized today was that following in her footsteps and being such a bulldog about my company…the way she is about hers… might have made me—"

She stopped, unable to think of the word without embarrassing herself.

"Made you?"

"I'm not sure. Stern comes to mind."

He laughed.

"Formidable."

"I like that one."

She took a breath. "Unapproachable."

He stopped the sauce spoon two inches from his plate. "Unapproachable?" He shook his head. "No. Even frazzled from exhaustion the night I met you, you were lovely." He smiled. "Actually, I saw you before the proposal began and I couldn't take my eyes off you. You were focused. But even trying to blend into the background you were beautiful."

Her heart stuttered and tears of joy tried to form in her eyes, but she wouldn't let them. *This* was what having an affair with a suave Italian billionaire should be. Compliments that touch the heart. Easy conversation. Discussions about things like vineyards and villas. And delicious pasta.

"Thank you."

"Eat your spaghetti. We got off on a serious topic when tonight was supposed to be all about you resting." He pointed at her plate. "And getting some carbs in you."

She laughed. Her shoulders relaxed. He was perfect for an affair. A short, happy fling that would help her to stop being so serious. Especially now that she understood how he'd formed his beliefs about marriage. There was no chance he'd ever love again, so she wouldn't allow herself to fall for him. She'd keep her goals in mind. Her need to loosen up and take time to enjoy life so that—as Marietta had said—when the right guy came along, she'd actually see him. Not be so tense. Be ready and open.

All she had to do was figure out a way to seduce Antonio.

No ideas came as they ate, but she refused to push. She was supposed to be relaxed, comfortable, open. Not tense. Not trying to figure everything out.

When their spaghetti was gone, Antonio rose to clear the table. As he gathered the plates and silver, she picked up the bowl of marinara.

"I'll put this in the fridge."

He paused on his way to the dishwasher. "Are you going to eat it tomorrow?"

She frowned. "I don't know."

"Why don't you freeze it? Then someday when you're hungry and you pull it out for dinner, you'll think of me."

"That sounds nice." It did. Everything about him tonight was warm and fuzzy. After two glasses of wine, she was a bit warm and fuzzy herself.

She headed to the cupboard to find a storage container for the marinara just as he walked by on his way to the sink. He looked up at the same time that she looked over and they both jerked to a stop.

He smiled. She smiled. This was what she wanted them to

be. Two people who knew each other and liked each other, gravitating toward more than friendship because of their attraction. Nothing strained. No confusion. Just letting something happen between them.

Once they cleared the table and cleaned the kitchen, they could watch TV together on the sofa and maybe, sitting close, their attraction would evolve naturally. No pushing. No fussing.

He motioned to the cupboard. His voice was deep and sexy when he said, "You go ahead."

"I'm just getting a bowl for the marinara."

He smiled again. His dark eyes glittered with desire.

Her skin felt like it caught fire. When he'd kissed her, she'd melted. She couldn't imagine how intense making love would be. But she wanted it.

She retrieved a container that she could freeze and walked over to the center island, giving him space to finish stacking dishes in the dishwasher. Her kitchen wasn't small but this thing that hummed between them made even the biggest space seem tiny, the innocent nearness of their bodies powerful.

She drew in a long breath. Anticipation scared her silly, even as it made her breathless. He finished the dishes. She slid the bowl of marinara into the freezer. She set it on a shelf and closed the door, but a realization struck her.

He'd asked if she would be eating the sauce the next day. As if he wouldn't be there. Was he going home? Tonight?

She told herself she was being silly, overthinking things. He would tell her if he was planning to go home. Her nerves were getting the better of her.

She followed him to the sofa, knowing if something was going to happen it would be on the sofa with them sitting close.

He picked up the remote but tossed it down again.

"You know what? You're tired and I have some calls to make."

She struggled not to gape at him. He was going to ignore this sizzle! She almost couldn't believe it—

Except she'd spent most of their relationship giving him negative signals. Somehow, she needed to turn that around.

"I'm not tired." She yawned. Damn it! Where the hell had that come from?

He laughed. "You are tired." With a wave of his hand, he directed her to follow him. "Come on. Let me walk you to your room."

She sighed internally. Marietta was right. She wasn't any good at this and she did need a fling to get her groove back.

"That's okay. I know the way."

"Agreed. But maybe I'd like to steal a kiss."

Her breath stalled. It seemed she'd read his suggestion that she go to bed all wrong. Saying she was tired might have been his way of getting them back to her bedroom?

He caught her hand, and they walked down the short hall. When they got to her door, he said, "Good night."

She smiled. This was sweet and romantic, but she was ready for more. "Good night."

He dipped his head to kiss her, and she slid her hands up his shirt front to his shoulders. She totally relaxed, let herself sink into the kiss. The feeling of his lips on hers. The solidness of his shoulders. The way their bodies brushed just enough to tempt and tease her. Every fiber of her being woke up. Her breath shivered into her lungs.

He pulled away suddenly. "This is awful."

She blinked. "Kissing me is awful?"

He groaned. "No. Having to stop is awful!"

She stepped close again. The time for signals and hints was over. She needed to be direct and honest. "You don't have to stop."

He held her gaze. "Yes, I do. You're coming down from the adrenaline of flying across an ocean to be with your mother, and two days of sitting at the hospital, worrying. You're not thinking straight."

"I'm pretty sure I've thought this through completely and I know what I'm doing."

"You're ready for an affair?"

She held his gaze. "Yes. I realized I've been all about work these past years and I'm in need of a real life. This," she motioned from herself to him and back to herself again, "the off-the-charts thing between us, is too tempting to be resisted. In fact, I'm pretty sure it's not supposed to be resisted."

"I agree. But—" He shook his head. "You thought it through while your emotions were all garbled." He took a breath and looked at the ceiling. "Making love is supposed to be wonderful. Sweet. Sexy. And mutually fun. Your whole world's been tossed up in the air the past few days. Give your emotions a chance to settle down."

Her chest tightened. Was that what these new feelings were? Her heightened emotions looking for release? She didn't know whether to be angry with herself or embarrassed.

Just when embarrassed would have won, he caught her elbows, pulled her to him and kissed her so sweetly she almost swooned. For a guy who didn't believe in love or the permanency of that emotion, he conveyed more to her in a slow romantic kiss than anybody ever had.

He pulled back. "Good night." With a flip of his wrist, he opened her bedroom door, then shifted to the right, giving her enough space to walk past him.

When she was inside her room, he closed the door and she stood frozen. Longing rippled through her. Kissing him always stirred up her hormones but tonight had been about more. She'd never felt closer to another human being than she had to him. What he'd told her about his mom, his parents, was the kind of thing you only revealed when you trusted someone.

He trusted her.

She liked him. And he liked her. The fact that he'd turned her down actually endeared him to her a little bit more.

She slid into pajamas and then into bed. She wasn't sure what would happen in the morning, but a warm feeling filled her heart. She fell asleep almost immediately, proving him right. She had been tired.

When she woke, she showered and dressed in jeans and a sleeveless blouse. After putting on a comfortable pair of sandals, she left her room and headed toward the kitchen. The door to the spare bedroom was open. The lights were off. But she saw the dim glow from the kitchen and smelled fresh coffee.

She pulled in a breath, straightened her shoulders and walked up the corridor, not quite sure what she was expecting when she stepped up to the center island.

Antonio leaned against it, reading his phone. Obviously having heard her enter, he looked up and smiled. "If I'd known you were waking so early, I would have made you a cup of coffee."

Her heart liquefied. He had no idea what a wonderful person he was.

"I can do it." She ambled to the cupboard and pulled out a mug.

Memories of the way he'd kissed her the night before drifted through her brain. The sweetness of it weakened her knees. Anticipation stole through her. She wasn't tired now. He would know that. If he kissed her again, this would be it. They would sleep together.

"I have to go back to Italy today."

Well, that wasn't what she'd been expecting. She stopped halfway to the coffeemaker. Then she remembered his suggestion that she freeze the marinara sauce and disappointment softened her voice. "You do?"

"I have meetings tomorrow morning that I can't miss. Italy

is seven hours ahead. The flight is seven hours. I'll get there fourteen hours after I leave here."

She plugged the pod into the one-cup coffeemaker, regret flooding her. She should have pushed the night before. He was leaving. She had to stay here. God only knew if they'd see each other again. They'd missed their chance.

Still, she said, "I understand."

But when she reached into the refrigerator for cream, her ring glittered up at her. She had decided she could get the ring cut off herself, but she didn't have to. Doing it together was a valid reason for them to see each other again. All was not lost.

Her mood brightened. "Besides, my mom is fine. Or will be fine shortly. You can report back to your grandmother that everything is good."

He snorted. "Yeah. That will cement my story." He took a quick breath. "Which reminds me. There's one more thing."

She poured her cream in her coffee and faced him. "What?"

"Yesterday afternoon, while you were at the hospital, I found a jeweler here in Manhattan. Rafe recommended him. If you and I can be there at ten o'clock this morning, he can remove the ring."

"Oh." Her brightened mood tumbled into genuine despair. Without the ring there was no reason to see each other.

"It just seems prudent to get this taken care of while we can."

"Yes. You're right. I'm sure my mom's doctor will be there well before ten. Plenty of time for me to talk to him and then meet you at the jewelers." She took a breath. Confusion and a need to get away from him so he wouldn't see her disappointment made her babble. "Actually, he's there at seven or seven-thirty. So, I should get going. I'll see him and have plenty of time to get to the jeweler. Text me the address."

"I'll send my limo for you."

She headed for the door. "Sure. Great. I'll see you there."

CHAPTER NINE

ANTONIO STOOD IN the office of Rafe's friend, Bruno, trying not to pace. The night before he'd sent Riley to bed—without him—after she'd made it clear she wanted to give in to their attraction.

He'd called himself crazy a million times. He'd gone over every event of the day, wondering what had held him back when everything he'd wanted had been at his fingertips.

And he got no clear reason for his hesitation.

He'd known she was tired, but making love had a way of invigorating people. Yet he'd walked away. Even after she'd very clearly said she understood anything between them would be temporary.

Something was definitely wrong with him.

Which was why he was handling the issue with the ring and returning to Italy. He had trouble enough maintaining a fake engagement for GiGi. He didn't need the added distraction of wanting to sleep with his fake fiancée, then walking away from the opportunity, making himself question his sanity. The truth was he was never supposed to see Riley again after his proposal. Instead, they'd been together nearly every day since their fake engagement. That was why everything felt so off.

He would go home and get back to normal. Without her around, the fake engagement would become nothing but telling GiGi that his visits to Manhattan were to see Riley. And his world would return to business as usual.

Bruno entered with a china cup on a saucer. Antonio hadn't really wanted coffee, but he was too antsy to make small talk with someone he didn't know.

"Your fiancée is here."

He took the coffee, setting it on the desk without even a sip. "She's arrived?"

"She's walking through the shop right now."

The door to the jeweler's office opened and Riley stepped inside.

She smiled.

His heart pitter-pattered. Tall and slender, she looked regal and elegant even in jeans. Her green eyes always sparkled. Her lips were full, perfect.

Regret tried to rise. He reminded himself that he needed to get back to behaving like himself. And he never seemed to do that when he was with her.

"Thank you for coming. How is your mom?"

"She definitely will be going home today." Riley laughed. "Her assistant has staff lined up to be with her 24/7. And she is in a mood." She laughed again. "She's awake and bossing everybody around."

"Then it's time for her to go home."

"Yes. Her assistant got her condo ready for her. I suggested my condo, but my mom refused." She laughed. "And not politely."

Antonio pictured her mother's reaction and laughed too.

Bruno said, "Shall we do this?"

Both Riley and Antonio said, "Yes."

Bruno had Riley sit at a small table by his cluttered desk. He slid a piece of plastic under the ring and caught Riley's gaze. "The plastic ensures that your finger won't be hurt."

She nodded. "I trust you."

"I've done hundreds of these."

He worked his magic and cut through the band, then pulled the two sides apart just enough she could slide the ring off.

She breathed a sigh of relief. "Thank you."

Antonio said, "Yes. Thank you." The same relief she'd obviously felt swelled in his chest. Their two-week engagement was over for her. He'd still be pretending. But now he had only his grandmother to manage. Not a grandmother, a fake fiancée and confusing emotions.

"The band can be repaired," Bruno said, handing the ring to Antonio.

He slid it into his jacket pocket. "Actually, I'm thinking of having the diamond set into a pendant for my grandmother."

Not really understanding, Bruno nodded.

Riley rose from the chair, brushing off the front of her shirt as if she thought it had been covered in dust from sawing the band.

But Antonio didn't see any dust. All he saw was the way her shirt cruised over the swell of her breasts.

He shook his head to clear it. "Can I drop you at the hospital?"

"No. My mom's room is full of people. She's holding court as they wait for her discharge orders." She took a breath. "I could use a break."

Antonio put his hand on the small of her back to direct her to the door. "Okay. I'll take you to your condo then."

"Thank you. I would appreciate that."

With their relationship ending, she was behaving the way she had the day she'd planned his fake proposal. Professionally friendly. He remembered how much trouble he'd had keeping his eyes off her that morning in her office—and the night before. Something about her classic beauty had drawn him in a way no woman ever had.

The hand he had pressed against the small of her back began to tingle.

She led him through the posh jewelry store and onto the street, where his limo waited. The driver opened the door. She slid inside. He followed her.

As the car pulled into the street, she faced him with a smile. "This feels weird. Different."

"Actually, it feels like the morning we planned our proposal."

"Really?"

"Yes. I feel like myself again."

"Because you're not engaged."

"*We're* not engaged."

She chuckled, but their gazes met.

Something like hot honey poured through him, heating his skin, setting his blood on fire. They weren't engaged. There was nothing between them except an unrelenting attraction.

His smile faded.

Her smile faded.

Before he really knew what was happening, he was kissing her. Her hands were on his back. His hands tried to be everywhere at once. They drifted from her waist to her rounded hips and then back up again. He couldn't believe he was actually, *finally*, touching her and that she was touching him back.

Here they were, in a limo…doing what they'd both been aching to do. And it did not feel wrong as it had the night before. It felt right. Perfect.

She pulled back and he realized they'd arrived at her condo. Her sparkly green eyes glittered. "What time's your flight?"

"In three hours."

"It'll take an hour to get to the airport."

He slid his fingers under her hair, kissing her deeply, his tongue mimicking what every other cell in his body wanted to do before he pulled away and said, "We have time."

They exited the limo and said hello to that day's doorman as they tried to casually stroll to the elevator. When the door closed behind them, he braced her against the wall of the little car, sliding his fingers through the hair at her nape, holding her head exactly where he wanted it so he could kiss her the way he'd yearned to for two incredibly long weeks.

The door opened and they kissed their way down the hall to her condo. She opened the door. They stepped inside and he caught her to him again. Knowing the way to her room, he turned them in that direction and kissed her until they entered her bedroom. Then he reached for the buttons of her blouse, and she slid his suit coat off his shoulders. It tumbled to the floor. He didn't care. Her blouse joined it, then she undid the snap of her jeans and stepped out of them and her panties. He followed suit with his trousers, unbuttoned the top few buttons of his shirt and pulled it over his head.

Naked, they faced each other, then as if they were a magnet and steel, they came together for a passionate kiss. Blistering heat consumed him, especially when her hands drifted over his skin. He kissed his way down her neck to her breasts and she groaned with pleasure.

Everything dissolved into a mist of desire. He wasn't entirely sure how they ended up on the bed or how he knew the exact minute to enter her. But the pleasure of it, the heat, roared through him. He understood why. He'd waited two long weeks for her.

Making love with Antonio was like stepping into a hurricane. At first, Riley thought she wouldn't be able to keep up, but something inside her snapped. Her days of being nice Riley, overworked Riley, driven Riley, were over. Except for making love to him. Then the desire that drove her to taste and touch him to her heart's delight was exactly what she wanted.

When the pleasure crested and exploded, she closed her eyes and enjoyed.

After a few seconds of absorbing every feeling, she sighed with contentment. "Wow."

He rolled over, dropping his head to her pillow, pulling her with him so they could nestle together. "Yeah. Wow. That was amazing."

"It was." She half sat up. "But I was referring to how you must really not like being engaged."

He frowned. "Excuse me?"

"You had the restraint of a saint until we weren't engaged. But I took off that ring and boom. Everything exploded."

He thought about that for a second. "Really?"

"That's exactly what happened. You turned me down last night, remember? Then that ring came off my finger and we weren't in the cab ten seconds before we were kissing. Like someone had flipped a switch."

He laughed. "I did have a really, really, really God-awful marriage."

She laid down again, snuggling against him, and placed her hand on his chest. "So you've said."

"Because it's true. It was bad. Even before my wife cheated on me, our relationship had crumbled. I didn't realize it until I looked back on things, but she'd been out of the marriage long before I even knew it was over."

"Really?"

"I should have seen it when she became difficult. She loved living in the family villa when we first married. But six months in, she made me buy a house for us." He snorted. "Which, six months later, she took in the divorce."

"Oh."

"Don't say 'oh,' snarky like that. It was about more than money. At least to me. Before we were married, we talked. We made plans. She even wanted children. I genuinely believe that she loved me for the year we dated and the year we were engaged. But her love grew cold quickly once we got married."

"Unless she was just infatuated with you. Or eager to be married?"

Antonio laughed. "Neither. She loved me. But after almost three years, a year of dating, a year engaged, and a few months of being married, her love died." He shrugged. "Maybe from boredom. Or maybe familiarity?" He shrugged again. "Whatever the reason her love grew cold, it almost doesn't matter because it did."

"How about yours?"

"Have someone treat you badly long enough and your love would die too."

"I get that."

"Really?"

"I might not have been treated abysmally, but the last guy I lived with behaved more like a roommate. After a while our feelings dimmed, then suddenly my life was empty even with him in it."

"So *you've said.*"

She laughed. "Yeah. But the same as your wife, Chad had left the relationship long before I asked him to move out. I'm absolutely certain, he missed my condo more than me."

He glanced around appreciatively. "It is a nice condo."

She laughed, then slapped him playfully. "I'm more than a condo."

He rolled her to her back. "You definitely are. And if I had you in my life 24/7, I wouldn't spend more time with your big screen TV than you."

He kissed her and her chest filled with happiness. But kisses soon became caresses. Caresses fueled the fire of their need. And the second time they made love was more passionate than the first.

She could not imagine a woman growing tired of this… of *him*.

But she wouldn't let her thoughts go any further than that.

This was about them living in the moment. If she let herself start believing it could become something more, she'd end up with a broken heart. He'd been very clear that he didn't want to marry again. She wouldn't let herself fall into the trap of thinking she could change his mind.

Antonio knew it was time to head to the airport. As it was, he would barely make his flight. But he didn't want to leave. Of course, there was another option open to them.

He ran his big toe up her leg. "Come to Italy with me."

She laughed. "Right."

He sat up. Caught her gaze so she would know how serious he was. "Please. We can't have one time together and hope we somehow run into each other again when we live on two different continents. Come to Italy with me."

Her eyes shifted, as she absorbed that. "What about your grandmother?"

"What about her?"

"I don't have a ring. She can't see me."

"If we run into her, we'll tell her it had to be resized."

She bit her lower lip. "It's not a lie."

"No. It's the truth." He ran his finger along her arm. "Plus, you still have vendors to investigate."

"I do. But I also have a mom who is getting out of the hospital today."

"You said she was fine."

"I'd still like to watch her the first day or two she's home."

"So come at the end of the week."

She inclined her head. "I suppose I could."

He took a breath, waiting for her to think this through. They might not be together forever, but they had something special. No matter how short-lived, he wanted to enjoy it.

When she didn't say anything else, he decided to pull out the Salvaggio charm. "We'll have the whole weekend." He nuzzled her neck. "Please."

She laughed "You're very hard to say no to."

"It's part of my charm."

"No. It's the result of your charm…and good looks…and that damned accent of yours."

He rolled out of bed, glad she'd agreed. But because this was supposed to be casual, he wouldn't push for or promise any more than that.

"All right, you figure things out while I'm in the air and I'll call you when my flight lands. We can make plans."

"Those plans are going to have to include me actually visiting the list of vendors Geoffrey made for me the other day."

It hit him in the oddest way that she called his assistant by his first name. It added a layer to what was happening between them that was fun and intimate. Though he would be careful with that. It was why he hadn't argued with her when she made the connection between getting rid of the ring and finally falling into bed together. It had given him a chance to further explain the story of his marriage. To make sure she understood why he would never again make the mistake of believing that love lasted.

After he'd redressed, she walked over and kissed him. "I'll miss you."

"I'll miss you too." He breathed in the scent of her, took in every detail of her face, memorized the sound of her voice… then kissed her good-bye.

She hadn't debated his view on love the way she had the night he'd slept on the chair in her little hotel room. She didn't make any proclamations or seek promises.

Finally, they were on the same page.

"I'm very glad things are working out between us."

She smiled. "I am too."

"And the fact that this is only us, in the moment, really doesn't bother you?"

She toyed with the button on his shirt. "I've been so serious for so long I think something fun and frivolous is what I need."

He kissed her. "It's definitely what I need." He kissed her again. "I'll see you on Friday."

And *that*, he decided, was the reason he felt comfortable with her now. Not the loss of one engagement ring. It was the release of expectations and pretense.

Now, they had none. Only each other.

CHAPTER TEN

ANTONIO DIDN'T CALL the second his plane landed. He'd slept through the flight and awoke groggy. He intended to call her when he got to the villa, but his grandmother was up and waiting in the family room for him.

"How is Riley's mother?"

Knowing GiGi sometimes had trouble sleeping since his grandfather's passing, he kissed her cheek. "She's good. Today, she woke grouchy and bossy so her doctor told her she could go home."

GiGi clutched her chest. "Really? A grouchy, bossy woman is well enough to go home?"

"She owns a home nursing agency. Half her staff will be at her beck and call."

"She will be cared for?"

"Probably better than the rest of us are after a hospital stay."

She breathed a sigh of relief.

Antonio walked to the bar and fixed himself an old-fashioned. "I'm glad I went to Manhattan to check on things though."

"I knew you would be."

"In spite of her mom being in the hospital, Riley and I had a good visit." He couldn't believe how easily conversation poured out of him. He knew his GiGi wanted details, wanted to feel part of things, and it was wonderful that he really did have facts for her. No lies. Nothing to worry about remembering. Except—

"The only problem is her ring is at the jeweler."

GiGi gasped. "Why?"

"Basically, it was too small."

"So, Rafe has it?"

"No. It's with a friend of Rafe's in Manhattan."

"Hmm."

He fell to the sofa and sipped his drink. "It's all good."

"I wouldn't think a resizing would take more than a few minutes. A day at most."

"Well, this one will."

"You should have let Rafe handle it."

"It's fine. Riley's fine. You'll see for yourself when she flies over at the end of the week."

GiGi brightened. "She's coming here again?"

Antonio fought a wince. Drawing on the truth was one thing, but he never should have told her that Riley was returning to Italy. This visit was for them—to stay in bed for a few days. Enjoy what they have. Now she'd have to at least come for dinner.

He downed his drink and decided to end the conversation before he fell into another easy trap. "We are a couple. We do miss each other."

She beamed. *"Si."*

He took his glass to the bar, kissed his grandmother's cheek again and went to his room. He shucked his jacket and loosened his tie, then sat on the sofa in the sitting area of his suite and called Riley.

She didn't answer until after the third ring. He laughed. "Playing hard to get?"

"That ship has sailed. Besides, I think this thing between us will only work if we're completely honest."

"Okay. In the interest of honesty, I told my grandmother

you were visiting at the end of the week, and she assumed that meant you'd be coming here for dinner."

She thought for a second, "I could come for dinner. I didn't take enough pictures of the potential proposal sites when I was there the other night. I didn't go into the winetasting room at all. Jake will need more than just my gushing descriptions when he updates the website. A visit over the weekend could kill two birds with one stone."

He laughed and relaxed on the sofa.

She relaxed on her sofa. For once a relationship didn't make her a bundle of nerves because it wasn't really a relationship. It was a short-term thing. She didn't have to worry about pleasing him beyond what came naturally. She didn't wonder if he wanted her condo. She wasn't on red alert trying to be a sparkling conversationalist.

She simply enjoyed him—enjoyed what they had in the moment.

They talked for another hour and that amazed her too. They were from two different cultures, two different worlds, but they had a million things to talk about. Making her believe the world really was getting smaller because of the internet.

She went to bed and woke early so she could visit her mom. To her surprise, Juliette was sitting at her dining table, with one of her staff serving her breakfast.

She pointed at her mother's plate. "Eggs and toast?"

"No one's worried about my cholesterol, Riley. It's my arm everyone wants to heal. And I'm taking advantage. I might even put jelly on my toast."

Riley laughed and took a seat at the table.

"Let me have Janine bring some eggs for you."

She almost said no but remembered what Antonio had said about her eating habits. That reminded her of the bowl of marinara sauce in her freezer and the groceries in her cupboards. Her heart filled with indescribable joy. Having some-one who thought of her needs was weird, but in a wonderful way. Their relationship might not be permanent, but it still had its good points.

"I could eat an egg or two."

Janine came in and her mom asked her to bring two eggs and toast for Riley. When Janine was gone, her mom said, "So what's the big smile for?"

"Nothing. Just glad to see you're okay."

"I'm fine." She picked up her toast. "Are you sure it's not your Italian god who's making you smile."

She laughed. "He's in Italy."

"Too bad. I would have liked to get to know him."

"Really?"

"At first, I thought it was sweet that he faked an engage-ment to help his grandmother, then he seemed to be around you a lot more than a fake fiancé should." She pondered for a second. "Almost like he thought the engagement was real."

"His grandmother insisted he come here when she heard you were hurt." Janine served Riley's breakfast. "If he hadn't come, she would have gotten suspicious."

"Um-hmm."

Riley frowned. "What does that mean?"

"I don't know. There's something about this whole situ-ation that makes me uncomfortable. A handsome guy who needs a fake fiancée? And why you? Why not bring one of his friends?"

"Because I was planning the proposal, he thought I would provide the fiancée and I thought he would bring a friend to pretend to be his fiancée. When we realized our faux pas, we also saw I was at the park and dressed like a woman about to be proposed to. That was your fault by the way."

"My fault?"

"You wanted me dressed up for your doctor dinner."

"Ah." Her mother frowned, then waved her fork. "You know what? Never mind. I'm on painkillers. All this suspicion is probably from being woozy."

"Probably."

Riley ate her breakfast, then left for work, where she got the totally opposite reception from Marietta.

Grinning like a fool, she caught Riley's arm and walked her down the hall to her office. "So? What happened?"

She frowned. "With my mom?"

"With the Italian dreamboat. What a great guy! So sweet and considerate."

"He is a good guy. But you were in on the ruse. We aren't really engaged, remember?" She displayed her bare hand. "In fact, we had the ring cut off yesterday."

Marietta frowned. "Really?"

"Yes! The thing was expensive, and it was weird walking around wearing it when it meant nothing."

"I don't know. I'm not sure it meant nothing. There was something about the way he looked at you that—" She shrugged. "Maybe it made me think there really was a spark between you."

There was a spark that had turned into a ridiculously hot flame. But Riley wasn't about to tell Marietta that. And there was indeed something odd about her relationship with Antonio, but it wasn't that he harbored real feelings for her. It was that Riley was doing something she never did. She had entered a relationship that didn't have a chance in hell of becoming permanent.

And she liked it.

She liked the freedom of it. No one, not even super romantic Marietta, was going to put doubts in her head, or turn her logical thought process into wishful thinking by suggesting that Antonio might want something more than a couple weeks or months of great sex.

He wouldn't.

She smiled at Marietta but as soon as her assistant walked up the hall to her office, her smile drooped, and she wasn't sure why. She and Antonio had a mutual agreement to keep things simple and temporary. And she *needed* a fling. Some fun—

Reminders of her real goals filled her head. Kids. Noisy breakfasts. Happy holidays—

She dismissed them. That was for another time. These next few weeks were for fun.

Friday evening, Italian time, she arrived in Italy to find Antonio waiting for her at the airport. He held a bunch of flowers, which he almost dropped when he grabbed her to kiss her hello.

He took her overnight bag from her and frowned. "I guess you're not staying long?"

She linked her arm with his. "Well, it's Friday night here, so technically, I can't do the work I wanted to."

"You won't be working this trip?"

"I'll work Monday and Tuesday…go home Wednesday morning, meaning I should be in Manhattan on Wednesday morning. I brought plenty of clothes, just packed everything into the bag snugly."

He grinned. "You're so clever, making time work to your advantage."

"I know!"

"Who's minding the store?"

"Marietta. I reminded her that your assistant had created a list of potential vendors for me." She shrugged. "I made it sound all business."

He laughed. "You're having too much fun with this."

She shook her head. "I don't think so. I missed out on a lot of fun. I think I'm just making up for lost time."

They reached his limo. The driver took her bag, and they slid inside.

"So, what's on our agenda?"

He settled back on the comfortable seat. "Tonight? Nothing. Tomorrow, GiGi is expecting you for dinner."

"So, we have tonight and all day tomorrow."

"Yes! And because we have all night and tomorrow, we're going to get dinner, then I'm going to show you at least some of the city before we retire."

They drove to her hotel where a bellman took her bag and the flowers Antonio had brought for her. He headed for her room and they went to the bar/restaurant with the glass wall.

"I hope we don't run into Marco again." He pointed at her hand. "You don't have a ring."

"It's at the jeweler," she said, smiling.

"Yeah. We might have to be careful with that. My grandmother mentioned that rings are typically resized in a day or two. It shouldn't take weeks."

"Okay. Maybe we just don't mention it."

He nodded. They ordered dinner, drank wine, ate a delicious meal, then took a stroll. The night air was perfect. June had become July and the temperatures had risen, but as darkness descended on Florence everything cooled. The scent of water filled the air.

"Is there a lake around here?"

"A river." He turned her to the right. "This way."

He led her down a few streets and a stone bridge came into view. "Ponte Vecchio."

"Oh... Ponte Vecchio," she said, mimicking his accent. "It sounds romantic."

"It means old bridge."

She laughed. "Apparently, people were more realistic when they named things back then."

"It's one of only a few bridges to survive World War II."

Arm in arm, they ambled over. "So, it's old and stubborn."

"Like my grandmother."

"She still hasn't scheduled her treatments, has she?"

"No. She's growing happier by the day though. I will keep up the ruse long enough for her to settle in, accept her happiness and get her treatments."

"As long as we're still, you know—doing this—I don't mind popping in to see her when I visit."

"Thank you."

"We'll have to figure out something about the ring."

"I still have it. Maybe I really will get it resized and you can slip it on when you visit."

"Sounds like a plan."

They stopped at a stone wall and leaned against it, looking at the reflection of the bridge on the water. Tourists milled around them. The sound of happy conversations floated on the air.

"This place is busy, yet it's peaceful."

"All of Italy is like that. There's a hum of something that rides the air. But it's something sweet and good." He chuckled. "Look at you, turning me into a poet."

"I think you could be anything you wanted."

"You do, do you?"

"You're smart. You're charming. And you seem to be in tune with everything around you." She paused and smiled. "You notice things like my bare cupboards. And you solve problems by doing things like filling those cupboards."

His expression grew serious. "*Are* you eating?"

"I've always eaten. Now, I'm actually thinking before I choose. I'm still grabbing a donut for breakfast, but I'm not skipping lunch and I'm eating something healthy for dinner like a salad."

"I have changed you?"

Her mouth opened, but she stopped herself from admitting he'd done more than change her. He'd helped her shift from being a workaholic to being someone who knew how to enjoy her life while she ran her successful business. In doing that, she'd realized she could trust her staff more. In trusting her staff more, she could see her business had more potential to grow in the future.

It was like dominoes but different.

Still, there was no need for him to realize the huge impact he'd had on her life. Especially since she was barely a blip on the radar of his. That reminder tweaked her heart. But she stopped the shimmy of apprehension. They'd slept together once. He shouldn't have serious feelings for her, and she needed to keep her feelings and worries in check.

She turned to face him, and he pulled her into his arms. "Yes. You changed me...or my thinking. And I am happier for it."

"Being with you makes me happy too."

That was enough for her. She didn't have to be the love of his life. He didn't want a love of his life. He liked relationships but had no expectations. Technically, in this space of time they were perfect for each other.

Just two people having fun.

They strolled back to her hotel, both quiet. He seemed to be enjoying the atmosphere of the city closest to his family's vineyard. She was contemplative. Old Riley would be wondering about the end of their relationship right now. How she would cope. What her next step would be. New Riley realized that the woman who hadn't taken a vacation in a decade was on her second trip to Italy. With a man she wanted to be with. She refused to think about the future because there was no future. This relationship was about teaching her to relax.

They walked through the hotel lobby and to her room.

When she opened the door, he sniffed. "Really? You picked the same room you had last time?"

"Hey, being with you doesn't mean I no longer have a budget. I'm expensing this. I don't want the Internal Revenue Service to think I'm padding my trips."

He laughed and kissed her softly. But as always, their kisses heated and unwanted clothing disappeared. He caught the corner of the comforter and tossed it back.

"I'll bet two weeks ago you never pictured us sharing this bed."

She blinked. Had it only been two weeks? Good Lord, in fourteen short days, they'd gotten engaged, she'd met his family, her mom had been hurt. Her employees were now doing half her work. She'd become a world traveler. She'd started an affair.

He tumbled them to the bed bringing her out of her reverie. Her back arched as need sharpened.

But her thoughts sharpened too. For the first time in her life, she felt like herself. Not playing a role. Not working so hard she didn't have time to feel bad about her past. She was simply herself.

Or was she? This relationship was nothing like what she'd always wanted—

No. It was what she wanted, *right now*. She hadn't given up her dreams. Only delayed them.

Antonio kissed her again, running his fingers along her thigh. Everything inside her stilled, then came to vibrating life and she pushed those thoughts aside.

A ringing phone woke Antonio the next morning. He groped along the bedside table and grabbed it. Pressing the button, he answered, "Hello?"

"Where are you?"

"GiGi?"

Beside him, Riley stirred.

"Yes. Where are you? I thought you were bringing Riley home from the airport last night."

He ran his hand down his face to wake himself. "We're at her hotel."

Riley sat up. He mouthed, *It's my grandmother.*

GiGi's voice brightened. "Oh, so she did come to visit?"

"Yes."

"Let me talk to her."

"She might still be sleeping…"

Riley nodded and reached for the phone. Antonio said, "Nope. Wide awake. Here she is."

"Good morning, GiGi."

She put the phone on speaker, which was what Antonio would have been smart enough to do if he'd been more awake.

"Good morning, Riley! How is your mom?"

Antonio said, "I already told you that."

"I want to hear it from the source."

"My mom is fine. Great really. She has a nurse with her 24/7 and she's still tired enough that she's actually taking it easy." She laughed. "But next week, when she feels better, we might have to tie her down to get her to continue resting."

GiGi chortled. "She sounds like a pistol. I can't wait to meet her."

Riley's eyes met his. Her expression said she didn't want to lie. So, he said, "Pace yourself, GiGi, one Morgan at a time. You barely know Riley."

"And whose fault is that?"

"Not mine. I'm bringing her to dinner tonight."

"Good."

"But I'm not just here to visit," Riley said suddenly.

He knew why. She liked keeping the conversation on her business, so they didn't accidentally stumble into discussions where they'd have to lie.

"Part of the reason I'm in Italy is that I'm scouting vendors and venues for my business."

"Oh, the event planning!"

"Yes. Depending on the event, I need flowers and musicians and sometimes choirs."

"What kind of events do you plan?"

"All kinds," Riley said, and Antonio rolled his eyes. He knew she was avoiding mentioning proposal planning because it was just too close to their ruse.

"So, you're bringing your business here and when you are married, you will move to Italy?"

Riley blinked and Antonio stifled a laugh. His GiGi knew how to set conversational traps.

But Riley craftily said, "I can't live in Manhattan if my man lives here."

Antonio guffawed with laughter. Mostly because Riley was as crafty as his grandmother. Her answer had not been a lie.

Riley swatted him. He rolled out of bed and went to the bathroom, leaving Riley on her own. He wasn't helping much anyway.

Before he closed the bathroom door, Antonio heard GiGi's voice fill with excitement as she said, "You can tell me all about it tonight."

"Okay."

A minute later, Riley came into the bathroom.

"I was just about to step into the shower."

"Oh, no. You're not stepping into the shower until you thank me."

He slid his arms around her. "For? You're the one who asked for the phone."

She sighed. "You're right."

"Besides you handled it brilliantly."

"She now thinks I'm moving to Italy."

He ran his hands down her bare back, luxuriating in the feel of her. "You do like it here. After you get this part of your business set up, you might actually want to move here. So, it's a possibility, not really a lie."

She kissed him, he was sure, to shut him up. Her moving to Italy was something they shouldn't even be considering. But unexpected happiness filled him at the thought, which wasn't at all what he wanted. What *they* wanted. This was temporary. And he would get them back to where they needed to be. Having an affair not thinking about the future.

Still kissing her, he reached into the shower and turned on the water, all thoughts of his grandmother forgotten.

CHAPTER ELEVEN

THAT AFTERNOON ANTONIO took the limo to the villa, giving Riley the afternoon to browse Florence while he went home to change clothes. She combined sightseeing with searching for the locations of the vendors on Geoffrey's list, though she didn't actually talk to any managers. She felt more like a tourist than a businesswoman today. Monday or Tuesday, she would make the contacts.

Today was for feeling happy. She refused to acknowledge the tightening of her chest when she remembered she'd never have any of the things she wanted as long as she was with Antonio. This was temporary. A respite. And she needed it.

When Antonio arrived to take her to the villa again, she was dressed in a pale blue sheath and white pumps. When he saw her, he whistled.

"You will wow my grandmother."

She glanced down at her dress. "No. This time I won't feel like a peasant."

He chuckled and they headed to the lobby, then out of the hotel to an Aston Martin convertible.

She stopped dead in her tracks. "Oh, my God."

"Pretty, isn't she?"

"She's... Wow."

"Now you see why I went home. I don't always like a limo. I love a drive in the country." He opened the door for her. "Climb in and get ready to enjoy the ride."

"How about if you climb in and enjoy the ride while I drive?"

He shrugged. "I don't see why not."

She just barely kept herself from gaping. Any guy who would trust a new person in his life with his fancy convertible either really liked her or he did not give a damn if she hurt his precious car.

Either way, she didn't care. She refused to think too deeply about anything when she was with him. That only led to reminders of what she would never have with him, and this wasn't the time for it. Right now, she wanted the luxury of driving his gorgeous car. She hopped in behind the steering wheel and pulled onto the street. He gave her a few quick directions that got them to the country road to the vineyard.

When they were out of the city, she hit the gas. The car took off like a rocket. The power was amazing.

She glanced over at him and shouted, "I love this."

"I love it too."

"It's titillating and relaxing at the same time."

"Exactly!"

The air swirling around them made conversation difficult, so Riley simply enjoyed driving, enjoyed watching the vineyards and villas that rolled along the gentle hills, the blue sky, the fresh air.

When they reached the Salvaggio mansion, they both climbed out. She walked around the hood of the car, caught Antonio by the back of the neck and yanked him to her for a hard kiss.

He laughed. "You're welcome."

"In bed tonight, you are going to be so glad you let me drive."

He laughed again and they entered his home. GiGi came down the curved stairway, again looking like mistress of the manor in a shirtwaist dress and pearls. She hooked her arm with Riley's, and they walked out to the patio.

"What did you do today?"

"Looked around the city. Antonio's assistant, Geoffrey, had created a list of venues for me. I didn't call them, but I did locate them." She took a deep breath as they stepped outside. "I just enjoyed being out and about."

GiGi smiled at her. "I hear Americans have difficulty relaxing."

"Antonio's helping me with that."

He walked to the bar, put wine on ice and rolled the cart to the chaises where they sat.

His grandmother shook her head. "He does know how to get everything done and still have a good time."

Antonio's father, Enzo, arrived a half hour later. He got another bottle of wine. Though Antonio held back from drinking because he had to drive to the hotel, GiGi, Enzo and Riley drank it, talking about how Riley was expanding her business. Enzo gave her some insights and she wished she'd had a pen and paper because the man was brilliant, showing her exactly where Antonio got both his good looks and brains.

The sun began to droop. Riley glanced over and saw that their table had been set. She looked at her wine glass, wondering just how many of these things she'd had. Then she decided she didn't care. She was with people she liked, enjoying the conversation—

She *was* with people she liked.

People she liked a lot.

An overwhelming sense of connection swamped her. Not just a connection to Antonio or his family or the villa and vineyard. To all of it. The sense that she was coming home filled her so strongly her breath stalled.

She belonged here.

She belonged here.

Was Antonio right? After she set up this arm of her business, would she want to move here? And if she did, would she be Antonio's mistress forever? One day at a time, it would be so easy to continue an affair that worked and was so much fun. Especially, since talking about the future was off limits.

The thought fried her brain. It couldn't take a step forward or a step back as that scenario played out in her head. Sleeping together. Going out to dinner. Visiting his family. But never going any further than that.

She tried not to think about it, but the genie was out of the bottle. And he had brought a million questions. Most importantly, would bringing her business to Italy keep her connected to Antonio—

And would staying connected to Antonio change the direction of her life? Her plans?

Her real needs?

Kids. Noisy breakfasts. Weekends of soccer games. Snow white Christmases packed with gifts and laughter. Would she lose it all? Never have what she wanted?

She stopped the waterfall of thoughts.

That kind of thinking was something old Riley would do. That Riley was always looking to the future, trying to determine costs and consequences. New Riley lived in the moment. Too much wine had to be why she'd slipped back into that pattern.

She drank water through dinner, joking and talking with Antonio's family about the ups and downs of owning a company. Most of their winemaking business was handled by managers, but they still went to board meetings and heard about employee disputes and customer complaints.

With dinner done, Antonio excused himself.

Enjoying the evening, GiGi leaned back in her chair. "Such a lovely night."

"Everything in Tuscany is lovely."

She nodded approvingly. "You make my Antonio happy."

"He makes me happy."

"And when you have children, you will be even happier."

After a night of keeping the conversation away from personal things by talking business, Riley only smiled. But her waterfall of doubts returned. If she moved here—even if she simply made regular trips here for her business—would Antonio be in her life forever? And if he was in her life forever, would she give up her dreams for herself one day at a time, one visit at a time?

Carrying a duffel bag, Antonio stepped out onto the patio again. "Not every couple wants children, GiGi. Don't forget Riley is a businesswoman."

GiGi batted a hand. "You can hire nannies."

Looking exasperated with her, he shook his head. "Always practical."

"No. Just trying to keep you from being alone."

Ignoring that comment, Antonio kissed his grandmother's cheek. "We're going now."

"You will be back tomorrow?"

"I think I'm going to take Riley on an official sightseeing tour." He offered her his hand. She took it and rose. He displayed the duffel. "That's why I'm taking extra clothes."

They left, ambling to the Aston Martin which still sat in the circular driveway. Antonio drove this time, happily shooting them up the country road back to Florence.

She appreciated the way Antonio had cooled his grandmother's expectation of children—promising the woman great-grandchildren when they might not even be a couple next year seemed more than one step over the line.

Then she remembered GiGi's response. She'd said she didn't want Antonio to be alone. Riley had realized that at the hospital, but hearing the emotion in GiGi's voice really cemented the idea in her mind. She didn't want great-grandkids as much as she wanted to make sure Antonio wouldn't end up alone.

But knowing GiGi as well as she was getting to know her, Riley also recognized that GiGi would adore any children Antonio had. She'd step into the role of great-grandmother like she was born for it.

Sadness for GiGi filled her. But she stopped it. That problem was Antonio's to deal with.

Just as her fear that she'd lose everything she wanted if she wasn't careful about this affair was her problem.

Suddenly, she couldn't stop herself from connecting what she was doing with Antonio to what her mom had done.

Was this what had happened? Her parents' affair had resulted in a pregnancy. They had a child. They committed—

But not legally.

And in the end her mom had been hurt. No. Her mom had lost everything.

She sucked in a breath, confused about why that comparison had popped into her head.

What she was doing with Antonio was different. There had been no promises. There would be no deciding they would get married "someday."

She would not lose everything, because she wouldn't allow herself to believe she and Antonio would ever commit.

Tooling around Tuscany the next day, she forgot all about that unfortunate comparison. What she had with Antonio was a straight up affair. She was having fun. Thinking such serious things was foolish—

Or old Riley ruining everything.

Luckily, Antonio made it easy for Riley to pause and enjoy herself as they puttered around town, ate lunch and did some touristy shopping. Monday and Tuesday, she worked with Geoffrey, interviewing vendors she could hire while working in Manhattan because no matter what impression she'd inadvertently given GiGi, she was not moving her company to Tuscany.

Not just because her engagement to Antonio was fake and therefore any planning that seemed to materialize when they were with GiGi was pure fiction; but because she was back to thinking realistically about this affair. Antonio had no place in her real-life decisions about her business. She was strong. She was smart. She had everything in perspective.

Especially the fact that she needed a frivolous affair. Something to get her sense of fun back.

All she had to do was withhold her heart. As long as she kept her wits about her, she could do that.

Wednesday evening, Antonio said good-bye to Riley at the airport and returned to the villa invigorated. It had been the best five days of his life. He couldn't ever remember working with such joy and efficiency. On Monday and Tuesday, he'd known he couldn't see Riley until the day's tasks were complete. So, he focused. And just when his jobs were complete, Riley and Geoffrey would return to the office, their visits to vendors done for the day.

She'd tell him about the vendors she'd found, the ideas she'd gotten, and they'd return to her hotel to make love. Then they'd wake up and do it all over again.

Every day had been fabulous, but he had to admit he was tired.

A voice in the back of his head reminded him that was irrelevant. Their affair was temporary, and he should enjoy it while he could. He and Riley would have fun for a few more weeks, a few more months...maybe even a year. Then it would be over.

His breath stuttered at the thought, but he reminded himself of his divorce, and his mother leaving and trying to get half the Salvaggio fortune. He remembered so much anger and pain. Strained silences in the villa.

The hurt of it rose as if both things had happened yesterday. He squeezed his eyes shut.

He would enjoy Riley while he could. Without dredging up those old memories. He did not need to be reminded that love didn't last.

In his own bed, he fell asleep and woke refreshed. Still, in the shower, alone, realizing he wouldn't see Riley that day or the next or the next, his mood plummeted. They hadn't made plans for her to return. He knew from her debriefings every day that most of her vendor investigations had been completed.

She didn't have any reason to come back.

He dressed, getting moodier by the second. They should have made some sort of plan, but they hadn't. Maybe she was already growing tired of what they had? Maybe it was time for him to bow out before he grew too fond of her, too accustomed to her—

The thought squeezed his chest.

GiGi and his father were already eating breakfast when he arrived in the dining room.

His dad laughed. "I'm hoping your mood improves before we have to meet with Marco this morning."

Not entirely sure what he'd done to clue his dad into his discontent, he mumbled, "I'm fine."

"No. You're not," GiGi said with a sniff. "You already miss Riley." She picked up her coffee cup. "Couples aren't supposed to be apart. You should get married."

Antonio choked on his toast. That brought him out of his funk really quickly.

"Married?" He almost reminded his grandmother that he and Riley had known each other three weeks—then he realized he'd led his family to believe they'd known each other longer.

Enzo frowned. "That's what engagements are for. Because eventually you intend to get married…" His voice trailed off as if that thought had reminded him of something. Or maybe because he was confused. Antonio's reaction to the word marriage had not been the reaction of a man engaged to be married.

Fear of getting caught rippled through Antonio. Before it could take root, he realized he was confusing their real-life affair and his pretend engagement. Talking to his dad and GiGi, he was engaged and should act that way.

He forced himself to perk up. "Of course, we're getting married. I was just thinking it would be more like next year. Or the year after."

GiGi sniffed again. "Two years?"

He dropped his napkin to his plate but took his coffee cup with him. He knew when a strategic retreat was necessary. It wasn't like him to get confused. It was time to leave and regroup. "This isn't a family decision. It's between me and Riley."

But just saying her name gave him a funny feeling in the pit of his stomach. As Gigi had guessed, he missed Riley. All those crazy memories about his marriage and his mom had pushed him in a bad direction and he'd reacted inappropriately.

He was *allowed* to miss her, but now that they were lovers, he was also permitted to do something about it.

"By the way, I'll be flying to Manhattan for the weekend. I hope we don't have plans."

Busy with his breakfast, his dad said, "No. No plans here."

His GiGi took a breath. "That's nice, but I was hoping she would come to Italy this weekend."

"She has a company to run and a mom who was just in an accident. We need to respect that. Plus, it's not very gentlemanly of me to expect her always to fly here. We'll be doing this fifty-fifty."

With that, he walked out of the dining room and returned to his room. He finished his coffee while talking to Geoffrey about flight arrangements for Friday. When the call was complete, he almost called Riley, but decided to surprise her.

Because that's what this relationship needed. Whimsy. Affairs were supposed to be fun, spontaneous. That's what he wanted. That's what she wanted. That's what they'd have. None of this worry that they would go too far. They wouldn't. He would see to it.

Even with video calls to her staff, the time Riley had spent in Italy had put her a week behind. She worked hard every day, then visited her mom every night. Not missing Antonio until she fell into bed exhausted.

Thursday morning, she wondered why he hadn't called and almost called him. She missed him. But this was an affair, not a relationship. Perhaps it wasn't proper for her to call? No. It definitely wasn't proper for her to call. Luckily, Jake came into her office with the prospective additions to the website, offering proposals in Tuscany. She shifted her mind off Antonio and onto work where it belonged.

Friday morning, she missed Antonio so much she knew she'd sound like a lovesick puppy if she called him, and he wouldn't like that. That wasn't their deal. She would not call him, not act like a real girlfriend. After all, she had plenty of work to do to get her mind off him. And she would do it.

But she still missed him.

Her company had a proposal in Central Park Friday afternoon and one at a restaurant Friday night. After the second one, she should have gone back to the office to continue catching up on work, but exhaustion and lethargy over missing Antonio forced her home.

This was the downside of a no-strings-attached love affair.

He owed her nothing. Not even a phone call. She had no idea when she'd see him again.

Actually, she had no idea *if* she'd see him again.

Having an affair suddenly sounded like the worst idea under the sun. A confusing roller coaster that wasn't as much fun as it had seemed to be when they were together.

She missed him.

She wanted to tell him.

She wanted to see him.

But that wasn't their deal.

Tossing her purse onto the center island of her kitchen, she headed back to her bedroom to shower off her misery, but there was a knock on her door.

She frowned. Oscar usually called her if someone was on their way up. Shaking her head, she raced to the door, looked through the peep hole and saw Antonio.

She whipped open the door and he caught her to him, kissing her so hard and so fast, she lost her breath.

"I missed you."

A little stunned, she blinked. "I missed you too."

He walked in and she closed the door behind him. The second she turned, he pulled her to him again. This kiss was slow and languid, turning her bones to liquid.

When he pulled away, he sighed. "I would immediately make good on the promise of that kiss but I'm hot and sticky."

"Hmm. I was just going to go shower."

He laughed and caught her hand. "We are very attuned to each other."

Joy filled her. Not just because he was there, in her apartment, but because he had missed her. Maybe more than she had missed him because she hadn't flown across an ocean to see him but, here he was…across an ocean to see her.

The pleasure that filled her at seeing him tripled as they soaped each other in between heated kisses. They came together in a frenzy of need that reminded her of why this affair was such a good idea. Then they made love again before falling asleep.

Still, she hadn't forgotten that this was just an affair. They could say they missed each other. They could be eager to make love. But after that an imaginary line formed. Not because he said so. Because this was what they had. Closeness but no commitment.

She enjoyed the closeness so much, though, that when they were together the lack of commitment seemed hazy, shadowy, so far off in the distance she refused to think about it.

She woke Saturday morning to the scent of bacon and grabbed a robe and stumbled up the hall to see him. She didn't want to miss a moment of him by sleeping away their time together.

When she walked into the kitchen, he kissed her. Realizing she was naked under her robe, he slid his hands inside, eventually easing the robe open so much that it puddled to the floor. He turned off the heat under the bacon and carried her back to the bedroom.

But while she enjoyed him being so hungry for her, he always seemed to be the aggressor, so she took over once they were in her room.

She leisurely helped him out of his shirt and pajama pants and when he would have pulled her to him in bed, she nudged his hands aside and straddled him.

"This is new."

She laughed, then kissed him. "You've pretty well taken control of things between us. It's my turn."

He laughed. She kissed him again, letting her hands roam. Then she slid her lips down his neck to his chest, enjoying the freedom he gave her to explore. But his hands slid up to her bottom, then up her waist to her breasts. She almost stopped him, but it felt so good she absorbed the pleasure even as she gave him pleasure.

But too soon he rolled her to her back and with a growl, nibbled bites down her neck. Her breath stalled, then jumped to double time when he entered her.

The heat and need and fun rolled through her like a happy symphony, until they reached the heights of excitement and anticipation and tumbled over the edge.

This was why she'd agreed to his insistence that this was temporary. She wanted fun. This was fun.

It was also why she could put her goal of a family on hold. This wouldn't last.

The following Friday, she flew to Italy. The week after that, he flew to Manhattan. Riley had promoted Marietta to office manager, and they'd hired a new assistant she and Marietta shared, as requests for proposals in Italy began to trickle in and their Manhattan business increased too.

Word of mouth was a powerful thing.

By the first week in October, they had a one weekend in Italy, one weekend in Manhattan schedule that they didn't even discuss anymore. Every Friday night he either showed up at her apartment door or the door of her hotel in Florence.

The hotel staff got to know them. The restaurant knew she liked ketchup with her eggs. They didn't go to the villa every time she was in Tuscany. Having to pretend to be engaged was killing the romance of their fling. But every other visit she had dinner on Saturday night. This trip was her stay without dinner at the villa.

He woke up extremely happy and knew the instant she woke too. Instead of sliding together in a blissful storm of need, she rolled over and nestled against his side.

"What do we have planned for the day?"

"Since we don't have to be at the villa tonight, I thought you might like to take the train to Rome."

She sat up, her eyes as wide as saucers. "I'd love to."

"Let's shower first."

She laughed and got out of bed. Before they reached the bathroom door, his phone rang.

"I'm not even going to look at it."

She sighed, heading back to the bedside table and his phone. "How about if we see who it is." She picked up the phone and winced. "It's your grandmother."

He took it from her hands, sucked in a breath and smiled before he answered, so she wouldn't hear the exasperation in his voice. "Good morning."

"Good morning. May I speak with Riley?"

"If you're going to try to sweet-talk her into having dinner at the villa tonight, don't."

She laughed. "No, I will not mess up your dinner plans. I would like to have *lunch* with Riley."

"We're going to Rome."

"Go after lunch."

He shook his head. "No. I want to leave this morning, take the whole day. See as much as we can."

She sighed. "Okay. How about lunch tomorrow?"

"Lunch tomorrow?" Antonio said, glancing at Riley as he said it. His grandmother had capitulated rather easily, but Antonio wasn't about to question his luck. Still, he wouldn't answer for Riley and sent her a questioning look. She did that gesture Americans sometimes did, where they raised both hands as if to say, "What could it hurt?"

"All right. Riley's giving me a sign like she wouldn't mind having lunch with you tomorrow."

"Excellent!"

"We'll see you at noon."

"Not, we," GiGi corrected. "I want to have lunch with Riley alone."

Warning bells rang. "We're sort of a package deal these days."

GiGi laughed. "You can survive one lunch without her. Have her text me the name of the restaurant where she'd like to eat."

It gave him an itchy feeling to think of GiGi alone with Riley, but Riley was a pro. She could handle one lunch on her own. Actually, some days she was better at the engagement charade than he was. He could trust her.

He could trust her.

The thought rattled through him, then made him smile. He probably trusted her more than he'd ever trusted a woman he was dating. Certainly, more than he'd trusted his ex. They had to trust each other to keep their affair brief and on point. He should not be surprised,

"Okay."

"Grazie."

Antonio and Riley had their shower time down to a perfect balance of lovemaking and cleanliness. But today for some reason it all felt different. Probably because of realizing he trusted her. She was beautiful, soft, warm and happy. Which made him happy.

So damned happy.

Adding his happiness to the knowledge that he could trust her somehow doubled both emotions—turned them into something like joy.

In a moment of unguarded honesty, he acknowledged that he'd never felt this way before. Never.

But that could be because this fling was temporary with no chance for an ugly, unhappy ending. When it was over, there might be sadness—

Of course, there would be sadness. He would miss her, and she would miss him, but that would be much better than embarrassment and court battles.

No matter what he was feeling, it was okay. *They* were okay. In some ways, they were better than okay. All because he wasn't counting on their relationship becoming something that didn't exist. It was the most delicious affair he'd ever had, but it was still an affair.

Content with that explanation, he dressed and got ready to take her to Rome, where he had a hectic but fun day planned. His limo dropped them at Santa Maria Novella where they boarded the train and found their seats in first class.

She glanced around like a happy child, then sunk into the plush seat. "This is fabulous!"

"It isn't just comfortable. The train is fast. We'll be in Rome in about two hours."

"That's amazing." She turned to the wide window, obviously ready to watch the scenery fly by. "I love that your leaves turn colors like trees in the US. So pretty."

Antonio said, "Uh-huh," but he wasn't as relaxed as she was. Now that he'd sorted through his feelings about Riley, his brain switched over to wondering about his grandmother's sudden need for a *private* lunch. He'd been so preoccupied with Riley's end of things, he'd forgotten that his grandmother was crafty...a wild card. And she probably wanted something from Riley.

"You don't think my grandmother has an ulterior motive for having lunch with you, do you?"

"She likes my company and seeing me once a month isn't enough?"

Antonio's brain tried to absorb that possibility. As much as he wanted to believe it, he knew his GiGi too well.

Riley sighed. "Honestly, Antonio, is it so far-fetched to think she wants to get to know me? She does believe you and I are getting married—"

"In two years."

Her face scrunched. "In two years?"

"That's what I told her, remember?"

"I do now." She huffed out a sigh. "And that's her ulterior motive! She's going to try to talk me into marrying you sooner."

He laughed.

"This is serious! A potential landmine—" Her eyes narrowed. "Unless she's suddenly pushing because she's figured out our engagement isn't real?"

"How could she think that when we see each other every weekend? And we have to fly across an ocean to do it. We're obviously crazy about each other."

Riley pondered that for a second. "Maybe that's the problem."

"Seeing each other isn't good?"

"We're acting like people in a new relationship."

"It *is* new."

"No. You're not seeing it. We're not acting like people who are established. Settled. People who know they are going to see each other every day for the rest of their lives, so they have a certain security."

"We're not?"

"No. We have that glow of blissful ignorance."

He laughed again.

"You're still not seeing it. We act like people who think there's no tomorrow."

Antonio sighed with understanding.

They acted like people who thought there was no tomorrow because there might not be a tomorrow. Neither of them knew when this relationship would end, but it would end. So they enjoyed every minute like it was their last.

She was right. They didn't have plans. All they had was emotion. "We're acting like people who are madly in love." His voice shifted when he said the word love and their gazes met.

Was that what his changing feelings were all about? Was he tumbling over the edge from liking her to loving her?

He could not let that happen. He didn't want it for himself. He also didn't want her feelings to grow so much she got hurt.

She licked her lips and spoke slowly enough that he knew she chose her words carefully. "I think it's more like infatuation."

He wasn't sure what she meant, but anything sounded better than love. "Infatuation?"

"You know. The shiny feeling at the beginning of a relationship. We don't see anything but good in each other and it makes us giddy. Engaged couples might be giddy but there's a substance to their relationship that tempers that."

"Oh." He saw it now. "And because we don't have that sense of being settled, GiGi thinks I'm postponing the wedding because I don't believe what we have is going to last?"

"Maybe."

His voice softened. "If she still has questions, she isn't buying this charade, is she?"

She shrugged. "I don't know."

He drew in a quick breath, as things fell into place in his head. "After three months of thinking I'm engaged, she still hasn't scheduled her treatments. Even with me and my father nudging her—reminding her that time is of the essence."

She caught his gaze. "Meaning, we're doing all this for nothing?"

"Not for nothing. She is happier. Much happier." He took Riley's hand. "And we do like each other."

She smiled. "We do."

"And tomorrow you have a chance to get her to talk. Maybe she'll tell you something? Maybe she'll explain why she's not getting her treatments. Maybe she'll alert you to the flaw in our plan?"

"Possibly."

"I think it's more than possible. If my grandmother wants to talk to you alone, it could be to get to know you better or trip you up. But think of it this way. That kind of conversation could lead her to talk about herself. And you could turn the tables. Be direct. Don't mince words. Ask the hard questions. And she'll either back off or explain herself. Either way we win."

"I guess."

"So, it's all good. Especially if you get her to talk. Then we can fix whatever she thinks is wrong." He squeezed her hand. "And today we can enjoy Rome."

Riley settled into her seat again. The idea that his grandmother wanted a heart-to-heart talk the next day was equal parts endearing and nerve wracking. So, she put it out of her head, determined to have a great day seeing Rome.

Seeing Rome.

A few months ago, she'd never left Manhattan, except for a few beach trips with her friends while on break from school. Today, she was on a train, watching the Italian countryside fly by. She'd come to Italy every other week for months. When Antonio came to Manhattan, they'd gone to Broadway shows, been to the Metropolitan Museum of Art, and most of the best restaurants in the city. Now, she understood what people meant when they said they were living their best life.

Four hours later, still awed by the scope of how her life had changed, she stood in Saint Peter's Square looking at the basilica on the sunny fall day. Antonio had rented a car so they could get in as many sights as possible. They'd stopped at the coliseum first, then driven to the Vatican.

Humbled by her surroundings, she glanced at Antonio who was trying to get a picture of her in the middle of the square alone. Every time he thought he had the shot, a tourist strolled by.

"Face it. You're not going to get a picture of me by myself. You're going to have to photoshop people out of the picture."

He gave up trying and took the picture as a mom and daughter walked by. "I forgot this is high season for tourists."

She strolled over and he slid his arm across her shoulders. "Because you're not a tourist."

He looked around. "Weather is perfect. Not hot. Not cold."

"So, people flock here," she said, interrupting him. "We're fine."

"That's what I like about you. No matter what's going on you find the good side."

"My mother taught me that."

"Oh, yeah?"

"She had to be positive." She shrugged. "Turns out it rubbed off on me."

"You are a ray of sunshine."

She laughed.

They visited the Vatican museums, the Sistine Chapel and the Vatican gardens, including Bramante's Belvedere Courtyard and the piece of the Berlin Wall. But by the time they were done, she was exhausted.

"That garden's huge."

He took a long drink of air. "And beautiful. Worth every step."

She laughed, then kissed him. She couldn't get it out of her head that she was in Italy, having fun, with a guy she really liked.

Thoughts of this relationship ending whispered through her brain, a gentle reminder to be careful. But she didn't want to be careful. For once in her life, she wanted to have fun. The kind of fun she could only have with a spontaneous, happy guy like Antonio. The affair would stop soon enough and that would be the time to be sad—or to actually begin looking for ways to accomplish her personal goals. Right now, she wanted every second of happiness she could have with him.

It was another twenty-minute walk back to their rental car.

When they finally reached it, she stretched her arms above her head and stretched her legs out as far as she could in the small vehicle. "I'm going to be so happy to get into a hot shower."

He laughed and drove to the train station. Peace and contentment bubbled through her. She could not describe the feeling of actually walking through places she'd only ever seen in pictures or on television. But it was amazing. Her entire life had been amazing these past three months.

When they were settled in their train seats again, she squeezed his hand. "Thank you."

He laughed. "Don't you know, it's every man's pleasure to show his woman his world?"

She smiled at the way he called her his woman. A feeling of complete contentment rose until it filled her eyes with tears. She'd never met anyone like him, and she suddenly knew she never would again. She began the litany of reminders she usually ran through her brain when her thoughts got away from her like this, but the way her heart swelled would not be denied.

Some day she would lose him. He would walk away, and she would never see him again. It was their deal. She never dwelled on it. She didn't want to open the door to that trouble. But today, after his planning this wonderful trip, shepherding her through Rome and making her feel like the most important person in the world, she didn't see simple loneliness when their time together ended. She saw heartbreak.

Real heartbreak.

The truth tiptoed into her thoughts before she could stop it. She *loved* him.

Oh, dear God. She loved him. Really loved him. She could see them spending the rest of their lives together. She could see their kids. Raising them on the vineyard. Taking them to Rome and Manhattan. Two different cultures, but culture all the same.

But he didn't want that.

Her heart squeezed and her breath stuttered.

She loved him and she had no idea what to do.

But she absolutely couldn't tell him.

Maybe it was a good thing she would spend tomorrow afternoon with his grandmother. She needed a pause to think all this through.

The real truth was it might be time for her to end it.

Her chest tightened so much she could barely breathe. How had she fallen in love with him when she knew it was wrong?

CHAPTER TWELVE

GIGI AND RILEY met at a restaurant Riley had suggested, somewhere close to her hotel, where she'd eaten lunch before. The day was cool, only in the high sixties, so she wore a yellow shaker knit sweater and jeans. But there was no breeze, so they could sit in the outdoor area, where GiGi already had a table.

GiGi rose to hug her and kiss her cheek. "Isn't this fun! Just the girls."

She laughed. Antonio hadn't talked any more about her lunch with his grandmother, but she was okay with that. She didn't want to have his suggestions and fears ringing in her brain during what might be a nice lunch with a woman she admired. She might not have to steer the conversation away from sensitive topics or ask difficult questions. GiGi might simply want a quiet meal with pleasant company.

That was what Riley wanted too.

After a good night's sleep, she had finally sorted out her feelings about her relationship with Antonio, realizing that when she'd come to her unwanted conclusion that she loved him, she'd been tired. They'd walked what felt like miles. The Vatican Gardens themselves were fifty-seven acres. Of course, she'd had some unexpected thoughts. She hadn't been on her game. Her emotions had swelled, and she hadn't been able to combat them.

But now she was fine. She couldn't love a man who would

never love her. Their affair would end. She would keep a lid on her feelings, so they could continue to enjoy what they had.

And she was happy to be having lunch with his grandmother.

"Is that why you didn't want Antonio to come with us? You want some girl talk?"

"That's part of it. You and I have never been alone long enough to have a real conversation."

"True." The waiter walked over, and she ordered a glass of wine, still looking at the lunch options.

GiGi handed her menu back to the waiter. "I'm just going to have a salad."

"Salad is good for me too," Riley said, also passing her menu back to the waiter. "What do you want to talk about on our girls' lunch?"

"Before we get into that. I did have an ulterior motive for keeping Antonio away."

She held back a wince. Maybe Antonio was right after all? GiGi had an ulterior motive in inviting her to lunch.

"I wanted to tell you that I'm planning a surprise birthday party for him."

She blinked. "Oh."

GiGi waited as if she expected Riley to have a useful comment on that. But she couldn't think of anything to say. If his birthday was soon enough for his family to be thinking about a party, that was probably something he should have told her.

The waiter came with their wine. Riley took hers and gulped a big swig, buying time. She had no idea when Antonio's birthday was and clearly GiGi thought she did. Plus, a party meant meeting all his friends and relatives. That might even be GiGi's purpose of having a party. To bring Riley even further into the family.

She swallowed her wine and smiled at GiGi. "Really? A surprise party?"

"Well, not until his birthday next month. But with the schedule you two devised, I thought you could tell me which of the weekends closest to his birthday you'll be in Italy."

Two things struck her at once. With the party being a surprise, she couldn't tell Antonio why his grandmother had wanted to have a private lunch with her. Second, she wasn't sure how she would explain arriving a day early or on the wrong weekend—depending on when GiGi planned the party.

Still stalling for time, she smiled.

Drat.

This would not stump a real fiancée. A fiancée would know when his birthday was.

GiGi said, "I mean, the fourteenth is the obvious date. But if you're not coming until the twenty-first, that could work too."

"Or the seventh," Riley said quickly, trying to look like she knew when his birthday was. "It's better to have the party *before* his birthday…that way the surprise is real. He won't be expecting it."

GiGi laughed. "I like how you think."

Riley nodded, hoping she actually had gotten herself out of that without telling his grandmother she didn't know his birthday. The first thing when she returned home, she was asking him when his birthday was—

No. She couldn't do that either without him wondering why she suddenly wanted to know.

"Anyway, with that out of the way, you and I can have our girls' lunch."

She quickly scanned GiGi's face for signs she was going to spring something else on her. Seeing only a happy grandmother, Riley smiled and said, "Yes. We can."

Their salads arrived and GiGi opened her napkin, setting it on her lap. "So, tell me about your relationship with my Antonio. How did you meet?"

Deciding to trust her instinct that Antonio's grandmother was sincere and really did just want to talk, she took a breath. "Actually, we met at one of my events."

GiGi laughed. "Seriously?"

"I had planned an event for someone at a restaurant and he was there with..." She winced. "A date."

GiGi squeezed her eyes shut. "He was hopeless before he met you."

"No. I think he was just popular."

"Maybe."

"Anyway, he came to my office the next day," Riley said, sticking to the truth of their story. No lies. Omissions maybe, but no lies. "We made a date to see each other the day after that, and then we sort of fell together. I don't think it was love at first sight, but when we didn't have a date, we kept running into each other."

Which perfectly described her having to fly to Italy to tell him the ring wouldn't come off and then him showing up in her building when her mom was hurt.

"It was those unexpected meetings where we really got to know each other. No pretense like there usually is on a date."

GiGi laughed.

"Anyway, we might have gotten engaged a little sooner than we should have."

"You said when it's right you know it."

"Yes, I did." And thank God she had. "When he asked me to marry him, it just all felt right."

Which was also not a lie. It had felt right that night in Dene Summerhouse. Weirdly right. But she wouldn't tell GiGi that.

"And you make good money with this business that you have?"

Riley smiled. She probably should have anticipated this question from the grandmother of a wealthy guy. She supposed a lot of women saw Antonio only in terms of his bank account. Riley could easily convince his grandmother she wasn't one of them. The man had her so bewitched she was worrying that she would fall in love with him for real. Their feelings for each other had nothing to do with money.

"Yes. My company is doing very well. With the addition of proposals in Tuscany, we're seeing an uptick in sales, but word of mouth for our New York business is also giving us new customers. Lots of people have events in Manhattan."

"I know. I've been to my share."

Surprise made her curious. "You come to New York?"

"I used to. My husband loved the city."

"So does Antonio! He said if there was a second place he would want to live, it would be Manhattan."

GiGi paused. "Oh."

"Not that we're thinking of living there," Riley said quickly. "I love Tuscany. Besides, we have plenty of time to think about that. Our wedding date is way in the future."

"I know."

From the sadness in GiGi's voice, Riley knew she disapproved. Maybe because of her grief over her husband, maybe because it seemed too far away to be real. That could be why she couldn't get excited enough to schedule her treatments.

She took a breath. She liked GiGi enough that she wanted answers as much as Antonio did.

"Is that why you haven't scheduled your treatments?"

GiGi could have been insulted by the question. Instead, she shrugged and said nothing. The woman who could talk for twenty minutes about a grape was suddenly tight-lipped.

Riley thought for a minute. There was really only one question that would bring GiGi right to the line of truth and force her to answer honestly. Difficult as it was, Riley decided to ask it.

"Don't you want to see our children?"

"Do *you* want to see your children?"

She assumed GiGi referred to the comment Antonio had made about them not having kids, and she knew she'd been right about pushing the conversation in this direction. Antonio had upset his grandmother with his offhand statement about not having kids.

That was why his grandmother had gone back to being depressed. She didn't not want to see Antonio alone for the rest of his life...and to an eighty-year-old grandmother, children were part of not being alone.

GiGi sighed. "Children bring happiness. Children speak of the continuity of a family. Your family is small, and you might not know this, but there is nothing like a child at Christmas. Or watching a toddler learn to walk. Or seeing the smile on their face when they see their mother."

Confusion overwhelmed Riley. She did know all that. She wanted a family so badly she'd tried to make three ill-fated relationships work. But Antonio had given his grandmother the wrong impression about her. Which might seem okay for the purposes of their fake engagement...but what if it wasn't?

Deciding to go with the truth, she quietly said, "I do want kids."

"You do?"

"Yes!"

"It's Antonio who is foot-dragging?"

She couldn't let his grandmother get that impression either. So she hedged. "We just got engaged. I think talking about having a family so soon made him jittery."

"Then maybe all this is just a matter of time for him to adjust?"

"Maybe."

She patted Riley's hand. "Definitely. Antonio might be stubborn, but he always comes around."

Riley laughed. "Antonio having a family really means a lot to you, doesn't it?"

"Of course! You and Antonio are so young you don't understand what it is to end your family's line, how alone he'll be. I have my son, Enzo. I have Antonio. But then our line stops. Enzo will have no more children, but he has Antonio. If Antonio doesn't create some heirs, he's going to be the one who is alone. Alone on our beautiful vineyard with no one to leave it to when he dies."

Riley opened her mouth to contradict GiGi, but nothing came out. If she fast-forwarded Antonio's life, if he continued to live the way he was now, he *would* someday be a very wealthy old man with a beautiful vineyard and no one to share it with—

Not her problem.

Not. Her. Problem.

The only thing Antonio asked her to do was figure out what was bothering his grandmother, and Riley believed she had. It was time to pull back. Not ruminate on GiGi's fears for Antonio. When she pictured him alone, those feelings she'd had the day before crept back and she didn't want them. She did not want to love him. She didn't want to feel so much for him that the end of their relationship would crush her.

She had to be smart.

"I'm afraid he gets this from his father, who also didn't remarry after a bad divorce."

Scrambling for a way out of this conversation, Riley said, "Oh, yeah?"

"Like his father, Antonio married a beautiful woman with no substance." She snorted. "Trophy wives, both of them. But I see the emotion in your relationship with Antonio."

Try as she might to stop it, Riley felt the emotion between her and Antonio too. She'd never had so many deep, important conversations with any of her exes. She'd also never had a boyfriend who cooked for her, cared about her mother—

She put the brakes on those thoughts. She could not keep

reminding herself why she liked Antonio. Why that liking was beginning to tumble over into deeper feelings. She had to establish some boundaries.

GiGi laughed suddenly. "You and Antonio are so perfect for each other. He will come around about having kids and I don't have to worry."

Riley smiled, her emotions under control again. She liked Antonio so, so much but she was holding her heart in reserve. Saving that for the guy who wanted to be her partner, the father of her children, the guy who'd laugh at her gag gifts at Christmas and take her and the kids to the beach for vacations. Yesterday's unwanted feelings were an anomaly. She was smart enough not to fall for another guy who didn't want what she wanted. Everything was fine. Better than fine because she now knew what had been bothering GiGi.

She managed to shift the conversation enough that they laughed through the rest of their lunch. They talked about fashion, the movies they'd seen and Antonio's Aston Martin.

She hugged Antonio's grandmother good-bye and was fine on the walk back to the hotel, but as she stepped into the lobby, guilt crept up on her. She might be fine. And GiGi might be fine. But the real bottom line to their conversation finally emerged through the haze of her thinking. GiGi didn't want Antonio to find a wife so he'd be happy. She was trying to make their family whole again. She wanted him to have children so he wouldn't be alone.

Meaning, when they broke off their fake engagement, GiGi would be back where she'd started from. Sure, she would probably be through with her chemo by then and be well again. But she would fall back into that black pit of depression.

Riley took a breath, weighing options. Really, this was Antonio's problem, but she couldn't help recognizing he didn't have many options. His first priority had to be getting his grandmother well. After that he would have time to deal properly with her grief and depression.

Her room was empty when she stepped inside, but she barely had time to wash her hands before Antonio walked in.

"How was lunch?" He tossed his jacket to one of the chairs by the little table with the phone. "Did she ask questions about us? Try to trip you up?"

"Your grandmother isn't an evil genius."

He laughed. "No. I think she's a normal grandmother. She just sometimes has a way of making conversations work for her."

She frowned. "I don't think she was doing that this time. She very sincerely told me that she worries you will be alone. She wants you to have children."

"Seriously?" His eyes widened. "*That's* what's bothering her?"

"Yes. One night after dinner, you casually said we wouldn't be having kids—because I'm a businesswoman."

He grimaced. "Yeah. I remember. I was just trying to stop her from steamrolling us."

"You might have stopped that but now she thinks you're always going to be alone."

He sat on the bed. "She's worried about me?"

"Yes. She sees you old and all alone on the vineyard."

"She's obsessing over nothing. I'll be fine."

Riley wanted to agree with him, but she saw what his grandmother saw. Young and handsome, he had no qualms believing his busy, happy lifestyle would last forever. But she knew it wouldn't. She'd lost her dad. She almost lost her mother. Life was tricky. One minute it could be fine and the next everything could fall apart.

"I'll just drop it into conversation one day that I think you and I will make great parents and that should fix it."

"It might."

"It might?" He frowned. "Are you thinking we should do something more?"

She shook her head. "Not we. *You*. How long's it been since you had a real talk with your grandmother?"

"About what?"

"I don't know. Your grandfather? How she feels about having lost him? Why she's so worried that you're going to be alone?"

He pulled in a breath. "We talked right after my grandfather died. We actually talked about you once. But it's been a while."

Guilt and sadness for GiGi filled her again. "Honestly, Antonio, I think she's lonely."

He ran his hand along the back of his neck. "Her best friend died last year."

"And she lost your grandfather this year?" She gaped at him. "She's definitely lonely. You need to spend more time with her. Quality time."

"You Americans and your quality time. Italians know how to be family. I will ace this."

She laughed and walked over to where he sat on the bed. He slid his hands up her bottom to her waist.

Ignoring the blissful sensations tumbling through her, she said, "You had better."

"Seriously. I'll talk to her. Maybe I'll even take her somewhere nice for dinner one night. Without my dad. I'll make it feel like a date."

She smiled, then kissed him. "You're a wonderful person." Was it any wonder her feelings were trying to shift from like to love? And was it any wonder it was getting harder and harder to stop them?

"If I were a wonderful person, I probably would have thought of this myself."

"Maybe."

He rose from the bed to kiss her properly and she gave herself over to it. But because it was Sunday, she pulled back.

"I have about an hour to get to the airport."

He sighed. "In all the worry about your lunch, I forgot you have to leave. Can't you stay another day?"

She shook her head. "No. There's a tsunami of Halloween proposals happening this week."

His face scrunched. "Halloween proposals?"

"Sorry. Everybody's obsessed with witches, zombies and skeletons these days."

"That's one of those things I'll never understand."

She laughed, kissed him, then started packing her bags.

On the plane, she settled in to fall asleep. Traveling to Europe every other week, she'd learned to book a seat in first class so she could make good use of the time. She arrived in Manhattan seven o'clock on Sunday night and putzed around her house, doing her laundry, beginning to tidy up for when Antonio would visit that weekend.

She'd talked herself out of falling in love—even stopped herself before she actually fell. Still, she liked him so much that she refused to waste any of the time they had together tidying up while he was visiting.

After all, any weekend could be the beginning of the end.

Their relationship had begun with a fake engagement to make his grandmother happy. Sure, they'd started a real affair, but it was still wrapped up in that fake engagement. If Antonio and his grandmother talked all this through, they wouldn't need the fake engagement anymore.

And the real-life affair might crumble with it.

She sucked in a breath as sadness rose at that thought, but she forced the feeling away. That was a worry for another day.

But the sadness wouldn't leave because deep down she knew they were at the beginning of the end.

CHAPTER THIRTEEN

ANTONIO TOOK HIS GRANDMOTHER to dinner on Tuesday night. He'd told her about the date on Monday morning, so she had time to prepare and anticipate. It was the happiest he'd seen her in months.

At dinner she talked more than she had since his grandfather's death. She didn't mention her grief. Her conversation revolved more around the past. What a precocious child he'd been. How she'd struggled to find her place in Tuscany's social circles. How Antonio's father had botched a marriage but become the best businessman she'd ever known. How Antonio clearly had his skills and abilities and would keep their companies thriving.

He didn't see the sadness Riley had seen. Tonight, she was bubbly. But he also didn't doubt Riley. If she'd said his grandmother had been struggling emotionally, then she had been.

As dessert was being served, he took her hand. "So, you are feeling better?"

She pulled back her hand and fussed with the linen napkin on her lap. "I'm feeling much better…thanks to Riley. The girl has nerve. She flat out asked me some questions like why I didn't want the chemo and she forced me to think."

He wasn't sure if that was good or bad. He sat back in his chair. "Oh. Have you made a decision?"

"Actually, I'm still thinking."

"How can you still be thinking!" Confusion overwhelmed him before he could stop it. "There's so much life to live!"

She shook her head. "You forget I've been through these treatments once already. I know how sick I'm going to be. I know the toll it takes. I'm nearly eighty. My brothers and sisters are gone. My best friend passed." This time she caught his hand. "Now, your grandfather is gone. He was not my reason for living. But I had a whole world of people when I went through chemo the last time. I had a good life. I had things I wanted to accomplish. Now, I wonder if my time is over. Other people took my seats on charity boards, and they are doing well. Your father is handling the company brilliantly. What he doesn't do, you do. I sit on a chaise longue and wait until it's time to dress for dinner."

She shrugged. "While I sit there, I think about the good life I had. The good things I've done and I'm proud. But I also see it's over."

He'd thought her reminiscence at dinner had been nothing more than a pleasant conversation. Now, he understood why she'd spoken of things long gone. She only saw her past. Not her future.

"It's wrong to think like that, when Dad and I need you."

"For?"

"Not *for* anything. *Because.* Because we love you."

"Oh, Antonio, I love you too." She shook her head. "So much. I remember you being born. I remember your coo. I remember your baby smiles." She chuckled. "It wasn't a hardship when your mother left. I was very happy to raise you."

"Then get the treatments for me."

She shook her head. "No. This choice is only mine. It's why I'm thinking it through so long." She laughed. "Though I have to admit, the thought of you and Riley having children does give me a boost of hope. Something that makes me want to see it."

"Then go get the treatments."

She took a breath. "I understand that to you this seems like an easy choice." She patted his hand. "When you are my age, if you are alone, if everyone who made your world a wonderful place is gone...only then could you understand."

"You're saying you're lonely."

"Give me a few more days to think about what I want. Not what *you* want. Not what your father wants. What I want. I will decide soon."

Friday night when Antonio arrived at Riley's condo, instead of their usual kiss, he just hugged her.

When he finally pulled back, he said, "She's not going to get the treatments."

Riley's eyes widened. "She's not?"

"Well, she says she hasn't really decided yet."

She studied his eyes. "Then there's still hope."

"No." He flopped down on her sofa. "We had a talk. A wonderful dinner filled with lively conversation. Then she told me that her whole world is gone. Everyone who made up her life has passed. The essence of the conversation wasn't that she had nothing to live for but that she was done. Her time was over."

She sat beside him and took his hand. "Yes. But she also said she hasn't made up her mind."

He bounced from the sofa. "This is hopeless! For months, I've been trying to get her to see reason and I had absolutely no impact on her."

She shook her head. "I'm going to have to disagree about your trying to get her to see reason. You haven't been trying to get her to see reason. You faked an engagement."

His face sharpened. "Excuse me?"

"We aren't engaged. We aren't going to have kids. You really haven't given her anything. Not a wedding. Not great-grandkids to spoil. If a person looks at this the right way, you tried to trick her into doing what you wanted."

"I tried to give her hope!"

"Yes. And that's commendable, but, Antonio, there really wasn't any substance there." The truth of that swamped her. "We aren't going to get married. We aren't going to have kids."

"Oh, God." All the blood drained from his face as if he finally saw her point. "You're right." He looked at her. "I feel so connected to you that I sometimes forget that our love affair is one thing, our fake engagement is another."

She squeezed his hand. "Don't feel bad. The other day, in Rome, I had this flash of love for you that was so real I had to worry that I was tumbling over the edge."

His face changed. "You thought you loved me?"

She couldn't tell if he was confused or concerned. "Don't worry. It passed."

"It passed?"

"I talked myself out of it."

His gaze lingered on her face as he digested that. A few weeks before, the very idea that she might have genuine feelings for him would have concerned him. Today, he said only, "Oh, okay."

She swore she saw a flash of disappointment, as if her loving him had pleased him. She wanted that to be true. Maybe so much that she could be imagining it, so she didn't allow herself to dwell on it and changed the subject. "But to get back to your grandmother, I think we have to admit the fake engagement failed and look for a new strategy."

"It's hard for me to believe it out and out failed when she seemed so happy at dinner."

"She was happy because she had *you* with her." The truth of that washed through her. *She* was always happier around Antonio too. She missed him when they were apart.

She shook her head to get rid of that observation, afraid of where it was leading. "You're someone to talk to. Someone she knows loves her. Maybe that's more of what she needs?"

"She needs more going out to dinner?"

"No. More of you talking to her. For real. Instead of a fake fiancée and pretending you'll give her great-grandkids, maybe she needs more of you?"

Again, she saw herself, not GiGi. That was the truth of what was happening to her. She desperately wanted to take the next step. Say she loved him. Consider a future together. That's why it was harder and harder to shove down her feelings for him. They were at the place where they should be taking the next steps—

But it wasn't what he wanted.

She rose and took a breath. "In fact, I'm starting to see something that we missed." They'd missed lots of things but right now they were talking about his relationship with his grandmother. This was what he needed to hear. So she stayed on topic though other things began to sort in her head. "She lost her best friend and her husband. What she needs is help building a new life. And I'm going to send you back to Italy right now to help her."

His face twisted with confusion. "Right now?"

"Right now. That was the real purpose for us getting together. You wanted to help your grandmother."

"And you're saying I need to help her rebuild her life?"

"Yes. Go. Help her for real."

He rose and caught her hand before she could turn away. "Come with me."

She smiled. "No. Think it through. She might like me, but you're her family. This is something you have to do."

"But she thinks of you as family."

"Because she thinks we're engaged. We're not. And I won't muddy the waters for her anymore." She took a sharp breath. Her thoughts cleared some more as logical conclusions began to form. "Even we had trouble keeping track of what was real and what was fake. I think it's time you get back to reality. Completely." Her chest froze, as the final pieces of the puzzle snapped together. She tried to avoid it, but she knew this was right. The thing he needed to hear. The thing *she* needed to realize. This was the end of their relationship. She wanted to take the next steps. He didn't. If she didn't end it now, she wouldn't be able to. She would hold on. Start hoping for things that couldn't be—

The pain of it steamrolled over her. But she held her head high and said what needed to be said. "The best way to do it is to stop seeing each other."

His face scrunched. "Are you saying we're through?"

It hurt her to think it, but no matter what her heart felt, her head knew this was it. The end. She'd fought so hard not to fall for him, trying to hold on to what they had or enjoy what they had that she'd missed the obvious. If she didn't end it now, it would kill her to lose him later.

"Yes. This is over."

"But we like each other. We're good together."

"Yes. But we said when it was over, we would know it and we would be smart."

He blinked at her. The strangest feelings washed through him. "You are breaking up with me."

"Antonio, we were never really together."

"We weren't? We've seen each other several times a week since June. It's October. That's *together.*"

"No. That was convenience and fun. Not commitment. We'd always known it would end. We made no plans because we each want different things out of life."

He studied her face. She was so sincere that it was difficult to believe she was the one ending things. Especially since she seemed so broken. Her words were blunt and to the point, but he saw the sorrow in her eyes. She'd said she'd worried she'd fallen in love for real and had talked herself out of it. But from the shadows in her eyes, he didn't believe she'd done such a good job.

She loved him.

Yet she was pushing him out of her life?

That didn't seem right.

The suspicion that hit him almost made him gasp. His eyes narrowed. "Are you angling to get me to ask you to marry me for real?"

"No!" Surprise replaced the sorrow in her eyes. "Even if you did, I wouldn't accept. You don't love me. You're just having fun. And, honestly, Antonio, there was nothing wrong with that. You're so happy when we were together that I loved being with you." She took a breath and the pain returned to her eyes. "But we've both always known that you don't want what I want. I want a partner, kids, a real family. You like your freedom. Standing here right now, knowing my feelings for you and that we'll never be on the same page, is killing me. So, I'm not just sending you home to do right by your grandmother. I'm sending you home because if we keep this up, we're going to hit a point where I'm not going to be able to come back from the hurt."

She blew her breath out. He could see the struggle going on inside her. "I'm going to take a walk. When I get back, you should be gone."

She headed for the door, but stopped suddenly and grabbed her purse from the center island. With money and credit cards she could slip into a bar and be gone for hours. She walked out into the hall and the door closed behind her, basically telling him there was no point in waiting for her to return.

They were done.

He stared at the door for a few seconds. Feelings, the likes of which he'd never before felt, bombarded him. He hated her pain. Hated that he was the one who had caused it. Wanted nothing more than to run after her and promise her whatever she wanted. But he couldn't. He couldn't walk into another relationship when he knew love always ended.

And she knew that. That's why she'd gone. They wanted two different things. Which was also why they'd so clearly defined their affair and knew it had a shelf life. Her feelings had crossed the line to love, but she understood that was a line he would not cross.

Now he also understood that his grandmother needed him more than he'd been around lately.

His affair with Riley might have been good intentioned, but he'd spent time with her that he should have spent with his grandmother.

Riley had seen that.

She'd told him that.

She'd sent him home for all the right reasons.

He grabbed his duffel and left, ignoring the tightness of his chest and the sadness that rippled through him.

He knew how to be strong. He also knew it was time to do the right thing for real.

CHAPTER FOURTEEN

RILEY RETURNED TO her condo building hours later, still shell-shocked that she'd broken things off with Antonio. The affair had been the best time of her life, but she'd known all along it wouldn't be permanent. When she'd made her arguments for breaking things off, she'd seen in his eyes that he didn't love her. As much as she recognized that his grandmother needed him, knowing that he didn't share her feelings—would never share her feelings—was what pushed her to send him away. If she didn't end things now, she'd one day find herself so in love with him that losing him would paralyze her.

Or she'd move her office to Tuscany and always be a mistress.

She tossed her purse to the kitchen island, not quite sure how that could be worse than what she felt right now. Ending what they had hurt so much she could barely breathe. Add her feeling of foolishness to that and she almost couldn't function the next day at Saturday afternoon's proposal and thanked God Marietta took over. She improved somewhat for Saturday night's proposal, but not much.

She'd thought she'd known better than to fall in love with him, but she obviously hadn't been as immune and objective as she'd thought.

But how could she not fall in love with him?

He wasn't just good looking and suave. He was kind, thoughtful, fun to be around.

But he was adamant about not falling in love again.

She'd seen that in his eyes when she'd asked him to leave. They'd been so preoccupied with his grandmother that they'd downplayed his insistence that he wouldn't fall in love or commit to another woman. Because he'd been hurt. And he'd drawn a line in the sand, a line he'd never cross again. While she'd fallen in love naturally, it hadn't even entered his mind.

She entered her condo and walked past the kitchen, refusing to turn on the lights. It might be a while before she could look at the kitchen without remembering him happy, charming, cooking for her.

Heading back to her room for a shower, she called her mother to check in.

"Where were you tonight? Out with Antonio?"

She would have laughed at the snarky way her mother said his name, but her mother had been right. At first, she'd laughed about the fake engagement but eventually she'd noticed that there was something off about their feelings for each other. Busy with physical therapy and running a company from her dining room, Juliette hadn't had time to interfere. Riley had seen it as a gift from the heavens. But just as Antonio had to be honest with his grandmother, it was time for her to come clean with her mom.

"You can rest easy. Fake engagement is ended."

"Really?"

"Why so surprised? You seemed to see right through it all along."

"What I saw was you actually liking someone, actually giving someone a chance. I honestly thought you'd come home some day and tell me you really were engaged."

She blinked. Had her mother not interfered because she was rooting for them? She didn't know whether that was sweet or confusing. "Nope. The opposite. Our deal is done."

"You broke off a fake engagement and you're sad?"

"It was a fake engagement and a real love affair."

"You slept with him."

"What did you think I was doing going to Italy every other week?"

Her mother took a long breath. "I don't know... I've been so busy the past months went by in a blur." She took another breath. "Catch me up."

"We thought the fake engagement was over, started a love affair and got dragged back into pretending to be engaged when I was in Italy. After a while it sort of got confusing. We were pretending for his grandmother that we were getting married and alone we were having fun."

"I can see how that would get confusing."

"Yeah, well, when his grandmother broke down and started explaining why she didn't want chemo, I saw that even her grandson getting engaged hadn't perked her up."

"Really?"

"Her husband died this year, but her best friend died six months before that."

Her mom sighed with understanding. "She's alone."

"Really alone. And instead of faking an engagement, her grandson should have been helping her build a new life."

"I get it."

"That's why I sent him home. I ended the fake engagement and the love affair. It wasn't going anywhere anyway."

"But you were happy."

"Yes and no." The answer made her think of Antonio and her heart hurt. She'd never had what she had with him. She'd never felt what she'd felt with him. Her feelings had been strong and real...no matter how much she'd tried to fight them. Which was part of why it hurt so much that he didn't return those feelings. It seemed wrong to love someone and not have them love you.

"I always knew what we had wasn't permanent. His first marriage was a mess. He doesn't believe in love or commitment."

"That *is* a mess. Maybe you're lucky to get out of it?"

She blinked back tears and said, "Yeah. Maybe I'm lucky." But she didn't feel lucky. She felt sad. Sad for his grandmother. Sad for him. Sad for herself.

Because the other thing she wouldn't let herself think about until now was that she might have fallen so hard so far because she was lonely too. Vulnerable.

She should have kept all that in mind before having a torrid affair with a handsome stranger who did end up breaking her heart.

Needing time to sort through everything Riley had told him, Antonio had kept his return to Italy a secret by staying in Florence that night and Sunday. But on Monday, he couldn't avoid his grandmother another day. Plus, he agreed with Riley. He needed to help her. Not avoid her. A little honesty would get them on the right track.

Rather than eat outside, they chose to have dinner in the formal dining room.

He kissed her cheek, said, "Hello," to his father and took his seat. Jumping in feet first, he said, "Riley and I broke up."

Looking shocked, GiGi said, "What?"

"You didn't notice that I didn't spend any time in Manhattan because I stayed in the city the last two nights."

His father said, "Why?"

"This was hard for me."

"Because you loved her!" GiGi said. "Fix this right now. Go get her."

"No. I'm a grown man, GiGi. I know when something is over, and this is over. Besides, she broke up with me."

His grandmother gasped. "I don't believe it. That woman loved you! For the first time ever, I thought you'd finally found real love and you're letting her get away?"

"She told me to leave." Just thinking that hurt him. Still, he wouldn't let himself examine that feeling. Their relationship was a jumble of odd things. First, pretending to be engaged. Then becoming friends. Then taking off the ring and having something that felt real—

Then her telling him to go back to Italy. Easily.

No. Not easily. He saw the hurt in her eyes. That's what had made him stop arguing. She loved him and he did not love her. The gentleman in him wouldn't persuade her to continue a relationship that was no longer equal. He would protect her from himself.

No matter how confusing the constant pain in his heart.

Two weeks later, he'd managed to stop the pain. Or at least dull it with logic. His grandmother no longer hounded him to call Riley. They'd had more than a few good talks. He'd taken her to dinner at fancy restaurants. Once at lunch he'd invited one of her old acquaintances and they'd talked for hours.

That's when he'd seen his grandmother's spark really coming back. She'd also decided to have the chemo.

Not for a chance to see her great-grandchildren…but because she was beginning to see the good side of life again. He'd shown her that. Because Riley had told him to do it.

He squeezed his eyes shut. Soon, he hoped, everything in his life wouldn't remind him of her.

When GiGi asked him to dress for dinner the following Friday, he'd complied, if only because it meant she'd invited a guest. Which was another good sign.

But as he walked down the corridor to the curved stairway, the pain hit him again. Out of the blue, the feeling of his heart being ripped in half stopped him in his tracks. Riley should have arrived that evening. He should walk down these stairs and see her entering the foyer.

The thought of it made his heart shimmy with longing, but he pulled himself together and continued the walk to the steps, confused that the foyer chandelier wasn't lit. In fact, there was no light in the foyer at all. He walked to the light switch, not wanting to navigate stairs in the dark. When he flipped it, he got a quick glimpse of a crowd of people before they yelled, "Surprise!"

He froze. His grandmother had planned a surprise party?

If that didn't say she was regaining her spunk, he didn't know what did.

He walked down the stairs happy. He might not like a fuss being made over him, but it was what the fuss represented that filled him with joy.

His grandmother had planned a party.

She stood at the bottom of the stairs and, when he reached her, he kissed her cheek. "Thank you!" He looked beyond her to the crowd and said, "Thank you all."

He scanned the crowd again.

Then again.

Looking for Riley.

He wasn't sure if it was his grandmother's insistence that Riley loved him that made him believe GiGi might have invited her or wishful thinking, but his heart sank when he didn't see her.

He put on a brave face, laughed and chatted with his guests, but his gaze constantly roamed to the front door.

It never opened until the guests began to leave. Then he became jovial again. He slapped the backs of old friends and business acquaintances. Shook hands. Thanked everyone for gifts.

And then found himself very alone in the foyer when the last guest had gone.

"You really thought she'd come, didn't you?"

He peered over at his dad. His powers of observation were what made him such a good businessman, but right now Antonio wished he hadn't said anything.

"Drink?"

Antonio cleared his throat. "Bourbon."

"Ah. The drink of men with broken hearts."

"I thought that was wine."

Enzo laughed and led the way into the den. "Wine is good for everything."

Antonio followed him, though he wished he'd simply refused the drink and gone upstairs to his room. He was tired from pretending to be happy.

His father handed him a glass of bourbon. "You think she's as sad as you right now?"

Once again, he went back to pretending. "I have no idea."

"Oh, son. You forget how much alike we are. I know exactly what you're thinking. And I know you are thinking about her. About love."

Antonio stared at him. "Really? Because the last time I looked you haven't been in love since Mom."

Enzo laughed and got comfortable on the sofa. "I was in love once." He peeked over at Antonio. "Before your mom."

Eager to hear that tale and forget about Riley, Antonio sat on a leather chair across from the sofa. "Really?"

"She was something."

"So why isn't she my mother?"

Enzo snorted. "Because I let her get away."

"Let her?"

"She wanted to study in Paris, and I told her I thought that was great, but I wouldn't go with her. I thought a visit or two would suffice and when her studies were over, she'd return home to me."

"But?"

"But she broke it off. Saw my not going with her as me not supporting her. I stubbornly stood my ground and she met someone else."

Not knowing what to say to that, Antonio just looked at his dad, waiting for details.

"You know that Riley's going to find someone else, right?"

Not wanting to think about that, he shifted on his seat and went back to pretending again. "Probably."

"Yeah. She's too pretty to stay single for long. Especially now that her business is established. I could read between the lines of her story. She threw herself into that company and now she's got something real."

"It's a solid company."

"And now that she knows that, I think she's realizing she can relax." He chuckled. "Dating you…coming to Italy every other week…was proof she trusts her staff enough that she can scale back. You know…go after what she wants."

"I wish her well."

"Oh, Antonio. You do not. You wish she was still here. And I'm not quite sure that she isn't."

"Because I can't give her what she wants."

His dad sat forward. "Really? And what is that?"

He knew better than to say, "Love." His dad would see right through that. A man didn't mope and pine for a woman he didn't love.

His breath stalled as that realization tried to take root. And he wouldn't let it. Watching his wife's love for him die and enduring the loss of his love for her were heartbreaking proof that love was temporary. He'd vowed he'd never risk that kind of pain again. He intended to keep that vow.

And his father should know that. "I can't give her a commitment."

Enzo frowned. "You lost me."

"Really? You must be forgetting Sylvia."

"Ack." He batted a hand. "She's your past. Riley could be your future."

"No, Dad. I'm not going down that road again and before you try to argue with me…clean up your own house. You did the same thing after Mom left."

He snorted. "So, because I made a big mistake, you're going to make the same mistake?"

"It wasn't a mistake. You protected yourself."

"I didn't protect myself. I hid. Then I never fell in love. There's a big difference between what happened with me and what's happening with you. *You're* wrong."

Tired, and only wanting to get to bed, Antonio rose. "Good night, Dad."

"Good night, Antonio. But just remember that Riley isn't Sylvia. Sylvia was like a butterfly. Beautiful. Fun. The kind of woman you like to make happy. Riley is the woman who makes *you* happy. The kind of woman you make a life with. She doesn't want your money. She has her own. The only reason she was with you was because she wanted to be." Enzo rose and headed back to the bar. "That's the difference. That's why you escape from one and keep the other."

The idea inched its way into his brain. He pictured himself with Riley for the rest of his life and there was no fear. Then he saw them having children and it felt as if an entire world, a world of possibilities, opened up to him. The firm foundation on which he believed he stood shifted and changed.

He wanted that.

All of it.

Not to please her but to have a new, happy life with her.

He didn't have to work to make her happy. They made each other happy.

He loved her.

He loved her...

And he had hurt the woman who made him believe in love again.

CHAPTER FIFTEEN

RILEY SAT IN the middle of the outdoor eating area of her favorite restaurant, just a smidge annoyed with Jake for keeping her at lunch for two hours. His where-is-my-life-going? crisis surprised her. She'd thought he was happy as the videographer for their proposals, but he seemed to want more.

At least that's what she thought this rambling conversation was about.

She could have guided him if he'd had a clearer understanding of what "more" was for him. But no. He had no idea what he wanted. So, she'd spent an hour detailing every job in her company and offering him the chance to train for different things. But he'd looked at his watch, then rolled into the possibility that he'd like to start his own company.

She'd listened to him prattle as long as she could before she'd motioned for the waiter to bring the check. She'd paid it, and they'd left the restaurant. Then, for a guy who'd been so gabby during lunch, he'd stopped talking. He'd sat beside her in the cab, playing a drum solo on the back of the passenger's seat in front of him, occasionally looking at his watch.

She could have swatted him. Instead, she started mentally running through that afternoon's work. Oddly, her schedule was clear. No proposals that afternoon. Nothing on the books to organize. She'd thought she had a prospective groom to talk to, but no. Somehow her schedule had magically cleared. She had no appointments or meetings. Otherwise, she could have gotten out of her conversation with Jake a lot sooner.

With nothing else to do, it was probably time to take a look at her notes from Italy and figure out how to beef up the rudimentary presentation she'd created for grooms who might want to propose while on vacation.

Or not. Up to now, she hadn't been able to look at her notes. Everything reminded her of Antonio and her broken heart. She wasn't sure today would be any different.

She couldn't believe she'd not only fallen in love, but she'd fallen in love with the worst possible person. She'd gone into her relationship with Antonio believing it would be an affair— and it had been a great affair until she'd connected with Italy as if she had been born to live there and saw another side of Antonio. The normal side: Not the billionaire playboy, but the man who loved the land and his family. The man who had so much to give but didn't see it.

The elevator door opened onto her floor. She plowed down the corridor and into the reception area of her office. Marietta jumped out of her seat. "You're back."

She grabbed the mail from Marietta's desk and began leafing through it. "Yes. Finally." She glanced behind her at Jake and winced. "Sorry. I know we didn't finish our conversation but maybe we can try again next week."

He gave her a sheepish look. "That's okay. I'll just keep thinking about my options here."

"Good. Because we can always hire another videographer, but you're beginning to understand the anatomy of a proposal now. You'd be great as someone who talked to clients and helped them decide what they want."

He grimaced, then sucked in a breath and smiled. "Sure. That sounds great."

He looked at Marietta as if seeking help.

Marietta glanced at her watch. "You know what, Riley?

There is something you and I need to do this afternoon. Central Park is making some changes to Summerhouse at the Dene."

The place where Antonio had fake proposed to her and where they'd had their first kiss? Her stomach fell, but not wanting to give away her real feelings she happily said, "Really?"

"I think you and I need to go down there and check it out."

Her heart stuttered at even the possibility of going back to the place where Antonio fake proposed to her. "We can't just call?"

"What if they're changing something major? We need to see it. We have four proposals there before Christmas."

"Wouldn't someone have called us if it wasn't available?"

Spreading her hands, Marietta shrugged. "Would they?"

Riley just looked at her. But she also realized she couldn't avoid that place for the rest of her life. Maybe it would be better to go back when she had nothing specific on the agenda, just wanted to see what changes they were making. She could go there, absorb all the memories, force herself to feel everything, then get herself on the real road to recovery.

She would love to feel better. She was tired of missing him, tired of wondering about what could have been.

Maybe what she needed was to see the place torn up, no flowers, no mandolins—just like her heart.

It really could be the first step to healing.

Marietta caught her arm and encouraged her out of the office. "Let's just go check it out. It won't take more than twenty minutes to get there and then we'll know for sure."

"Yes," she agreed as Marietta pushed her out the door. "After this we'll know better."

She liked the sound of that.

They caught a cab to Central Park. Riley paid the cab driver and followed Marietta into the park. The whole place had the oddest feel to it though. She decided that was because the world was caught between fall and winter. The early November air was cooling. Leaves had changed color and were drifting off trees. Everybody was preparing for Thanksgiving. People were living normal, everyday lives.

Exactly what she wanted.

Now she just needed to see Dene Summerhouse getting an overhaul and it would be the symbol of her getting on with her life.

Marietta said, "This way."

"Really? I thought it was that way."

Marietta smiled. "You can get to it a lot of ways."

"Okay."

As they walked up the path, voices floated to them. Probably subcontractors.

Laughter unexpectedly filled the air.

Which began to feel different again. She swore the whole place reeked of the anticipation of a proposal. Her favorite feeling in the world. And she probably felt it because she'd done more than a few events here.

The voices hushed.

They walked a few more feet and she could clearly see Dene Summerhouse. "There are no contractors here," she said, confused.

"Just keep going."

They walked up to the gazebo space and Marietta gave her a nudge. "We can't see much from back here, why don't you go check out the inside, see if you can tell what they're doing."

She frowned, wondering why Marietta wasn't coming with her. But it didn't matter. The place looked fine. Whatever Marietta had heard was wrong.

She walked into the gazebo and three violinists appeared out of nowhere. They began to play something soft and romantic.

She turned, confused, and ready to go back the way she had come, but she saw Antonio. And Jake, filming everything.

Her heart stumbled as Antonio climbed the steps. No one would ever be as handsome to her as he was. The love she felt for him filled her heart, but she also remembered that he didn't want what she wanted.

She opened her mouth to say, "What are you doing here?" But she only got out the "What—"

Antonio got down on one knee, pulled a ring box from his pocket, and said, "I love you. Will you marry me?"

Her heart pounded in her chest. The weirdest sense of déjà vu filled her. She wanted to say yes, as she had in the fake proposal, but she knew this wasn't what he wanted.

She leaned down and whispered. "What are you doing?"

"Asking you to marry me."

"You don't believe in love. You never want to marry again."

He rose, slid his arms around her and pulled her close enough that he could whisper in her ear. "I changed my mind. When you left, I looked around and realized the whole world was dimmer. Duller. I was lonely without you. Nothing had meaning. And that's when I saw it."

She pulled back so she could look into his eyes. "Saw what?"

"What you knew about love and connection and partners."

She studied his eyes which had darkened with sincerity.

"Love—getting married—isn't about sex and romance—though that part is fun—it's about believing."

"Believing?"

"Life is common unless you have someone or something you believe in. You make my life richer. You make me believe in possibilities again. You have shown me that I do have a future."

"Oh."

He bumped his forehead against hers. "So will you marry me?"

Her lips trembled but her heart filled. "Yes."

He pulled the ring out of his pocket. "Nothing starts until the ring is on your finger."

She laughed. "It is usually the cue."

He slid the ring on her finger and tears filled her eyes. "It's a different ring."

"The other one was for a fake proposal. This one is very real."

She nodded. "And it fits."

Then he kissed her. Having his lips on hers was like coming home. She could picture them raising their kids on his family's villa and coming to Manhattan for holidays and Christmas with her mom. She could see them growing old, watching their children take over the vineyards and the companies that had been built by Carlos, GiGi and Enzo.

But most of all, she could see their love, their commitment, enduring.

He broke the kiss, and the sound of the alleluia chorus filled the area. Thirty singing judges danced their way onto Dene Summerhouse and made a circle around them. Marietta and Jake stood off to the side applauding.

Her eyes filled with tears again. "I'm not a judge."

"No. But these judges clued me in that you were a proposal planner and that's why I approached you. I thought it fitting that they should oversee our real proposal."

She laughed. "Maybe this one will hold up in court."

"This one will hold up forever."

She brushed a light kiss across his lips. "That's exactly what I was thinking."

He turned to look behind him. "Jake, is this all on video?"

He waved his small camera. "Got it."

She realized then that Jake had stalled her at lunch so Marietta could throw all this together and she laughed. "Do you really think your GiGi's going to believe this?"

"Yes and no."

"Yes and no." She frowned. "I seem to remember somebody dissing me for not being able to make up my mind."

He pointed to the right, and she saw GiGi, Enzo and her mom standing together, clapping. The first thing she noticed was the bandana on GiGi's head.

"She started her chemo."

"Yes. I wasn't sure she should come but she insisted. We chartered a jet and came with a nurse. So she could see it all."

Riley laughed. "Seeing is believing?"

"I think the strength of her belief might depend on us getting married."

She stood on her tiptoes to kiss him. "The sooner we get married, the sooner I move into the villa."

"That," he said, "will seal the deal."

She loved the sound of that, loved that her life had fallen into place. But most of all she loved that he felt the same way about her that she felt about him.

EPILOGUE

ANTONIO STOOD AT the bottom of the exam table, glancing around at all the "things" in the room where Riley would have an ultrasound to determine the sex of their first child. They were in Manhattan. The pregnancy had been a surprise, and she hadn't found a gynecologist in Italy yet. But they'd figure it out. Eventually. Not that he was nervous.

Much calmer than he was, Riley lounged on the piece of furniture that looked more like a chair than a table.

"Relax."

He faced Riley. "I'm fine."

"You're nervous."

He thought about that for a second. His case of jitters was not for himself but for her. He couldn't imagine being pregnant, let alone going through childbirth. Women were braver than any warrior for the challenges of bearing a child.

"I'm not nervous."

"Maybe you should be. A baby is going to change our lives."

He walked over and took her hand. "For the better."

She smiled. "I think so." Then she frowned. "But he or she comes with a lot of noise."

"GiGi will love that."

"We've taken her very quiet, sedate life and turned it upside down already."

"So having a child can't be that much more disruptive."

Her eyebrows raised as if she were about to argue, but the doctor walked in. "Are we ready?"

They both said, "Yes."

He washed his hands, then strolled over, pulling on his rubber gloves before he grabbed the wand. After a few seconds of prep work, he ran the wand over her stomach. Antonio expected him to say *It's a boy!* or *It's a girl!*

Instead, he frowned. "Well, Riley…" He glanced over at Antonio. "Antonio. It looks like you've got a twofer."

Antonio said, "Twofer?"

"Two for the price of one."

His eyes narrowed. "Two what for the price of one what?"

Riley gasped and squeezed his hand. "Oh, my God! Twins?"

The doctor grinned. "Twins."

Riley laid back and laughed. "Wow."

Antonio saw the whole situation through her eyes. She'd been an only child, didn't know her father's family, felt like an outcast. Then she heard the doctor say they were having twins, and her laughter came naturally, easily.

The man who didn't believe he'd ever have a family was about to become the father of twins.

She caught his hand. "It's great, isn't it? What we want?"

"It's exactly what we want." He squeezed her fingers. "Gi-Gi's going to be over the moon."

He could tell from the expression in her eyes that she'd pictured it. "Yes. She is. So are my mom and your dad."

"Our family."

He squeezed her fingers again. "Our family." And a great adventure. He'd never thought of having kids. Never thought of marrying again. Now, it felt like the whole world had opened up to him.

So many possibilities. So much love.

* * * * *

HIGHLAND FLING WITH HER BOSS

KARIN BAINE

MILLS & BOON

For anyone who needs to hear it—you are enough.

xx

CHAPTER ONE

BONNIE COULD ALMOST hear the carriage wheels trundling over the stone bridge, the clip-clop of horses' hooves, maybe even a piper at the entrance of the castle to welcome visitors. BenCrag Castle certainly didn't look as if it had changed in the three hundred years it had stood proudly on the Scottish Ayrshire cliffs, yet she trusted it had been modernised inside. Otherwise the chocolate shop she was about to open in it was going to look very out of place.

'You'd think they'd have sent someone to meet me,' she muttered to herself. What she wouldn't do now for a horse and carriage, or even a lift on the back of a tractor.

It had been a long walk from the bus stop, down through the trees, sun blazing, carrying all of her worldly possessions. Not that she had much to call her own. Ed had paid for everything during their relationship, that was how he'd wooed her, by treating her like a queen and lavishing her with gifts. To an only child, who'd been wrapped in cotton wool by her parents, it had been exciting to have Ed pursue her, taking her places she'd never been before. They'd dined in fancy restaurants, gone on exotic holidays, and he'd bought her new clothes to go with her exciting new life. The family home and chocolate shop her entire world up until then.

Looking back, she'd been naïve. Probably because she'd been so protected from the world. Ed had seemed like the handsome prince in her childish fairy tales come to life, whisking her away from a life of drudgery working in her father's chocolate shop to a happy ever after with the love of her life. He couldn't do enough to make her happy and she'd felt like the luckiest girl in the world. It had been an easy decision to move out of her home and go to live with him, even if it had caused a rift between her and her family.

She'd discovered too late that Ed thought she was just another one of his possessions. Before long, he'd isolated her from the few friends she'd had, and begun criticising her appearance and questioning her every move, until she'd barely left the house. Cut off from everyone, she'd thought she had no choice but to remain in the relationship, until he'd started pushing her for a family, and she'd known she couldn't subject a child to the same treatment. Then he'd raised his fists…

Bonnie shivered, despite the heat. It had taken some planning to make her escape, saving the little money she had and reaching out to a domestic abuse charity, who'd eventually convinced her to press charges and found her a refuge to stay in. That was when she'd seen the ad for the café in the castle and persuaded the duke she could go one better with a chocolate shop, finally putting the skills she'd learned in the family business to good use.

She'd even managed to convince him to let her live on site, giving her the impression he was quite lonely up here in his castle. A castle! Bonnie couldn't believe this was going to be her new home for the foreseeable future. After the nightmare she'd been living for too long, it seemed like a fairy tale. She just wished she'd been able to get hold of him before she'd made the journey. It had been weeks since he'd answered any of her calls or messages, but she supposed he was busy with the summer season coming up, and she had a contract. There was no backing out now.

Trailing her trolley suitcase behind her, she took a deep breath and crossed through the archway into the courtyard, marvelling at the turrets and ramparts towering above her. She marched up to the large oak door with iron hinges and studding, and lifted the lion-shaped knocker, the sound of which seemed to reverberate through the whole building when she let it fall again.

Bonnie straightened herself up, tried to flatten her wayward chestnut curtain of hair, and waited to face her new employer. And waited. She knocked again. By the third attempt she was beginning to lose patience, wondering what kind of set-up she'd got herself into if they didn't even have enough staff to open the door. It didn't bode well for getting customers into her new chocolate shop.

The sound of clipped footsteps on hard flooring sounded behind the door, marking someone's journey to meet her. Then a scowling man yanked the door open and barked a 'What?' at her.

'I, er, I'm looking for the duke,' she stuttered, thrown by the hostile reception.

'We're closed,' he spat, and slammed the door shut, the din scaring the birds from the neighbouring tree tops.

Bonnie took a step back, startled by the brief, brutal interaction. Although these months on her own had been building her confidence again, she still found a domineering man triggering. The scars from her relationship with Ed were still raw. Even though she'd had counselling at the refuge and Ed was currently serving four years in prison, it was difficult to get past those wounds. Though, deep down, she knew now that she wasn't to blame for what had happened, that he'd manipulated her and abused her trust, she naturally remained wary of other men. More aware of the need to protect herself.

Tempted though she was to slink away again, she had nowhere else to go. Besides, as another member of staff, she had as much right as the grumpy butler to be here.

She knocked again. When there was no forthcoming answer, despite her presence having been acknowledged in some capacity, she decided to try and find another way inside.

Of course, the duke wouldn't open his front door himself, but she was sure he was in residence and would be able to clear up any confusion over her arrival. All she had to do was bypass the surly gatekeeper standing in the way of her new life.

With renewed purpose she turned and made her way around the side of the castle, looking for the back door. There was always a secret tradesman's entrance in these places, so the lowly staff didn't sully the eyeballs of the well-heeled residents by being seen. Although she got the impression times had moved on and the duke was much more accommodating, her presence had already apparently upset someone.

However, her new nemesis was interfering with her plan b, gathering some freshly cut logs from the woodpile near the back door. He rolled his eyes and tutted when he saw her approach. Bonnie swallowed down the rise of bile in her throat, and braced herself for the confrontation she knew she had to have if she was going to get her new start.

'I need to see the duke. He's expecting me.'

'Oh?' Now that he'd stopped frowning, raising an eyebrow only, she could see he was quite handsome in that outdoorsy, farmhand kind of way.

She noted that he wasn't actually wearing any sort of

formal uniform, dressed in worn denim and a checked shirt with the sleeves rolled up, teamed with an auburn mane and red beard—he definitely had that lumberjack vibe going on. Still, he wasn't the reason she was here. The only man she was interested in was the one who was giving her a job and a home.

'Yes. I'm taking over the café. Turning it into a chocolate shop. Now, if you don't mind, could you tell your boss I'm here, please?' She had hoped to have a shower and change before meeting her new employer, but, since no one seemed to know she was coming, Bonnie doubted her room was even ready.

'My boss?' He was openly laughing at her now, only furthering the rise in her temper and need to get away from him.

'Yes, your boss. The duke. The owner of this castle, and the man I've been corresponding with.' Her sigh was full of frustration, exasperation, and all the stress she'd been going through for months. She didn't need any more hassle. Especially when this was supposed to be the new, shiny version of her life. Bonnie Abernathy 2.0.

The castle handyman-cum-butler-cum-pain-in-Bonnie's-backside carefully set the logs back down and stood up straight. 'That was probably my father. I'm sorry to say he passed away last month. I'm the new owner. The new Duke of Arbay.'

Although the smile had gone from his lips now, her tormentor continued to cause her anguish. A whole range of emotions and questions bombarded her at once as she processed this new information. She was sorry she'd never got to meet the man who'd given her so much confidence by believing in her and giving her a new start, and wondered what had happened to him. Most of all she was concerned about where the duke's death left her. Of course, it seemed selfish in the wake of this man losing his father to think about herself first, but without this position she had nothing. Her fate was in this man's hands. Definitely not a position she was relishing.

'I'm so sorry for your loss. He seemed like such a lovely man.'

Ewen had witnessed the shock, and the concern, cross the woman's face. These past weeks had been a whirlwind for him, so he knew how the news about his father's passing could disrupt a person's life. The least he could do was offer her a cup of tea to get over the shock.

'I'm Ewen. Ewen Harris.' He held out his hand, ignoring the comment about his father, and the fact he'd slammed the door in her face only moments earlier.

'Bonnie Abernathy,' she said, shaking his hand limply, her earlier fire seemingly having dissipated.

'Why don't you come in and I'll make us both a cuppa?' He opened the door, led her into the kitchen, and pulled out a chair for her before putting the kettle on.

Bonnie settled herself at the kitchen table whilst he tasked himself with finding some clean cups.

'I'm still trying to find my way around. It's a long time since I lived here.' Ewen opened and shut the cupboards looking for the good china, but making do with the chipped mugs he'd been using since moving back. He'd had more to sort out lately than appropriate dishware for unexpected visitors.

'Were you here when he died? Sorry. That's too personal a question. Forget I asked. I'm still trying to process the news.' She wrapped her hands around the mug of tea he poured for her, staring at it, apparently lost in her thoughts.

'It's okay. No, I wasn't here when it happened. I don't

think anyone was. Heart attack in his sleep apparently.'
Naturally he felt guilty about not being there, but Ewen's
issues with his family went back further and deeper than
just his father's passing.

'At least it was quick, and peaceful.'

'Yes. I'm thankful for that.'

Her analysis, whilst true, brought back thoughts of his
brother Ruari's death, which might have been quick, but
hadn't been peaceful. For any of them.

'So you're the new Duke of Arbay?'

'Yes. By default. My older brother, Ruari, died in a car
accident twelve years ago.' Something he'd never forget,
and something his parents had never forgiven him for. Because he'd been driving. It didn't matter that the road had
been icy, that he'd only just passed his test—important
points he'd reconciled with over the years and learned to
forgive himself for. As far as they'd been concerned, he
was responsible for the death of their firstborn.

It was that guilt, that blame, that had spurred him to
leave for university in England, unable to live with his parents' blatant hatred, and why he'd never come home. Until
now. Until forced by his father to live in this castle for a
year before he could sell it and rid himself of the reminder
of that terrible time for ever.

'I'm so sorry.'

'It was a long time ago.' He shrugged, not wishing to get
into the sordid details with someone he'd just met.

'And you're here on your own? No other family? I
thought you would at least have staff.'

Her forthright questions made him smile. It was refreshing to have someone be so upfront with him. Especially
after Victoria, his partner of two years who'd apparently
been pretending to love him to enjoy the benefits of his

wealth. He'd become a success in his own right, creating an app that he'd sold later for millions. A one-stop shop for businesses that synced with their needs. Taking care of everything from contacting suppliers when the office copier ran out of ink, to linking directly to recruitment agencies when they needed staff. Basically, a digital office assistant.

Selling it, making his own fortune, had meant he'd had no reason to come back home. It had suited everyone. He hadn't had to face the empty place where Ruari should've been, and his parents hadn't needed the reminder that Ewen existed. He got the impression they'd been happier believing they'd lost both sons in the crash than admitting they blamed Ewen and couldn't bear to look at him.

'My mother died ten years ago. I've been estranged from my parents for some time.' He hadn't come home for the funeral. Too busy in negotiations over the sale of his app. And, if he was honest, hadn't wanted to face his father. It would have felt hypocritical to turn up and mourn for his mother when they hadn't had any contact for years at that point. He'd only found out about his father because his solicitor had tracked him down. Only came back to tie up loose ends, then hopefully he'd be done with this place, and the memories for good.

He wasn't comfortable being here. In a way he was thankful for all the things keeping him too busy to dwell on the past, despite the inconvenience of it all. Dealing with his father's legal and financial affairs were practical things he could manage, but it was the emotional fallout from being back here that he feared.

He'd worked hard to be a success, to put the pain of his parents' rejection and the loss of his brother behind him. The death of his father, and his subsequent demands, had forced Ewen to live within these walls again, reliving those dark times, reminding him of the loneliness he'd felt at a time when he'd needed his family more than ever. Now he had no one.

'I'm sorry for your loss. I know something about being separated from parents. I haven't spoken to mine in quite some time.'

When he looked at her, expecting the reason, she simply shrugged. 'They didn't like my boyfriend. I left home to be with him, it didn't work out, but I don't want them to know they were right about him.'

He was about to offer his commiserations on the matter when she carried on, denying him the opportunity to butt in.

'Anyway, that's why I came here. For a new start.'

'I'm sorry things haven't worked out the way you expected. Do you have anything else in the pipeline?' He knew what it was like to have your life disrupted so suddenly and unexpectedly. A few weeks ago he'd been living in London with Victoria, not knowing he'd end up back in Scotland, single, and taking up residence on the family estate. The last surviving member of the Harris line. Although it was bad luck for Bonnie too that his father's death had clearly impacted on her plans, he was sure she'd find another job soon.

She didn't have the same conviction, sitting blinking at him, apparently stunned. 'No, I don't have a backup plan. This is it. My new start. Everything I own is in this case. I'm homeless, penniless, and apparently now jobless.'

Ewen frowned. He hadn't really paid much attention to the small trolley case until now, figuring it might have contained some small personal items she wanted for the café. It hadn't crossed his mind that she was carrying all her worldly possessions in it. To have so little told a story in itself, but she'd mentioned problems with a boyfriend and her parents, so it was obvious she'd gone through a rough time. Unfortunately, he was going through one of his own and didn't have room in his life to deal with someone else's troubles. Especially when she would have to move on.

'I don't understand…surely you had accommodation lined up to come here?' It didn't make any sense to him as to why it was his problem she had nowhere to go and no money to her name. He felt sorry for her, of course, but it wasn't any of his business, and he wanted it to remain that way. Victoria had made him wary of any beautiful woman now wishing to get close to him, in case they were only using him for his money and status. And here was a complete stranger turning up on his doorstep with a sob story, just as he'd become a duke and inherited the estate… He'd be a fool to be taken in a second time by a damsel in distress.

'You really know nothing about this?' She sighed, setting her cup down as though she were preparing to go into battle and needed her hands free.

'No. I've been busy with my father's funeral and sorting out his affairs. The staff are off until I'm ready to reopen to the public. There has been no mention of a new café manager, and quite frankly I don't see why your struggles are suddenly my problem. My father hired you, not me.'

Yes, he was being abrupt, but he still had a lot to sort through, and, technically, he was still grieving. It didn't matter that he and his father hadn't spoken in years, his death was still having a huge impact on his life, and there were things he needed space and time to process. He wasn't in the right frame of mind to start bringing strangers into the family home, or take on new staff. It was going to be a challenge dealing with the ones that were already employed here.

'I have a contract, written and verbal, to say I would have a place to stay here. I wouldn't have come otherwise.' She bit her lip before she said anything else, but Ewen had heard the rising panic in her voice and realised there was more going on than her being inconvenienced.

He wondered if it was something to do with the ex she'd mentioned. A break-up perhaps? Whilst she had his sympathy, something she probably didn't want or need, she wasn't his problem. He had enough of those to deal with and he didn't need to take on another one. Especially one in the form of an attractive brunette spitfire.

'That contract was with my father. I'm sorry but I'm not under any obligation to honour that.' Ewen was being harsh, but there was no room in his life for more complications, and that was exactly what this pretty stranger represented.

He didn't know why his father had decided to open the family home up to the public, or if he was even prepared to carry on with the tours. It didn't feel right taking on another member of staff when he wasn't sure what the future held for him or the castle. What Bonnie was asking for went beyond an extra pay cheque. After looking into the castle finances, he could tell they were sufficient to cover staff wages. His predicament had been whether or not to continue in that vein. And now Ms Abernathy had presented him with the added pressure of a possible resident.

It was difficult enough for him to be here after all this time, dealing not only with his past, but also his father's business affairs. On top of that, he was just getting over a break-up himself. He wasn't good company, not in the mood to have to pretend otherwise to a complete stranger who thought she had the right to live in the castle. The upheaval of his move here and his new, unwanted position was already stressful, and he didn't need the role of landlord/housemate added to his current workload. She should not be his responsibility.

Her full lips thinned into a determined line. 'I came here in good faith, hired by the Duke of Arbay to work in BenCrag Castle—'

'The previous Duke of Arbay...' he clarified.

'Nevertheless, the castle is still standing, as is the shop, and I'm here now. It would seem a little churlish on your part to send me away just because you're on a power trip.' She tilted her nose into the air, and, though she was fast becoming a pain in the proverbial, he kind of admired that fighting spirit in her.

Another red flag should he need it. The only positive thing to come out of this mess was that it was a distraction from his disastrous love life. He did not want a reason to like this pretty brunette, especially when she was trying to establish herself in this strange new life he'd been thrown into. When he inevitably sold up and moved on, he didn't want any ties or recriminations. The whole idea was to be finally done with this place and all the bad memories it represented. Not add more.

'Look, I don't even know if I'm going to open the café again. There's more going on in my life right now.'

'I appreciate that, but I'm sure your father wouldn't want to see me out on the street.' The sickly sweet smile as she batted her eyelashes was just as disarming as her warrior pose.

'That may be so, but he's not here, and he's left me to make the decisions regarding the castle's future.' Goodness knew why. Mrs McKenzie the housekeeper, Richard, the estate manager, or even the local students who volunteered in the gardens probably had more interest in that than he did. They would certainly have appreciated it more. Though he wasn't sure if even they would've agreed to letting an outsider live in the place rent-free.

Bonnie leaned forward. 'I don't want to make this a legal thing. I mean, we wouldn't want the press to get a hold of the story. It wouldn't look good for the new Duke of Arbay.'

Legally, he was sure she wouldn't have a leg to stand on if he decided to dispute the contract. After all, it was his father who had employed her. A legal battle would be lengthy and of no benefit to either of them in the end. However, he couldn't afford any bad publicity if he was going to open the castle again. Not when he already had a task ahead trying to win over local opinion of him. All anyone knew about him was that he was the driver of the car in the crash that killed his brother, and that he hadn't come home when either of his parents had died. It wasn't going to help his reputation if Bonnie went around telling people that he'd thrown her out on the street after his father had promised her a life here. She'd backed him into a corner, leaving only one option open to him.

'I'll give you a trial. If it doesn't work out, you'll move on.' He'd make sure it didn't work out, that she would hate being around him so much she'd move on of her own accord.

'Deal.' She was so quick to hold her hand out and shake on it, Ewen was beginning to have second thoughts about the whole idea. It felt as though he was losing control all over again.

'There aren't any rooms ready for you...' He was grasping for reasons to delay sharing his living space now, regardless that he'd agreed to it in the end.

Even though it was true. He was sleeping in his childhood bedroom and had yet to venture into any of the other rooms, including the one his father had passed away in.

'That's fine. Just point me in the right direction and I can sort one out for myself. I have a lot of work to do anyway if I'm going to open my chocolate shop. Do you have a date for the castle reopening?' Bonnie appeared brighter, sitting up taller in her chair, now that she had secured her job and accommodation again. Ewen, however, was becoming more unsettled by the second.

'No, I've just been taking one day at a time.' He'd been a little overwhelmed by the situation and his answer had been to dismiss the staff so he could be alone to deal with things. His go-to defence, harking back to Ruari's death when he'd had to work through the guilt and trauma of the accident by himself because his parents had been too wrapped up in their own grief to help.

'Well, I think it's about time we made some plans. Or else it's just going to be the two of us rattling around this big house for the rest of our days, and you don't want that, do you?'

No. No, he didn't. This fiery yet vulnerable stranger with big brown eyes who'd turned up on his doorstep had just upended his world all over again. Far from coming here to brood alone about the turn his life had taken, he had now found himself a housemate and a business to run.

Ewen didn't know what had prompted his father to make the decisions he'd made, agreeing to let a complete stranger move into the castle, and forcing his estranged son to stay in residence for a year. It felt as though he were still trying to punish him from beyond the grave. Testing him, pushing him to the limits of his patience, and waiting for him to break.

Only time would tell if he could rise to the occasion, or prove that the wrong son had died all those years ago.

CHAPTER TWO

'MORNING,' BONNIE SAID brightly as she helped herself to the cereal in the cupboard and added a generous pouring of milk.

'Morning,' Ewen replied, barely looking up from his phone.

Regardless of his less than enthusiastic welcome, she joined him at the kitchen table. The one in the staff quarters, not the huge one upstairs she'd spotted in the dining hall on her quick tour of the castle that the duke was probably supposed to use. She felt more at home down in the modest farmhouse-style kitchen and she supposed he did too.

It had been an odd few days. Although they were living together, there was plenty of room to actively avoid each other, save for this room when they drifted together at mealtimes like this. She'd used the time to make her bedroom feel more like home, unpacking her few possessions and making the bed with the linen she'd found in the cupboard. Although she was aware she could be out on the street at any given moment.

She knew she didn't have a binding contract with Ewen, and it was clear he didn't want her here. In other circumstances she might not have pushed so hard, but without the job and the room here she had nothing. There was no way she was going back to the refuge when she'd so been looking forward to having a life of her own again. The centre had been her sanctuary, her escape from her ex, but it wasn't a home, living with a group of women all left traumatised and frightened by abusive partners.

At least here she could start over and not be reminded of the situation she'd been in for too long. Once she was earning enough money, able to put something by every month, she hoped she'd have enough for a deposit on her own place. All she had to do was not annoy Ewen too much so he'd let her stay until then. Not that he was making it easy. Every time he made it obvious that he didn't want her here, when it looked as though her new life was in jeopardy, she came out fighting.

They'd definitely got off on the wrong foot when she'd threatened legal action and bad press to force his hand, but she hadn't seen any other choice in that moment. His father had offered her a lifeline at a time when she was desperate for a new start, and she wasn't prepared to give it up without a fight. She'd had her fill of domineering men dictating what happened to her, and her time away from that oppressive situation with Ed had taught her she didn't have to put up with it.

'I'll replace the cereal and milk later when I do a shop. I just haven't had a chance to get any groceries yet. I don't want you to think I'm a bad housemate.' She was rabbiting to fill the silence between them that was only punctuated when she took a mouthful of bran flakes.

'Make sure you do. We're not housemates. You're more like a squatter I'm powerless to get rid of.' Ewen didn't look up, wearing that scowl that seemed to be omnipresent in her company.

She knew he'd just lost his father and had a lot to deal

with here at the castle, but it was difficult not to be affected by his bad mood and clear dislike of her. Given her circumstances, she had to put up with it, but the tense atmosphere was something she'd hoped she'd never be forced to endure again. Just like living with Ed, one wrong move and she'd face the consequences. Except this time it was less about verbal and physical abuse, and more to do with losing her job and accommodation. Ewen held all the cards and she was powerless, save for her strong will, which had got her in the castle door at least. Hopefully once the other staff and visitors were trooping through his home, her presence would be a minor irritation he would eventually forget about altogether.

'Harsh, but perhaps I'll be able to win you over with my chocolate skills. There will never be a shortage of chocolate around here now. Speaking of which, I want to talk to you about plans for the shop. I wondered if there was a budget for the refurb? Although it's going to be a chocolate shop, I wondered if we should get one of those fancy coffee machines installed and encourage people to stay. Perhaps I could even branch out to making chocolate-based desserts.'

Ever since she'd agreed to take over the café her mind had been working overtime on what she could do. With this new independence she felt as though the world were her oyster, if only she had the money to achieve everything she wanted. Bonnie knew she was on thin ice with Ewen, but she was counting on him wanting the business to be a success too.

He glanced up at her this time, the scowl so deep she was sure it would leave a permanent indent. 'Let's not get carried away. We don't know how the chocolate shop is even going to go. I don't want to pour money into something that mightn't even be around in another year. Concentrate on what you're here for. Write a list for the basic equipment and ingredients you need, and we'll work from there.'

Finally putting his phone away, Ewen got up from the table and placed his dirty coffee cup in the sink.

Bonnie took a deep breath and counted to ten. 'Whatever you say, boss.'

She wasn't going to let his pessimism dampen her enthusiasm, or stop her from dreaming. For now, she'd bite her tongue and be grateful he'd conceded this far. Even if it had been under duress. It wouldn't do her any favours to butt heads with him again so soon. Besides, once he saw how good she was, Bonnie knew it would be easier to persuade him to invest more into the enterprise. In fact, once Ewen tasted her chocolates, he'd never want her to leave.

'I think the counter top and cash register we already have will do just fine for now,' Ewen insisted as he and Bonnie stood surveying the interior of the castle café a week later.

He could've done without the distraction and complication of having her living in the house with him. Not only was he tortured with the sight of her in the mornings wearing little more than a dressing gown that barely covered her round backside, there was no escape from her constant pushing for big changes in the castle. It was understandable that she would be ambitious, wanting to make the most of this opportunity, but he needed to be cautious. In both his personal and professional life.

He didn't want to be attracted to any woman at present, and certainly not a stranger wanting him to invest his money in her dream. Victoria had taught him a hard-learned lesson to be cautious when it came to his money and relationships. For all he knew, Bonnie was just another gold-digger deploying her feminine wiles to make him lose all common sense and think with other parts of his anatomy rather than his head. She'd made it clear she had no money, and from the outside he must have seemed like a stable financial prospect. Victoria had obviously thought so when they'd got together. It was all very well appreciating a woman's beauty and spirit, but he needed to be cautious about even entertaining the idea of getting close to someone again, to protect his heart, and his assets.

On a practical, business level, if things went to plan he was going to be selling the castle as soon as the conditions of his father's will had been met. He'd already made enquiries with an estate agent about putting the place on the market. So it would be pointless investing more money into the business now, and he definitely didn't need to do it to impress Bonnie when he needed to give her reason to leave. And soon.

'Can I at least redecorate?' she huffed, arms folded, clearly not impressed by his answer.

'Sure. Why do you think I'm here?' He hoisted the tin of paint he'd stashed there earlier onto the table.

Bonnie peered at it, wrinkling her nose in disgust. 'Beige?'

'Yes, beige.'

'I don't get a say?'

'You're the manager, not the owner. The place still needs to be in keeping with the rest of the castle. Nothing ostentatious, but subtle. We don't know how business is going to go, so I don't want to be left with sparkly pink walls and rainbow-coloured carpet if this doesn't work out.' It would make it difficult to sell on to any potential buyers.

'What makes you think I would be so OTT?'

Ewen looked her up and down, taking in the azureblue dress she was wearing, emblazoned with bright yellow sunflowers, and the matching yellow wedges on her feet. He loved that she was expressing herself, her vivid wardrobe livening up the interior of the otherwise drab building. However, he had to draw the line when it came to the castle aesthetics.

'Okay, point taken, as long as you don't expect me to start wearing some generic dull uniform. I've had my fill of being told what to wear and how to behave.'

The comment grabbed a hold of Ewen and wouldn't let go. He wasn't going to pry, but Bonnie's past had clearly left its mark on her. He couldn't imagine anyone trying to tame her, or wanting to. Perhaps whatever had happened to her was partly to blame for them butting heads, along with his frustration at being forced to live with her in a place he couldn't wait to escape from.

If she'd been with someone who'd dominated her, it was no wonder she was rebelling against Ewen putting his foot down and asking her to fall into line with his wishes. He understood her blatant need to assert her independence, he'd done the same when he'd moved away from home. Keen to escape the burden of guilt his parents had tried to heap upon him, he'd moved quickly to start a new life for himself at university, almost becoming a completely different person in the process. He was no longer a naïve, privileged rich kid, but a jaded, older-than-his-years man who'd had to be proactive about securing a financial future away from his family.

However, it was also important for him now to remind Bonnie he was her boss, or he'd make a rod for his own back in the future. Victoria had spent most of their time together splurging his cash for her own benefit, leaving him with the bills when she moved on elsewhere. He wasn't prepared to let that happen a second time.

'You can wear what you like. If it makes you happy you can put whatever paintings you want on the walls.' A few pictures could always be taken down and wouldn't cost the earth. He hoped the compromise would keep her happy and give her some sense of control over her work environment.

For a split second her eyes lit up and he thought he'd won her over. Then she pulled a face, clearly not wanting to seem as though she was caving too easily.

'You're *too* generous.'

'I know,' he said, ignoring the blatant sarcasm. 'That's why I'm devoting my spare time to painting the place myself.'

She rolled her eyes. 'Because you're *so* generous and not at all a tight-ass.'

That made him laugh. He didn't know how, or why, anyone would want to dampen Bonnie's spirit, but he was glad she'd broken free from whoever had tried to control her. She was certainly going to keep him on his toes around here. Since the split from Victoria he'd felt as though he was alone in the world, his entire family now dead save for him. But he wasn't sure if it was any easier for him having Bonnie in situ. He'd become accustomed to being on his own, only making decisions concerning himself. Now he was beginning to feel responsible for her too. More than that, he was beginning to like her, and he couldn't afford to let either get in the way of his plans.

The staff had begun to filter back to the castle to get ready for the reopening—the groundskeeper, and the estate manager, as well as maintenance—but they went home at the end of the day. Though he didn't actively seek Bonnie out at night, her room was only a few doors down from his in the part of the castle that was closed off to visitors, so he often heard her walking in the hallway, or singing to herself. Enough for him to remember he wasn't alone with his ghosts. Not that he wanted to get too used to having her around when he intended to sell the place and move on when he could. Something that would certainly not endear him to Bonnie, but he hoped by that time she would be ready to move on to bigger and better things too. This was merely a stopgap for both of them.

'Feel free to help. It will get done quicker with two of us.' He opened the lid on the paint and offered her a paint roller.

'No, thanks. I've plenty to do in the kitchen. Recipes to finesse, chocolate to temper and sample. You know, all the real hard work.' She grinned before turning on her sunshine-yellow wedges and sashaying towards the kitchen at the back of the small room.

Ewen couldn't help but admire the sway of her hips in the figure-skimming jersey dress and the proud way she carried herself. This was a woman reclaiming her confidence and the person she was. Someone he was beginning to admire more with every interaction, regardless of the inconvenience. When he let his eyes dip to the fullness of her backside he knew it was time to occupy his thoughts elsewhere.

He covered the floor with the dustsheet he'd brought, picked up the paint roller, and did his best to block out the sound of her happy singing in the kitchen.

Bonnie had arranged the kitchen the way she wanted it, made some of her staple chocolate truffles and started to build her basic stock for opening day. She could give out a variety of milk, dark and white chocolates as samples to any potential customers, though she wanted to work on something special. A signature creation specially for the castle. Something with whisky perhaps, linking to the

Scottish heritage, or a lavender base as a nod to the purple beauty in abundance by the castle walls. She wanted to put her little chocolate shop on the map. With visitors paying an entrance fee to get into the castle, she wasn't likely to get repeat custom yet, relying on rich tourists flocking in en masse. So she needed something eye-catching and palate-pleasing to get them to spend their money.

Her plan was to eventually have a website selling online, maybe even doing personalised corporate orders. Whatever it took to make the business a success and make a name for herself in the chocolate world. Then all of those weekends and holidays she'd spent working in her father's business wouldn't have been wasted after all. And it would certainly boost her self-confidence to have a purpose again.

Of course, she'd have to get it past Ewen first. A minor hiccup. Despite his gruff exterior Ewen would do what was best for the shop, and the castle. After all, she'd managed to persuade him to let her stay and work here. He'd even spent the day painting the shop walls that unattractive beige colour, which she was going to be sure to cover up as best she could with the permitted artwork she would now be on the hunt for.

Her stomach grumbled. They'd worked through lunch, but since she'd spent all day in the kitchen she didn't fancy standing making dinner down in the depths of the castle staff quarters.

'Do you fancy a takeaway?' she shouted across the short distance between them, leaving her spotless kitchen to seek out her boss. 'Although, we should probably eat it somewhere else. The smell of paint fumes is making my eyes water.'

Although they weren't the closest of housemates, primarily because he made it obvious he didn't want her there, it made sense to share the meal. Not only could they split the cost, at a time when she was counting every penny, but it saved on waste. She wasn't the sort of person who liked to microwave takeaway leftovers the next day. Also, despite their clash of personalities at times, they'd got along fine today.

If she was honest, the company would be nice for a change too. It had been a while since she'd shared a meal with anyone, and even longer since she'd enjoyed one without the threat of her companion's temper spoiling it. She could handle Ewen's tendency towards grumpiness if it meant she had someone to talk to other than the walls for one evening. He'd almost been congenial today, even if he was only painting the shop to save money.

Bonnie was wondering how he'd managed to work all day without getting high or passing out, when she saw him sitting slumped over one of the tables, his head in his hands.

'Ewen? Are you okay?' Her heart sank at the thought that something had happened to him and she'd been completely oblivious.

Yes, she'd battled against him on nearly every decision since her arrival, but that was only to be expected given her limited history with men. To have another male telling her what she could and couldn't do had been a trigger, inciting that need for her to fight for her independence. Okay, he was her boss, and, as such, she had to make compromises, but she was damned if she'd go back to being that submissive woman who'd simply fall into line or face the consequences. She hadn't realised she'd become so feisty in the short space of time since she'd left her ex until meeting Ewen. There was a lot to begrudgingly thank him for, even if she had backed him into a corner, and she certainly didn't want him to come to any harm.

It was only when she came to touch him on the arm she realised he was sitting in front of his laptop, his earbuds in, oblivious to the outside world.

He jumped when she made contact with him and pulled out his earbuds. 'Sorry. I didn't hear you.'

'I didn't mean to scare you. I thought you'd passed out from the paint fumes. I didn't spot the laptop, or the earbuds.'

'I was just going through the calendar for the year trying to figure out how I'm going to honour all of the bookings my father apparently took. Is there something I can do for you?' He closed the laptop as though there was something he didn't want her to see, or no longer wanted to deal with.

'I thought you might like to get some takeaway rather than cooking tonight. It's been a long, hard day for us both and we could do with putting our feet up.' There hadn't been much interaction between them outside castle and shop business, but ordering food for one seemed a step too far. They weren't in high school, they weren't going to catch anything by being in the same room, and she was sure they could manage a civil conversation over some fast food. It might even begin to feel as if she was back in the real world.

Although she'd left Ed, moved on from the refuge, and found a place of her own—albeit part of a castle—she had yet to fully immerse herself in her new reality. She didn't know if she could still function as a human being. If she'd ever feel comfortable around people again, or if she was always going to feel on edge. Waiting for something bad to happen.

Making small talk with Ewen would be a start. A gentle lead in to dealing with members of the public. Having worked in retail at her parents' place when she was a teenager, she was aware it required her to be amiable and approachable. As the face of the chocolate shop at the castle, she had nowhere to hide. After years of her being in the background, cowed by her partner, running a shop was like being thrown into the deep end in terms of socialising again. A challenge she was more than willing to take on when it meant finally getting her life back under her control.

'Sure. I've got some menus downstairs if you want to have a look and decide what you want? I can make the call and we can eat it in the lounge. It'll be much more comfortable, and warmer, than the kitchen.'

It also meant crossing over into Ewen's private quarters. So far their interactions had been confined to the communal kitchen and the parts of the castle open to visitors. She had her own room and en suite bathroom but, most likely, he had a few rooms to call his own that were closed to the public.

Her hesitation was based purely on the idea of breaching that invisible line between work and their personal lives. They'd had their differences of opinion, but he'd never forced her to submit to his will. She liked that they were able to compromise, that, despite initial appearances, he was a reasonable man. He was also going through a difficult time and she was sure that had a lot to do with his mood. Something she could easily relate to—she was more defensive than usual too.

Even though she knew she was safe around Ewen, that he was no threat to her, it was still a big step to socialise with a man alone. It had crossed her mind when coming to live here that she'd find it difficult to live with another man in any circumstances. That she'd never be able to let her guard down in case someone else tried to take advantage of her. Or hurt her. But he'd given her a job and somewhere to live when he really didn't have to, and she got the impression he was every bit as alone as she was.

'Okay. Let me get changed first. I'm covered in chocolate. I'll see you down there in fifteen minutes.' It gave her a little breathing space, time to regroup, before venturing into unknown territory.

Although she knew sharing some food with her boss was nothing to fear, or be anxious about, it was another big step out of her comfort zone. One she knew she needed to take in order to move on.

CHAPTER THREE

EWEN JUMPED IN the shower and scrubbed off as much of the paint as he could see, then donned a pair of jeans and a clean tee shirt. Victoria would be mortified by his wardrobe these days, though he'd found it quite liberating to swap city suits for comfy casuals. He supposed once the castle was reopened he'd have to dress the part, but he drew the line at wearing a kilt to keep the tourists happy. A shirt and tie would have to suffice. He wanted to look smart for his new role as the duke, and in control of what was happening on the estate. Even if that seemed out of reach at present.

The sound of Bonnie rapping on the door forced him out of his reverie. Despite being in the same space, they'd managed to avoid each other for most of the day. That was what had made her suggestion seem so out of left-field. Yet, he'd agreed before he'd had time to think it through properly, desperate for some company.

He'd known moving to the castle was going to be an upheaval, but he hadn't realised he'd end up here alone, with nothing, or no one to go back to. Once Victoria had gone he'd sold up, hadn't seen the point of keeping an expensive, empty apartment in London for a year. It meant whenever he was finally able to get rid of the castle and the other problems his father had left, he had nowhere else to go. In that sense, he understood where Bonnie was coming from. He knew, unlike her, he had options, money to go anywhere, but he had no friends or family around him. Another thing they seemed to have in common. He supposed it wouldn't hurt either of them to have some company once in a while.

The sight of her when he opened the door made him smile. Her hair was still damp from her shower, the curly ends wetting the shoulders of her slouchy grey sweatshirt, and she'd swapped her dress for a pair of comfy jogging bottoms. Clearly marking the distinction between work and play. Victoria had always dressed to the nines, with full make-up and coiffed hairdo, which was her prerogative, but had made him feel slightly on edge. As though he always had to be on display too, in case he let her down by appearing in an outfit she didn't deem acceptable. At least he could relax tonight.

'Hey. Come on in.' He opened the door to let Bonnie in. It seemed a bit strange when they were ostensibly living in the same house, if in separate areas. Housemates who rarely interacted.

'Sorry I don't have a bottle of wine or a bunch of flowers to offer for your hospitality,' she said, ducking inside. It was then he noticed her pink fluffy slipper boots. She really was going for comfort tonight. At least it showed she felt she could be herself around him, and it made it easier for Ewen to relax, knowing she wasn't likely to mistake this evening for anything other than a meal together. Getting the sense that she'd recently gone through a break-up too, he didn't imagine either of them were interested in a relationship of any kind. Not that having dinner with one another constituted a commitment beyond cultivating a more harmonious working environment.

He supposed he should be happy that he seemed to raise her hackles every time they spoke. It would make it easier in terms of scaring her off, and relieving him of any responsibility towards her. But he was emotionally drained by recent events and simply wanted a quiet dinner in some company for a change. At least if they were eating, they wouldn't get caught in another verbal battle of wills.

'No need. I have some wine here and I've had so many sympathy flowers delivered recently I could open my own florist shop. Besides, technically we live together, so dinner isn't that big a deal.'

'You're right. Now, where are those menus? Because I need to eat.' With that, she walked on into the lounge and threw herself down onto the settee, making herself at home.

Ewen did the same, pulling out his phone and the stack of menus he'd found earlier. It was the most normal he'd felt in weeks.

They'd opted for Italian in the end. Bonnie figured the carb overload of pasta and creamy sauces was the ultimate comfort food they both needed. Though she might not need to eat again for another week.

'Would you like some more wine?' Ewen held up the rest of the bottle of white they'd already enjoyed with their dinner, and she nodded as he topped up their glasses.

Regardless of being in a castle, surrounded by antique furniture and valuable paintings, it felt like a cosy night in. Normal. Not a night in a room no bigger than a cell, sharing a building with other women afraid of their own shadows, too traumatised to socialise. Nor another evening trying to be as invisible as possible so as not to antagonise her other half by simply breathing. Neither scenario had been any sort of life, and though no one could call this exciting, it was exactly what she needed right now. Simply chilling out with good food, good wine and good company. Bonnie couldn't remember the last time she'd felt so contented, and relaxed.

That was when the doubt crows began to circle, pecking her head with their sharp beaks to remind her that it couldn't last. Her whole life had been dictated by men telling her what to do. Ewen was her boss. Tonight was nice, but, by the very nature of their relationship, he had the power. Something he'd demonstrated already, and once the castle was back up and running as a business it was going to be tough for her to fall into line again. Who knew how long this new way of life was going to last? Ultimately, her fate was still at the mercy of another man, and, after everything she'd been through, that didn't sit well with her.

'Uh-oh,' Ewen said, leaning forward, his forehead wrinkled into a frown.

'What is it?' Her stomach knotted at the thought that she'd done something wrong. Something to upset him. A throwback to the life she'd lived with her ex, when she'd constantly been on eggshells, waiting to find out what she'd done to trigger his anger.

'I can see you're lost in your thoughts, and they don't look to me as though they're very happy ones.'

She offered him a reassuring smile. Something else she was used to doing to make the peace. However, on this occasion, Ewen's observation, combined with his concern for her, made it a genuine reaction for once.

'Just thinking about things, and people, I left in the past.'

'And that's where they should stay. Although, it's not that easy when they're still dictating your everyday behaviour, is it?' Ewen knocked back the rest of his wine, almost as though he was trying to blot something out too.

'What makes you say that?' Bonnie took a sip from her glass, her hand shaking, jolted by his apparent insight into her innermost thoughts. She wanted to know if she'd done anything to give him the impression she'd been left dealing with a deep-seated trauma by her ex, or if he'd had his own experiences.

He set his glass on the coffee table, creating a barrier between them, and leaned forward, his forearms resting on his lap. 'When you arrived, you were homeless, penniless, and defensive. I know it's none of my business, but I get the impression you went through more than a breakup. Whatever happened, I do know how incredibly brave it was to come here and start over.'

'Thank you, but I'm fine,' she whispered, trying to hold it together. The reminder of how much it had taken for her to walk away in the end, and the fact he was acknowledging that, were bringing up all sorts of emotions.

She hadn't intended to share anything about that with anyone, never mind her new boss. As well as being painful to recall those memories, it was humiliating to share the details of that relationship. Ewen had seen her only at her fighting best after counselling had bolstered her confidence. She didn't want him to see her any differently. Certainly not as the weak woman who'd let herself be used and abused for way too long. Yes, she knew now that she wasn't responsible for Ed's behaviour, but even she didn't recognise the young woman who'd been taken in by a pretty face and some attention. These days she was more worldly-wise, not to mention cynical.

Only the women at the refuge had known what she'd been through. By that stage she wasn't in contact with any of her old friends, or her parents. She'd had no one to turn to, and no one to tell her she'd done the right thing, the brave thing, at the loneliest, most frightening time of her life. The help she'd received from the charity had saved her. But she was trying to move on and didn't want to keep looking back. From now on she had to be more careful about her choice of words around Ewen.

Ewen sat back in his seat again, giving her back the personal space she needed in that moment. 'I didn't think I'd ever come back here myself.'

'Oh?' It was the first time Ewen had opened up to her about his personal life. Whether it was the effect of the alcohol, the cosy atmosphere that had developed between them tonight, or that he felt he needed to share something of himself to even the score, Bonnie didn't know. But she was ready to listen. It was clear he wasn't happy about being here. For someone who'd just inherited land, a title, and his father's fortune, he seemed as though he had the weight of the world on his shoulders.

'I've been estranged from my family since I was eighteen. I went to university and very rarely came back. I made a life of my own. My father's death forced me to return, to take up the role I never wanted.' The pressure he was feeling was there to see in his slumped shoulders, and, now she was looking closely, there was a smudge under his blue eyes that told of his sleepless nights.

'Perhaps this was your father's way of making amends?' Of course, she didn't know the circumstances, nor was she privy to anyone else's thoughts or motivations, but it was a possibility. Whatever had happened between them had been serious enough for Ewen to stay away all these years, but his father leaving everything to him in his will seemed to her to be an act of contrition.

Ewen shrugged. 'Then why not come to me before he died? Why lumber me with all of these bookings to honour? I've got a wedding, craft fairs, and then there's the matter of the annual ball...what would make him take on these commitments? He didn't need the money, so I don't understand why he'd want so many strangers traipsing through the house.'

'From the couple of times I spoke to him, he seemed lonely. When I enquired about accommodation he jumped at the chance to have me here. I think he was looking forward to having someone else in residence. Unlike you.' She dared to tease him, watching for his reaction. Relieved when he didn't appear to take offence. It was refreshing, and novel, to be able to joke around without fearing any potential consequences.

'It's nothing personal. I'm not really the best person to be around right now. I broke up with my girlfriend before I came here. Then, of course, there's the knowledge that I will never see my father again, that we won't have a chance to reconcile. If this wasn't one last chance to dig the knife in deeper...'

Bonnie felt for him. She knew what it was like to have no one to turn to for support. To feel utterly alone and full of regret. She'd been so wrapped up in her own personal issues, she hadn't recognised Ewen might be struggling too. That he was hurting just as much as she was, and perhaps that was why they'd clashed so much at the beginning, only to spend the next few days in isolation licking their respective wounds. She hoped going forward they'd be able to give each other more consideration.

It made her think too about her own family circumstances. Of how she'd left things with her parents, and how she'd been too hurt, too embarrassed by what had happened with Ed to get back in touch. She didn't know what it would do to her if they died without ever having the chance to build some bridges. Perhaps when she was feeling stronger, was more settled in her job, she could offer an olive branch and see if there was a relationship worth salvaging. Unlike Ewen, she still had a chance to reconcile, or get some closure on that part of her life.

'I haven't spoken to my parents for eight years. They knew the man I was seeing was bad news, but I thought they just didn't want me to be happy. That they were trying to control me. Of course, now I know they were right, but I don't want them to know that. It sounds petty, but I'm not ready to face the "we told you so" conversations.'

A lot of hurtful things were said on both sides out of anger and pain. In hindsight, and with a more mature attitude to the situation, Bonnie knew they were only acting out of love. Perhaps all the control issues she'd had with them came down to that—they'd only wanted her to be safe, even if the way they'd gone about it had been difficult to take. She was worried that though she might be ready to forgive and regret, they might not be. They might decide life was better without her in it, and that rejection would be too much for someone still so vulnerable and fragile.

'Trust me, you don't want to be left with regrets. Those conversations you have in your head, of all the things you should've said, how they might have reacted, how different things could have been, will drive you mad. I'm sure they just want you to be safe. Maybe try reaching out with a text or a call first before confronting them face to face.'

What Ewen was saying wasn't unreasonable. A text message wouldn't be too painful. Just a hello to start with, to see if they responded, should suffice for now. As soon as she worked up the courage to send it. After all, she'd done the hard part by leaving the man who had physically and emotionally caused her harm. She should be ready to tackle anything.

'I might do that. Thanks.'

'No problem. At least it will make me feel as though I've achieved something here if I save you from making the same mistakes I did.'

'So what are you going to do about the bookings?' Although she was naturally curious about what had happened to cause such a split in the family, she wasn't ready to share details of her own personal life in return. It was better to focus on the future instead of looking back, especially when he was so concerned about what he was taking on at BenCrag. It was a huge responsibility to pick up where his father had left off, and he seemed convinced he was going to fail.

Even though Ewen had been estranged from his family, to her mind his father had passed on the reins to him because he'd believed he was capable. The best man for the job. All that was needed was for Ewen to have the same belief in himself. She would understand if he didn't honour the bookings, but she didn't see him as someone who gave up at the first sign of trouble. Hopefully he'd realise that continuing with his father's business plans was the right thing to do.

He stretched out his legs with a sigh, crossing his feet at the ankles, and folding his arms across his chest. A real mixed message about being open, and closed, at the same time. He was conflicted. It was only natural when making the big calls. She'd had her fair share of wobbles and worries until she'd eventually worked up the courage to pick up her ready-packed bag and leave her ex.

'That's the million-dollar question, isn't it? If I cancel, it'll ruin the castle's, and the family's, reputation. Not to mention letting down my father. If I honour these bookings, even though I'll have no clue what I'm doing, it's extremely likely I'll let a lot of people down anyway. It's a lose-lose situation for me.'

It might seem like an insurmountable mountain to climb, but if Bonnie had taken that attitude, she would never have made the break from her toxic relationship. Dealing with huge life-changing decisions wasn't easy, but she was willing to help. They needed visitors, and good word of mouth, for the sake of both their jobs. 'Let's start with the wedding…when is it?'

'Next Saturday,' he said with a grimace, which Bonnie matched.

'And you haven't been in contact with the bride and groom yet?' The way he'd been stressing over forthcoming events led her to believe he had yet to make contact with any of the parties involved.

'No. I know, I should've dealt with it, but I really don't know where to start.'

'Well, it's definitely too short notice to cancel a wedding party now. I'd suggest contacting them, telling them the castle is under new ownership and asking for all relevant details about the day. You know, timings, caterers, florists—find out what's already been arranged. Have a look and see if your father has any info too. He's bound to have a record of these things. The housekeeper and estate manager will have information too, I'm sure. Use them. They've probably dealt with this kind of thing before. You don't have to do this alone, Ewen.'

As they were preparing to reopen the castle, the staff had begun to filter back to make it presentable. Bonnie had met a few of the key staff, and they'd been helpful and welcoming. They also seemed to be aware of her appointment on staff too, which helped her feel less like an intruder. She was sure they'd all pull together to make a success of whatever was planned.

Ewen was nodding his head to everything she said. 'You're right. I didn't give anyone a chance to tell me what was in the castle diary, sending everyone away the moment I got here. Hopefully, they won't hold that against me.'

'I can only imagine, given how warmly you greeted me.' She raised an eyebrow, wondering how many other feathers he'd ruffled in the process of becoming the new duke. 'However, you're grieving. I'm sure people will make allowances for that. I did. Because at the end of the day, we're all making our livelihood from this place.'

Despite her honesty, she thought she saw a fleeting look of disappointment cross Ewen's features as she spoke. As much as she was sure everyone on staff loved the castle, they were still employees. They relied on it being a success to get their wages and pay their bills. Not everyone was lucky enough to come from a privileged, wealthy family.

'I deserve that rap over the knuckles.' He stretched out his arm, and Bonnie gave him a playful slap across the back of the hand.

'Yes, you do, but I wasn't on my best behaviour either, so let's leave it in the past.' She'd come out swinging the second he'd confronted her on his doorstep, lashing out like the injured animal she was. Although she still had a long way to go, her defences were gradually being lowered, the claws retracting. That was the only reason she would ever have agreed to be here in his apartment tonight.

With the new truce in place, Ewen clapped his hands together. 'So, any suggestions to make the day special and really put us on the map again?'

Bonnie blinked at him, wondering how she'd managed to get him to get on board so quickly, and get herself involved.

'Well, as long as there are no dietary requirements I need to know about, perhaps I could make some sort of chocolate centrepiece for the reception. It could add something special, and advertise the new shop.' It would also give her more than truffles to showcase her expertise with, if they ever did venture into online marketing with the chocolate shop.

'You could do that? It would give me something positive to lead with when I talk to the couple, in case they're worried about the changes going on.' Ewen was suddenly enthused, sitting up straighter in his chair, his blue eyes bright, and there was a new nervous energy about him. As though, instead of his dreading the forthcoming nuptials, she'd given him something to look forward to.

She didn't want to give him false hope that one chocolate sculpture was going to save the day, but she liked to see him looking more energised about business prospects at the castle. The last thing she needed was the new heir to decide it was more hassle than he wanted to deal with and sell the whole place on. Bonnie was prepared to put in whatever work it took to maintain her new independence. Even if that meant forging a new alliance with her boss. Now it seemed as though she was very much part of the upcoming wedding, and its success…

For the first time since he'd taken over at the castle, Ewen was feeling optimistic. Sitting down with Bonnie tonight had given him a new perspective on things, as well as a chance to get a few things off his chest. Although he hadn't gone into specific details about his break-up with Victoria, Bonnie was the first person he'd actually had a conversation with about it.

Bonnie had also helped to allay some of his fears over the wedding booked for next week, on a practical level. When he'd been confronted with those bookings he'd gone into something of a tailspin, wondering how he was going to pull it all off. Not realising he didn't have to do it all on his own. His father certainly hadn't. He had a team around him who, as Bonnie had pointed out, would have experience dealing with these things. Since leaving home he'd been so used to doing everything for himself, it hadn't occurred to him that there was help available. All he had to do was work with everyone, take their ideas and comments on board, as he had done with Bonnie tonight. It could make the world of difference.

She already had.

He might not have wanted her here, but she'd been a help to him tonight.

'I can't wait to see what you come up with for the centrepiece.' As an app designer, he had some level of creativity, but he was looking forward to seeing what Bonnie's imagination conjured up.

This was clearly important to her. She wanted to make the chocolate shop a success, as much as he did the castle reopening. Goodness knew he didn't want to be seen as a failure in the eyes of his father's friends and peers, when they'd probably heard all sorts about him over the years. None of it likely to be good, given the non-relationship he'd had with his parents. This could be his one and only chance to prove himself, to finally be an asset to his family.

'I'm a bit rusty. It's been a while since I tackled anything on this scale, and I was never allowed to freestyle in my father's shop. With that level of jeopardy, it should make things interesting to say the least.'

Ewen knew she was teasing, but he didn't mind. He could see her testing boundaries with him, pushing to see how he reacted, no doubt ready to fight back if necessary. She was being provocative, wary of the sort of person he might be, but he liked her honesty. Victoria's betrayal had made him cautious about trusting anyone again, but Bonnie was acting in her own best interests as well as his. This new life was all she had and she wanted to protect it. So he was trusting her not to mess things up, for both their sakes.

CHAPTER FOUR

'Yes, I'll look for it later, Mrs McKenzie.' Ewen took a note of his housekeeper's request for his father's address book. It was bound to be in the study, but he had other matters to attend to.

'It's very important, Your Grace. That book contains all of your father's important contacts. We'll need that for the guest list. You know, for the ball.' Her not-so-subtle hint that he'd yet to make a decision on that particular bugbear stopped him mid tread on the staircase.

'Please, call me Ewen. I haven't agreed to that yet. One thing at a time.' He'd prefer to see how this wedding went before he committed to anything more. At least the happy couple had hired a wedding planner who had a very detailed schedule planned down to the last tea rose, so all he had to do was turn up and add an air of nobility to proceedings.

Of course, they needed to ensure the castle was looking its best, but Mrs McKenzie and the estate manager were employing all of their skills to make that happen. Everything seemed to be in hand. Except for the spectacular chocolate centrepiece he'd promised to deliver, which had yet to appear.

'But—but all the residents so look forward to coming here to celebrate every year. It's tradition.' The matronly figure who'd been here when he was a child looked distraught at the very notion celebrations would be postponed. He didn't want to upset her when she was helping him find his feet at the castle, but neither did he want to give her, or the rest of the village, false hope.

'Look, Mrs McKenzie, I appreciate everything you're doing for me. I really do. But hosting a ball is totally different from someone using the castle for a wedding venue. The wedding planner has organised everything for this, co-ordinated the deliveries and the caterers. I'm merely decoration for this.'

'I would help you, as I'm sure Ms Abernathy would. She seems very keen to be part of life here at the castle.' It appeared Bonnie already had a fan, though it came as no surprise when she'd really thrown herself into the castle reopening.

As well as stocking the display cabinet with all sorts of tasty treats, she'd been greeting their visitors with some samples as they arrived for the castle tours. He had no doubt she would jump at the chance to help him host a ball here too, but Ewen wasn't sure if he wanted that. The ball was a gathering for all of the nearby residents, along with some of his father's high status friends. Ewen didn't want to be a hypocrite, throwing an elaborate party and befriending the locals when he planned on selling up at some point. Getting to know people and their circumstances would make it more than a simple business decision and he didn't want any more obstacles in his path. Once his year here was up he'd be moving on somewhere for a completely new start, with no obligations or ties. He certainly didn't need to carry any more guilt with him. It was better that the sale went ahead without any emotional attachments that could potentially throw a spanner in the works.

'Speaking of which… I need to go and make sure she's ready for the big reveal on Saturday. Once the wedding is over, we'll talk again about the ball. And yes, I'll look for the address book,' he called over his shoulder, already continuing his ascent towards the chocolate shop, leaving the sighing housekeeper far behind him.

Much like the rest of the castle now, the shop was empty when Ewen got there. It wasn't surprising, as they'd stopped admitting visitors an hour ago, but they'd been open for a few days and business hadn't exactly been brisk. Even though he wasn't intending to stay beyond the required amount of time stipulated in his father's will, he still needed it to be a viable business to make a profitable sale, and it was concerning. More so if Bonnie wasn't getting the sales she'd hoped for either.

He'd invested in the chocolate shop, buying whatever equipment and ingredients she needed. But it was more than a financial issue. He wanted the shop to be a success for Bonnie's sake. It went against the notion of chasing her away so he could have peace of mind, but he got the impression she needed that confidence boost. The more time they spent around one another, the more he was able to see past her defensive exterior and see that vulnerable centre. Like him, she'd clearly been wounded, and he reckoned they both needed a break.

With no sign of her out front, he walked towards the kitchen. Just in time to hear a clatter on the floor and a short burst of expletives. He gave a cursory knock on the door before he opened it and found Bonnie on her hands and knees on the floor picking up broken shards of chocolate.

'Is everything all right in here?' he asked, eyeing the counter tops littered with trays of chocolate and used equipment. It looked as though a bomb had literally gone off in a sweet shop.

Bonnie shoved her hair out of her eyes to look up at him, smudging chocolate onto her forehead in the process. 'Just dandy. I've lost the castle wall.'

She gathered up the two large flat, broken slabs of chocolate and deposited them into the waste bin with a heavy thud.

'Okay…dare I ask how it's going?' He needed to know, after making promises to the wedding party, that they'd produce something spectacular in chocolate. With a lack of any structure in sight, and the fact she had yet to even mention what she was working on, his anxiety levels were rising dramatically.

Bonnie glared at him, then held out her hands like a disgruntled magician's assistant pointing out the mess surrounding her. 'I need about six pairs of hands to get this done. Every time I try to stick the walls together, another one falls down. I need something to hold them in place whilst I work.'

'What is it you're making?' He wandered around the worktop to have a closer look, where he could see it wasn't simply a mess of broken chocolate and dreams, but very carefully crafted slabs and domes sitting waiting to be assembled.

'Can't you tell?' She grinned, so he didn't feel so bad that he'd failed to recognise whatever it was she'd been slogging over.

'I…er…'

'It's the castle.' She turned the two-dimensional shapes into 3D, lifting up some of the slabs to form walls, and give him a better idea of what she had planned.

It *was* the castle. He could see the turrets waiting to be

added, and she'd even formed a tiny replica of the door knocker on the original oak front door.

'That's amazing.' Although there was a long way to go before completion, he could see the vision she'd had for the final piece. A complete scale model of the castle. All made out of chocolate.

'It might be, if I can get the walls to stick together,' she said, carefully laying down the slabs again.

'Can I do anything to help?'

'Are you serious?'

Ewen nodded. 'We're on the same team, remember? Just tell me where you want me.'

He took off his suit jacket, hung it on the back of a chair, and gave his hands a quick wash and dry at the sink.

'Great! If you could hold this, and this, it leaves me free to try and stick them together.' Bonnie guided his hands with hers to hold two of the larger slabs at an angle.

Her touch was soft, but firm, showing him where he needed to be. It was the closest they'd managed to stand to each other since she'd arrived. Her chestnut hair tickled his nose and he inhaled a deep breath, taking in her scent of vanilla and cocoa, and everything that reminded him of his happier childhood days. Back when his mother used to bake chocolate-chip cookies with him and Ruari in the kitchen. When she used to love him.

Bonnie took a bowl of melted chocolate, using it like a glue to adhere the walls together, then smoothed away any excess with a palette knife. She took out a canister and sprayed the area where she'd just worked.

'What's that, some sort of edible glue?' It looked like a can of spray paint, or something you'd use to oil a creaking joint. He'd hoped that though the sculpture was going to be primarily for show, it would still be edible.

Bonnie smiled. 'It's freeze spray to speed up the process, or else you'll be standing there all night waiting for that chocolate to set.'

She peeled his fingers away and they waited tentatively to see if the structure would hold fast. Sighing their relief when it did.

'Now we just need to do that about a hundred more times,' she said with a grin.

'Whatever it takes. Have you been working on this all day?' He wanted to gently broach the subject of footfall with her to get some idea of sales. If she'd been working mostly in the kitchen today, it suggested she hadn't been particularly troubled at the counter.

'In between sales. There's been a steady trickle of customers since the castle reopened. I think most people stop by, but there's no incentive for them to hang around and spend money, you know? I think we should at least start doing teas and coffees again. I've got all the equipment here, and if business picks up, we could look again at expanding into desserts et cetera. I'm not giving up.'

It was obvious in the set of her jaw that she was determined to put in whatever hours, and work, it took to make this viable. Ewen wasn't going to stand in her way, though he still had to be practical about things pertaining to his side of the business.

'Don't you need hygiene certificates and food-safety awareness before you do that?'

'All of which I have. I needed those even to come here. This was everything I wanted, so the moment I knew it was a possibility to run my own chocolate shop I did all the courses I needed.' Whatever she'd gone through prior to coming here, Bonnie had obviously channelled her strength into something positive. Making plans for her future. Something he had yet to do beyond his obligatory year in residence at BenCrag.

'I suppose we can start with the beverage side of the business and see how it goes from there. Am I done here?' She'd started adding the turrets now the walls were standing without his support, and, now he was satisfied she was going to produce something newsworthy on the day, he could rest easy.

'I can do the rest of the castle myself, thanks. However, I do have about two hundred raspberry and chocolate hearts to make for the wedding guests, if you'd like to assist me?' She pulled out the plastic moulds she was going to be using and set them on the counter in front of him.

Ewen knew to refuse help would seem churlish after promising to support her. It wasn't tiredness, or a lack of interest in the process, that made him hesitate. There was just something, a little warning light going off in his head every time he spent time with Bonnie, that told him to be careful.

Although he knew the end of his relationship with Victoria was best for him, he still missed having someone to share his life with. He didn't want to mistake that loneliness for something else.

With each revelation about Bonnie's courage, her work ethic, not to mention her company, he worried about getting too close to her. They both had baggage to deal with, and he certainly wasn't ready to get involved with anyone again. Not when he was emotionally battered from Victoria's betrayal, and having to relive the way his parents treated him at BenCrag after Ruari's death. The rejection and subsequent abandonment from people he loved, people who were supposed to love *him*, were too great to risk going through it all again with someone else.

Apart from anything else, he didn't know where he was going to be this time next year. Something he knew wasn't going to go down well with Bonnie when this place had been a lifeline for her. Before that happened, he was going to make sure there were provisions for her either here with the new owner, or somewhere more beneficial. Perhaps he could even get her started in her own premises in town. Whatever happened, he wasn't going to let her down the way she had been in the past. Starting with learning how to make raspberry chocolate hearts apparently...

Bonnie could tell he wasn't comfortable being the pupil in this scenario, but, since he'd offered his assistance, she wasn't going to send him away now. It was the only way she was going to get everything done in time without pulling an all-nighter. She'd lectured him on accepting help to achieve his goals, so it would be foolish not to take heed of her own advice. Especially when the stakes were so high.

Although the castle reopening under new ownership had drawn some interest, the already dwindling numbers suggested they couldn't sustain that novelty value for too long. She hoped that the summer holidays would provide more tourists, but they needed something to really pull in a crowd. Working on this showpiece was her way of highlighting her abilities, and making people aware of the shop's existence. Although she had been wondering if she'd bitten off more than she could chew until Ewen had showed up. Now the castle cast in chocolate was beginning to take shape, she was regaining her belief in herself.

Taking a leaf out of the book of other, similar businesses, she wondered if offering chocolate-making classes for children, or even a romantic couples evening of truffle-making, would increase interest and profits. The next initiative, once she proved to Ewen that she was capable of making teas and coffees. Her head was full of ideas and incentives, but he would need convincing that she could produce the goods. Further motivation to get this castle finished.

Ewen rolled up his sleeves as he awaited her instructions. Bonnie couldn't help but smile to herself, enjoying this little bit of temporary power. Tonight she was in charge, a complete role reversal for them both.

'I'll show you how to do the first couple, then you can do the rest. That'll free me up to finish the showpiece.'

Ewen nodded, his brow creased with concentration, obviously taking this more seriously than she'd expected.

'I hope I'll get credit for these when the time comes.'

'Certainly. Especially if they're not up to my standard.' She ignored Ewen's glare to retrieve the bowl of dried raspberries she'd put in the fridge earlier.

'Just show me what I need to do. How hard could it be?' The challenge was there in Ewen's mischievous blue eyes, but Bonnie wasn't going to rise to the baiting. She knew exactly how difficult it was to create something of a high enough standard befitting a wedding. Otherwise she wouldn't have spent the better part of a week perfecting her techniques before tackling this project. Ewen would find out for himself soon enough how much skill it took for something so simple.

And yes, she was running the risk of Ewen making a mess of the treats she'd planned for the wedding guests, and giving herself extra work fixing it all. It would be worth it though, just to see him sweat.

Ewen was sweating already. Bonnie, of course, remained cool as a cucumber as she toiled away on her architectural masterpiece. He'd sprinkled some dried raspberry into the circular moulds, and had now been tasked with tempering the chocolate, via the use of the microwave and a thermometer.

'You should check on that chocolate, Ewen,' she called over her shoulder. 'If you leave it in there too long it could crystallise and you'll have to start over again.'

He definitely didn't want that, when he was already feeling the pressure to get this right.

'Yes, boss.' He knew she liked him to call her that because it made her smile. And, because it made her smile, he'd been saying it frequently. He found himself wanting to please her.

This seemed to be her happy place, working in her chocolate shop, building something spectacular, and he wished he could promise it for ever.

'Check the temperature now,' she instructed as she removed the bowl of chocolate for him and replaced it with a bowl of white chocolate to be zapped.

Once the thermometer registered the required temperature, he checked with Bonnie before proceeding. 'Okay, I think that's it ready now.'

'So, you want to pour that into this thing that looks like a funnel and decant the chocolate into the moulds, until it reaches just below the surface.' Bonnie demonstrated, carefully controlling the amount of melted chocolate dispensed using the lever on the side of the device, before handing it over to him.

Ewen took control, with Bonnie watching from over his shoulder, and squeezed the lever to release the flow of molten chocolate. Worried it was going to come out too fast, he let go, shutting off the steady stream. 'How's that?'

He could hear the grimace in her voice without looking

at her. 'It's a little shy. We need them all consistent, so you can afford to add a little more.'

'Very diplomatic.' He dripped in an extra layer before moving on to the next one, taking his time to get it right. Too much time apparently.

'You need to speed up before the chocolate begins to set and it becomes harder to get out of the dispenser. It doesn't matter if it gets messy, we can tidy that up later.' When she moved to retrieve her own chocolate, Ewen took the opportunity to fill the rest of the tray without an audience, with some varying degrees of success.

'Not bad,' she noted, whilst stirring and testing her own batch, before putting it back in the microwave. Then she took the chocolate dispenser and topped up every single mould to the exact same level. It told of years of practice and expertise that he obviously didn't have, and never would.

'Okay, I admit it, this is harder than it looks.' He held his hands up and watched the smile of triumph cross over Bonnie's lips.

'And?'

'And you're the expert, not me. Clearly.'

As if to show him up even more, she took a spatula, drew it across the back of the mould in one swift move, cleaning away all the excess chocolate to leave perfectly shaped hearts. 'We'll leave those to set and you can get on with doing the rest.'

Ewen groaned, faced with the empty moulds laid out before him, and another bowl of chocolate ready to start the process all over again. Bonnie swirled some green food colouring in with her tempered white chocolate then set to work with a paintbrush, dabbing some moss onto the castle walls and the cliffs below. She truly was a master at work. Now everyone else would get to see it too.

Bonnie was enjoying herself. Now the castle was finally coming together, and Ewen was knocking out the heart-shaped chocolates, with her help, she wasn't feeling the pressure as much. Okay, so trade wasn't where she wanted it to be, but it would take time to build the business and her reputation, so she wasn't going to stress over it yet. Not when she was having so much fun watching Ewen eat humble pie.

Her stomach rumbled with the thought of food. The constant aroma of cocoa and vanilla often quelled her appetite, and she'd worked through lunch today to try and get her centrepiece finished. Ewen's help meant she had a little breathing room and had given her an appetite.

'Have you eaten? I might make an omelette if you'd like one?'

'Sure. Do you need me to get some stuff from the kitchen?'

'No need. I have some supplies here to keep me going through the day. There should be enough to make a couple of omelettes. Ham and mushroom okay for you?'

'Add some cheese and I'm yours for ever.'

Bonnie knew he was only joking, that they were only talking about food here, but Ewen's words sent a shiver along her skin. She grabbed her cardigan from the back of the chair and shrugged it on, refusing to believe the goosebumps could be attributed to anything other than the cool kitchen climate. Certainly not because she was thinking about Ewen's strong, thick forearms, and how it would feel to have them wrapped around her…

'Onion?' She tried to focus on the job at hand, and ended up shouting out randomly, earning her a bemused stare from Ewen.

'Yes, please,' he shouted back.

She turned on the extractor fan, more to cover her embarrassment than to diffuse the smell, and fumes, of her cooking. On autopilot, she diced up the ingredients and added them to the beaten eggs already cooking in the pan. A sprinkle of herbs, then she folded it over, before scooping it onto a plate and setting it in front of Ewen.

He was staring at her.

'Where's yours?'

'I'm going to make it now.' She gestured back at the ingredients spread out on the worktops ready for round two.

He was still staring at her.

'What?' She was worried now that she hadn't cooked it the way he wanted, or had made some sort of social faux pas. It was true, she hadn't cooked for anyone in a long time, so it was possible she'd done something wrong.

'You don't have to serve me, Bonnie. Sit down and eat your dinner first. In fact, I'm a grown man. I can make my own.' He seemed to get increasingly agitated, to the point where he got to his feet and pushed his chair back.

When he came towards Bonnie, she instinctively flinched, drawing a scowl from him in response.

'Sorry,' she squeaked, seeing the look on his face.

'You have nothing to apologise for. I just wanted you to sit down and enjoy your food.' Ewen pulled out the chair for her to sit on and took a step back, letting her reclaim her personal space.

Though Bonnie appreciated the gesture, she hated that he now felt the need to do it. To treat her as something fragile he needed to tiptoe around for fear of breaking her. She had only herself to blame. As usual. He wasn't aware that it was a reflex when a man came near her.

'Thanks.' She sat down, and, though her appetite had

diminished, she stabbed the omelette with her fork. Damn her ex for still having the power to make her feel this way, cowed even by a man she'd battled with nearly every day since they'd met and who'd never once posed a threat to her. Flinching, in anticipation of a blow, was a reaction she didn't know if she'd ever grow out of. It also made her wonder if she'd ever let another man close to her, either as a friend or more. She hated that Ed continued to impact her life without even trying.

She swallowed down her bite of omelette along with the tears she was determined not to shed. Her ex didn't deserve any more of them.

Ewen turned away to make himself some dinner and she was grateful to him for not pushing her for an explanation of her behaviour. She wasn't ready to share the details of her life before BenCrag just yet, if ever. Perhaps being around him would help her realise that not all men acted the way Ed had. She felt more like herself around him. At least until just now, when she'd reverted momentarily to that submissive housewife role she'd been forced to assume for most of her adulthood.

She sawed into the rest of her omelette, forcing herself to finish it and deny Ed another victory. Okay, so he'd broken her, but that didn't mean she was fragile. She was still here, surviving without him, soon to thrive. Proving to him and everyone she wasn't a victim, but a warrior who would fight back with everything she had in her. It helped that Ewen could see that in her, even when he'd known her for only a short while. Letting her know that the old Bonnie was still a part of her.

'This is becoming something of a habit,' Ewen said, sitting down at the table opposite her with his burnt omelette offering.

'Pardon me?'

'Us. Having dinner together.' Ewen prodded his omelette, inspecting it before he dared to eat any of it.

'Well, it's weird pretending we're not ostensibly living together. I don't suppose it hurts to have some company every now and again.' Especially if she was going to freak out every time she was alone with a man. At least socialising with Ewen might go some way to helping her learn to trust again.

'Don't flatter me too much.' He feigned offence, but Bonnie could tell he wasn't too bothered.

Although he'd been spiky when they first met, often stressed over the happenings at the castle, he didn't strike her as someone who would go out of his way to hurt anyone. So far tonight Ewen had been nothing but considerate of her feelings, and her emotional hang-ups, despite not knowing all the details. The hallmarks of a good man.

'As if I would,' she sparked back, and moved to the sink to deposit her dirty dishes.

When she felt him moving behind her to leave his now empty plate in the sink too, she tensed, though did her best not to react the way she had earlier.

'I don't know what happened to you in the past, Bonnie, but I would never hurt you,' he said softly, his kindness undoing her so that tension in her body melted away.

She turned around to face him. 'I know.'

The small space between them was suddenly filled with an air of expectation and anticipation. A feeling that something was about to happen.

'Would it be okay if I gave you a hug?' he asked, though he didn't move.

'I'd like that.' She loved that he was asking permission to even comfort her. Understanding that she needed to take control of who touched her body, how, and why, without knowing anything of her circumstances. Realising that right now a hug was a huge step for her. As was trusting a man to touch her without expecting anything in return or lashing out if she didn't acquiesce to his needs.

Ewen wouldn't take offence if she walked away right now, seeking sanctuary alone in her room. Except an unconditional hug was everything she'd needed for such a long time.

When he opened his arms wide, she went willingly to him. Let him wrap her up in his strong embrace and hold her close to his solid chest.

'You're safe here, Bonnie.'

It wasn't clear if he meant safe in the castle, or in his arms, but she knew she wanted to remain in both for the foreseeable future.

CHAPTER FIVE

'HAVE YOU SEEN the bride?' Ewen sidled up to Bonnie and whispered into her ear.

Since letting him hold her two nights ago in the kitchen, she'd learned to enjoy the warmth of his body near her, rather than fear it. Even if the moments after had proved a little awkward. She'd thanked him for his help with the chocolate making, before retiring back to her room out of harm's way. Where she'd had to deal with the new emotions he'd brought to the fore.

It wasn't just that it was a new experience to have someone show her so much compassion, there was something more beneath that solace he provided. She liked him. Yes, he was handsome, as illustrated by the Harris tartan kilt and jacket he was wearing today. But there was also a bond forming between them, despite their obvious differences. He was wealthy, upper class, whilst she was broke and essentially homeless without his assistance. Yet there was a vulnerability she recognised in him. He'd been hurt too. Not physically perhaps, but he was nonetheless scarred. They were both battle weary, yet it seemed as though they'd begun to open up to one another. Ewen was making her transition back into the real world a little easier. And had she mentioned how hot he was in the formal outfit he'd begrudgingly put on for the wedding today?

'Earth to Bonnie. Did you hear me? The bride has apparently gone AWOL. That wedding planner is going nuts outside.' The concern in Ewen's voice drew Bonnie's attention away from his thick, hairy legs to the real reason she was standing here at the entrance to the function room.

She'd only come to watch the ceremony from a distance, not play a part, except that of chocolatier. Unlike Ewen, who was playing genial host, she was background staff only. So she didn't know why he was coming to her now with this news.

'I'm sure she'll turn up. The bridal car has probably just been held up somewhere.' With the money that had been spent on this event, there was no doubt in Bonnie's mind that it would be going ahead.

'The car is already here. The bridesmaids said she went to the bathroom when they got here and disappeared. What am I going to do, Bonnie?' The panic was evident in his voice and his wide eyes.

She wanted to tell him it wasn't her problem, hell, it wasn't even his problem. However, he'd dug her out of a hole on two occasions now. It was also important to both of them that today went well. The least she could do was help him look for their runaway bride.

'Okay. I'll check the ladies' bathroom, then meet you out front in the garden.'

Ewen nodded at the suggestion, probably glad for something productive to do rather than letting pure panic set in. There was a room full of expectant wedding guests, a groom sweating at the end of the aisle, and a bewildered registrar constantly checking his watch, probably because he had another ceremony to go to after this one. At least the pianist, who'd been drafted in along with his very expensive piano just for the occasion, was managing to entertain the waiting congregation with a selection of popular show tunes in the meantime.

'Janey? Are you in there?' Bonnie ducked her head into the bathroom and called out, but there was no one inside. The halls of the castle appeared to be littered with worried bridesmaids tottering on impossible heels, attached to their phones.

Assuming by the hysterical voices that the blushing bride hadn't come out of hiding, Bonnie left the band of cerise-silk-clad worrywarts behind and headed outside. Ewen had wandered down by the beautiful wisteria-covered pergola. The sun shining through the lilac blossoms created a fiery red halo effect around his head. He looked quite the romantic lead and could almost have passed for the groom himself. Though she was sure he wasn't any more interested in getting married than she was. Bonnie suspected it would take a great deal of trust for either of them ever to enter into a long-term commitment like that again.

'Any joy?' he asked as she made her way over to him.

She shook her head and watched the hope die in his eyes. 'If she's changed her mind, shouldn't we leave her be? Clearly she doesn't want to be found.'

This was apparently more than a bride having a bathroom break. If Janey had seen some last-minute red flags and decided not to tie herself to this man for the rest of her life, Bonnie wanted to respect that.

'It does suggest that she's upset and I wouldn't want to leave her out here alone.'

Damn it, he was so logical sometimes, as well as considerate.

'Okay, I'll help look for her, but I want you to promise we're not going to force her to go back there. I don't want her to feel under pressure to do something she doesn't want to.'

'I totally understand. I just want to make sure she's all right. Cross my heart.' He made the action of the cross on the left side of his chest. That was enough to convince Bonnie they weren't going to be complicit in aiding another toxic relationship.

'Well, if it was me running away from my groom and a room full of people, I wouldn't be standing under this photo-op pergola in full view. I think we should look somewhere a little more inconspicuous. You know this place better than I do—any suggestions?' They were a tad isolated up here on the cliffs. A bride in a full wedding dress would have been noticeable running down the driveway, so she imagined Janey had retreated into the trees, seeking shelter like a lost lamb.

In a way that was probably what she was. There'd been plenty of times when Bonnie had felt alone, not knowing where she was going, or how to get out of the situation she was in. Ewen was right. She needed someone to reassure her, and, if necessary, book her a taxi out of here as soon as possible.

'There are a few hidden gems further back in the trees where we used to hide out when we were kids.' It wasn't more than a brief mention of his brother, but Bonnie knew it was bound to cause him pain. Whilst that wasn't something she could assist him with, she was able to help him in his current quest.

'Lead the way.' She hung back and let him forge a path down to the trees along the estate boundary, following behind and wishing she hadn't worn heels.

Away from the expertly trimmed lawns, and carefully tended gardens around the castle, the surrounding woods were a wild tangle of trees and brush. It would have been a haven for two young brothers to explore. Bonnie wasn't sure how well it suited a bride in a full meringue gown when even she was in danger of having her modest, not at all poofy, strappy floral sundress torn to shreds. Ewen, on the other hand, was striding through briar and bramble in his kilt, looking every inch a true highlander. He had such a capable strength about him that she couldn't imagine him ever being hurt by anything, yet someone had clearly wounded him deeply. It made her wonder if that tough exterior was the armour he chose to wear now to prevent further injury, and what he'd been like before all of the heartache.

Not that it mattered to her, when he was still the man who'd held her in his arms, given her a job and a place to stay. The person he was now was everything she needed. She just wished he'd never had to go through the things he had to get here.

'We used to have a den down here made out of broken branches and bits of old fencing. It was nothing more than a lean-to, really, that would have collapsed on top of us with little effort. But it was special. It was ours, you know?' He stopped long enough to give her a hangdog look that said he missed those simple, carefree days.

Bonnie didn't remember having any of those. Even as a child she'd had her father telling her what to do, spending her spare time working in the shop, which had felt like a punishment then. Now she was grateful for the skills she'd learned in his chocolate shop. She was glad Ewen had some happier memories to look back on.

'Did you come down here a lot?' She was sure life in a castle had been much different from growing up above a chocolate shop, but things were never as much fun as they appeared from the outside. Her friends used to be jealous

of her easy access to the sweet stuff, and yes, she had pur-
loined some of the stock to buy friends with at times, but
life at home had always been hard work.

'Whenever we could. We'd take food from the kitchen
and bring our comics down here to read. All Ruari's doing,
of course. Believe it or not, he was the troublemaker, leading me astray.' His lopsided smile told of how close he'd
been to his brother, and just how much he missed him.

Bonnie wanted nothing more in that moment than to
offer him comfort, but she knew from experience coming
into close contact with him wasn't something easily forgotten. A hug wasn't just a hug when she never wanted to
leave his embrace. A frightening revelation for her when
she needed to assert her independence, and not throw her
lot in with another man.

'I'm not going back.' A voice sounded somewhere from
the trees, interrupting Bonnie and Ewen's heart-to-heart
before she did something she might regret. Bonnie was
grateful for it.

'Janey?' It took a moment before Bonnie realised where
the voice had come from. Then the bride appeared, re-
splendent in white lace and satin, from an old arbour hidden in the thicket.

Janey hitched up the train of her dress as though she was
getting ready to run again.

Ewen held up a hand to appease her. 'We're just here to
make sure you're all right.'

'You don't have to do anything you don't want to, Janey,
but you can't stay out here for ever.' There would come a
time when she would have to face up to her situation and
make a decision about her future. Bonnie just hoped she
didn't take as long as she had.

'I know. I'm sorry if I've spoiled the day. I suppose everyone's waiting for me back there.' Janey sat down on the wrought-iron seat that had been hidden from Bonnie's view by the ivy-covered trellis around it.

She took a seat beside the anxious bride and took her hand. 'Don't worry about anyone else. If you've decided you don't want to go through with this, I'm sure we can get a car to take you some place away from the madness.'

Bonnie looked to Ewen, who nodded. 'I have my car. Just give me the word and I'll take you anywhere you want to go.'

'I just need a minute to think things through and make sure this is really what I want,' Janey explained, and Ewen and Bonnie both fell silent.

Except a million thoughts were running through Bonnie's head that she could never live with herself if she didn't voice out loud. It mightn't make any difference, just as her parents' opinions hadn't mattered to her before she'd committed to the wrong man, but Bonnie thought it worth trying.

'Has Lawrence done anything to…to hurt you?' She knew it was a difficult subject to tackle, but one she couldn't in good conscience shy away from.

Janey stared at her. 'You mean like cheated, or anything? No. He's very loyal.'

'No… I mean has he ever…physically hurt you, or tried to tell you what to do, how to behave?' She could feel Ewen's eyes burning into her, looking for answers as to why she should ask such a question. Though she hadn't intended on sharing details of her past with anyone, it was more important to save Janey from making the same mistakes she had.

There were always warning signs of a potentially controlling partner, even if that blinding love often masked the problems at first. In hindsight, her ex was always calling, checking in with her, seeing who she was with and what she was doing. Young and naïve, she'd liked the attention, believing it was his way of showing how much he cared. That he was always thinking about her. She hadn't seen him gradually exerting control over her until it was too late and she had nowhere else to go.

Ewen coughed discreetly, his subtle way of telling her not to interfere. Perhaps even that she was crossing a line, but she didn't know where she would've ended up if she'd actually married her ex. If Janey was having doubts now, it didn't bode well for the future.

'What? No?' Janey was frowning at her, obviously outraged.

Bonnie blushed, aware that she'd projected her own issues onto the woman. Though she supposed it was good news that Lawrence wasn't a potentially abusive scumbag. 'Sorry. I just wanted to check that this wasn't a cry for help.'

'I didn't ask for help. I came here for some time alone. Lawrence is a kind, loving man I am lucky to be marrying.' In a fit of pique, she gathered up her skirts and stomped off out of the woods, leaving Ewen and Bonnie staring at one another.

Ewen couldn't keep the look of concern from his face. 'Are you okay?'

'What? Yes. I'm fine,' Bonnie huffed, embarrassed that he'd witnessed her epic fail, revealing way too much of her own issues in trying to help the bride. It appeared she still had a long way to go with her own healing, as well as her social skills.

'Bonnie, I get the impression that something happened before you came to BenCrag. Do you want to talk about it?'

'No. The bride's gone back to her groom, that's all that

matters.' Her eyes were prickling with tears because of the memories she'd conjured, all in vain apparently. It was clear she hadn't left the past entirely behind after all. Especially when Ewen could tell she was keeping some sort of big dark secret to herself. Bonnie didn't want him to know she'd been weak and let someone take advantage of her to the degree that Ed had, but clearly keeping it to herself hadn't worked.

In an effort to retain some of her dignity, Bonnie attempted to flounce off too. Only to stick her foot straight into the end of a log lying in her path. She found herself falling forward, feeling as though it were happening in slow motion as she did her best to maintain her balance, though she knew the end was inevitable. Her dignified exit was going to end up with her face first in the dirt. With Ewen there to watch her further humiliation.

Except, before she got a face full of moss and twigs, a strong pair of arms grabbed her around the waist from behind and pulled her back upright. Ewen knocked the wind out of her as she hit his chest with a thump.

'Sorry. Did I hurt you?'

'No. I, er…you've got quick reflexes.' She blurted out the second thing that came into her head. Glad she didn't voice the first. Otherwise Ewen would know how much she liked the intimate feel of him against her. Although her almost purr might have given it away…

'I wouldn't want you to turn up to your big event with mud on your face.'

Maybe she was imagining it, but she thought Ewen's voice was deeper than usual as he spoke directly into her ear. She definitely wasn't flinching any more when he came close to her. If anything, her body was responding to him in a way she hadn't felt in a long time. Being around him had made her realise not all men were to be feared, and that had let other sensations take over. Excitement. That the awareness of a solid male body could awaken more than terror inside her. *Desire*. Something she didn't know if she was ready to explore again, and certainly not with her boss.

He eventually let go of his hold on her and she brushed herself down. Wiping away the feel of him against her, and all of those emotions she wasn't ready to deal with yet.

'My big event…' She gave a fake laugh. 'I'm not the one getting married.'

'No, but it's a new chapter in your life too. I know you'll want to look your best.' He gave her a smile and Bonnie could see he genuinely cared. Ewen seemed to understand what she needed, and when. Always there to catch her and put her back on her feet. If she wasn't careful, she'd come to rely on him, and that was when the trouble would really start.

'You can talk to me, Bonnie.' Ewen didn't want to let the matter drop. He could tell she'd been through something traumatic and wanted to help. There'd been certain comments that had raised his suspicions about her ex, added to the circumstances of her arrival when she'd come to Ben-Crag homeless and broke. Then there was the way she'd flinched in the kitchen when he'd come near her. He'd held back from asking at the time, wanting only to reassure her he wasn't a threat, to support her and offer the hug they'd both needed.

Now, hearing her counsel someone else about the dangers of an abusive partner, things were beginning to add up to an unpalatable scenario. He could no longer hold his tongue, and wanted her to know he was there for her.

Though their relationship had been antagonistic at the

start, they were clearly two lonely, wounded people. He knew what it was like to suffer emotionally, with no family or friends around to turn to. It was human nature to want to help Bonnie and he tried not to read any more than that into it.

'About what?' She blinked at him, feigning an ignorance that didn't suit her.

Ewen narrowed his eyes. 'You. Your ex. It doesn't take a genius to work out something seriously bad happened there. I just want you to know I'm here if you want to talk about it.'

Bonnie stared at him, her eyes filling with tears and something that looked very like fear. He swore and wrapped his arms around her in a hug. Despite her defensive nature, there was something about her that made him want to protect her, now more than ever. As though he knew she was just as vulnerable inside as he was.

Only when her face was buried in his chest did she deign to speak. 'I let Ed control me for ten years. Who I spoke to. What I wore. Everything. And it still wasn't enough to make him happy.'

'Did he hurt you?' Ewen's jaw tightened even as he said the words. He hated to think of any man thinking it was okay to raise a hand to a woman, but to imagine Bonnie cowering in terror under the threat of violence made his blood boil.

She was such a feisty spirit, the level of control it would have taken to make her submit to someone else's will was unimaginable.

He felt her nod against him and his heart broke into a thousand pieces for her.

'I'm so sorry. Is there anything I can do?' It seemed like such a clichéd thing to say, but he felt powerless in the circumstances. He wanted to make things better for her, to take away the pain, all the while knowing it was impossible.

Bonnie pried herself away from his body, and, though he wanted to keep her safe in his embrace for ever, getting her to open up was a huge step. One she likely needed to take so she could begin to heal.

'He's in prison. The women who took me in at the refuge persuaded me to report him to the police. So he won't be free for some time. There's no need to turn vigilante on my account.' She gave him a half-hearted smile, which did little to persuade him she was okay. For her abuser to end up in prison suggested it had been a serious assault. Something Bonnie did not deserve under any circumstances.

'I'm so sorry you had to go through all of that, and for how I treated you on your arrival here. I can only say I'd just gone through a break-up too. Nothing as serious as yours, of course, but I was licking my wounds when you turned up, and not in the mood for company. You deserved better and I'm sorry.'

He understood now why she'd been so combative at the time. She'd been fighting to keep hold of the new start that had been promised to her, trying to leave all the bad stuff that had happened behind. Yet instead of providing support, he'd done everything to try and get rid of her. Adding to her stress because he'd wanted to wallow alone.

'It's not your fault. I guess we were both a bit tender at the time. So, did your partner not want to become lady of the manor, then?' Bonnie was angling for some information and it would be churlish of him not to share after she'd poured her heart out to him. Even if it was embarrassing to admit he hadn't been good enough for Victoria.

'She never got the opportunity. By the time I'd heard about my father, Victoria had already found someone with a bigger bank account and title. I think I was just a place-holder until someone better came along.'

'Well, I'm sure she's kicking herself now.' Bonnie offered him a bright smile that was much nicer to see on her face than the pain of reliving her recent troubles. The one positive to come out of his humiliating love life.

'I don't know about that, but I do believe we weren't right for each other.' In hindsight, he'd always been holding a part of himself back. He'd been hurt so much by his parents' rejection he'd been afraid to give his heart completely. The only part of Ewen Harris Victoria had really known was the successful businessman. He hadn't shared anything of his family life, or the strained relationship he'd had with his parents. Bonnie hadn't been here long and she knew more about him than Victoria ever had, illustrating the fact that he'd never felt comfortable enough around her to just be himself. Perhaps he'd been so keen to fill the void left by his family that he'd clung onto the relationship even when it clearly hadn't been working. It had taken being around Bonnie to understand that.

Victoria wouldn't have settled for takeaway in front of the telly, or chased runaway brides with him. And he certainly had never felt able to open up emotionally to her. The split was probably a blessing in disguise, it had simply taken him this long to see that. Now all he had to worry about was what this bond between him and Bonnie meant for the future he'd planned away from the castle.

'You did a good job with Janey,' Ewen whispered as the happy couple took their seats at the top table. After the short delay, and with the congregation none the wiser about the bride's emotional breakdown in the garden, or their hosts' heart-to-heart, Janey and Lawrence had exchanged their vows and joined together in holy matrimony.

Bonnie narrowed her eyes at him, as though she was waiting for the punchline, but she'd been brave in asking the questions she had. It had focused Janey on the important things too, helping her realise she had a good man, and it was just wedding-day jitters after all. Hearing of her experiences had also given him a better insight into the woman he was working with. Given him more reason to admire her, even though his head was telling him to fight against it.

'I'm serious. They look happy.' He supposed he was envious of that, though both he and Bonnie had reason to be sceptical about romance when they'd been conned by it in the past.

'I'm pleased for them.'

Now it was Ewen's turn to look sceptical.

Bonnie nudged him with her elbow. 'Hey, I'm sure it works for some people. And if you're going to be vying for wedding venue of the year, then you need to start playing the role of host with a little more enthusiasm.'

'You want me to start weeping tears of joy? I'm afraid I'm not the sentimental type.' Finding out about Victoria's betrayal had made him cynical about the whole idea of marriage.

Once upon a time he'd imagined they'd get married, have children, and be a family. Something he hadn't been part of for a long time. Looking back, he could see she wasn't the type of woman who would've been content with the vision he had for two-point-four children and a Labrador. Victoria enjoyed the party lifestyle too much to give it up for cosy nights in, and she'd never professed otherwise. Ewen had been the one who'd pretended to be someone he wasn't to impress her. Splurging on luxury holidays abroad, partying with the rich and famous, when all he really wanted was someone to settle down with. Now he'd had some time and space to see things more clearly, he realised Victoria hadn't been entirely to blame for the breakdown in their relationship. She might have cheated on him, but he hadn't been honest with her about who he was, or what he wanted. The family he'd been missing for so long.

Now he didn't think he'd ever let anyone close enough to even think of marriage again. He could only imagine the pain he'd endure if he married someone, shared his life with them, and they later cheated on him. Once was enough. Further proof that he wasn't worthy of love, on top of his parents' rejection. Well, he didn't intend to put himself through any more heartache. Single life seemed the way to go if he was ever going to have peace.

'I don't believe that for a second. Otherwise you wouldn't be doing this in the first place.' Bonnie reminded him that hosting this wedding hadn't been a foregone conclusion. He would've been within his rights as the new owner, not to mention a grieving son, to cancel the booking. Fulfilling the obligation had been more about honouring his father's wishes than appeasing the couple making a lifetime commitment to one another.

Perhaps he and his parents hadn't had much of a relationship in Ewen's adult years, but he had hoped, by honouring his father's commitments, he would find some sort of closure. So far, it remained elusive.

'Well, I guess I can only try to hold it together. Looks like it's showtime.' As the guests babbled excitedly at the table, waiting for the speeches to begin, Ewen knew it was expected of him to say a few words first.

His hands were sweating as he walked up to take the mic, even though he was used to speaking in public. Setting up his own business, and subsequently selling it, had meant having to be vocal, able to sell himself. After leaving home he'd had to do everything himself, and he'd learned to control his nerves in this kind of situation. But championing newly-weds was definitely out of his comfort zone given his recent history.

He felt Bonnie's hand on his back. 'Go get 'em, tiger.'

It put a smile on his face, and a want to forget all the other people in the room and stay with her. Every time they touched he was reminded he had an ally, that he was no longer on his own. It didn't matter that Bonnie was technically an employee, only here due to the fact she had nowhere else to go, because they had a connection beyond that. Despite all his intentions otherwise, he had let someone in. He'd only known Bonnie a matter of days, yet he felt more comfortable talking about his feelings with her than someone he'd lived with for years. It was both refreshing, and terrifying.

And that was before he even tackled the way she made him feel. Beyond his admiration, and the kinship, that she evoked in him, there was something more primal awakening inside him. A want to protect her from any more harm, but also a desire he knew he could never follow up on. That night in the kitchen he'd enjoyed having her in his arms, her soft warmth pressed against him. Today, catching her in the woods, he'd wanted the same again. He'd resisted not only because it would complicate things when they were working and living together, but also because he didn't think Bonnie would welcome it. Although she'd gone willingly to him for comfort once, it didn't mean she was ready for anything more. He knew he wasn't either.

Never mind that he wasn't prepared to risk his heart on anyone again, he also didn't have any intention of sticking around longer than necessary. After everything she'd been through, Bonnie wasn't the kind of woman who could be picked up and dropped at will. She deserved more. Nothing good could come out of acting on whatever these growing feelings for her were. Experience had told him that getting close to anyone only ended in heartbreak for him. The best he could hope was that these feelings would gradually fade away and save them both the pain that seemed to come with emotional attachment. For him at least.

For the time being, romance had to be reserved for paying customers at the castle only.

Ewen took the microphone and addressed the assembled guests, his eyes firmly on Bonnie at the back of the room to keep him grounded. 'Good afternoon, everyone. I'm the owner of BenCrag Castle, the current Duke of Arbay, and I'd like to thank you all for joining us to congratulate the marriage of Lawrence and Janey.'

He started a round of applause and turned to give a nod to the couple of the moment, continuing his speech once the clapping finished. 'I just want to wish you both the very best for the future. Love doesn't come around for everyone, and you're very lucky to have found it with each other. Thank you for sharing your big day with us at the castle, and as a gift from us to you, to mark the occasion, we have a special treat. Our resident chocolatier, Bonnie Abernathy, has created an entirely edible scale model of the castle for you.'

Bonnie took her cue and unveiled her chocolate masterpiece with a nervous smile. As he'd hoped, the reveal was met with a chorus of oohs and wows, along with a loud round of applause.

'We also have raspberry chocolate hearts for everyone, made by our very own duke.' She clapped and directed attention back to him.

'I'd like to raise a glass and toast our happy couple before I hand you over for the speeches. To the bride and groom.' Ewen helped himself to a glass of champagne from a tray nearby and lifted it into the air, the rest of the guests joining in. He was glad when he was finally able to hand over the microphone to the wedding party, and jog back to Bonnie.

'Good job.' She patted him on the back as though he'd been the one who'd been slaving away for days, rather than someone who'd simply microwaved a bowl of chocolate and poured it into moulds.

'Hey, I did the easy part. Everyone can see where the real work was. Fingers crossed it leads to extra business for us both.' In these days of social media, and the obsession with photographing everything, Ewen hoped the guests would share images of the day far and wide.

'I've left some business cards on the table beside the chocolates. Maybe next time we should open the shop, or set up a stall in the hall for passing trade.'

Ewen knew she was joking, but he loved Bonnie's entre-preneurial spirit. It showed her ambition for the future. One he was sure he wouldn't be around to be a part of, and suddenly he was having second thoughts about his own plans.

'Ugh. You mean we have to do this all over again? You want to go to the bar? I think I need a drink.' Anything to blot out thoughts about the tasks he had ahead, and how much Bonnie was going to hate him in a year's time. He wanted to enjoy her company whilst he still had it.

CHAPTER SIX

'THANK GOODNESS THAT'S OVER.' Bonnie sat down opposite Ewen with a glass of white wine and kicked off her
shoes. It was the first time they'd had a chance to really
relax. With the bride and groom off to start their honey-
moon, and taxis steadily arriving for the rest of the guests,
the pressure was off.

Of course she could have left once she'd delivered her
part of the deal, but Ewen had seemed as though he could
use the backup. Once the formalities were over, and drink
had been consumed, he'd been besieged by guests all wanting selfies with the handsome, kilted duke. She'd had her
fair share of attention too with people congratulating her
on her work and making enquiries about other custom creations. A sideline she would have to run by Ewen if anything came to fruition. The day had been a lot for two
people who'd been rattling around the castle on their own
for some time.

'Thanks for sticking around. I appreciate it.' Ewen held
up his whisky and clinked his glass to hers.

'Where else would I be? I mean, the sound in this place
really travels so I may as well be here, watching you
schmooze your fan club.' Bonnie was poking fun at the
attention he'd received, mostly from the female members

of the wedding party, but she could hear the tinge of bitterness in her voice.

Seeing him smiling and posing with his arm around random, glamorous women had woken something inside her. Something green, territorial, and beating its chest with rage. She didn't want to see him touching anyone else. Perhaps that was part of the reason she'd stayed on. To scare off potential suitors. Okay, and she also wouldn't be able to rest in another part of the castle thinking he was here partying with everyone else, without her. It was clear she was becoming closer to Ewen than she'd been prepared for, and she didn't know what to do about it.

'Hi. I really wanted to say what an amazing job you did of the chocolate. The raspberry hearts were amazing.' A young blonde, wearing a short turquoise strapless dress and a phenomenal amount of fake tan, approached their table.

'Thank you, but it was Ewen who made those...' Bonnie trailed off when she realised the woman wasn't even looking at her, her eyes locked onto her companion.

'They were yummy.' The blonde's now husky voice didn't sound as though she was still talking about the chocolates. Especially with that look in her eyes that said she was ready to devour Ewen, whether Bonnie was there or not.

'Feel free to drop into the shop to buy more any time. Bonnie has a wide variety of flavours in store.' Bless Ewen, he was doing his best to big up her shop, when it was clear Blondie had no interest in anything but him.

Bonnie didn't think he could be oblivious to the woman's interest. She wondered if he was just being polite, or if he didn't want to make a play for her in front of Bonnie. Either way she wasn't going to stick around to watch. She drained her glass and got up to leave.

'Can you take a pic of me and the duke?' Ewen's admirer thrust her phone at Bonnie and proceeded to sit in his lap. He didn't do anything to dissuade her.

Bonnie snapped a couple of pics then tossed the phone back at her. 'Here. I'll leave you two to it.'

She walked away, jaw clenched, hackles rising, and confused about why. Ewen wasn't hers, and she wasn't in any position to claim him even if he wanted her. He was the first man she'd really had contact with since leaving her ex. The only one she'd had any interest in. It terrified her that she was even thinking about opening her heart up to someone else when she was hurting already simply by being in the same room as him.

She didn't want to have these feelings for her boss and landlord, who already had more control over her life than she was comfortable with. If she lost herself to him, and things didn't work out, she would lose everything again. A relationship simply wasn't possible when there was so much at stake. Especially so soon after she'd left the last one. Her life at BenCrag was supposed to be a new start, her time to find herself again, and she wouldn't do that if she was mooning over someone she couldn't, and shouldn't, have. She only wished she could walk away from her feelings as easily as the scene at the bar.

She was about to climb the marble stairway up to her room when someone grabbed her arm. Ewen.

'Where are you going?'

'Bed.'

'Oh…did I do something to upset you? I thought we were having a nice time.' He looked genuinely puzzled as to why she'd want to leave.

'No offence, but I didn't want to be a gooseberry. You looked as though you were having a better time with your new friend.'

A slow smile across Ewen's lips. 'Wait...are you jealous?'

Bonnie shrugged his hand off her arm, not wanting him to touch her when she needed to be mad at him, instead of enjoying the contact.

She spat out a laugh. 'As if. It's nothing to do with me if you like having women drape themselves over you for attention.'

His smile grew broader until he was flashing his even white teeth, clearly enjoying tormenting her. 'You are. You're actually jealous.'

Bonnie couldn't even deny it when it was so obvious. So she gave him an eye roll and an exasperated tut, before attempting to walk away again.

'Wait. I'm sorry. I was only teasing. I didn't mean to be rude and leave you feeling like a spare part. I'm just not used to this. I've never really had to play up the whole family-connection thing before. It's a novelty for people. I don't take it too seriously. You shouldn't either.'

Bonnie didn't want him to be upset when he'd been having a good day. A rare thing for both of them, she suspected.

'When we first met I saw you as more of a Viking lumberjack. All outdoorsy and intimidating. Now I know you're really a homebody who likes takeaway in front of the TV.' Somebody she felt comfortable with, who made her feel as though she wasn't alone any more.

'Shh!' Ewen put his finger to her lips. 'That doesn't make me sound very glamorous.'

Despite the teasing tone, the energy between them had become something altogether more serious. He was standing so close, his finger was practically the only thing between their lips. She was very tempted to push it out of the way. Instead, she put a step even farther over that line.

'It's all I need.' She held eye contact with him, saw the darkening of his pupils, the tic in his jaw as he clenched his teeth together. There was a power in knowing, seeing, that she affected him just as much as he did her.

Her gaze fell to his mouth. She wanted to feel his lips hard and insistent on hers. His beard grazing her skin, turning her insides to mush in the process. It was nice to feel something other than fear being this close to a man again. Even if it still represented a danger of sorts. Though, in that moment, she didn't care about the repercussions of straying beyond the boundaries of their working relationship. All that mattered was the notion that he was about to kiss her.

'Your Grace, the last of the guests are leaving. Do you need me to stay on?'

Their moment was interrupted by the arrival of the housekeeper, who was either oblivious to their current situation, or too discreet to make a big deal out of it. She stood patiently waiting for a response as Bonnie and Ewen scrambled to regain their personal space from one another. The sudden separation and change of mood left her head spinning. Ewen, too, seemed flustered, not at all his usual confident self.

'Mrs McKenzie…we were just, er, discussing the, er—'

'We'll tidy up. You go on home.' Bonnie couldn't bear to watch him try to come up with an excuse and jumped in. Then realised that she didn't have any authority to say any such thing. 'That's if it's all right with you, Your Grace?'

'Yes. Of course. That's just what we were discussing, Mrs McKenzie. You've done so much already, it wouldn't be fair to expect you to stay any later.' Ewen was a bad liar, stumbling through his explanation so much Bonnie couldn't help but smile.

She liked that manipulating the truth to suit himself

didn't come easily. It wasn't likely he did it on a regular basis when he was rambling so much just to cover up the fact they'd almost kissed. It was reassuring after being with a man who drove her crazy twisting her words until she hardly recognised the truth. She didn't imagine he was someone who felt the need to exert control over her, or any-one else, with lies. Or his fists. In any other circumstances Ewen would seem like the perfect man, but it was difficult to get past the fact he held all the cards in the relationship they already had. To throw her heart into the ring along with her financial stability would be madness.

Even Mrs McKenzie could see through his poor attempt at an excuse, folding her arms with a sigh, eyeing Bonnie with some suspicion. Goodness knew what she'd seen at the castle over the years when this little interaction didn't raise any more than an eyebrow.

'The caterers are packing away their dishes now, so there shouldn't be too much mess left.' She took her leave, only to turn back a second later. 'Oh, and any more thoughts on the annual ball, sir?'

Ewen grimaced. 'I'll get back to you on that, and yes, I'll take another look for that address book. Goodnight, Mrs McKenzie.'

'Goodnight.'

'So I guess I'm not going to bed, then?' Bonnie resigned herself to the fact she'd be spending the rest of the night cleaning up the mess left behind by the inebriated wedding guests, and nothing more exciting.

Even if she and Ewen had decided to lose their minds and act on the attraction brewing between them, Mrs McK-enzie's interruption had given her an opportunity to think things through more clearly. The moment had passed now she remembered they still had to live and work together.

She wasn't ready for a relationship with anyone, least of all her boss. Nor was she the sort of person to go for one-night stands. Especially when they'd have to see each other every day at work. Giving into temptation now would only make things awkward between them in the future. She didn't want that, not when she'd found someone who made her feel safe for the first time in years.

'I'm sorry if you felt pressured into volunteering for clean-up duty.' Ewen walked back down the stairs with Bonnie, watching as the last of the staff, including Mrs McKenzie, left the building.

'It's okay. What else would I be doing anyway?' Other than perhaps making the second biggest mistake of her life, sleeping with her boss, and ruining the best thing to happen to her in a long time. She was trying not to think about the pros of that scenario, and how they might be working up a sweat under more exciting conditions.

He locked the doors, leaving them alone for the first time that day. Bonnie didn't want to wait around for that lightning to strike again. They mightn't escape it a second time, and ran the risk of getting frazzled in the process.

She walked into the function room which looked as though a tornado had swept through. Although the caterers had cleared away the dirty glasses and dishes, there were still empty bottles, food mess, and even confetti, littering the tables and floor.

'I'll get a broom.' Ewen disappeared, presumably to raid the cleaning supplies Mrs McKenzie kept locked away.

Bonnie busied herself clearing away the rubbish using the bin bags she found behind the makeshift bar that had been set up for the day. Separating the recyclable items from the rest to make it easier to dispose of.

'Who said life with you wasn't glamorous?' she said,

scooping a pile of mashed potato off the table and dumping it into the rubbish bag.

'I did try to warn you it wasn't all champagne and waltzes around the salon floor. Sometimes you have to get your hands dirty too.' He scrunched his nose up as he picked up a single dirty sock between his thumb and forefinger and deposited it into the makeshift bin.

Bonnie's mind boggled as to how anyone had lost it without noticing, and what the circumstances for taking it off had been. She supposed a long day combined with alcohol consumption led to some dodgy decision-making. After all, she'd just been caught about to kiss her boss by another member of staff. Hopefully the trusted housekeeper could be relied upon for her discretion. It would be soul-destroying to lose everything now over a stupid crush. So Ewen was attractive. There was no point denying that when he'd had most of the people here today drooling over him. He was also the only man to have shown her any consideration in her entire life. Little wonder then that she'd confused that for something more.

Naturally her emotions were all over the place after being put through the wringer with Ed, who'd made her think she was going crazy by manipulating her feelings. If she didn't want to ruin the new life she'd set up for herself here at the castle, she needed to get a handle on these emotions, and keep her relationship with Ewen strictly professional.

'So what is this ball I've heard mention of? That sounds more in keeping with my idea of castle life. Do we wear gowns and waltz around the salon floor at that one?' Despite all the joking around, Bonnie had to admit the idea held some appeal for her. She couldn't remember the last time she'd had a chance to dress up and have fun. Today didn't count when they'd had to put in so much work and were currently reduced to cleaning duties.

Ewen kept sweeping the floor, piling up the debris at the far end to be disposed of later. Regardless of the privileged upbringing she imagined he'd had growing up here, he wasn't afraid to do his share of hard work. Bonnie thought back to the day she'd arrived when he'd been out the back doing his lumberjack impression, now here he was sweeping up whilst dressed in his full duke attire. It was no wonder he had women falling at his feet. All he needed was a photo op with a baby on his bare chest and they'd have a stampede at the castle door.

Bonnie made a mental note to suggest a topless calendar in the new year. There was no way of knowing how he'd take the idea of being a pin-up, but it was bound to get them some new sightseers around the place keen to sneak a peek at the hot duke. She'd just have to get over the idea of other women gawping at him, along with the images of him posing in various states of undress…

Ewen paused and leaned on the top of the broom. 'The family hold a ball every year for all the residents of the village, as well as local dignitaries. It's much more salubrious than today's event. A black-tie affair with a champagne reception and formal dinner.'

'Is there waltzing?' She wanted to picture the scene the way she'd always imagined those Regency-style balls, ladies flirting up a storm behind their fans, whilst handsome gentlemen vied to add their names to their dance cards.

Ewen sighed. 'Yes, there's waltzing, and fox-trotting, and my dad was even known to do the highland fling after a wee dram or two of whisky. Can't say I was ever really a part of it. Ruari and I were too young to be allowed to stay up late when I lived here. And, as you know, I didn't spend much time here as an adult.'

'So you're not going to keep up the tradition?' She could see why he wouldn't be inclined to continue with the event, but could understand why people would be upset. It might not earn him any brownie points with the locals if he put an end to something they'd been enjoying for years, at a time when he probably needed all the friends he could get.

'I haven't decided yet. Mrs McKenzie is nagging me about it and she wants me to look for Father's contact list to send out the invitations, but it would be a big commitment. We only just pulled off today, and that was with a wedding planner doing all the organising.'

'Surely Mrs McKenzie will have contact details for people who've worked it before?' She knew it would be a daunting task, but she was sure there would be caterers and musicians, or whoever they used for such an event, who knew the score.

'Oh, yes. I just need to make the call on whether or not it's happening. If I still want to be part of that.' The sag of his shoulders said he didn't, that he wanted to shrug off the ties to his parents, but given his position it was impossible. Living here, taking on his father's title and responsibilities, he would be living in his shadow for ever. Perhaps it would be healthier for him to accept all that came with the role, and do it to the best of his ability, rather than to rail against it. It didn't do anyone any good to hold onto those bad memories or feelings.

'You still have to make a life for yourself here, Ewen. It won't help if you alienate the locals. Perhaps you can still host but put your own twist on things?' She wanted the best for him, and the castle. Not only because her future was tied up in both, but because she *cared*.

'Hmm, we'll see.'

'When is it? You can't put it off for ever.'

He ducked his head, and, looking up at her under his long eyelashes, said, 'Next month.'

Bonnie immediately dropped the now full rubbish bags onto the floor. 'In that case...no more stalling. I'll help you find your father's list of contacts, then we're going to start organising your version of the annual ball.'

'Yes, ma'am.' Ewen let his broom fall to the ground and saluted her.

Bonnie wasn't usually this bossy, but she had a feeling he needed to move on just as much as she had. That could only happen when he confronted his problems. It wasn't easy, but she wasn't going to let him do it alone.

'You can give me the guided tour. I haven't seen much of the place behind the red velvet ropes.' She linked her arm through his, not caring if it took all night to find that book and start making arrangements. Ewen needed it, and she wanted to do something that would make them feel good. Preferably something that didn't involve them getting naked together and messing things up between them.

CHAPTER SEVEN

EWEN KNEW HE was dancing with danger extending his time with Bonnie. Yet when he wasn't with her he felt lonelier than ever. He'd had time on his own in the apartment after Victoria had left, spent weeks in the castle with just the ghosts of the past for company. But that was before Bonnie had arrived. Before he'd got used to having her to talk to, to share dinner with, to think about even when he wasn't with her.

Today had been a success, but it might not have happened if he hadn't had her to push him forward and think about the future of the castle. Even if he wasn't around for long, the place would hopefully still be standing here for another few hundred years. Regardless that he'd effectively be turning his back on his family heritage by selling up, he nevertheless wanted it to survive without him. The only hitch in his plans now was Bonnie.

Not only was he going to upset her when she discovered he intended to sell up and move on, but it was going to be more of a wrench for him now when the time came. He'd thought it would be easy to rid himself of the family home and all the bad memories he associated with it. Being lumbered with it was a headache he'd imagined he'd be happy to shake off. Then Bonnie had moved in and changed everything.

She was part of the fabric of the castle now. He wouldn't want to make a deal on the sale of the place unless he knew she would still be okay. Then there were the new memories he was making with her. The silent, awkward dinners with his parents after Ruari had gone now replaced with thoughts of her in his apartment sharing Italian on his couch. Those lonely nights in his room, staying out of sight to avoid upsetting anyone, fading against the fun he'd had with Bonnie in the kitchen making chocolates.

Then there was that moment on the stairs, leaning in to kiss her. That was what he'd think about every time he climbed the staircase, instead of his mother standing there wailing about the loss of her son and snarling at the one she still had. Bonnie was exorcising his demons one by one. Perhaps he needed to go through the castle room by room with her...

Images of what that could entail flashed in his mind. New fun memories they could have created together if they hadn't stopped themselves from giving into temptation.

Taking her into his father's study and letting her even further into his private life wasn't going to help his resolve. Yet he didn't want to do it alone.

'I haven't touched anything in here yet.' He opened the door for only the second time since he'd come back. This time he stepped inside instead of simply shutting the door on it again.

'Wow. It's like something out of a fairy tale.' Bonnie stood in the middle of the study, spinning around like a kid lost in a fairground.

'I've never really thought about it that way, but I suppose it is impressive.' Ewen tried to look at the place through her perspective. A floor-to-ceiling rainbow of colour-coded books was something he'd taken for granted growing up.

Especially when several of the rooms in the castle had their own mini library. A lot of the books had been inherited, some added by his father, none to be touched. And now they were his.

'Feel free to take one whenever you want.'

'Really?' She was already running her fingers down the leather spines, caressing first editions that probably hadn't been read in decades. Touched only by the people who came to carefully clean them every now and then.

'That's what they're supposed to be for. Don't ask me what we've got, I never had permission to as much as look at them until now.' It seemed absurd now to find he was the owner of the entire collection, free to do with it as he chose. He was surprised his father hadn't made separate provisions for the collection rather than let him take control of it. Perhaps he hadn't hated Ewen as much as he'd thought. Or, more likely, he hadn't expected to die when he had.

'That's a pity. I suppose that was something that had been drummed into your father too. I mean, this collection must go back generations, and, I've got to say, some of your ancestors look pretty fierce to me. I don't imagine they encouraged anyone to touch their things. No offence.' Bonnie gave a nod to the portraits above the marble fireplace of the stern dukes who once ruled the roost. She had a point.

'None taken. They were long before my time. I'd like to think I'm not as…controlling.' He was thinking in terms of the rules of the house, but he could see the impact that word had on Bonnie.

There was a flash of something fearful and disturbing in her eyes, before she moved to his father's desk and focused on it instead. 'I suppose if your father's contact list is going to be anywhere, it would be here, right?'

Ewen moved over beside her. 'Sorry, Bonnie. I didn't mean to bring up any bad associations for you.'

Her smile as she looked up at him was a little too bright to be believed. 'It's fine. I got out. I got away from him. And I'm here with you.'

'I'm not sure that's any consolation for you.'

'Trust me, being with you is like being at a holiday camp compared to life with Ed.' Those big brown eyes were now glassy with tears, the trauma still there looking back at him.

'What did he do to you, Bonnie?' He kept his voice soft and low, not wanting to spook her, but knowing she needed to get this out.

Although she'd told him something of what had happened, he couldn't help the way she needed him to if he didn't know the trauma she'd gone through. Not that he would push if she wasn't ready to share it with him, but he hoped she was. She was such a different person now from the one she described in her past.

She was silent for what seemed like for ever and he was on the brink of apologising again, deciding to leave her past where it belonged. Then her small voice broke through and smashed his heart.

'They have all sorts of names for it these days. Coercive control, gaslighting, and generally making my life hell. He isolated me from my family. Which was all too easy to do when I'd already been looking for a way out from my over-protective parents. Talk about out of the frying pan…' Her bitter laugh was so uncharacteristic it made Ewen angry on her behalf.

'I'm sure he didn't show his true colours when you first met. Men like that are sneaky and manipulative. I've met a few in my time.' The business world was full of egos and megalomaniacs, all out for themselves. He'd seen how they operated, trampling over whoever it took to get what they wanted and make themselves feel good. It didn't make it any easier imagining his strong, feisty Bonnie as a victim of one of those people.

'Yeah. Promised me the world, showered me with gifts, made me think I was moving on to something better. Anyway, I was young and naïve, thought that when he wanted to keep me at home to himself it was his way of showing me he loved me. Even after the first time he hit me, I convinced myself it was for my own good. That I must have failed him and needed to do better if I wanted to keep him.'

She talked in such a matter-of-fact manner about the mental and physical abuse it was almost as though she'd disassociated from it, and the person she'd been. Perhaps it was for the best, her way of dealing with it. Ewen, on the other hand, was becoming increasingly distressed at the thought of what she'd been through, and that she'd ever blamed herself.

'None of it was your fault. I hope you realise that. These men thrive on breaking people down. Usually strong ones at that. What happened was a sign of his weakness, not yours.' He wanted to hold her, hug her, show her the tenderness she deserved, but it would be overstepping the mark in all sorts of ways.

'I know. I realised that eventually. After a couple of black eyes, broken ribs, and a split lip. That's why I didn't hang around to start the family he was trying to pressure me into having. I wasn't so far removed from reality that I thought that would be a good idea. I suppose it made me wonder why I was putting up with his behaviour if I wasn't prepared to subject anyone else to it. Anyway, I don't want to let him take up any more room in my life. He's in prison now, where he belongs.'

From that he understood she didn't want to talk about it again. She'd told him her story, and he was grateful that she'd felt able to share it with him. Though he'd winced at the description of her injuries, had got angry at the man who thought he had the right to inflict such horrific damage on such a wonderful person, it wasn't his right to feel any of those things.

He was simply grateful she'd found the strength to report him and get away for her own sake. It helped him better understand what had brought her here and gave him more of an insight into the amazing person he already knew her to be.

'I understand. We'll never speak of him again, but thank you for sharing that with me. I know how painful it must have been, and I think you're incredibly brave. Onwards and upwards for both of us from now on.' He only hoped when the time came for him to move on from his painful past she would understand too.

'Starting with this annual ball. No more procrastinating, Mr Harris, you need to find this book.' Seemingly done with the topic of her abusive ex, Bonnie got back to the task at hand—busting his chops.

Ewen groaned and set to work searching his father's desk. Something else he'd been forbidden to touch when he was younger. 'He used to do everything at this desk. Opening his mail, meetings with his tenants, writing in his journal.'

'And now it's yours.'

Ewen looked at the fountain pen lying where his father had last left it and the neat pile of papers waiting for his attention. It was like a time capsule, a moment of his father's life captured for ever. Tasks he would never complete.

'I'm not sure I would ever feel comfortable in here. It's

a little too formal for me. I'm more a "laptop on my knee in front of the telly" kind of guy.' He couldn't imagine working in here, always thinking his father was looking over his shoulder disapproving of whatever he was doing.

'It seems a shame not to use it. It's such an amazing room.'

'Maybe I'll open it up to the public. After I take out any of his personal papers, of course.' He was sure any visitors would react the same way Bonnie had upon seeing his father's study. They would get a lot more from having access to this room than he would.

That wasn't to say a new owner wouldn't completely gut the place and turn it into a games room if they chose, and there would be nothing he could do about it. A notion that bothered him more now than it used to.

'You haven't gone through any of this yet?' Bonnie began to open the drawers in the desk, revealing stacks of notebooks and Manilla envelopes, all of which he would have to sort through at some stage.

'Not yet. All of the important legal papers were with his solicitor. This is probably his journals and the records to do with his family history. He was big into that. If we empty everything onto the desk, I'll get some boxes tomorrow and pack it all away.' To deal with at a later date.

He flicked through the loose papers sitting on the desk to make sure there were no outstanding bills, but they'd all been settled. Whether that was his father's doing, or the estate manager, he didn't know.

'He was so organised,' Bonnie remarked as she stacked the neatly labelled files on the desk.

'I don't remember him being like that. The place was usually cluttered with papers everywhere, and I don't think anyone has been in here since he died.' He was sure if Mrs

McKenzie had tidied things away she would have mentioned it.

'Perhaps he was getting his affairs in order to make it easier for you to deal with. It's a lot to take on. Especially when you were estranged for so long.' Bonnie's take on his father's sudden predilection for housekeeping hit hard. Although his death had been unexpected, according to Mrs McKenzie, he'd had heart problems in the past, and hadn't been in great health towards the end. Organising his personal affairs so he didn't put Ewen to too much trouble wasn't in keeping with the idea of a father who didn't love him. Perhaps, at the very least, he hadn't hated him as he much as he'd thought.

'Maybe he had an attack of conscience after all these years and realised not everything that happened was my fault.' He couldn't help but feel aggrieved regardless. A better way to show remorse and regret over their lost relationship would have been to reach out before it was too late to make amends. If Ewen had had any hint that he would've been welcomed here he might've been persuaded to visit and at least speak to his father before his death. Instead, he'd remained oblivious to his thoughts and health issues, still an outcast.

'Are you okay?'

He heard the concern in Bonnie's voice before he saw it in her eyes or felt it in the touch of his arm. Until now he'd kept the family circumstances to himself, but she deserved an explanation for the mess she'd walked into, and was now living in. More than that, it was time he finally opened up about what had happened, had to if he ever hoped to move past it, and he knew Bonnie would understand. She knew how it was to walk away from a toxic relationship.

'There's something I haven't told you...' He'd got over

the guilt of the accident a long time ago, but he'd lived with other people's condemnation for so long he hesitated before spilling the details.

Then he saw the sympathetic tilt of her head and knew Bonnie would hear him out without judgement.

'The reason I wasn't in contact with my parents for so long was because they blamed me for my brother Ruari's death.' He watched for a flinch, a sign that she was wary of him even before he told her the details, but she simply waited to hear him out.

'I was driving when the crash happened. I'd only just passed my driving test and the roads were icy. The car slid out of control and there was nothing I could do.' Even talking about it now brought him back to that night, the helplessness as he tried to steer the car away from danger, then the horrible crunch of the car hitting the tree, and the jolt as he was thrown forward at the impact. He'd never forget the silence that followed. That terrible quiet that told him his brother was dead.

'It was an accident. Surely your parents understood that.' Bonnie's voice gently brought him back to the present.

Ewen shook his head. 'They were completely blinded by their grief, couldn't bear to even look at me. So I went to university and never looked back. Until now.'

'Perhaps this was your father's way of making amends. By leaving you everything here he was making sure you're set for life.'

'I suppose that's how it looks from the outside, but I'm successful in my own right. I created an app and sold it for enough money that I'd never have to work again if I chose.'

Bonnie's eyes widened at that and Ewen blushed a little. He didn't make a huge song and dance about his wealth, especially since Victoria had made him more careful about sharing those kinds of personal details. Never knowing who might try to take advantage of him again. In this context, though, it was an important detail.

'Lucky you,' Bonnie said with a grin.

He was aware mentioning his financial status was somewhat tone-deaf given Bonnie's circumstances. 'It's not my intention to boast. I'm just saying my father must have had an ulterior motive in leaving this castle to me. I'm just not sure what that is yet.'

'You're still his son, Ewen. Maybe he realised he was in the wrong and this was his way of showing you that he still cared about you.'

'I love your optimism, but I'm not convinced. My father had years after my mother died to reach out and build some bridges. If he had, things could have been very different.' As it was, Ewen felt only resentment that he'd been forced back to BenCrag.

Bonnie contemplated his take on the matter and seemed to accept it, not putting forward any further argument. Instead, she set to work helping him go through his father's things, looking for the elusive address book.

They systematically went through the papers on top of the desk before starting on the contents of the drawers.

'Ewen?' Bonnie lifted out an envelope from one of the drawers and handed it to him.

His name was etched in ink on the front in his father's unmistakable scrawl. Ewen's blood ran cold, as though he'd just been touched by icy fingers from beyond the grave. His father was finally reaching out to him for the first time in over a decade after all.

He took the envelope, holding it carefully as though it were a bomb about to go off. For all he knew it might be. His legs unsteady, he collapsed into the leather office chair where his father once sat and stared at the letter, realising that once he opened it there was no going back. Whatever his father had to say to him, it would likely dictate what he thought about him for the rest of his life. There was no way of knowing if it was simply a written account of the blame he felt Ewen deserved for Ruari's death, or regret that they never got to say the final goodbye they should have had in person.

'I don't know if I can...' Good or bad, this was the last thing his father ever had to say to him, and he wasn't sure if he was ready for it. He was glad at least to have Bonnie with him.

She perched on the edge of the desk, a move that would seriously have infuriated his father, but ultimately made him smile. 'Do you want me to do it?'

It was tempting to let her have the dubious honour of opening the letter and reading whatever his father had to say to him. 'No. He left it for me. The least I can do is read it.'

He took a deep breath before attempting to disarm the explosive device beneath his fingertips, sweat breaking out on his forehead. Even Bonnie seemed to be holding her breath, waiting for the fallout from the blast.

If the sight of his father's familiar handwriting hadn't knocked the breath out of him, the *Dear Son* opening did. He dropped the letter on his lap and drew in a shaky breath, trying to compose himself.

'Let me do it.' Bonnie gently reached out and took the letter. He didn't try to stop her, afraid if he read any more he'd break down in front of her. Although she wouldn't want a replica of her violent ex, he doubted she'd be impressed by a tearful, grieving duke either.

'"Dear Son, If you're reading this, I'm already gone. We

*didn't get to say goodbye. I didn't quite manage the cour-
age to reach out to you in the end, and for that I'm sorry.
Along with everything else.'"*

Bonnie looked up to see how he was handling it so far.
She knew he was doing the macho male thing, thinking it
was a sign of weakness to show any emotion. Not that he
was especially good at hiding it, nor would she expect him
to be. This was a big deal.

She hadn't been aware of his difficult family circumstances, but it must've been horrible bearing the unjust
burden of his brother's death. It wasn't fair that he'd shoul-
dered the blame all these years, lost his parents along with
his brother. It was an accident. Although she'd lost all of
her family and friends too after one stupid mistake in the
form of her ex, so she guessed that gave them one more
thing in common.

It was also where the similarities ended. He wouldn't
get proper closure, or a chance to repair those damaged relationships, but she could. Maybe one day, when she was
stronger, successful, and her ex was nothing more to her
than a bad memory, she would go back waving an olive
branch. It wasn't too late.

Being estranged from her parents too, she knew how difficult it was not to have them for important milestones, or
emotional support when needed. She knew if she had any
sort of contact from her own parents asking her to come
home, she'd be reduced to a sobbing mess.

Ewen gripped the sides of his chair and waited for her
to continue, apparently steeling himself for more.

*"'I know the accident wasn't your fault, and deep down
your mother knew that too. We just couldn't seem to find
a way out of our grief, and I'm ashamed to say we took it
out on you. These last years on my own have made me re-*

flect on how we treated you, and how we let you down. I wanted to apologise to you, Ewen, and often thought about contacting you. In the end, I was too much of a coward. You were doing so well on your own. I could see you didn't need me to bring you down. Yes, I've kept track of your achievements over the years, and if it's not too late I want to say I'm proud of you. I'm proud that you're my son."'

Bonnie heard her voice cracking and took a moment to clear her throat. It was evident this had been written by a man full of regret in his last days, but still unable to show his son how much he loved him. It was a tragedy all around.

The least Ewen deserved was to hear what his father had to say without her crying all over him.

"'I hope you can forgive me, and your mother, for everything. I suppose it's a fitting punishment for me to die believing you still hate me, but for your own sake, Ewen, don't live the rest of your life with hate in your heart. Your mother was bitter after Ruari's death, it tainted everything, and that's what killed her in the end. So, I'm leaving you everything, hoping you'll realise I did love you, and that I trust you to make all the right decisions when it comes to the castle. I'm only sorry I left it too late to make amends in person. I wish you a long and prosperous life, son. But, more importantly, I hope it's a happy one. With love from your father."'

As Bonnie finished reading the letter aloud, the room fell into silence, both of them processing the contents. Ewen dropped his head, the weight of trying to stay strong apparently becoming too much.

It was instinctive to move closer to him, wrap her arms around his neck, and offer some comfort. The same way he'd done for her in the past. He buried his head against her stomach and hugged her closer. He didn't make a sound, but she knew he was hurting. As much as he'd needed to hear that apology, it wasn't going to bring back his father or repair their relationship. It would only add to his regrets.

'He loved you, Ewen. Just hold onto that.'

He tilted up his face to look at her, those blue eyes so full of pain and grief that he could no longer hide. 'And now he's gone, who do I have?'

Bonnie recognised that loneliness and her heart ached for him. It didn't seem fair to let him think there was no one left in the world to care for him when she knew otherwise.

'Me,' she said, cupping his face in her hands, and dropping a soft kiss on his lips. They'd been dancing around the attraction, and their growing feelings—at least she had, and Ewen's actions to date would suggest he was having the same problem. Circumstances had thrown them together and they'd found comfort in one another. She wondered why that was such a bad thing, given the ordeals they'd both been through recently.

Ewen pulled her closer, until she slid off the edge of the desk and was sitting astride his lap. There were no words needed, only actions. They both wanted, *needed*, this, and it didn't look as though either of them wanted to stop it this time. She wrapped her arms around his neck, he grabbed her backside with both hands, and they let their mouths find each other again.

Bonnie leaned into the kiss, into Ewen, letting him carry her away on that wave of passion she'd known was waiting to crash over both of them. Their want for one another apparent in their grinding bodies, and insistent mouths. She didn't want to listen to that nagging inner voice trying to protect her from herself, insisting that this was a bad idea. So she focused instead on the sensations Ewen was introducing her body to. The languid kisses that she couldn't get enough of, and that ache at her very core she knew only he could remedy.

She was so lost in the taste of him, the hot feel of his mouth meshed with hers, that it took her a moment to register that he'd stood up and was setting her back down on the desk. When she attempted to extricate herself from him, worried that she'd missed his cue that the moment was over, he grabbed her legs and wrapped them back around his waist.

'I didn't want us to stop. I just thought we needed a bit more room.' He was kissing her neck, slipping the straps of her dress down her bare shoulders, and doing everything to steal her breath away.

Then he cupped her breasts in his hands, and almost rendered her catatonic. His assured touch, combined with his hot breath on her skin, was just the thing to make her remember she was more than a victim, or a survivor. She was still very much a woman with needs.

With greedy hands of her own, she stripped away his shirt to explore the dip and rise of his muscular physique. Marvelling at the hard muscle and solid strength beneath her fingertips. The very essence of masculinity. Even more so because he didn't feel the need to assert his dominance over her like every other man in her life. Sufficient to turn her on even if he hadn't unclipped her bra and was now... oh...

She tilted her head back as waves of ecstasy crashed over her, Ewen sucking one nipple, then the other. Arousal was coursing so hard and fast through her body she thought it would burst through her skin. Then everything stopped. Ewen took a step back, abandoning her, leaving her restless and frustrated.

'What's wrong?' Her voice was husky with unfulfilled

need and concern as she fought to remember Ewen's feelings in all of this. He was bound to be emotional and confused, and perhaps she'd taken advantage of his moment of vulnerability.

He fixed her with his cutest hot-guy smile. 'Given the circumstances, doing this on my father's desk seems a little disrespectful. And weird. Do you mind if we take this somewhere else?'

Bonnie's relief was quickly overtaken by her returning desire as he wrapped her legs back around his waist, her arms around his neck, and lifted her from the desk.

'Not at all,' she gasped, her breasts pushing against his bare chest and stoking that fire within her. That intimate contact, a promise of more, only pushed her further towards the brink of madness with every step he took.

Ewen carried her into his bedroom and laid her on his bed, coming down onto the mattress with her. Here in his own space he seemed to lose what was left of his inhibitions, kissing her all over as he stripped her naked. Leaving her exposed and wanting.

She watched with increasing hunger whilst he discarded the rest of his clothes, reaching for him once he was magnificently naked before her. He left her momentarily to find some protection, giving her the opportunity to marvel at his naked form. All honed muscle, no doubt from the manual labour he wasn't afraid to do. A true Scottish warrior who deserved his fine physique to be captured for prosperity on the side of a shortbread tin. Albeit a more PG image.

He had that tall, proud body she could imagine striding through the highlands, and for tonight, at least, it was all hers.

Ewen caught her watching and smirked, prowling along the bed back towards her.

'You look pleased with yourself,' Bonnie remarked, anticipation of what was to come making her a little nervous. Her sheltered life before her ex meant she had scant experience in the bedroom department, save for what she'd had with Ed. Given the playful, passionate lead-up with Ewen so far, she was beginning to realise she had a lot to learn. And that she'd been missing out.

'Just enjoying being objectified. You're looking at me the way the wedding guests were eyeing your chocolate today.'

'It's true. I haven't had a thing to eat for ages,' she said, shifting her body so it was perfectly positioned beneath his.

Ewen looked stricken by her comment. 'I'm sorry. I didn't think. We can go get something now if you need to eat.'

Bonnie loved that he was so considerate, if a little slow on the uptake. Willing to set aside his wants to make sure she was okay. A real man. Though clearly her pillow talk needed some work.

When he straightened up as though to leave her, she moved quickly, wrapping her arms around his neck to keep him anchored to the bed with her.

'The only thing I'm hungry for is you.' She kissed him with renewed fervour to prove he was the only thing on her mind.

He sagged against her, the weight of him reassuring her he wasn't going anywhere unless she requested it. And she hoped neither of them were leaving his bed for the foreseeable future. Not when he was worshipping her with his tongue, and his mouth, touching her with a tenderness she'd never experienced before.

Every soft kiss as he travelled down her body, covering all erogenous zones, taught her a new way of loving. Her ex hadn't cared too much about her needs, or feelings, helping himself as though she was nothing but a possession to be used at his will. Now she looked back, sex had never been a particularly enjoyable part of their relationship. Simply something expected of her to keep him happy. To show him she loved him. She didn't recall ever receiving the same consideration in return.

Ewen, on the other hand, appeared to be on a mission to drive her wild. In a good way. With all of those feel-good endorphins colliding with this all-new lust coursing through her veins, she no longer had any control over what was happening to her. Though in these circumstances she was happy to let Ewen take the driving seat. He seemed to know what she wanted, needed, and was determined to serve it to her on the tip of his tongue.

Bonnie arched up off the bed with a gasp as he dipped inside her core, holding her steady with his hands on her thighs. Her climax took her by surprise with the speed and force with which it came, leaving her head spinning, and her body limp.

'You okay?' Ewen asked, before dotting kisses along her inner thighs, starting that fluttering sensation across her skin all over again.

'Yeah… I'm just…' She didn't know how to thank him for making her feel loved without sounding pathetic. 'I'm, er, not used to this, that's all.'

It wasn't easy to admit she was practically a virgin, that there were still a lot of unknowns, uncharted territory, for her when it came to sex. Bonnie felt a flush spread from the top of her head down to her toes, the heat of her embarrassment tinging her pale skin pink.

Ewen frowned, not quite understanding. Then she watched as realisation dawned and he let loose several choice words about her ex. He came up to lie beside her.

'I don't want to do anything you don't want to do. I just want to make you feel good.' With a gentle kiss on the lips, and the slow sweep of her hips with his hand, he started that build-up of pressure inside her all over again.

'Oh, I don't want you to stop…' Emboldened by Ewen's desire to keep her happy, she reached between their bodies and took hold of him. His gasp at her confident power play only encouraged more of this new, wanton Bonnie.

She moved her hand along his shaft, revelling in the evidence of his desire for her, and the ragged breaths she was drawing from Ewen as he fought to regain control. It was powerful knowing she could make him feel this way about her. They might regret this in the morning, when they were thinking clearly enough to realise the consequences. That it was going to make working and living together complicated. For tonight, at least, she wanted to forget he was her boss, and for a little while at least pretend she was the one in charge.

Ewen was doing his best to treat Bonnie as tenderly as she deserved. Though she was making that a challenge when she was touching him the way she was, straddling his lap now, and testing his restraint to the max.

After hearing a little about her selfish ex, he wanted this to be good for her. He knew he was probably the rebound guy in this scenario, but he couldn't ask for more than that. To do so would put their working relationship in jeopardy and he was coming to rely on Bonnie more and more. Tonight had proved that. He'd opened up to her more about his family than he ever had with anyone else, but that was also why this couldn't be any more than sex. Relationships never worked out for him and he wasn't ready to lose Bonnie when he'd just found her.

His father's letter had knocked him for six. He'd never expected an apology, especially posthumously. It was bittersweet to receive one when it was too late to do anything about it. They'd wasted so much time and thrown away a relationship. Giving up on one another too easily, at a time when they'd probably needed each other more than ever. With his father's health in decline, and Ewen's relationship with Victoria on the critical list too, they could have leaned on each other.

Now there was no going back. He didn't want to make the same mistake again with someone he cared about. Yes, despite years of telling himself otherwise, he'd still loved his parents. Since they'd seemed happier without him in their lives, it had been easier to convince himself he didn't need them. It was only now his father had confessed it was fear that had kept him from reaching out that Ewen could admit the same. Except he also hadn't wanted to face the same rejection, which had bordered on hatred, that he'd received at the time of Ruari's death. So he'd stayed away, and now it was too late to repair the damage.

It was a bitter pill to swallow. And a reminder not to waste time. He didn't want to live with any more regrets. Tonight he wanted to be with Bonnie, to express those growing feelings he had towards her. All the self-recriminations could wait. He just wanted to feel good, and it seemed as though Bonnie was overdue some loving too. Although she was doing her best to make him forget any chivalrous behaviour, grinding against him. Teasing him until he was ready to explode.

Then she bore down on him, joining their bodies together, and Ewen knew he was lost to her. With one hand braced on his chest, the other stroking between his thighs, Bonnie had him at her mercy. It was all he could do not to

flip her onto her back and thrust into her like the Nean-
derthal she brought out in him. But she needed this. She
needed to be in control. To find out what she liked. To learn
how to enjoy sex, and no longer feel as though it was something merely to be endured.

It was part of life he certainly enjoyed. Especially right
now with this firecracker riding him and discovering the
joys for herself. Head thrown back in ecstasy, her breath
no more than excited pants. Even if he wasn't aroused beyond rational thought, the sight of her taking pleasure
from his body was certainly an aphrodisiac. He needed
that boost after the way Victoria had so cruelly discarded
him. This brought a whole new dimension to his relationship with Bonnie. Bonnie, who was sweet and attractive,
and so damn sexy.

Her breathy moans as she grew closer and closer to the
end finally undid him. Ewen thrust his hips up to meet hers
and forced a gasp from her. So he did it again, and again,
until his blood was thundering in his veins and Bonnie was
crying out her release. As she crashed over the edge and
slowly came back to earth, rocking gently now, he was finally able to take control once more.

He shifted their bodies, until Bonnie was beneath him,
and drove home again. She tightened her inner muscles
around him and shattered what was left of his composure.
That overwhelming bliss managed to blot out all the pain
he'd endured tonight, leaving him satisfied and content to
lie with Bonnie, the miracle worker. He couldn't help but
think she might become a habit he wasn't going to be able
to break. However, like all vices, he worried that his desire for another fix might begin to affect all other aspects
of his life.

For now, though, he was going to enjoy the high.

'What are we doing, Bonnie?' he asked, brushing her tangled hair from her face.

The satisfied smile across her kiss-swollen lips was tempting his weary body back to life already.

'If you don't know that then you're more naïve than I am.'

That made him laugh. 'You know what I mean. Tonight has been amazing, but what happens tomorrow?'

Ewen didn't want things to get awkward between them, the dynamic changed for ever, and not in a good way.

'Well, I'm not the boss, but I think it's pretty much the same as every day. We open the doors, people pay their entrance fee, you charm them, and I try to get them to buy some chocolate.'

'Ha-ha. Very funny. I just… I don't want to ruin things.' He had a lot to deal with in the not-too-distant future: the clean-up, the ball, and the emotional fallout from his father's letter still to come. Things he could do on his own, but would much prefer to have Bonnie by his side for if he could. She made everything better.

She turned onto her side and fixed him with a serious stare. 'I don't see why this has to be anything. We don't need to label spending time together. I doubt either of us is ready to jump into any kind of relationship. Surely we're adult enough not to make a big deal of just sleeping together. I don't want anything serious.'

'Does that mean we can still have some fun?' He threw an arm around her waist and pulled her closer, hooking her thigh over his so their most intimate parts were flush once more.

Ewen knew he could never get enough of her. This was exactly where he wanted to be, with her full breasts pressed tightly against his chest, her body wrapped around his. Where he felt wanted.

He didn't want this to be the last time.

'Keep it casual?'

'If that means you'll stay the night without either of us panicking that the other will read more into it, then yes, let's keep things casual. By day we'll be mild-mannered work colleagues, at night, red-hot secret lovers.'

'Ooh, I like the sound of that.' Bonnie started kissing her way along his neck, then drew his earlobe into her mouth.

Ewen felt a familiar stirring in his groin and he was glad they were in no rush to get back to reality. Tomorrow, they could deal with any repercussions he was currently not letting have access to his brain. Because that was totally consumed with thoughts of how they were going to spend these next few hours together.

CHAPTER EIGHT

'ARE YOU SURE you don't want to get in with me?' Bonnie was lying with her head against the old copper bucket-style tub, which Ewen had filled with soothing hot water for her tired body.

'I'm not sure there's any room left for me.' He scooped some water from the bath in the gold-rimmed ewer he'd taken from the dressing table, and poured it over her hair.

With the only light in the bathroom coming from the candles he'd lit around the tiled room, the scent of rose and honey in the air, he was romancing her after the fact. The opposite of how her ex had worked. A sign that he wasn't pretending to be someone he wasn't just to get his own way, because she was his any time he chose. He'd proven himself to be supportive, considerate, and loving. All the things Ed had pretended to be in order for her to fall in love with him. Bonnie just had to make sure she kept some perspective with Ewen. She didn't want to fall for someone who didn't want her in his life. That would almost be as tragic as staying with someone who'd emotionally and physically damaged her. Just a different form of abuse. Albeit self-inflicted.

'I'll make room.' Though she was enjoying her impromptu pampering session. After another enthusiastic bout of bedroom gymnastics, Ewen had insisted on drawing her a bath.

She wasn't some damsel who needed taking care of, but it was nice to have someone treat her so well. He was good for her body and soul. A soothing balm for the trauma scars her ex had left on her. Ewen was helping her undo some of the damage, showing her she was worth desiring, caring about. That being with someone didn't have to mean pain and upset. He gave her space to work through her feelings, and at the same time was there for her when she needed company or support.

Keeping things casual reduced expectations on both sides and she was happy enough with that for now. It was early days, for her relationship not only with Ewen, but with herself. She needed time to trust again, to explore the sort of romantic entanglement she did, or didn't, want. Ewen was showing her a kindness and tenderness she wasn't used to and she was happy to simply enjoy his attentions in the meantime. Ed might not be representative of all men, but that didn't mean she was ready to jump into something serious with anyone else again. Some time exploring her freedom was enough for now.

'It's okay. I think it's about time someone took care of you for a change. Besides, we both need a recovery period. You can have too much of a good thing, you know.'

'Really? Because I think I have a lot of lost time to make up…' Whilst she didn't want to be a slave to another man's whims, her aching body was still craving Ewen. She hadn't known someone could ever make her feel this way, and it made her sad for the version of her who'd put up with so much less for so long. Now she knew she was worth more than being a punchbag for a bully, she would never accept anything less than the way Ewen treated her. Like a duchess.

These past months, she'd proved to herself that she was independent, and courageous, and all the other words the women's charity had used to try and instil some confidence into her. It was only coming to the castle and setting up her new life that had helped her to start believing it. She didn't need anyone else to give her life meaning. Although Ewen had shown her that sometimes it could still be fun to share her life when it suited her. Like tonight.

She felt like a born-again virgin, discovering sex for the first time. Keen to explore every new position, along with her new-found sexuality. It had been an awakening, one she was glad to have had, but that also worried her. What if Ewen had spoiled her for ever? If he was the new standard, any other man had a lot to live up to. She wasn't even sure she'd want anyone else. The memories they were making now might be enough to sustain her for ever. That was why she didn't want it to end.

'We're not in any hurry, are we? Casual means just that. We can pick this up again whenever we choose.' Ewen took a detour with the soapy sponge he'd been washing her down with, paying particular attention to her nipples, before dipping lower under the water.

She closed her eyes and gave herself over to the sensation. 'Hmm, we might have to hold that thought. I think I'm going to have to take that time out we talked about.'

Although her mind was willing, her body pleasantly numb, she'd clearly reached her orgasm limit for the night. A yawn slipped out of her mouth unbidden, reminding her that it had been a busy, energetic day.

'Right. I think we're done for the night.' Ewen grabbed a couple of towels and helped her out of the bath. Once she was sufficiently dried, he wrapped her in a big fluffy white robe.

'You have your own private spa in here,' she teased, then found herself wondering how many other women had enjoyed the same treatment. Though it was none of her business, and she had no claim on Ewen, she wanted to believe he'd done this only for her. That she was special.

'I guess there are some perks to living in a castle. I just haven't availed myself of them in a long time. We do a personal chauffeur service too,' he said, putting her mind at ease that this hadn't simply been part of his usual seduction technique.

'Well, I'm not planning on going anywhere for the foreseeable future.' She gave another yawn and stretched as he tied the robe around her waist.

'Oh, I think you are.' With a mischievous glint in his eye, he scooped her up in his arms.

Her little scream of protest in response was in contrast to the way she was wrapping her arms around his neck and snuggling into his chest. She'd never been so romanced, felt so wanted and sexy, and she had Ewen to thank for everything.

The only blot in her perfect romantic fantasy was when Ewen kept walking past his bed and down the hallway, carrying her away from the prospect of more time with him tonight.

'Where are you taking me?'

'To bed. Your bed.'

'Oh.' A cloak of disappointment settled around her shoulders that it had all come to an end. He'd made the decision for both of them. Despite their talk about continuing on a casual basis, who knew when they'd get to do this again, or if they could ever hope to replicate the magic they'd shared tonight?

'You need some rest. So do I, come to think of it.' He

gave a self-deprecating laugh. 'Besides, we don't want Mrs McKenzie seeing us slipping in and out of one another's rooms, do we?'

'I guess not.' He had a point. She was already the outsider on the staff, and, though they were pleasant enough, she didn't want to alienate herself by becoming too cosy with the boss. He too was still trying to make his mark here, had a lot to prove, and it probably wouldn't do his credibility any good if it was public knowledge he was sleeping with the hired help.

It didn't mean she wasn't going to feel the loss once he left her here alone.

Ewen set her gently down on the bed and went to take his leave.

'Can you stay with me for a little while? At least until I fall asleep?' She didn't want to appear needy, but this was the first night since leaving her ex, maybe even before then, when she hadn't felt alone. It would be nice, just for once, to fall asleep knowing someone was there with her. Someone she didn't have to fear.

'Sure.' He climbed onto the bed so they were lying face to face.

'Thank you. It's been a while since I felt this safe and happy. I just want to make it last.' The fact that Ewen hadn't already run in the opposite direction from all of her baggage made her comfortable with the admission. He knew about her past and he was more understanding about her needs than she could ever have hoped for.

'I get it. It's no fun going to bed alone at night.' He plumped up the pillow and settled in beside her, not in any hurry to leave her at all.

'Why aren't you married?' She hadn't intended to say it out loud, but it was hard to understand why someone like

Ewen hadn't been snapped up. He was handsome, rich, had a title, and a conscience, all of which were rare enough, but he was also kind and loving. If she hadn't just come out of her nightmare of a relationship, she would probably be hoping for something long-term herself. But she didn't know if she'd ever want that with anyone. If she could ever trust a man enough to completely open up and share her life with him. She had a feeling this was the closest she'd ever get.

Ewen sighed, and he seemed to drift off somewhere else for a moment. A place that tightened his jaw and robbed him of his dreamy smile. Bonnie was already regretting the question.

'Not my choice. I did think it was on the cards, along with a family of my own. I thought those things were important to Victoria too, but I was wrong. It turned out she was more interested in my bank account, or, more specifically, one that was bigger than mine. She didn't want to move here with me, and found herself another man to fund the life she was accustomed to in London.'

'I'm so sorry. Clearly she wasn't the right woman for you if she didn't appreciate the man you are.' More fool this Victoria if she didn't realise what she'd thrown away. It was hard to find a good one like Ewen, and he certainly deserved being treated better than a cash machine.

'Story of my life.' He had that bone-weary tone she was familiar with. That feeling that nothing was ever going to improve. Luckily she knew that wasn't true.

'So you've no ties left in London?'

'Nope. I sold everything to come here. There's nothing left for me in the city any more.' Although she was sorry he'd endured the pain of a bitter break-up, she couldn't help but be happy that his life was here now. His future was wrapped up in the castle along with hers for the time being.

'What about you? I know you left a bad relationship behind, but you still have family don't you?'

Bonnie screwed her face up. It was a difficult subject,
not least after Ewen's discovery about his own father tonight. 'It's complicated. It was my father who taught me
everything about being a chocolatier. I spent weekends
and holidays working in the shop, helping him with his latest creations. He made everything himself and our whole
house smelled of melted chocolate. It was heavenly. Looking back, my parents treated me like their little princess,
but instead of appreciating their love, I decided it was suf-
focating. I wanted to prove I was grown up, no longer their
little girl. Then Ed came along... I wouldn't hear a word
against him, packed my bags and left. I haven't spoken to
my parents since I moved out.'

'Is there any hope for a reconciliation?'

'Honestly, I don't know. I never thought I'd want anything to do with them again. They tried to warn me about
getting involved with Ed, but as far as I was concerned,
I was right and they were wrong. Of course, I know differently now, and I suppose, if my father reached out the
way yours did, there might be a glimmer of hope for us as
a family. Some day I might even find the courage to swallow my pride and make that first move...'

'Don't let that prevent you from getting your family
back. My situation should be a cautionary tale. I left it too
late, don't make the same mistake.'

'We're a right pair, aren't we?' Bonnie moved in for one
last cuddle, thankful she had someone, at least for a while,
who understood her circumstances, who'd gone through
something similar. It made her realise she wasn't some
sort of freak who couldn't manage any sort of normal relationship. All families had their issues, but maybe she had

a chance of resolving hers. She wondered if by setting up her own chocolate shop she'd been trying to recreate the innocence and security of her childhood, before Ed had destroyed everything.

'At least we have each other for now.' He hugged her close and kissed the top of her head.

The only thing spoiling the moment, that feeling of security and bliss, was *for now*. Right now, she didn't want this to ever end.

Ewen nuzzled into Bonnie's mussed hair, the scent from last night's bath evoking some very happy memories. Spooning her naked body with his was the perfect way to start the day. He didn't know when her robe had been dispensed of, but he was grateful for the curve of her buttocks now resting against his groin. She began to stir as he kissed her neck, shifting her position ever so slightly, but enough to tease his body wide awake.

'I hope you're well rested,' he whispered into her ear, gaining a little shiver in response.

'Hmm mmm.'

He'd barely had time to congratulate himself for taking the next step with Bonnie, when he heard voices downstairs. Followed by the sound of a vacuum cleaner. He sat bolt upright.

'What time is it?'

Bonnie groped for her phone and showed him the screen as she fought to open her eyes.

'Seven o'clock?' He swore and tossed back the covers.

'You stayed all night?'

'I didn't mean to.' He swore again. 'Mrs McKenzie has her own key. She probably let the cleaning crew in.'

'A cleaning crew?' she asked, an eyebrow raised at the admission.

He'd known all along they were coming to clear up after last night's revelry, but when Bonnie had offered her services, he'd seen a chance for them to be alone again and taken it. 'Er, yes. So sue me for wanting to spend more time with you. Anyway, I'm not sure it would be a good look if I was caught naked in bed with a member of staff.'

It was his own fault. He should have left her in her bed and gone to his own room. That was more in keeping with the idea of a casual fling than crawling into bed beside her and cuddling until they'd both fallen asleep. It had just felt so good, the best night's sleep he'd had since moving home. Warning signs that he was getting too comfortable with this arrangement already. If he was going to have the best of both worlds, being with Bonnie, without risking his heart, he had to keep to the boundaries of their casual arrangement.

'Take the robe, or you'll cause even more of a scandal.' Bonnie failed to suppress her amusement as he paced the room naked, wondering how he was going to get out of this.

Ewen grabbed up the robe from the floor and threw it on to cover his modesty.

'I'm sorry. I have to run. I'll see you later, okay?' He paused for one last kiss, aware he wouldn't get to touch her again for the rest of the day. It was going to be torture when he knew every inch of her amazing body now, how soft her lips were, and how well they fitted against his. All of which wasn't going to help him avoid embarrassing himself in front of his staff right now.

'Yes, boss.' Bonnie saluted him with a smile that made him want to slide back into bed beside her and forget about everything outside the bedroom door.

With every ounce of strength in him he opened the door and walked out.

The sound of real life going on downstairs filtered upward. The castle coming to life reminded him that he had priorities over his libido. He crept down the corridor, body pressed to the wall, trying to keep the robe closed so he didn't accidentally expose himself. The scene was probably like something out of a farce, but it made a change from tragedy.

His night with Bonnie had been incredible, something they had been building up to for a while. That attraction sizzling away until it was sure to catch fire, and it had. Spectacularly. However, there was a part of him that wondered if it had also been a way to block out the earlier revelation of his father's letter. A nice distraction for a time, but without Bonnie in his arms his mind was already beginning to think about less appealing things than the sexy curve of her hips under his fingertips.

She wasn't going to be there all day, every day, to take his mind off the time he'd wasted, the mistakes made, and the regrets he was going to have to live with. He was going to have to find another way to deal with this renewed grief.

Ewen showered and changed as quickly as he could to take up his rightful position, overseeing the work going on in the castle, instead of hiding away pretending it wasn't happening.

'Morning, Mrs McKenzie. You're in early this morning. No hangover?' he teased the housekeeper who looked as though she'd slept standing upright last night, wearing the same crisp grey tweed, and not a hair out of place. Whereas he was sure he had bags under his eyes and had thrown on the first pair of jeans and tee shirt he'd found.

She turned her head away from the cleaning crew she was supervising in the function room to give him a withering look. The same one she used to give him when he was younger after he and Ruari had been caught doing something they shouldn't. Like the time she'd found them putting salt in the sugar bowl before one of their parents' big fancy dinner parties. Mrs McKenzie never had to raise her voice to get him to confess to anything, or make him feel bad about his actions. She only had to give him the look.

She turned away again. Point made that she didn't think he was humorous. 'We have to be ready for opening. The whole place doesn't shut down after one event.'

'I'll remember that. It's hard to get used to treating this place as a business rather than a home. Though I don't know if it was ever that either...'

Mrs McKenzie tutted. 'You boys never knew how lucky you were. I know your parents took out their grief on you after your brother died, but they loved you. Your father would never have left you all of this if he didn't.'

'I know. I found a letter he left me in his study last night. Too late for me to do anything about it, but he finally apologised.'

Mrs McKenzie dropped her folded arms and stiff upper lip as she faced him. The tears in her grey eyes making her look more human than her usual ice-queen appearance.

'You two were as stubborn as one another. I lost count of the amount of times I tried to get him to contact you. He read me every article about your business success. He was so proud of you.'

'If only he'd told me that. I might have come home sooner.'

'I think he was afraid of you rejecting him. He might have looked gruff on the outside, but he was sensitive. That's why the loss of your brother hit so hard. Don't hate him.'

'I don't. Not any more. That's why I've decided to go

ahead with the annual ball in his honour.' It was his way
of trying to make peace with the past, as well as giving
him something to occupy his thoughts other than Bonnie.

Mrs McKenzie clapped her hands together in an uncharacteristic display of enthusiasm. 'That's great! Oh,
there's so much to organise…what about your father's address book? Did you find it yet? We're going to have to get
invitations sent out, and book caterers…'

'No… I er, I got distracted by the letter.' He tried not
to think about what had followed, not when he was determined to keep his personal life separate from his position
at the castle. At least during the day.

'Well, why don't we go find it now? There's no time to
waste.' A smiling Mrs McKenzie hooked her arm through
his and started walking towards his father's study.

There seemed little point in resisting now he'd committed to the idea of having the ball. He'd been putting it off,
unwilling to deal with the emotional baggage lying in that
room, but since confronting it with Bonnie, there was no
reason to avoid the place any more.

It was only when they entered the room he started to
panic. Mostly about any evidence of their passionate tryst
they might have left behind last night.

'We…er… I already went through his desk.' He moved
quickly to gather the pages and files that had hit the floor
in the midst of their late night clinch.

'So I see.' She arched a thin eyebrow, surveying the
scene, with Ewen hoping she didn't realise what had actually gone on. That she didn't see the butt-shaped space
between the papers scattered on the desk, or at least mis-
took it for destruction by a grieving son.

'I think there's a filing cabinet over there somewhere.
You could try that, and I'll tidy this.' He set to work tidy-

ing the mess he and Bonnie had made last night, memories coming thick and fast, and making him ache for her all over again.

Mrs McKenzie moved slowly, eyeing him suspiciously. Just the way she used to do when he and Ruari had been up to no good. She always knew when he was hiding something. In a lot of ways she'd been more of a mother figure to him growing up than his own parent. After the crash, she'd been the one to hug him, to hold him when he'd cried, and reassure him it wasn't his fault. It was his own mother and father who'd convinced him otherwise.

'I'm sorry I didn't keep in touch with you either, Mrs McKenzie. You were always good to me, and you've made my transition here easier than it probably would have been without you.'

He watched her face soften with a smile.

'Things were complicated. I knew you weren't at fault for what had happened, but your parents were too grief-stricken at the time to see things clearly. My loyalties had to remain with your parents. I'm sorry you were left on your own to deal with everything.'

The pain he saw in her eyes was disconcerting for a woman who'd never been anything but a pillar of strength. It only made his heart ache a little more, realising that he hadn't been the only one hurting this whole time.

Without a family of her own, their housekeeper had devoted her life to the castle and its dysfunctional residents for as long as Ewen could remember. The only one here for his father's dying days, holding things together until his reluctant replacement took over. Even now, she was the one Ewen was turning to for guidance in his new role.

'That's my job. To keep this place standing.'

Strictly speaking, that was the estate manager's job, but

everyone knew Mrs McKenzie was really the one in charge. The estate manager had apparently been drafted in when his father had opened the castle up to visitors and the workload had become too much. Not that she would ever have admitted any such thing. Still, he appreciated her sticking around even in the most difficult of circumstances, when she was likely grieving too.

'Thank you for being there for him at the end.' He was glad she'd stayed for his father's sake as much as his own, knowing she would have been a comfort, as well as a practical influence.

It had crossed his mind that she might have had something to do with the farewell letter, a final cleansing of his father's conscience, which he was sure had helped his father die at peace. The way she'd pushed him about looking for the address book might have been a cover to get him to come in here and find it. He supposed it wouldn't have had the same impact if she'd just handed it to him. He'd needed to be ready, in the right headspace to deal with it. It had taken being with Bonnie to get him where he'd needed to be. He just didn't want to come to rely on her. Not when he was going to be moving on again.

He hadn't changed his mind about that, despite his night with Bonnie. If anything, it had only cemented that idea that he had to leave. Becoming too attached to her, to the castle, was pain waiting to happen. At the minute she was exploring her independence, finding her way in the world again, and losing his heart to her was a bad idea when she might decide she didn't want it. He didn't have a good track record when it came to personal attachments. It was safer for him, and his heart, to keep to the original plan and sell up when the time came.

'I know he wasn't always the father you deserved, Ewen,

but he was a good man. He filled this place with so many guests and visitors in an attempt to fill that hole in his heart left by you. Don't get me wrong, I know that's not your fault, but he did miss you. And your brother. I'm happy you're going ahead with the ball in his honour. He would've loved that.' She patted him on the arm.

'I'm just sorry we didn't get a chance to make up when he was here. I want to do him proud.'

'As long as you do your best for this place, and for the family name, I'm sure he will be.'

Her words were like knives jabbing at his conscience. She clearly wasn't aware of the stipulation his father had made in his will. That the only reason Ewen was even at the castle was because he'd been forced into it, and he planned to sell it on once the year was up. It probably wasn't the best thing for the castle, or the family legacy, but he was sure it was the right thing for him. Or at least he had been until recently. The longer he spent here, the more complicated things became.

'We'll start with the ball and see how things go from there. All I can do is try.' He didn't want to commit to anything beyond that when it might serve as a farewell party too.

'I'm sure that's all your father is asking of you too. Just don't let any distractions get in the way of that.' She nodded towards the mess still littered on the desk with that knowing look, and Ewen felt the heat rise in his cheeks.

Warning received loud and clear. This might be only a casual fling with Bonnie, but it was already interfering with the running of the castle. His focus had to be on making it a viable business proposition for the next owner, leaving it in the best possible position so he wouldn't spend the rest of his life feeling guilty about everything he'd walked away from. Perhaps he needed to pull the brakes on his love life now before everything spun out of control. He owed his father that at least.

Ewen knew he couldn't afford to get carried away by this thing with Bonnie for his own sake too. Their connection had happened so quickly, perhaps he needed to slow things down and take stock of what he was really getting himself into. He was drawn to Bonnie for the type of person she was, but he couldn't be sure if it was the same for her. Perhaps her circumstances had coloured her judgement. He'd been the one to offer her a way out after her ex had left her in such a precarious position after all. Either way, he had to be careful that he didn't get too attached to Bonnie, only to end up wounded and alone again.

From now on it was strictly sex. No cuddling until the morning, or thinking about her when he should be planning his future away from BenCrag.

His aim was to leave it behind for ever, not find reason to stay.

'I should go.'

Bonnie had barely got her breath back from another mind-blowing orgasm before Ewen was scrambling out of bed and grabbing his clothes. She'd known what she was getting into by agreeing to a casual fling, but it was beginning to feel like more of a series of one-night stands when he left so soon after sex. It had been a couple of weeks since they got together and at first it had been exciting, snatching kisses out of sight of everyone, sneaking in and out of each other's rooms at night. But, despite her promise not to let her feelings get in the way, she wanted more.

'You don't have to. We're adults. Staying overnight doesn't have to mean anything. No one needs to know.'

Bonnie didn't want to seem desperate, practically begging him to be with her, but she felt as though he was pulling away from her.

As much as she was enjoying the physical aspect of their relationship, they didn't do as much talking as they used to. She was beginning to realise that sort of intimacy was as important to her as the sex. Ewen's hurry to leave was making her think he didn't feel the same.

'Yeah, but it's probably for the best that we keep to separate rooms. We don't want to fall into something that neither of us is ready for.'

'No, of course not.' Bonnie swallowed down the sudden swell of nausea, knowing she was already in deeper than she'd intended.

Though she was enjoying her job and her freedom, the highlight of her days was getting to spend time with Ewen. She was falling for him. It wasn't something she'd expected, or wanted, but it had happened nonetheless. Ewen had shown her how being with someone could be fun and exciting, without having to live in constant fear. She hadn't expected to want another relationship with someone, but spending time with Ewen made her think about exploring the possibility. He was clearly still wary after being hurt by his ex, but she hoped that some day he might start to lower his defences too. Then they might have a chance at something even more special.

As long as she didn't scare him off in the meantime.

'I guess I'll see you around.' Ewen paused to give her a brief kiss on the lips.

Clutching the bed covers to cover her nakedness when her emotions were making her feel vulnerable, she offered him a bright smile as he left. Pretending that being a convenient lay was enough for now. Though her body was satisfied, the rest of her was decidedly antsy. She'd grown close to Ewen and was beginning to think she was ready for more than a casual arrangement.

If Ewen didn't come to feel the same way, her whole world could be in jeopardy once again.

Ewen threw himself down on top of his bed, not bothering to undress again. He hadn't been able to get out of Bonnie's room quick enough. The sound of his heavy breathing filling the dark room was only partly to do with his physical exertions. It was fear that had his heart beating so fast he thought it might explode.

He'd done his best to keep his emotions at bay around Bonnie. Convinced himself that having a purely physical relationship would protect him. So why had it been on the tip of his tongue to tell her that he had feelings for her?

He could put it down to the euphoria of the moment. Making love to Bonnie made him feel like the king of the world, there was nothing on earth like it. Therein lay the problem. It wasn't just sex any more. As much as he'd tried to keep their encounters passionate, with no room to discuss those deeply personal matters that had brought them so close in the first place, it was all to no avail.

In those moments when he wasn't kissing her, touching her, or sharing her bed, he was thinking about her. He was invested in her. That was why he'd had to leave her tonight. Before he confessed his feelings, his want for something more than a fling. Because that went against everything he'd been trying to do to protect his heart.

He couldn't leave himself exposed like that. Waiting for her to reject him and abandon him like his family, like Victoria. This was a transition stage for Bonnie. She'd just come out of an abusive relationship and the timing certainly wasn't ideal for either of them to enter a serious commitment. He could take a chance, but he knew what he felt for Bonnie was so strong already that it would kill him if she rejected him too.

As always, Ewen's response when things got complicated was to retreat somewhere alone to deal with his feelings. He had a lot to think about and he could only do that with a clear head, away from Bonnie.

'Can I have a selection of the orange blossom and dark chocolate ones and...some praline swirls?'

'Of course.' Bonnie waited as the customer perused the glass case, making the crucial decision about which chocolates she wanted.

'I might take a few back for my husband too...'

It always took people a while to choose when there was such a wide range, but it was Bonnie's favourite part of her job. Watching people enthuse over her work, mouths watering, eyes wide, like children on Christmas morning not knowing which present to open first. Despite losing out on a childhood to follow in her father's footsteps, she was glad now to have a skill she was able to fall back on.

Bonnie carefully dropped the chocolates into the gift box with her tongs and sealed it with a sticker emblazoned with an image of the castle. Branding that made her products exclusive to castle visitors, and a tasty souvenir of their visit. Something she hoped to make available to a wider demographic at some stage. Her past had made her wary of getting too optimistic about the future, but with her new job, and Ewen in her life, she had a lot to look forward to.

Nights with Ewen were wonderful. Being in his arms, not having to go too far to get to work at a job she loved, was everything she could have wanted. However, experience had taught her things weren't always what they seemed at first. Not to take things at face value. Handsome, successful Ewen might appear to be the perfect man, certainly everything she needed at the moment, but he had his own emotional baggage. The last thing she needed was to get involved in anyone else's drama when she'd just escaped her own. As long as they kept things low-key, and they didn't get carried away with the idea of romance, things might be okay. After all, it hadn't worked out for either of them in the past.

'Thank you so much.' She took payment from her customer and handed over the bag of goodies, just as another group of excited elderly ladies walked in.

It was good to keep busy, so her thoughts weren't fully occupied with Ewen. Her new life shouldn't revolve around one man. She'd learned that lesson the hard way.

'I have a few free samples here, ladies, if you'd like to try before you buy.' Bonnie walked out from behind the counter with a tray, knowing no one could resist free chocolate.

A chorus of 'oohs' filled the little shop as she passed through the queue.

'Did you make these yourself?' one curious woman asked as she inspected a milk chocolate, caramel parcel, probably looking for flaws.

'Yes. All made in the castle kitchen by my own fair hands.' Strictly speaking it was the café kitchen, but people liked the romance.

'What flavour is this one?' another of the ladies asked after popping a whole truffle in her mouth.

'That's a Black Forest truffle. These ones are red velvet, and we have a cappuccino-flavoured one for the coffee lovers.'

The prospective customer turned her nose up at that one,

then proceeded to help herself to each of the others. Bonnie had a feeling this was going to be one of those times when they treated it like a buffet rather than a sample, so she'd be left holding an empty tray. It ate into her day's profits when people got greedy, but she couldn't say anything or she ran the risk of losing a sale, so she had to grin and bear it. She could always whip up some more during that quiet period between lunchtime and closing.

'Do you have any more of those white-chocolate, whisky ones?' A familiar voice sounded from the doorway, and her heart gave that extra kick at the sight of Ewen. Even when her head was telling her not to read too much into their new dynamic, her body betrayed her true feelings.

'I always save some specially for you, Your Grace. Ladies, this is our very own duke.' She set the sample tray down on top of the counter and went in search of the whisky-flavoured truffles he was so partial to. Leaving Ewen to be mobbed by some excited tourists.

'Morning,' he said, shooting daggers at her over the top of their heads.

Bonnie blew him a kiss and grabbed a bag of whisky truffles.

'Ooh, can I get some of those too?'

'Me too.'

'My husband would love those.'

Attention shifted to the small bag of chocolates now in Ewen's possession. They obviously thought this was some sort of under-the-counter, only-for-the-duke, secret stash. Bonnie didn't have the heart to tell them she just hadn't restocked the display yet.

Ewen took a seat at the back of the shop and waited whilst she parcelled up the rest of her whisky-flavoured stock. She didn't know what had brought him here, but he clearly wanted to talk, since he was willing to give up part of his working day to wait for her. Once all the purchases were complete, and the ladies had said goodbye to her, and their new favourite duke, Ewen came up to the counter.

'Business been good today, then?' There was something in his demeanour that had definitely changed since she'd last seen him. He was stiff, and awkward, and acting more like a boss than someone she'd shared her bed with last night.

'Yes, it's been pretty steady.'

'I've decided to go ahead with the annual ball,' he said, out of nowhere, taking her completely by surprise.

'That's great news! I'm sure Mrs McKenzie is delighted. What convinced you to go ahead with it?' The news gave her a little buzz of excitement. If he was planning to continue the tradition, it said that he was beginning to settle into his role here at the castle, adding to her security too. There was also the anticipation of being in attendance, of getting to dress up and dance and live out the fantasy of life at the castle.

She could just imagine Ewen in a tux waltzing her around the floor, her fabulous chiffon gown swishing around her strappy heels. It was a fairy tale come true, and she didn't even have to run to catch her pumpkin coach home before midnight. As long as she didn't expect her happy ever after with the handsome prince, it should be a perfect night.

Ewen dropped his gaze to his feet. 'I thought it was the right thing to do. I want to honour my father, my family, and my new position. It's what he would've wanted. I, er, also think it's about time I focused on the reason I'm here.'

When he eventually looked up at her again through lowered lashes, his shoulders slumped with resignation, she had a feeling she wasn't going to like what he had to say next.

'I thought things were going well? The wedding was a success and visitors are coming back to the castle. What's the problem?' She was aware the sharpness in her tone matched the defensive body language as she folded her arms, but her defence mechanism kicked in quicker these days.

'There's no problem. I just… I don't want to get distracted. We had a good time, but I don't think we should mix business and pleasure any more.'

Bonnie's stomach plummeted into the floor. So much for her lovely new life. A lot of her happiness was wrapped up in him, and the expectation of spending her nights with him. She'd invested her heart in him, in them, when clearly Ewen hadn't.

'You don't want to see me again?' She hated how small and pitiful her voice sounded, but this felt more brutal than anything her ex had inflicted on her. Maybe because she cared about him, wanted to be with him, it hurt so much more.

'I'll still see you every day.' He gave her a half-smile, which only made her sadder. 'It could never have been anything serious anyway, so it's probably for the best that we end things now before anyone gets hurt.'

'Sure.' She plastered on a bright smile for his benefit, and to preserve the last dregs of her self-respect.

In that moment it didn't matter that he was right, that if they let things go on the way they were she'd only fall harder, deeper, for him. All that mattered was the loss she was already experiencing.

It was then she decided she really needed to work on those defences more. She'd only just left one damaging relationship and she was already hurting again. So she steeled herself, hardened her heart, and tilted her chin in the air.

'Is that all you wanted? Because I have some whisky truffles to make.'

Ewen flinched as though she'd actually hit him, but if all he wanted was a working relationship, then that was what he would get. She wasn't about to jeopardise her home and her job if he thought she was going to make things difficult around here. It would be better for both of them if she acted as though their time together hadn't meant anything to her either.

'Okay, then. I should probably go and help Mrs McKenzie with this guest list. We've only got a few weeks to get ready and I'm going to need that time to brush up on my dancing skills.' His attempt at a joke fell flat without an engaged audience. Bonnie simply didn't have the energy to fake laugh when she'd effectively just been dumped.

'Are staff permitted to attend?' That would be the cherry on the cake if she wasn't allowed to take part in the festivities, forced to watch from the sidelines like an unwanted wife locked in the attic. She at least wanted the dressing-up part to look forward to. There hadn't been much call for glamming up in the refuge, or any money to do it. Once she got paid, she was treating herself to a haircut and a shopping trip.

'Of course.' He looked wounded that she'd even asked, but clearly she didn't know what went on in that head when she'd thought they were going to be spending another night of passion together. Not reverting to mere work colleagues, avoiding each other as much as humanly possible.

'In that case, I'll see you there.' She turned her back on him and walked back into her kitchen. The one place she did have control. The only place she needed to be.

Today's development was going to take the shine off the fairy-tale ball, but she had to remember why she was here. It wasn't to jump into another relationship, or tie herself to another man. Especially her boss, who had the ultimate power over her, when she was only living and working here because he'd allowed it.

From now on she was going to concentrate on her position at the castle too. Everything that had happened between her and Ewen would have to remain nothing more than a passionate interlude. A reintroduction into the real world, which would hopefully set her up for the future now she knew she didn't have to fear every man who crossed her path. That sex could be fun, mutually enjoyable for both participants. As long as she didn't let emotions get in the way.

CHAPTER NINE

'WELCOME. IT'S SO good to see you. Thank you for coming. Yes, it is a shame about my father, but I hope I can do him proud this evening.' Ewen greeted everyone as they came in with a clammy handshake.

Although he could legitimately call the castle his home, and he'd invited all these people here, there was still an element of unease that wouldn't let him enjoy the night. He had a lot to prove to these people, who only knew part of the story between him and his parents. His father might have apologised in a letter to him, but he certainly hadn't made the admission of his mistakes public or accepted his responsibility for their estrangement. Most of these people likely saw Ewen as the problem child who'd left his ailing father to die alone, and simply waltzed back to claim the inheritance. There were always two sides to a story, but most people were only too happy to believe the one they heard first, not interested in the backstory. Grief wasn't as sexy as the scandal of a rebellious son who killed his brother in a crash and ran away from home.

Tonight was hopefully his chance to prove he could fill his father's shoes, and that he wasn't some bad seed who was going to blow the family fortune. He'd certainly been putting all of his time and effort into making this a success tonight. Not that it was all for the benefit of others.

He'd needed tasks to fill his days with something other than yearning after Bonnie and wondering what could have been.

This past month had been torturous in so many ways, seeing her every day and pretending that his feelings for her had never happened. They were civil and professional towards one another, but in a way that was almost as devastating as if she had walked away from him altogether. He'd lost a friend and a confidante, as well as a lover.

During the long, lonely nights lying awake in his room his mind was thoroughly made up about selling the castle and moving on. Then he'd see Bonnie happy in her shop and yearn to have her back in his arms. When he had her beside him this place felt more like home than it ever had. He was conflicted over his plans for the future, and, left alone to brood, he'd read and reread the letter his father had left him.

Ewen had been so engrossed in what had happened between him and Bonnie that he hadn't fully processed the contents of the note. Now he'd analysed it in greater detail, his father's words had given him a new perspective on life at BenCrag. Past and present.

His father had wanted to renew their relationship, but that same fear of rejection Ewen suffered from had prevented him from doing so. Causing them both unnecessary pain. Ewen wondered if he was making the same mistake with Bonnie. If he was hurting himself by not being with her, instead of taking that leap of faith and telling her how he really felt. He didn't want to spend the rest of his life with regrets like his old man.

Now all he had to do was get Bonnie alone and find the courage to open up. Not an easy task on the biggest night of the castle's year.

Mrs McKenzie sidled up to him, wearing a blue and green dress made from her family tartan, a brighter alternative to her usual dull tweeds. The smile was new too. 'It's so wonderful to see the castle coming alive again, isn't it?'

Ewen was tempted to remind her they'd had visitors coming for weeks now, not to mention the wedding that had taken over the castle and its grounds. But he didn't want to rain on her parade when he knew how much this meant to her. It was a reminder of the old days, and happier times. The only difference was the duke holding the event. He didn't know how she would cope if he did leave and all ties to the family were severed. Depending on what happened tonight, this could be the last ball in the castle. Though he couldn't even tell her that. He could only try and make it as memorable as possible for all involved.

'I hope you've got your dancing shoes on, Mrs McKenzie. I have you pencilled in for a reel.'

She lifted her skirt and turned her ankle, showing off a pair of sturdy heels. 'I'm looking forward to it.'

A couple came through the doors that she seemed to recognise, and she left Ewen greeting the guests at the door to go with them into the main hall where the dance was being held.

Everyone was in their finery, the event an excuse for people to dress up and enjoy themselves. He could see why it was a highly anticipated day on the calendar. Regardless that the decision to hold it had been last minute, all the RSVPs had come in thick and fast. It seemed the regular attendees had kept their diaries open just in case, and for that he was thankful. It wouldn't have been quite the same if it had been only him and the castle staff in attendance.

He glanced back at the familiar group banded together at the back of the room, clutching their drinks and chatting among themselves. Specifically letting his gaze fall on Bonnie, who looked amazing.

She'd really gone all out tonight, her hair cascading onto her shoulders in soft chocolate waves, her smoky eye make-up and the slick of crimson lipstick highlighting all her best features. Along with the off-the-shoulder, slinky satin red dress, with the train at the back skimming the floor. It clung to her full breasts, the indent at her waist, and her curvy hips. The epitome of a siren, calling to every man in the room who couldn't take his eyes off her. Including Ewen. Though he didn't even try to fool himself that this was for his benefit, when she'd been brusque with him on the occasions that they had interacted.

She'd taken to having her breakfast half an hour earlier than he did, eating dinner in the shop at night, so they didn't have to make awkward small talk in the castle kitchen. It was what he had asked for, space to concentrate on events at the castle. Except numerous phone calls, meetings with suppliers and auditioning ceilidh bands hadn't managed to take his mind off her.

Seeing her tonight wasn't going to help with that. Every part of the castle seemed to have her imprinted on it. The kitchen, his apartment, the stairs…now even the ballroom. He missed her. It had been his idea to call things off before they had a chance to begin, but he'd spent just as much time thinking about her as if he'd simply let things play out. The only difference was that he was miserable inside because he couldn't be with her. He'd be lucky if she'd even give him five minutes of her time tonight.

'Aren't you coming in, Your Grace? The dance is about to start.' One of the volunteers who helped with the gardens, a horticulture student from the local college, touched him lightly on the arm.

She was the last to arrive, windswept and alone, and clearly a little anxious about walking into the party on her own.

'In that case, may I escort you inside, Sara? I think I saw some of your friends in there.' He angled his arm and offered it to her in support, though he was glad he wasn't walking in solo either. The idea of having to succeed, of making a good impression on his father's friends and acquaintances, was a lot of pressure. Part of the reason he'd invited the junior members of staff too, young enough not to hold a grudge against him.

'Thank you, Your Grace,' she said, slipping her arm into his and clinging on for dear life.

'Just call me Ewen.' He grimaced every time someone addressed him according to his status. It reminded him of his father, and wasn't a title he was sure he lived up to yet.

The other guests were milling around the room, enjoying the glasses of champagne and drams of whisky being passed round by the waiting staff. Everyone was dressed in brightly coloured gowns and tartans, but his eyes automatically went to the flash of red in the corner. She was talking to Richard, the estate manager. The handsome, *single* estate manager, who currently had his hand on Bonnie's arm.

Ewen found himself steering Sara towards them, enjoying the flash of irritation in Bonnie's eyes.

'Good evening. Richard, Bonnie, this is Sara, she's one of our gardening volunteers.'

'Hi, yes, I think you bought some of my dark chocolate lavender creams the other day.' Bonnie offered her a welcoming smile in stark contrast to the dark look he'd received upon his approach.

'They were a present for my granny and she loved them. I think I'll have a standing order now.' Sara laughed.

'Nice to see you again, Sara. We met when we were landscaping that overgrown land behind the old stables,' Richard explained to Ewen and Bonnie.

'Yes, how is that coming?' Sara enquired, dropping her arm from Ewen's, her attention now on Richard.

'I have some pictures on my phone if you'd like to see. You should stop by next time you're here. I'd like to get some new eyes on the project.' Richard pulled out his phone to show Sara what he'd been working on, and the couple drifted away from Bonnie and Ewen.

'You look amazing,' he told her, unable to ignore the obvious now his buffer had disappeared.

'Thank you. You've done a great job putting all of this together,' she said, gesturing around the room.

'Well, Mrs McKenzie had a lot of input, but I'm happy with the turnout.' His main worry had been that no one would show up, unwilling to give him a chance, like so many people in his life. But he'd underestimated the enthusiasm for the annual event. He had Mrs McKenzie to thank for persuading him to go ahead, otherwise he might never have won people over.

An uneasy silence descended between them, highlighted even more by the chatter going on in the room around them. He hated this new awkward dynamic when they'd been so close at the beginning. As close as two people could be. That was probably why he'd backed away, afraid things would develop into something more serious than he'd anticipated. Those wounds Victoria and his parents had left upon him preventing him from even taking a chance. Afraid of further rejection and heartbreak. Of being left alone again.

However, as he'd found, it wasn't as easy to simply shut off those emotions and forget how she'd made him feel. Why else had he barrelled straight over at the sight of her talking to another man? A possessive move he knew would horrify her, and only made him despise himself more. It was no one else's fault but his if she did move on with someone else.

'How've you been?'

'Do you have any other events planned?'

They stumbled over each other's words, adding to the pain in his heart. They couldn't even be around one another now without things being awkward, and that wasn't going to improve the longer they dodged around each other both inside and outside work. It was probably only a matter of time before she decided to move into her own place where she was free to come and go as she pleased without fear of running into an ex. A scenario that should have suited him too, not having to be reminded of what he'd thrown away at every turn, but which also saddened him. He didn't want to imagine living in the castle on his own again.

They exchanged embarrassed half-smiles.

'I'm good. Busy getting the website up and running. Thank you for agreeing to that, by the way. I've already got some custom orders coming in, so plenty of work ahead.'

'It wasn't a problem simply adding a link on the castle main page. I'm glad you're getting some interest. You deserve it.'

'Thanks. I trust you've more events planned, since they seem to be such a success.' She probed into the castle's future again, but Ewen didn't want to look too far ahead. At least not beyond the things his father had pencilled in for the rest of the year.

'I think we've got a few craft-fair weekends planned out in the grounds, weather permitting, and maybe a New Year's bash if this goes well.'

'Hogmanay, at the castle. That sounds like a definite

winner.' Her smile lit up the dark corner of the room, but also squeezed his heart like a vice. Not only because he missed her, but also because he wasn't sure if he'd still be in the castle beyond Hogmanay.

'Ladies and gentlemen. Dinner will now be served in the main dining room, if you'd care to make your way there.'

Before Ewen cracked and told her how much he was missing her, dinner was announced, and all the attendees began to file out.

'Shall we?' He held out his arm to escort Bonnie to the dining room. Hoping it wouldn't be the last time he'd get to touch her.

The whole scene was something Bonnie had never dreamed she could ever be part of, chandeliers sparkling from the arched, ornamental ceilings making everything look so much more magical. Her heart was beating frantically with every step they took, but she was glad Ewen had taken it upon himself to escort her to dinner. Even if it was merely out of politeness.

She missed his touch, missed being with him. It was difficult living and working in the same place, unable to escape the memories or feelings associated with him. She'd have to find her own place soon, before he started seeing someone else and completely broke her heart.

'It's all right. I've got you,' Ewen whispered, sensing her unease as they walked into the dining room. As always, doing his best to take care of her feelings.

It was daunting being in a room full of people, most of whom she didn't know. Especially when she was dressed the way she was tonight. At first, the idea of glamming up had been thrilling, something she'd looked forward to. The shine somewhat wearing off when Ewen had called a halt to their fling so early on. With a little time to herself, she'd decided it was a chance for her to dress the way she wanted for once.

After years of being told what she couldn't wear, of not being able to look how she wanted, she'd gone a bit mad with power. Now she wondered if the vamp look had been overkill, and if it had been to get Ewen's attention. Either way it appeared to have worked. Okay, so she had wanted him to see what he was missing, but he looked better than ever too in his formal tight-fitting tux jacket and kilt.

The weeks since their night together had been lonely. Though she'd proved to herself, and everyone else, she was more than capable of looking after herself, it had been nice to have his company. Nicer still to share a bed with someone who took care of her needs as well as their own.

Being with him had been the happiest time of her life. Ewen had shown her she was capable of having a normal relationship, that she didn't have to settle for someone who treated her badly. She'd stopped flinching every time someone raised their voice, enjoyed being touched without wondering when it would turn to something violent. Thanks to Ewen she could be comfortable around men again. But there was only one she wanted. It was a shame he couldn't give her the serious commitment she knew she wanted now.

She'd liked being in a relationship, even for a little while. Enjoyed having someone to spend her evenings with, to talk with about her day over a shared meal. But she wanted a partner who wasn't afraid to show his emotions. Who didn't freak out at the thought of spending the night with her. She deserved someone who would love her completely, and apparently that wasn't Ewen.

'I think that's your seat there.' Ewen unhooked her arm

and led her to her name card on the vast banqueting table laid with shining cutlery and crystal-clear glasses.

'Thank you.' She took her seat and watched as he walked down to take his seat at the end of the table.

It would have been easier for her to have him sitting beside her, regardless of their current awkwardness, rather than the two strangers who sat down either side of her. She consoled herself that at least he was still in her eyeline, close enough that she could hear him, giving her some sense of familiarity in the situation.

'You're a new face around here.' A deep voice sounded from the seat next to her.

She turned to find an elderly, distinguished gentleman peering at her through horn rimmed spectacles.

'I just moved here. I run the chocolate shop in the castle.'

Her dinner companion frowned, and she wondered if he was the type who thought the hired help shouldn't be dining at the table. 'Are you the lass that made the chocolate castle? I was a guest at the wedding here last month. Incredible work.'

Bonnie let out a sigh of relief. 'Yes, that was me. Thank you.'

It was always nice to get positive feedback on her work, and she hoped the little treats she'd made to give out to the guests at the end of the evening would earn her more future custom too.

'It's good to have some new blood at the castle. It would be a shame if it fell into more commercial hands, and it lost the local charm. I knew the late duke…a terrible loss to the community.'

'So I understand. I never actually met him, but he was very kind in taking me on.' She had him to thank for everything.

'What do you think of the son? He's a new face around here too.' The gentleman sniffed.

Bonnie was uncomfortable engaging in any negative conversation involving Ewen when her personal feelings were so wrapped up in him and everything at the castle. She couldn't bear to hear anyone talk ill of him either, when they didn't know the full, painful family history. So she tried to be as diplomatic as possible.

'Ewen is doing his best to honour his father's legacy under some very difficult circumstances.'

'Yes, I understand there was some bad blood between them after the eldest was killed. A car crash, I understand.'

'An accident, which I think left the whole family grieving. I think he was very brave to come back and pick up where his father left off.' She had to defend him when she knew what had gone on behind the scenes to get him to this place. Ewen would never make the contents of his father's letter public, which would have exonerated him of any wrongdoing, because he was too proud, and protective of the family name. He wouldn't want to air the family's dirty washing in public.

Ewen was a man of honour. A hard worker who tried to do the right thing by everyone. Not to mention amazing in bed. Okay, so that might have coloured her view a little, and was information she wouldn't be sharing either, but it didn't take away from the fact he was just a wonderful person.

'He has big shoes to fill, but, if tonight is anything to go by, I think the community will welcome him back with open arms.' The gentleman toasted the new duke with his dram of whisky before taking a sip, and Bonnie was relieved Ewen was beginning to win people over. He deserved his place here, and she knew he'd work hard to do what was best for the castle, and the people employed there. Including her.

The sound of his laughter from the head of the table caught her attention. He was laughing at something the woman on his right had said. Bonnie slowly zoned out from the conversation she'd been in to try and hear what had amused Ewen. She was experiencing the same irrational envy now as she had when he'd walked in with the pretty young blonde earlier, regardless that they obviously weren't together.

It was that want to be the woman making him laugh, to be with him, that made her realise she'd fallen for him. Given that they hadn't been together for weeks, the damage had clearly already been done. Now she was doomed to watch him from the sidelines as he captivated other women. She wasn't looking forward to meeting his next conquest over the breakfast table.

Ewen caught her eye and gave her a heart-racing smile. A private moment just between the two of them in this room full of strangers that made her wish they were alone. That he'd never ended the best thing to happen to her in years.

Ewen took a swig of whisky to steady his nerves before he got to his feet. He didn't think he'd get heckled at his own dinner, but that didn't make it any easier to stand in front of his father's friends and acquaintances and make a speech.

'Ladies and gentlemen, could I have your attention, please?' He waited until the hubbub of conversation subsided. 'Thank you.'

'You've had my attention all night,' one of the more inebriated female guests shouted to make him blush. The interruption raised a few titters around the table and broke the ice for him.

Ewen glanced over at Bonnie, who was sitting tight-lipped, glaring daggers at the new member of his fan club. It made him smile that she should be outraged on his behalf, or might even have been touched by the green-eyed monster at the thought that someone else should be interested in him. Perhaps he hadn't completely ruined things with Bonnie. She hadn't flinched when he'd offered to escort her to dinner, and had almost looked disappointed when she'd found she wasn't sitting with him. His pulse picked up along with his spirits. All might not be lost after all.

Deciding to ignore the vocal adulation, Ewen cleared his throat and continued. 'I just wanted to take this opportunity to thank you all for coming tonight. It's been a difficult time for everyone who knew my father, and an upheaval for those working at the castle.'

He gave a nod to all the staff currently seated, grateful that they'd all stayed on to help him keep the place running. 'I'd have been lost these past weeks if you hadn't all pitched in to show me the ropes, so thank you.'

He raised his glass and toasted his new friends to a chorus of approval from the rest of the guests.

'Anyway, tonight is about honouring my father, and he would want us all to eat, drink, and dance the night away. So if you'd care to raise your glasses, I'd like to make a toast to my father, the duke.'

'The duke.' The room echoed with the sentiment and Ewen found himself becoming choked up.

As always when he was struggling, feelings of grief and remorse overwhelming him, he sought out Bonnie to centre him. Her eyes were glistening with tears as she gave him a wobbly smile and raised her glass to him. Ewen knew it wasn't just his father she was toasting and he wanted to hold her in his arms more than ever.

Before he could go too far down that rabbit hole, the sound of the band filtered through the air. The upbeat tempo of traditional Scottish folk music immediately altered the mood of the place, and he was grateful for it. He would've hated to be responsible for a maudlin atmosphere at what was supposed to be the highlight of the year in the village.

'It sounds as though the party's starting without us, so if you'd all like to make your way back to the main hall, we'll get our dancing shoes on.' He gave everyone permission to leave, and took a minute for himself, watching as everyone headed out of the room. With one notable exception.

Bonnie hung back until everyone had left before moving towards Ewen. 'I know that couldn't have been easy for you, but you did a good job. Of everything. Your father would've been proud.'

Ewen didn't realise how much he'd needed to hear that, how much he needed Bonnie, until she hugged him. It was a brief, empathetic reaction to something she knew was an emotional matter for him, but it was the contact he'd been yearning for. He didn't want the night to end, didn't want to go back to the real world, avoiding each other at work because it was too painful otherwise.

'Thanks. I suppose I should really go in there and start shaking my stuff.' He deployed some humour to try and defuse the situation.

Bonnie made a *tsk* sound. 'I'm not sure you'll want to do that. I think that might be enough to start a stampede of drunk cougars headed your way.'

Ewen loved the tinge of jealousy he swore he heard in her voice as they made their way towards the sounds of the ceilidh. It proved she still cared.

The dancing was already under way, and as they en-

tered the room Ewen could feel all the men stand up a little straighter. All eyes on Bonnie. He wasn't ready to let
her go again.

'May I have this dance?' he asked with a bow and his
hand extended towards her.

'I'm not sure I'd make a good partner. I haven't danced
in a long time.' She hesitated, but he was sure it was due to
her lack of experience rather than who was asking.

'Perfect! Neither have I.' It would be expected of him
to take part, and he knew he'd feel much more comfortable in the spotlight if Bonnie was with him. Although he
wouldn't push it if she really didn't want to accompany him
onto the dance floor.

Given her history, he would never force her to do anything she didn't want, and he hoped she understood that.

He was about to leave, resigning himself to making a
show of himself solo, when she threw her hands up in the
air.

'Sod it. You only live once, right? You were brave
enough to go ahead with this tonight, so I'm sure I can
cope with making a fool of myself on the dance floor.' She
took his hand and walked forward, chin held high.

Ewen was proud of her. This was a woman who'd been
through serious trauma, who would have had every right to
hide away from the world. But that wasn't Bonnie. Instead,
she was throwing herself out there, being the true version
of herself—strong and beautiful. An amazing woman he
couldn't believe he'd almost let slip through his fingers.

They joined the throng on the floor, who'd already arranged themselves into two lines facing one another. Ewen
and Bonnie broke into the lines, holding hands with their
fellow dancers and asking each other what they'd got them-

selves into. Luckily there was a caller to remind them of the dance moves.

After a short countdown, the dancing couples advanced towards one another, then retreated. Ewen and Bonnie were lagging behind a little trying to keep up with what was happening.

They split into parties of four, hands in the middle, spinning around one way, then the other.

'Now, do-si-do!'

Following the caller's instruction, and the others around them, Ewen and Bonnie passed each other back-to-back, arms folded. They weren't slick, or co-ordinated, but neither was anyone else, the free bar obviously having an effect on the quality of dancing. But everyone was having fun, and the sound of Bonnie's laughter made everything worthwhile.

'I think I need a drink,' he shouted over the music once the dance had ended, a tad out of breath.

'Just one more dance,' Bonnie begged, tugging him back onto the floor.

How could he refuse when she looked so happy, and it was another chance to be close to her?

They linked arms and spun around with the rest of the guests. Clapped and whooped, and skipped the length and breadth of the hall until they were both red-faced and out of breath. For more than one dance. When it finally came to a gentle waltz, Ewen took Bonnie into his arms with some relief. Neither of them had hesitated to partner up with each other for the slow dance. He took it as a positive sign that she didn't hate the sight of him altogether, since she'd been content to dance with him for most of the evening.

'Have you enjoyed yourself tonight?'

'I have. I was worried about socialising with so many

people I don't know. I've been a bit isolated these past few years.'

Even though her grin said she was joking, Ewen knew it was also something of an understatement. From everything she'd told him she'd practically been a prisoner in her own home. He could only imagine how overwhelming this could have been if she hadn't confronted it so head-on. Even he'd had sleepless nights over having a bunch of strangers in his home, judging him and his actions, and he was used to the bustling streets of London until recently. For Bonnie to be such a part of his big night meant a lot to him, and spoke volumes about the special kind of person she was. The sort of woman he should've snapped up when he had the chance.

'I miss you.' The words fell from his lips into her ear as they slow-danced around the floor.

Bonnie stiffened in his arms and he immediately regretted opening his mouth.

'Sorry. That wasn't fair of me. Forget I said anything.'

She locked her eyes onto his. 'It was your idea to call things off. Not mine.'

'I know, and I've been kicking myself every day since.' That bud of hope threatened to fully bloom when she reminded him that she'd been happy with the set-up. It opened up the possibility that she would be willing to give him another chance.

At least in his head.

'What is it you want from me, Ewen?' Bonnie didn't know if the ache in her heart was from false hope or fear she was giving him an opportunity to hurt her all over again by even entertaining whatever he had to say to her.

They'd spent most of the evening together. Something

she hadn't planned, but had enjoyed nonetheless. When he said things like he was missing her, it only set her up for more heartbreak if nothing more was going to come of it. It was only when he'd called things off that she'd realised the true depth of her feelings for Ewen. Knowing if he'd expressed an interest in making things serious, she would've been prepared to risk her heart on him. Except he'd ended things instead.

She'd missed him every minute of every day, but had to get on with things as best she could, because that was what she did. What she'd been doing for years. And she was afraid to expect more.

'I don't know,' he said honestly, which didn't do anything to help her. 'I just know I want you back in my life as more than a member of staff who's constantly trying to avoid me.'

His smile was heartbreaking. She'd taken steps to protect herself, eating at different times so she didn't have to see him all the time and be reminded of their nights together. It hadn't occurred to her that it might be hurting him just as much.

'We're leaving. I just wanted to thank you for such a wonderful evening. Looking forward to the next one.' A tall, well-dressed man tapped Ewen on the shoulder to get his attention, interrupting his heart-to-heart with Bonnie.

He gave her a look of apology, but she understood he couldn't ignore his guests. They broke hold so he could shake hands with the man, and his partner.

'Thanks for coming. I'll see you out.' He turned back to mouth an apology to Bonnie and she nodded an 'okay' in response. It was part of his duty as host, she knew it was nothing personal when he'd been keen to talk to her.

Bonnie moved to a seat at the side of the room, glad to take off her shoes and rest after the earlier energetic dancing. She saw little more of Ewen as more and more couples took their leave. Every time he appeared at the door, someone else was keen to say their goodbyes and shake hands with the now popular duke. Whatever preconceptions they'd had about him had obviously been put to rest over the course of the night, and she was pleased he'd achieved his objective, along with honouring his father's memory.

It showed a lot of restraint, and social etiquette, that he hadn't felt the need to explain himself, to lay the blame for his estrangement from the family at his parents' feet, when they'd treated him so appallingly. She wasn't sure she would've been so magnanimous in the circumstances. Although she was in similar circumstances with her own mother and father, she knew she had to shoulder some of the blame for her actions. They'd just been trying to protect her. Even if they'd gone about it the wrong way. If they had as many regrets about their actions as she did, she thought it might be worth trying to salvage a relationship before it was too late and she was left in the same emotional turmoil as Ewen appeared to be in.

Bonnie watched as the room gradually emptied. The band packed up their instruments, the lights came back on, and it began to feel as though she'd been stood up on a date, people looking at her with pity. In the end, weary and wanting to hold onto a shred of dignity, she decided to go to bed. If Ewen really wanted to speak to her he could find her. He knew where she worked and lived. She'd spent enough of her life being dangled like a puppet on a man's whim.

On her way up the stairs to her room she noticed the door was ajar. Ewen was outside holding court and laughing with a group of revellers. She didn't begrudge him the chance to make new friends and acquaintances, or enjoy his new status, having charmed everyone in the village. However, it was a reminder she wasn't a priority in his life. Something he'd made clear the last time they'd been together. She was only worthy of a casual fling, nothing more serious. And, whilst it had been by mutual agreement at the time, now she realised she deserved more.

If she was going to share her life with another man, it had to be someone who treated her feelings as a priority, not an afterthought. What these past weeks had shown her was that she was more than capable of taking care of herself, so why should she open herself up to someone who thought he could pick her up and set her down when he chose?

She stomped her way back to her room as much as her bare feet would allow, stripped off her dress, wiped off her make-up, and put on her comfy pyjamas. The knock on her door didn't come as a complete surprise, and she realised her quick change had been out of defiance. If she hadn't been enough to capture his attention in all her finery, she was done making the effort.

'I'm sorry. I'm sorry. I'm sorry,' he said when she opened the door.

She cocked an eyebrow at him and folded her arms across her chest. 'I know you didn't expect me to sit around like some love-struck schoolgirl waiting on you all night.'

'Of course not. I really wanted to talk to you. It's just… people wanted to chat, to share memories of my dad and the nights they used to have here at the castle. I didn't want to be rude and walk away, but I am sorry I let you down.' The sincere remorse was evident in the slump of his shoulders, and the puppy-dog eyes begging for forgiveness made her wilt.

'It's okay,' she relented, remembering that this whole thing had been about remembering his father, not her love life.

'Trust me, I would much rather have been spending that

time with you. You looked amazing tonight.' He was leaning against the door jamb, his voice seeming to drop an octave as his eyes swept over her. Making her feel as though she were still wearing her sexy red dress and heels, not her fleecy, sloth-covered pjs.

Her heart started that dangerous arrythmia that followed every time he looked at her. More apparent now they were alone and he wasn't even trying to disguise the fact he found her attractive.

'Sorry. I changed as soon as I got in. I thought the moment between us had passed.'

He dropped his head as though he'd been punched in the gut. 'You still look amazing, but I should've waited until everyone had gone before I tried to start that conversation. You deserve my undivided attention, Bonnie.'

The way he was looking at her, she knew she had it now.

Bonnie swallowed hard, trying not to slide into a puddle of want on her doorstep.

'So, what was it you wanted to talk about?' She did her best impression of a woman holding it together, indifferent to the man standing in front of her begging her to hear him out.

'Us.'

'There is no us. That was your decision, Ewen.' She wasn't going to let him get away from that fact lightly.

'Well, I'm not known for making the best decisions, am I?' Another flash of that endearing smile and the twinkle of his eyes ensured she would at least hear him out.

'And ending things between us was…?'

'A big mistake. Huge.' He gave her a self-deprecating grin that almost convinced her to let him off. Except she needed more convincing she wouldn't be the one full of regret if she relented now.

'Ewen, I've had time to think too, and, you know, I don't think a fling is enough for me. If I'm going to be with someone it'll be because they want to be with me, not because I'm convenient. We work together, we live together, and I just think it should be all or nothing. I'm not saying I want to get married and have babies, but I'm saying I do want some level of commitment. I think I deserve that at least.' She didn't think it was too much to ask to have some sort of security in a relationship. Something normal, that wasn't limited to within the walls of the castle.

'You do. I know we rushed head first into things, but I would like to try again. We've both been hurt in the past, and I think we chose a casual arrangement because it felt safer. I ended it because I knew I would want more and I didn't think I was ready for that. Ready to risk my heart on someone again. Being without you these past weeks has been torture and made me realise I'd rather take that risk than not be with you at all. We can take it slow if that's what you want. If you're even willing to give me another chance...'

Bonnie scrunched her face up. 'I don't know... I think I have a few demands which need to be met before I agree to anything.'

'Your wish is my command.' He stepped farther into her room, sliding his hands around her waist, and sending her hormones into overdrive.

'Not those kinds of needs. Although... I'm sure a little sweetener would help seal the deal...' She tilted her head back as he began kissing his way along her neck, the friction of his beard against her skin making her shiver with delight.

'Tell me what you need, Bonnie.' His voice was thick

with longing, his breath hot in her ear, and her entire body seemed to ache for him.

'I want...' Bonnie fought to find words through the fog of desire currently consuming her. She closed her eyes and tried to focus on her thoughts rather than the sensations rushing through her body.

'I want to go out. To date. To be part of a couple. All the fun things I've missed out on for so long.' Any good memories she had of the early days with her ex when he'd been wooing her were now tarnished with the realisation he'd been lulling her into a false sense of security. Now she wanted the real deal.

'Done. We can go steady.' He paused his perusal of her skin with his mouth. 'Does that mean you want me to go now? To forget what we've already had and start from scratch?'

She thought about it briefly, and discovered her head and her heart differed greatly on the matter. In the end she went with the feelings she was having somewhere lower than her gut.

'No.' She grabbed him by the shirt collar and pulled him fully inside the room, kicking the door shut behind him.

There was no point pretending their time together hadn't happened. Certainly, she didn't want to. There was nothing to be gained from being coy now, and she had a lot of lost ground to make up for in the bedroom department.

'Good,' he growled, and backed her towards the bed.

Perhaps she was making it too easy for him, but this was what she wanted too, and there was no better way to get over her past than by taking control of her own wants.

Ewen was unbuttoning her pyjamas whilst he kissed her, taking his sweet time about it. The graze of his fingers travelling down her body flooding her with arousal.

She was more impatient, tugging at his jacket, unbuttoning his shirt, until he got the message and pulled them off himself. His clothes quickly followed by hers as they tumbled onto her bed.

'I'm sorry it's not quite the same standard as your room,' she muttered against his lips.

'I wouldn't care if we were in the dungeon, I'd still be happy as long as I was with you,' he said, palming her breast and teasing her nipples into tight buds.

'There's a dungeon? Is that a duke kink?'

'Not yet.' Ewen playfully grabbed both of her wrists and held them above her head in one of his large hands.

It could've been a macho display of strength used to intimidate her, but she knew that wasn't Ewen. She wasn't frightened or cowed by his actions, merely turned on. Not least because, whilst she was incapacitated, he was kissing his way all over her body, driving her nuts when she couldn't touch him in return.

When he did loosen his grip, his attention diverted towards her breasts again, she took the opportunity to break free.

'Condoms. We need condoms,' she said breathlessly, pushing herself up off the bed.

'I didn't think to put any in my sporran,' Ewen said with a grin as he moved aside to let her get up.

'I have some in the bathroom cabinet. I thought when we decided to have a casual fling that we might need them.' She had no need to be embarrassed. It was the sensible thing to do. Yet she didn't want him to think there had been anyone else. She supposed the fact that he hadn't been carrying protection around with him suggested perhaps he hadn't been sleeping around either. The thought comforted her as she retrieved a foil packet from the bathroom.

When she came back into the room, Ewen was lying gorgeously naked on her bed waiting, arms behind his head, looking as though that was exactly where he was meant to be.

'What?' he asked.

'I was just thinking you look very at home. I mean, I know the castle *is* your home, but you look comfortable in my bed.' She straddled him and handed over the shiny prize.

'Not comfortable, per se, in my current state,' he joked and drew her attention to his impressive arousal. 'But I am very happy to be here.'

'So I see.' She bent down and kissed him on the mouth, reconnecting, and picking up where they'd left off.

Except something had changed between them. The earlier frenzied passion replaced with a tenderness. A new softness in the kissing that suggested this was more than just sex now. They didn't have to rush, or hide away any more. If they were embarking on a new relationship, they had all the time in the world to explore one another. Along with their feelings.

Bonnie rolled over onto her back, taking Ewen with her. She wanted to feel loved tonight, to let him take control.

'I need you, Ewen.'

He stopped kissing her long enough to check that was what she wanted. 'Are you sure?'

She arched her hips up off the bed to meet his. 'I'm sure.'

That was all the confirmation he needed as he sheathed himself and slowly filled her. Bonnie gasped, adjusting to that initial union of their bodies, and Ewen paused. Kissing her so tenderly any tension in her body immediately melted away. She wanted this, wanted him, for as long as possible.

When she'd left her ex she'd never have believed she'd want to be with anyone else again. It said a lot about Ewen that she was willing to open up her heart and her life to him so soon. She was putting all of her trust in him not to hurt her. He let her make her own choices, didn't try to exert control over her the way the other men in her life had. Although it was early days, she had a good feeling about their relationship. They'd already been through so much, she knew neither of them wanted any more drama or deceit. Hopefully they were going into an honest, easy relationship, with no nasty surprises lurking in the closet. What she saw was what she got with Ewen—a handsome, sexy, hardworking, loving man. It was a bonus that she got to see him every day, working in a place she loved.

For once, her future was bright.

CHAPTER TEN

EWEN FORCED HIS eyes open, though he had no desire to leave this cosy cocoon he and Bonnie had made under the covers. Especially when she was naked, and curved so invitingly against his body. He groaned as the rest of his body began to stir, knowing he had no time to indulge the carnal urges Bonnie had awakened so vigorously in him.

He knew the physical side of their relationship was so spectacular because it was about more than sex. They had a connection he'd never had with Victoria, who'd always remained a little aloof. Now he realised she'd been keeping secrets, with one eye on a better prospect. Perhaps had indulged in a few more dalliances than he was even aware of. Not that he cared any more. His life was here at the castle, with Bonnie. He'd made the decision to stay permanently in the early hours of the morning, when he'd wakened briefly with her in his arms with a feeling of contentment that he never wanted to lose again.

The castle had always represented a difficult past, but now he wanted to make plans for a future with Bonnie. He had the events side of the business to run, and she had the chocolate shop. Their life was here, and now they had each other it would start to feel like a real home again.

Trying his best not to disturb her, he eased himself away, and slid to the edge of the mattress.

'Where are you going? Afraid Mrs McKenzie won't approve?' she mumbled, her back still to him.

'Not at all. We're both adults, and my private life is nothing to do with the staff. At least, the rest of the staff.' He was aware their relationship might raise a few eyebrows, but if he and Bonnie were happy that was all that mattered. It had been a long time since he'd felt loved and wanted, and he wasn't about to throw that away simply because of someone else's opinion. He was done living his life afraid of what people thought about him. The only person's opinion that held any sway over him was Bonnie's, and after their night together he was pretty sure he'd made her happy. Several times.

'Then get back into bed.' She threw the covers back again and patted the empty space behind her.

'I wish I could. Trust me, I could happily spend the rest of my life in there with you. Unfortunately, I have a business appointment this morning.' It took every last drop of his energy to refrain from climbing back into the bed and snuggling up behind her again. However, he had an appointment this morning that he'd left too late to cancel. There were decisions to be made that were going to dictate his future, and that of the castle, now he was certain of the direction he wanted both to take.

He dropped a kiss on a sleepy Bonnie's forehead, taking a mental snapshot of her lying here so he remembered exactly why he was doing this.

'Go back to sleep. I'm just going to grab a shower and change into something less comfortable than my birthday suit.' He grabbed his clothes up off the floor, separating them from Bonnie's pyjamas, which he left on the end of the bed for her.

'I happen to like your birthday suit,' she muttered into her pillow, making Ewen laugh.

'Don't worry, I'll wear it again later. Just for you.'

With his modesty covered by the bundle of clothes in his hand, he made a dash down the hall to his room, hoping it was early enough to dodge Mrs McKenzie's eagle eyes.

Whilst he still maintained his private life was no one else's business other than his and Bonnie's, that didn't mean he was ready to face her disapproving glare. He wanted her to know they were in a committed relationship, not just bed-hopping. It would be the more mature call to talk to her, rather than let her find out for herself.

He was sure that was what he wanted now with Bonnie. A secure, committed relationship, and a future to look forward to at the castle. These last weeks, he'd been floundering to find somewhere he belonged, and a purpose in life. The castle had held so many bad memories his knee-jerk reaction had been to sell it on. Working to get the castle up and running again with Bonnie, Mrs McKenzie, and the rest of the staff had filled that void in his life. He'd found his family.

By the time he'd showered and changed, Mrs McKenzie was already buzzing around downstairs setting the place to rights.

'Good morning. A Mr Argyle has just arrived. I've shown him into the study. That's where your father held all of his business meetings. I hope that's all right?'

She met him at the bottom of the stairs. He was sure she'd been in a dilemma about whether or not to come up and wake him. Probably worried about what she might find.

'Yes, that's fine.' Although he'd been dealing with companies involved in the events side of castle business, it had mostly been over the phone. Or, in the case of the ceilidh band, over video call. He supposed he had to find his own rhythm, but it would be a shame not to utilise the space his father had carefully curated for business purposes.

Apart from anything else, he wanted the privacy. It would upset the current status quo around here if it became common knowledge that he'd considered selling the place. He didn't need that kind of discord when they'd just started working together as a team.

'Mr Argyle, it's a pleasure to meet you.' Ewen walked over to the premier estate agent he'd forgotten he'd even contacted about the sale of the castle. The slick suited and booted visitor stood to shake his hand.

'Thank you for inviting me over. It's such a wonderful opportunity for my company to be involved in a property with such history.' He reached for his briefcase and began unpacking files onto the desk. His enthusiasm making Ewen flinch.

'I'm afraid it might be something of a wasted journey.' Ewen took his seat at the desk, making sure there was some distance between them when he broke the news that there wouldn't be a mega commission coming his way after all.

'I know you said you wouldn't be selling until next year, and you just wanted me to put out a few feelers for possible interest in the property, but I couldn't help myself. I took the liberty of mocking up a brochure using some of the photographs and information available online. I think if we spark some interest now you might get a bidding war on your hands.' An enthusiastic Mr Argyle handed over a slick property brochure inside a leather binder.

Everything about this man screamed money and Ewen began to think he'd had a lucky escape. If money was his sole motivation, he might not have had the castle's best interests at heart. The staff could've found themselves unemployed, with their workplace sold on to property developers for a pretty penny. There was enough land on the property to build an entire new housing development. Ewen doubted this man, or his contacts, would've had any interest in the history of the castle, or the people who lived and worked there.

He couldn't imagine the beautiful surroundings he'd grown up in being bulldozed to throw up high-rise apartment blocks, squeezing every penny out of the available land. Exactly what his father hadn't wanted to happen when he'd entrusted the family estate to him. The actions of the ne'er-do-well son he'd purported not to be. Ewen was glad he'd come to his senses. Happy that Bonnie had crashed into his life and given him some happy memories here, and the promise of making a lot more together.

He looked at the glossy photographs, essentially a sales catalogue of his family home, and felt nothing but revulsion that he'd even considered the idea of flogging his heritage to the highest bidder. It was the only link he had left to his family, and though at one time he would've been thankful to be rid of even that, the letter from his father had healed some of those old wounds.

He looked at the photographs of his father's study where they were currently sitting, of the desk where he and Bonnie had finally taken a chance on their feelings for one another, and was certain of his next move.

'The castle is not for sale. I'm sorry for wasting your time, and I'll pay for all the work you've done thus far, but I've changed my mind.' Ewen tossed the brochure back across the desk.

Mr Argyle blinked at him, temporarily stunned into silence. Ewen surmised he probably wasn't used to being told no, and watched as the stunned expression turned to something darker.

'I'm aware you weren't ready to sell just yet. Apologies if I've jumped the gun. I'm sure you just need some time to think things through properly.'

Ewen got to his feet, deciding the meeting was over. 'Sorry. I'm not going to change my mind. I'm staying on at the castle for good. It's my home.'

He shook hands with Mr Argyle, who clearly wasn't going to give up without a fight. 'I'll leave the brochure with you anyway, and you have my number if things don't work out the way you plan.'

Ignoring Ewen's protest, he removed the paperwork from the binder and left it on the desk. Ewen saw him to the door, confident their paths would never cross again.

'Is everything okay?' Mrs McKenzie walked up beside him, hands fidgeting with the buttons on her cardigan as she watched Mr Argyle get into his flashy sports car.

Ewen didn't know how much information his visitor had shared with her, but it was clear she was anxious.

'Yes. I was on the verge of doing something stupid, but I came to my senses.'

Mrs McKenzie's worried frown smoothed out into a smile. 'Bonnie's been good for you.'

His housekeeper's astuteness still had the ability to surprise him. 'How did you…? I thought you didn't approve.'

Mrs McKenzie patted him on the arm. 'It's not that I didn't approve, Ewen. I was concerned. I didn't want you to make any rash decisions that might jeopardise your future here. But I can tell she's helped you make the right ones.'

She gave him a squeeze before walking away, leaving him staring after her in disbelief.

'I'm just heading out to see my solicitor. I'll be back later,' he called out, grabbing his coat on his way out of the door.

He didn't want to lose her or Bonnie, the two most important women in his life, and he was going to take steps to make sure of that.

Ewen was conspicuous by his absence and Bonnie hadn't been able to settle in the shop, worried he'd had second thoughts again. After all, it was a big jump from a supposed casual fling into an actual relationship, and he'd been antsy first time around.

'Thank you. Have a good day.' She handed over another paper bag full of her chocolates and watched her last customer disappear out of the door.

Business had been steady this morning, but it appeared to have died down again, so she made the call to take a quick break. She turned the closed sign on the door, locked the shop, and decided to go looking for Ewen. If they needed to have 'the talk' she would rather do it soon than spend the rest of the day wondering and worrying.

Bonnie ventured downstairs, among the new crop of visitors making their way into the castle. Ewen often liked to mingle with the guests and provide a more personal touch to their tours.

'Are you taking an early lunch?' Mrs McKenzie, with her ninja-like stealth, appeared in the sitting-room area beside her without making a sound.

'Something like that. I was looking for Ewen…the duke. I know he said he had an appointment, but I thought he would've been finished by now.' She'd be lying if she said she wasn't curious about the nature of his meeting, but not everything that happened at the castle was her business.

It was early days in their relationship. So early she was already doubting if they had one. It would probably take a while before he thought to include her in any decision-making, if ever. Though Bonnie would like to feel a part of it all if they were looking towards a future together. Especially when this was her home and livelihood too.

'Yes, he had a meeting in the study earlier, but I think he said something about going out to see his solicitor.'

'Okay, thanks. I'll catch up with him later.'

Before Bonnie could leave the group currently marvelling at the huge fireplace, and paintings of men on horseback that covered the walls from floor to ceiling, Mrs McKenzie caught her arm.

'He's thinking about the future of the castle, but he also needs to do what's right for him.'

Bonnie nodded in agreement, even though she didn't know what the woman was referring to. Mrs McKenzie and Ewen were close and he'd obviously confided in her about whatever he was up to today. Whilst Bonnie was glad he had someone to look out for him, who'd known him his entire life, it irked that he hadn't been able to confide in her. Especially after what they'd shared, and when they'd planned to be in a committed relationship. Now she wasn't sure of anything.

She made her way to the study and knocked on the door.

'Ewen?' When there was no reply, she took a peek inside in case he'd fallen asleep after his nocturnal exertions last night.

There was no sign of him, but he'd left the windows open, causing a breeze to chill the room. When she went to close them, she noticed some papers on the floor that must have blown off the desk.

She hadn't meant to look, and she was sorry she did in the end. It was a sales brochure for the castle. As her heart broke into a million shards, she flicked through the pages of glossy pictures offering her home as an amazing property investment. Not an important, historic site, or a castle that had been on the land for generations of the Harris family. Or her home, the place she'd imagined a future with Ewen.

Worse than the idea of the place being sold, possibly to a property developer who'd likely swamp every inch of surrounding land with new houses, was the fact that Ewen had been keeping this from her. Once again, she'd been lied to, conned into a relationship by someone who'd purported to want the best for her. He'd let her get comfortable, let her defences down again, believing she'd found someone she could trust, in a place she'd come to call home. Then spectacularly broken her trust.

She knew then it was over.

Tears clouding her vision, she ran to her room and immediately started to pack her case. She had a few more clothes than she'd first arrived with, but she managed to squeeze everything in. Minus the red dress, which was hanging up in her wardrobe, because she knew she couldn't look at it without thinking of the ball at the castle, and Ewen. All of which she'd lost with the discovery of his betrayal.

She didn't understand why he was doing it. The castle was his home, his business, the last link to his family, and it wasn't as though he were short of money. Mrs McKenzie had talked about him making the right decision for his future, and perhaps that meant moving on somewhere else.

'Well, good for you!' she shouted into the empty wardrobe. This new life he was setting up clearly didn't involve her, when he was making plans to sell her home from under her without as much as a discussion.

Bonnie heaved her case off the bed, grabbed her jacket and handbag and made her way downstairs.

'Bonnie? Where are you off to?' Mrs McKenzie met her on the staircase.

She had hoped to get out of here unseen, with a short note to tell Ewen she'd gone. It was clear the housekeeper wanted more information, but she didn't have any to give.

'Honestly? I don't know, but I can't stay here any more with someone I can't trust.' Ewen had fooled her into thinking he was different, that he wouldn't hurt her. With that false sense of security, she'd given him her heart, taking a leap of faith that he wouldn't break it. Only to find he'd betrayed her already. Manipulating her, taking advantage of her feelings for him, was everything she'd been afraid of happening.

She should never have let her guard down so easily when he'd toyed with her feelings once already. Only a fool would have given him a chance to do it again. She certainly wasn't going to stick around and find out what else he was capable of.

With her eyes on the front door, she continued her escape, unwilling to be delayed in case she did run into Ewen and couldn't control her emotions. Whether they would manifest in tears or anger she couldn't predict and would rather not wait to find out.

Mrs McKenzie hurried down the stairs after her. 'Please, Bonnie, wait and talk to Ewen. He at least deserves that.'

Bonnie hesitated at the open door. 'I don't owe him anything.'

If her last relationship had taught her anything it was that she wasn't beholden to anyone. She wasn't going to let another man manipulate her emotions, using guilt and charm to keep her in a toxic relationship. The fact that he was already hiding the truth from her so early on set off so many alarms, and this time she was going to listen to them.

With a final act of defiance, she slammed the front door shut, and closed another painful chapter of her life. Whilst she'd had some good times within the castle walls, and a business she was proud of, she loved herself more, and needed to leave for her own sanity.

The wheels of her case clattered over the cobbles as she made her way down the tree-lined lane towards the main road. It was only then she realised she didn't know where she was going.

There was one place she'd contemplated returning to one day, and right now she was out of options. If that didn't work out, she'd have to start over somewhere else. She'd proved she could live independently, manage her own workplace, and survive the toughest of circumstances. Though she didn't relish the prospect of moving to a new town, setting up again, she knew she was capable of doing it. She didn't need anyone, but she also knew how comforting it was to have someone who felt like home.

Bonnie took out her phone and dialled her parents' number, hoping they hadn't changed it in the intervening years. Her heart was in her throat as she listened to the dial tone, waiting to speak to people who might not forgive her behaviour and could very well add to her pain. But she was willing to take the chance and admit she'd been wrong if it meant healing their broken relationship. Her parents had had her best interests at heart, it had simply taken her a long time to recognise that. They'd loved her once, and she hoped, if she explained everything she'd been through, they could find it in their hearts to do so again when she needed them most.

'Hello?' The voice answering the phone almost broke her and she had to swallow down the sudden welling of emotion. All she wanted to do was throw herself into her mother's arms and cry out her heartbreak, but she knew there was a long way to go until then.

'Mum?'

'Bonnie, is that you?' When the sound of her mother promptly bursting into tears quickly followed, Bonnie knew she at least had somewhere to go.

'You sit there, Dad. I'll go and make you a cup of tea.' Bonnie helped her father into an armchair, waiting patiently as he huffed and puffed his way into a comfortable position.

'What about the shop?'

'The shop's closed, Dad. Remember?' It had broken her heart to come back and find the place boarded up. Worse still, to discover how badly her father's health had deteriorated during their years of estrangement. He seemed to have aged rapidly, skin and bone compared to the robust, imposing figure she remembered from her youth. Her mother too now looked old beyond her years, caring for her ailing husband clearly taking its toll.

'Oh, yes. I got too old for it and you weren't here to take over the way I always hoped you would.'

The guilt pierced her very soul at the mess she'd left behind. Perhaps if she'd come back sooner she could've salvaged the shop, maybe even something of her parents' health. Now she counted herself lucky she at least got to see them, and hadn't ended up like Ewen, full of regret and remorse.

'Well, she's back now and that's all that matters.' Her mother bustled in with the tea already made, fixing the tray on her father's lap, and giving Bonnie a grateful smile.

All the animosity between them had dissipated the minute they'd been reunited, her parents so tearfully happy to see her again.

'I'm going to have a look later and see if I can get some part-time shop work so I can contribute. It would give me

time here too to help you with things around the house.' The
family home, which had once been spotless, was now cluttered, laundry and dirty dishes dotted around, her mother
clearly struggling to cope with everything.

It wasn't the life she'd planned for herself, but for whatever time left her parents had, she wanted them to be comfortable. They were her family after all.

'I'm so glad you're home. We thought we'd never see
you again.' It was the umpteenth time her mother had ut-
tered the same sentiment over the past week, always teary
when she did.

Bonnie hadn't left any contact details when she'd had
her rebellion, running off with Ed, the worst thing to happen to her. Then fear and manipulation had prevented her
from getting in touch and admitting her parents had been
right all along. After cutting her off from anyone who'd
loved her, Ed had convinced her no one would want her
back. That she wasn't worthy of love and they'd been glad
to be rid of her.

She could see now by isolating her in such a manner it
had made it easier for him to control her. Making her believe he was the only person in her life who cared about
her, despite the opposite being true.

According to her mother, her father had become very
introspective after their only child left, parting on less than
favourable terms. They'd missed her, regretted any harsh
words spoken in the heat of the moment, but hadn't been
able to make amends because they'd had no idea where
she'd gone.

Even though it had been difficult for everyone, she'd
been honest about what had happened between her and Ed.
She hadn't thought it necessary to tell them all the grue-
some details, but enough for them to understand why she

hadn't been in contact. There had been tears and apologies on both sides, and she'd felt a huge weight lifted off her shoulders as she'd opened up. As if she'd finally left the past behind her.

The past seven days had been spent trying to make a dent in the housework, and helping take care of her dad. It was at night in bed her thoughts turned to Ewen and the life she'd thought she had at the castle. That was a loss she didn't think she'd ever get over, but she hadn't had a choice but to leave it all behind.

She didn't want to spend another decade trapped in a relationship with another man who thought he could play games with her heart, and who obviously didn't respect her. Why else would he have made plans to sell the castle without telling her? Perhaps he hoped she'd simply go along with whatever he decided, or, worse, would drop her once someone more suitable came on the scene. He was ambitious, where she just wanted somewhere she felt safe and secure. Ewen had ruined all of that.

At least coming back here, helping her parents, was a decision she'd made herself. It wasn't something that had been imposed upon her.

'You sit down too, Mum. I can sort out the washing.' She didn't want her mother's health impacted too, and was doing her best to lighten the load. At least when Bonnie was busy with laundry, or washing dishes, she didn't have time to dwell on her broken heart.

Once she got her mother seated, her feet up, with a cup of tea, Bonnie set to work in the kitchen. In the middle of her loading the washing machine the doorbell rang at the front of the house.

'Typical,' she muttered to herself. 'I'll get it, Mum. Don't get up.'

She deposited the wash basket with the rest of the dirty clothes onto the kitchen worktop to resume once she saw off whatever visitor was at the door. In a fit of pique, she yanked the front door open.

'Yes? What do you want?' The frustrated words died on her lips when she saw who it was standing on the step.

'Ewen?'

'That pleasant tone brings back so many memories...' He grinned, making her confused about whether she wanted to hit him or hug him for showing up here unannounced and breaking her heart all over again.

'What do you want?' she repeated, arms folded, chin tilted up into the air, denying him the knowledge that she cared.

'You.'

The fluttering in her stomach went ignored, because she clearly couldn't trust her instincts around handsome men.

'Too bad.' She went to slam the door in his face to show him she remained out of reach, but he stuck a foot in the way, and stepped inside instead.

They were toe to toe in the cramped hallway and she took a step back to regain some personal space and a clear head.

'Do you know how hard it was to find you?'

'No, and I don't care.' Bonnie tried to convince herself it didn't matter why he'd felt the need to follow her. He was probably miffed because she hadn't fallen into line, that she'd decided what happened in her future instead of him.

'We both know that's not true, but I'll tell you anyway. Since you neglected to answer any of my calls or messages, I had to do a bit of detective work. I remembered you telling me your father had a chocolate shop, so I did a bit of digging and found an old listing for this address.' He looked so pleased with himself she couldn't wait to wipe the smile off his face.

Coming here was supposed to mark the end of her time with Ewen, the beginning of her new relationship with her parents. Now he was blurring those two definitive lines in the sand that she'd made, with his big stompy boots.

'Doesn't sound *that* hard. You've found me. Whoop-de-whoop. It wasn't a treasure hunt, X doesn't mark the spot, and you don't get a prize.' Unfortunately, she didn't find the satisfaction she'd hoped for in watching his face fall.

'You are the prize, Bonnie. You always were.'

'Yeah? I felt more of a convenience.' The pain and anger she'd been bottling up since that afternoon came bubbling to the surface now she finally had an outlet for it.

'That's not true. I wanted to come after you sooner, but I thought you'd decided you didn't want to be in a relationship with me after all. I knew it had to be serious when you left the chocolate shop behind. That's why I gave you some space. I just didn't want you to think I didn't respect your decision.'

'Yet here you are…'

'I missed you. You have no idea how much. The castle hasn't been the same without you. I can't even bear to open the shop. Life is so lonely now you're not part of it, and I just need to know why. All you said in the note was that you weren't prepared to let another man dictate your life. Whatever I did, or didn't do, I'm sorry. Mrs McKenzie was in a terrible state after you left too. I think she was as heartbroken to see you go as I was.' He scrubbed his hands over his scalp and she could see his obvious distress, her defences gradually crumbling with every utterance of remorse.

'I would've thought it made things easier for you. I'm sure it's more difficult to sell a property with a sitting tenant.'

Ewen's forehead knitted into a frown. 'What are you talking about?'

Bonnie let out an exaggerated sigh. 'Don't pretend you don't know. At least do me the courtesy of being honest. It doesn't matter now when I've no intention of going back.'

Gaslighting her into thinking it was all in her head didn't work on her any more. She'd since learned it was a preferred tool of the controlling male.

When he continued to stare at her with that puzzled expression, she lost the last of her patience.

'You were selling the castle, my home, and my business from under me. Apparently, I wasn't even worthy of a discussion over my future.'

Ewen let out a long breath. 'I'm not selling the castle.'

'I saw the brochure. Mrs McKenzie said you were making some big decisions on your future. It didn't take much working out.'

'It might have looked that way. I suppose I haven't been upfront about everything at the castle.'

Bonnie *tsked* at the eventual confession, knowing she'd been right all along. Now he was going to try and worm his way out of it, the way her ex always had.

'Part of my father's will stipulated that I had to stay at the castle for a year before I could sell it on. When I first arrived, I was grieving for him, angry at myself and my parents. Mostly at him for forcing me to stay somewhere that held such painful memories. So I had made enquiries about selling up when the time came. That was before you came into my life, Bonnie. Before everything changed.'

Her heart began to pitter patter, the sliver of hope that she hadn't lost him for ever, that he wasn't like her ex after all, shining brightly. 'You had a meeting that morning, presumably with the estate agent, and Mrs McKenzie said you'd gone to see your solicitor. What was I supposed to think?'

'That I love you and was making plans for our future.' He took her trembling hands in his. She was barely holding onto the last of her defences.

'I had a long-standing appointment with the estate agent I forgot to cancel. He'd taken it upon himself to make a mock-up property brochure. I told him I'd changed my mind. That I was staying on.'

'And the solicitor?' Slowly, the reasons she'd thought she'd had to leave were being shot to pieces, and she was clinging onto the theory he hadn't had her interests at heart before she completely capitulated.

It was the first time he'd said he loved her. Words that had been used in the past to control and coerce her, and she was afraid to believe now. Once she trusted in his feelings, she would have to be open with her own, and that left her vulnerable to more hurt.

Ewen's smile tried to convince her everything was okay, that she'd worried for nothing, but she'd been burned one too many times to let that sway her.

'I did go to discuss business at the castle, and my future in a way. I had a contract drawn up to sign over the chocolate shop to you. It's your business now, and I had hoped it would help you feel more secure at the castle.'

He pulled a wad of papers from inside his wax jacket and handed them over to her. 'The offer's still there. Even if you don't want to give me another chance, you have a place at the castle.'

It was a commitment she'd never expected, and, though she wanted to jump at the chance, her circumstances had changed.

'I can't leave my parents. Dad isn't well, and Mum is

struggling to care for him. They had to close the shop. I can't just walk away again.' Her conscience wouldn't let her, even if her heart was elsewhere.

'In case you didn't hear me, Bonnie, I love you. I'll do whatever it takes to keep you in my life. Your parents can come too. There's plenty of space, and we can get them whatever help they need. I promise you, I was making plans for our future together. In hindsight, yes, I should've consulted you first, but I think I've learned my lesson. Do you think you can forgive me?' He slipped his hands around her waist and pulled her closer, and Bonnie knew she already had.

'I do have some stipulations,' she said, not wanting to appear too easily won over. There needed to be a precedent set for the future.

'Of course.'

'I want to move into your apartment.'

'Naturally. If we're living together, I want us to be together, not sleeping in separate rooms.'

'I'll expect you to run me a bath at least once a week. Dinner together every night.'

'As long as that includes the odd takeaway.'

Bonnie nodded. 'And a promise to continue with the annual ball.'

'I think that's a definite anyway, or I'll never hear the end of it from Mrs McKenzie. How about the promise of the first dance?'

'Done.' Bonnie held her hand out to shake Ewen's hand, but once the handshake had sealed the deal, he pulled her closer, and took her in his arms.

'Please don't leave me again.' His kiss, so full of love and desire, made her wonder why she ever had.

Now that he'd made that commitment, assured her of

his feelings, Bonnie was able to finally speak hers aloud without fear.

'I won't. I love you too much.' She hugged him tight, never wanting to let go.

Bonnie had finally found the unconditional love she'd been looking for her entire life, and she knew her future was safe in Ewen's hands. He was invested in their relationship, and their life at the castle, as much as she was.

EPILOGUE

'CAN I STEAL you away for lunch?' Ewen appeared in the shop once all the customers had gone.

Bonnie ruefully glanced at the now empty shelves in the display case. 'I can't. We had a run on the whisky truffles.'

They'd become a firm favourite in the shop, probably due to the duke's favourable reviews, which he liked to share with the visitors before they stopped by.

'You go. I can restock with the ones you made earlier.' Her mum gave her a nudge, not that it took much to convince Bonnie to take time out to be with Ewen.

It had been five months since she'd reunited with her parents. Four months since they'd sold up the house and shop to move into the castle with them. Since then, they'd all been finding a new way of life. Her mother's workload had considerably lessened now there were cleaners on hand to take care of the communal rooms, and they'd even got some home help to assist with her father's day-to-day care.

With Bonnie's chocolate shop beginning to flourish, she'd needed an extra hand to help meet demand. When her mother had expressed an interest in working a few hours, it had seemed like the perfect fit. After all, she'd had experience working in the family shop too. Meeting new people and finding an interest of her own had reinvigorated her mother, and Bonnie was glad to see her enjoying life.

'If you're sure?' She was already taking off her apron and heading towards Ewen. Even though they were living together in his apartment, she never liked to miss an opportunity to be with him. It was safe to say they were loved up.

'I thought we could eat in,' he said cryptically, leading her to the study.

'What on earth...?' The desk had been covered with a red and white gingham cloth and was laid out with plates of delicious food.

Bonnie wandered over to take a closer look, spotting the bottle of champagne cooling in the ice bucket, the bowl of scrumptious-looking strawberries, the dainty finger sandwiches and home-baked scones. Her mouth was watering already.

'Did you do all of this?' She helped herself to one of the fresh strawberries and took a bite.

'I had some help...'

Mrs McKenzie, she presumed. The woman had been so much more than a member of staff to both of them, helping Bonnie's parents settle into their new surroundings. As well as helping her mother take care of her father, she often escorted him to the chocolate shop to enjoy a cup of tea and a sweet treat whilst he watched her mother work. With his heart problems and his early-stage dementia, there was no way of knowing how long they'd have him here, but Bonnie wanted to make sure he was happy and comfortable for whatever time he had left. Certainly, this was the most relaxed she'd ever seen her parents.

'Well, it's all appreciated. I'm starving.' She didn't take gestures like this for granted and it felt to her that Ewen went out of his way every day to make sure she knew she was loved. Something she would never tire of, and took comfort from on a daily basis.

He poured two flutes full of champagne, but before he handed one to her, he turned and took her hands in his.

'I can't tell you how much these past months have meant to me, Bonnie. Having you all here has made me feel like part of a family again.'

She didn't know what had brought on this outpouring of sentiment, but it was further confirmation that the arrangement was working well for all parties. A commitment many men would've shied away from, especially so early on in their relationship. But Ewen had bent over backwards to accommodate her parents, giving them rooms large enough for whatever possessions they wanted to bring with them. If she was honest, she'd expected some resistance from her mother and father to being uprooted and transported into the middle of a local tourist attraction, but they'd been on board from the start. It had taken a weight off their shoulders and given them all an opportunity to build some bridges. All thanks to Ewen.

'None of it would've been possible if you hadn't been so accommodating. Thank you.' She tilted her face up to kiss him full on the lips, expressing her love for him the best way she knew how.

'Marry me.'

'What?'

'It's not quite how I'd imagined this going, but I'm in the moment. Go with it.'

Bonnie opened and closed her mouth, speechless. Suddenly it all made sense, the romantic lunch date, the champagne, and a very eager Ewen.

'Ask me again.' She wanted to know she hadn't imagined it or misheard him.

Ewen disentangled himself from her and got down on one knee, leaving her in no doubt about his intentions.

'Bonnie Abernathy, will you do me the honour of becoming my wife and the new lady of the castle?'

There was only one title that mattered to her, and that was becoming Mrs Harris. She was simply very fortunate she got to call this place home too.

'Yes. A million times yes. I love you, Ewen, and I want to be with you for ever.'

He gathered her up in a hug and swung her around, his joy as palpable as her own.

Bonnie's future was bright. It was with Ewen, and she couldn't think of a better man to spend the rest of her life with.

* * * * *

COMING SOON!

We really hope you enjoyed reading this book.
If you're looking for more romance
be sure to head to the shops when
new books are available on

Thursday 11th April

MILLS & BOON

MILLS & BOON®

Coming next month

SECRETLY MARRIED TO A PRINCE
Ally Blake

She watched as a dozen thoughts tangled behind those pale hazel eyes, before he said, 'I am Prince Henri Gaultier Raphael-Rossetti.'

He pronounced his name *On-ree*.

A burr of pain settled behind her ribs. For while she'd known next to nothing about him, she'd thought at least he'd given her his true name.

Then her brain stuttered and she backtracked a smidge. 'I'm sorry, did you say *Prince*?'

He nodded. Thought it was more of a gentle bow. Elegant, practiced, princely.

Matilda blinked. 'Since *when*?'

'Since birth,' he said, a flicker at the edge of his mouth that might have been a smile. Or a grimace. 'Though I have been Sovereign Prince of Chaleur for the past two years.'

Matilda looked at the ancient sandstone structure, the burly bouncers hovering nearby, Henri's gorgeous car, and the beast parked in behind it. She remembered the crowd in the street, surrounding him, calling his name.

Then she looked back at *him*. The way he held himself, the way he dressed, the way he spoke. How educated and hungry for knowledge he had been back then. That *je ne sais quoi* that had drawn her in from the very first moment.

'Are you freaking kidding me?' she asked.

'I'm not. Freaking or otherwise.' Again with the flicker at the corner of his mouth. This time it came with a slight thawing in his gaze.

The requirement of anonymity, the money, the access, the way they had breezed through Europe with absolute entitlement. It all made sense now. It hadn't been a weird hazing thing, or bored rich kid thing. It had been about protecting Henri.

A *prince*.

A prince that she had fallen for. Had married. Which made her…

No. Nope. Nope-ty nooooo. There was no point getting ahead of herself. Not until she had legal paperwork before her own eyes. Legal enough to satisfy George Damn Harrington.

As to the rest? Part of her wanted to kick him, right in the shins, for keeping such a thing from her. Then again, she had vowed to love him for a lifetime, before bolting to the other side of the world.

Maybe they were even.

Continue reading
SECRETLY MARRIED TO A PRINCE
Ally Blake

Available next month
millsandboon.co.uk

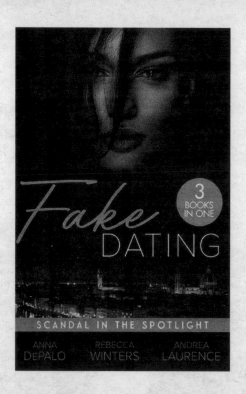

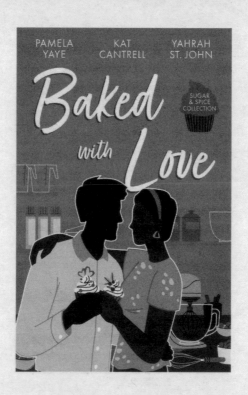

LET'S TALK

Romance

For exclusive extracts, competitions
and special offers, find us online:

 MillsandBoon

 @MillsandBoon

 @MillsandBoonUK

 @MillsandBoonUK

Get in touch on 01413 063 232

MILLS & BOON

THE HEART OF ROMANCE

A ROMANCE FOR EVERY READER

MODERN

Prepare to be swept off your feet by sophisticated, sexy and seductive heroes, in some of the world's most glamourous and romantic locations, where power and passion collide.

HISTORICAL

Escape with historical heroes from time gone by. Whether your passion is for wicked Regency Rakes, muscled Vikings or rugged Highlanders, awaken the romance of the past.

MEDICAL

Set your pulse racing with dedicated, delectable doctors in the high-pressure world of medicine, where emotions run high and passion, comfort and love are the best medicine.

True Love

Celebrate true love with tender stories of heartfelt romance, from the rush of falling in love to the joy a new baby can bring, and a focus on the emotional heart of a relationship.

HEROES

The excitement of a gripping thriller, with intense romance at its heart. Resourceful, true-to-life women and strong, fearless men face danger and desire - a killer combination!

###

From showing up to glowing up, these characters are on the path to leading their best lives and finding romance along the way – with plenty of sizzling spice!

To see which titles are coming soon, please visit

millsandboon.co.uk/nextmonth